Leif G.W. Persson is Scandinavia's most renowned criminologist and a leading psychological profiler. He has also served as an advisor to the Swedish Ministry of Justice. Since 1991, he has held the position of Professor at the National Swedish Police Board and is regularly consulted as the country's foremost expert on crime.

Persson is the author of ten bestselling crime novels for which he has won many awards including **The Glass Key, The Piraten Award, The Swedish Academy of Crime Writers' Award** (which he has won three times), **The Finnish Whodunnit Society's Annual Award for Excellence in Foreign Crime Writing, The Petrona Award for Best Scandinavian Crime Novel,** and **The Danish Academy of Crime Writers' Palle Rosenkrantz Prize.**

Praise from around the world for Leif G.W. Persson and his novels:

'From a country known for terrific crime novelists, Sweden's great crime writer Leif G.W. Persson brilliantly takes the reader into a world of fascinating mystery and secrets'
Joseph Wambaugh

'Persson is more authentic than Stieg Larsson'
La Repubblica, Italy

'Persson shines a light on Swedes and their society, and in that broader sense may be the most interesting of the novelists in the current Swedish crime boom'
Barry Forshaw, *Crimetime,* UK

'Persson outperforms most of his competitors in the Swedish crime genre by miles . . . hardboiled, clever, suspenseful'
Svenska Dagbladet, Sweden

'Leif G.W. Persson's books are both brilliant and unique – stylish crime requiems marked by pitch-black humour and an unparalleled satirical sting'
Hakan Nesser

'Persson's novels contains everything you expect from good crime literature: an irresistible plot, subtle storytelling and interesting characters'
Crimezone, Netherlands

'[Persson] remains unthreatened as the King of Swedish crime writing. Period'
Kvällsposten, Sweden

By Leif G.W. Persson

THE DYING DETECTIVE

The Story of a Crime series
BETWEEN SUMMER'S LONGING AND WINTER'S END
ANOTHER TIME, ANOTHER LIFE
FALLING FREELY, AS IF IN A DREAM

The Bäckström series
LINDA – AS IN THE LINDA MURDER
HE WHO KILLS THE DRAGON
THE SWORD OF JUSTICE

The Sword of Justice

Leif G.W. Persson

Translated from the Swedish by Neil Smith

BLACK SWAN

TRANSWORLD PUBLISHERS
61–63 Uxbridge Road, London W5 5SA
www.penguin.co.uk

Transworld is part of the Penguin Random House group of companies whose addresses can be found at global.penguinrandomhouse.com

Originally published in Sweden as *Den sanna historien om Pinocchios näsa* in 2013 by Albert Bonniers Förlag

First published in Great Britain in 2016 by Doubleday
an imprint of Transworld Publishers
Black Swan edition published 2016

A CIP catalogue record for this book
is available from the British Library.

ISBN
9781784160050

Typeset in 11/14pt Giovanni Book by Falcon Oast Graphic Art Ltd.
Printed and bound by Clays Ltd, Bungay, Suffolk.

Penguin Random House is committed to a sustainable future for our business, our readers and our planet. This book is made from Forest Stewardship Council® certified paper.

1 3 5 7 9 10 8 6 4 2

This is a wicked tale for grown-up children, and if it hadn't been for the last tsar of Russia, Nicholas II, the British prime minister Sir Winston Churchill, the Russian president Vladimir Putin and Detective Superintendent Evert Bäckström of the Western District Police in Stockholm, these events would never have occurred.

In that sense, this is a story about the cumulative and final results of actions performed by four men over a period of more than a hundred years. Four men who never met one another, who lived their lives in different worlds, in which the eldest of them was murdered forty years before the youngest was even born.

As on so many previous occasions, and quite regardless of the company and circumstances he may have ended up in, it is Evert Bäckström who will bring the story to a close.

LEIF G.W. PERSSON
Professorsvillan, Elghammar
Spring 2013

I

The best day of Detective Superintendent Evert Bäckström's life

1

It was Monday, 3 June, but even though it was a Monday and he had been woken in the middle of the night, Detective Superintendent Evert Bäckström would always think of it as the best day of his life. His work mobile started to ring at exactly five o'clock in the morning, and because the person who was calling refused to give up he didn't exactly have many options.

'Yeees,' Bäckström answered.

'I've got a murder for you, Bäckström,' the duty officer with Solna Police said.

'At this time of day?' Bäckström said. 'So it's either the king or the prime minister?'

'Even better than that, actually.' His colleague was barely able to hide his delight.

'I'm listening.'

'Thomas Eriksson,' the duty officer replied.

'The lawyer,' Bäckström said, having difficulty concealing his surprise. It can't be true, he thinks. It's far too good to be true.

'The very same. Considering all your past dealings, I wanted to be the first to pass on the good news. It was actually Niemi at Forensics who called and said I should wake you. So, sincere congratulations, Bäckström. Congratulations from all of us here at the station. You got the last laugh in the end.'

'He's quite sure it's murder? And that it's Eriksson?'

'No question, Niemi's one hundred per cent certain. Our poor victim looks pretty terrible, apparently, but it's still him.'

'I'll try to find some way of dealing with my grief,' Bäckström said.

This is the best day of my life, he thought as he ended the short conversation. He was also wide awake, his head clear as crystal, and on a day like today you had to make sure you made the most of every moment. Not miss a single second.

The first thing he did was put his dressing-gown on and go off to the toilet to ease the pressure. That was a routine he had picked up early in life and had been careful to maintain. Easing the pressure before he went to bed and as soon as he got up, regardless of whether or not it was necessary, and in marked contrast to what his prostate-tormented male colleagues seemed to devote most of their waking hours to.

A superb high-pressure jet, Bäckström thought contentedly as he stood there with the super-salami in the firm grip of his right hand and felt the water level sink in his well-proportioned nether regions. High time to restore a bit of balance, he reflected, concluding with a couple of sturdy tugs on the salami to squeeze out the last drops that had gathered there during the course of an entirely dreamless night.

Then he had gone straight to the kitchen to prepare a hearty breakfast. A proper stack of extra-thick slices of Danish bacon, four fried eggs, freshly squeezed orange juice and a large cup of strong coffee with warm milk. A murder investigation wasn't the sort of thing you embarked upon on an empty stomach, and carrots and oatbran were almost certainly one contributing factor to why his malnourished and cretinous colleagues fucked up with such depressing regularity.

After that he had gone, happy and sated, into the bathroom and stood in the shower, where he carefully soaped himself in sections as the warm water coursed over his pleasantly rounded and harmoniously constructed frame. Then he dried himself thoroughly before shaving with the assistance of a proper, old-fashioned razor and generous quantities of shaving foam. Finally, he had brushed his teeth with his electric toothbrush and, just to be on the safe side, gargled with some refreshing mouthwash.

Eventually, with aftershave, deodorant and other pleasant smells carefully applied to all the strategic parts of his temple of a body, he had dressed with great care. A yellow linen suit, a blue linen shirt, black, handmade Italian shoes and a colourful silk handkerchief tucked into his breast pocket as a final fond greeting to his murder victim. On a day like this it was important not to be sloppy about details, which is why – in honour of the momentous occasion – he had swapped his usual Rolex for the one in white gold that he had been given as a Christmas present by a grateful acquaintance whom he had been able to help out of a minor inconvenience.

In front of the hall mirror he had conducted one final check: the gold note-clip, with a suitable amount of cash; the little crocodile-skin wallet containing all his cards (both of these in his left trouser pocket); his key-ring and mobile in the right pocket; his black notebook with the pen clipped to the spine in his left inside pocket; and his best friend, little Sigge, tucked securely in the ankle holster on the inside of his left leg.

Bäckström nodded with approval at the finished result. All that remained was the most important thing. A suitable dose of malt whisky from the crystal carafe on the hall table. Two throat sweets in his mouth the moment the delightful aftertaste had subsided and another handful in the side pocket of his jacket, just in case.

When he stepped out into the street the sun was shining in a cloudless sky, and even though it was only the beginning of June, the temperature had to be at least twenty degrees already. The first proper summer day, and just what you had the right to expect on a day like this.

The duty officer in Solna had sent a patrol car containing two young officers, skinny, spotty creatures, but the one who was driving had at least picked up the basics when it came to the authority's management practices. He had both held the door open and moved his seat forward so that Bäckström could sit in the back seat without having to sit where suspects usually sat, or crease his neatly pressed trousers.

'Good morning, boss,' the driver said, with a polite nod. 'Not a bad day.'

'Yes, looks like it's going to be a real scorcher,' his partner agreed. 'A pleasure to meet you, by the way, Superintendent.'

'Ålstensgatan 127,' Bäckström said with a curt nod. To fend off any further observations he demonstratively took out his black notebook and made his first note on the case. 'Detective Superintendent Evert Bäckström leaves his residence on Kungsholmen 0700 to visit the crime scene,' he wrote, but the message evidently didn't get through, because the youngsters started up again before the car had even pulled out on to Fridhemsgatan.

'Odd business, this. The duty officer said that it looks

like our murder victim is that lawyer, Thomas Eriksson.'

The driver nodded before carrying on.

'That must be pretty unusual – someone murdering a lawyer, I mean.'

'Yes, it hardly ever happens,' his colleague agreed.

'No, sadly,' Bäckström said. 'Unfortunately, it happens all too infrequently.' Two more fuckwits, he thought. Where do they all come from? Why don't we ever run out of them? Why do they all have to join the police?

'Do you think he could have been mixed up in something dodgy, boss? He was a lawyer, after all, so there's probably a risk of that sort of thing, if I can put it like that?'

The silly sod had turned round now as well. He was speaking directly to Bäckström.

'That's exactly what I was planning to think about,' Bäckström said wearily. 'While you gentlemen drive me to the crime scene in Ålstensgatan. In complete silence.'

At last, he thought. Ten minutes later they stopped outside a large, bright white modernist brick villa from the fifties, with its own mooring, boathouse and jetty straight on to Lake Mälaren. It must have cost its owner more than an ordinary cop would earn in a lifetime, before tax.

Not a bad crime scene. Wonder what the sod was doing here at this time of day.

Otherwise, things looked the way they usually did. The blue and white tape of the cordon surrounding both the property itself and a good portion of road on either side of the house. Two patrol cars and a mobile coordination unit, and at least three cars from the Crime Unit, far too many unoccupied officers just standing around with the others who had already gathered there. A few journalists with accompanying photographers, and at least one cameraman from one of the television channels, a dozen or so nosy neighbours, considerably better dressed than they usually were, and a striking number of them with one or more dogs, of varying sizes.

But the expression in their eyes was the same. An underlying hint of fear, but mostly anticipation and the hope that was nurtured by the suspicion that, if the worst had happened, at least it hadn't happened to them. Compared to a whole life, what do all these days matter, apart from one? Bäckström thought. A whole life containing the single day that ended up being the best of your life.

Then he had got out of the car, nodded to his spotty-faced driver and his equally spotty colleague and contented himself with merely shaking his head at the vultures from the media as he set off towards the front door of the house that had, until just a few hours ago, been his latest murder victim's home. Not the first walk of this sort that he had made in his life, and certainly not the last, but this time it was a welcome duty and, if he had been alone, he would have tap-danced up the steps to the victim's house.

II

The week before the best day was an entirely ordinary week. For good and bad

2

Monday, 27 May, a week before the Monday that was to be the best of his life, had been like Mondays usually were, possibly even slightly worse than an ordinary Monday, and it had begun in a way that challenged human comprehension even for a man as insightful and noble as Evert Bäckström.

In a purely literal sense, it involved two insane cases that, for unfathomable reasons, had ended up on his desk. The first concerned a maltreated rabbit that had been taken into care by the county council. The second involved a smart gentleman with connections to the royal court, who, according to an anonymous witness, had been assaulted with a sale catalogue from the renowned auction house of Sotheby's in London. As if this weren't bad enough, the crime was also supposed to have taken place in the car park at Drottningholm Palace, just a couple of hundred metres from the room in which His Majesty the King of Sweden, Carl XVI Gustaf, ordinarily enjoyed his nightly slumber.

Several years ago Detective Superintendent Evert Bäckström had worked in the Western District of the Stockholm Police as boss of the department that was responsible for the investigation of serious violent crimes.

It wasn't a bad patch, and if it had been in the USA, where ordinary people get a say in things, Bäckström would obviously have been a shoo-in as their elected sheriff. Three hundred and fifty-five square kilometres of land and water between the large inland Lake Mälaren to the west and the Baltic Sea to the east. Between the old toll gates of central Stockholm to the south and Norra Järva, Jakobsberg and the outer archipelago to the north.

He used to think of it as his very own Bäckström County, with almost three hundred and fifty thousand inhabitants. At the top of the pile were His Majesty the King and his family, residents of the Royal Palaces at Drottningholm and Haga. Besides them, there were a dozen billionaires and several hundred who were each good for a few million. At the other end there were several tens of thousands who didn't have enough to feed themselves, who were forced to live on benefits or beg and commit crime to get from one day to the next. And then there were all the ordinary people, of course. All the people who minded their own business, took care of themselves and didn't make a fuss about the lives they were living. At least, they rarely did anything that risked landing on Bäckström's desk in the large police station in Solna.

But, unfortunately, not everyone who lived there was made that way. During the course of each year almost sixty thousand crimes were reported in the district. The majority of them, admittedly, were simple cases of theft, criminal damage and drugs offences, but there were also a few thousand violent crimes. If you looked at criminality in the Western District as a whole, it stretched right across the social spectrum. From a handful of gangsters in pinstripe suits who committed financial crimes worth hundreds of millions to the many thousands who stole everything from steak and sausage to make-up, beer and headache pills from the big supermarkets in the district's shopping centres.

And, in almost every instance, they didn't involve Bäckström at all. Bäckström worked with serious violent crimes. He had done that for the whole of his life as a police officer, and he intended to continue doing it until that part of his life came to an end. Murders, assaults, rapes and armed robberies. Plus all the other wonders hidden in among them, in the form of pyromaniacs and paedophiles, menacing behaviour, hooligans and various assorted lunatics. Even the occasional flasher or peeping Tom could be imagined to nurture more corporeal ambitions. There were also more than enough such cases. Thousands of reports each year, all ending up in the department for serious violent crimes. And it was all these cases that gave content and meaning to his life as a police officer, and if he was to be able to accomplish anything on that score, it was all a matter of distinguishing between the things that mattered and those that didn't. On the Monday before the Monday that would be the best day of his life, he had, sadly, been less than successful in this regard.

In Bäckström's department for violent crimes, the week always started with a morning meeting where they summarized the human misery that had taken place during the preceding week, bolstered themselves in advance for what was to come that week and chewed over a few old cases that had sat and mouldered for too long simply to be carried off to the archive and forgotten about.

To assist him, Bäckström had twenty or so co-workers,

one of whom was both silent and fully functional and half a dozen who at least did as he told them. The rest were pretty much as could be expected, and if it hadn't been for Bäckström's firm hand and strong leadership, not least his ability to distinguish between the things that mattered and those that didn't, then, obviously, the bad guys would have got the upper hand from day one.

A new week, morning meeting, high time for Detective Superintendent Evert Bäckström to wield the sword of justice once again. He was happy to leave all that fiddling with the scales of justice to the large number of do-gooders and paper-shufflers higher up the police hierarchy.

3

'Please, sit down,' Bäckström said as he sank down in his usual place at the end of the long conference table. You useless, lazy bastards, he thought, looking round at his colleagues. Monday morning with empty eyes behind heavy eyelids, and considerably more coffee cups than notepads or poised pens. What's happened to the force? Detective Superintendent Evert Bäckström wondered. Where have all the proper cops like me gone?

Then he had handed over to his right-hand man, who, naturally, was a woman, Detective Inspector Annika Carlsson, thirty-seven. A terrifying figure who looked as if she spent most of her time in the gym down in the basement of Solna police station. Probably in other, more nocturnal basements as well, for that matter, but he preferred not to think about that.

She did have one advantage, though. None of the others dared argue with her, which was why they had quickly got through the list of what had happened the previous week and over the weekend. Resolved and unresolved, successes and misfires, new information and tip-offs, tasks and commendations that awaited them over the coming week. As well as all the other stuff of a more practical and administrative character that everyone in the department was expected to absorb.

The whole thing had gone swimmingly. Done and dusted in less than an hour, and Detective Inspector Carlsson was even able to crown her run-through by telling them that the murder that had occurred three days before had been cleared up, with a full confession, and handed over to the prosecutor.

The perpetrator had turned out to be an unusually accommodating drunk. On Friday evening he and his now deceased wife had started arguing about which television programme they were going to watch. Then he had gone out into the kitchen, fetched a carving knife and put an end to the discussion. After that he had rung at his neighbour's door to borrow his phone to call for an ambulance.

The neighbour hadn't been particularly helpful. Past experience had taught him not to open the door, and instead he had called the police. The first patrol arrived just ten minutes later, but by the time the uniformed officers had got into the flat there was no longer any need for medical intervention. Instead they had cuffed the newly widowed man and called in Forensics and detectives to deal with the more intricate aspects of the police work.

At the very first interview the following morning the victim's grieving widower had confessed. He wasn't particularly clear about the details, because, obviously, he'd had a few drinks that evening, but he was still keen to let the interviewers know that he was already missing his wife. She may have been stubborn, resentful and generally impossible to live with – largely because she drank like a fucking fish – but, in spite of all her faults, he still wanted to make it clear that he actually missed her.

'Well, thanks for that,' Bäckström said happily, and that was probably the point when he, caught up in the elation of the moment, made a mistake. Instead of simply concluding the meeting, withdrawing to his office and taking his time preparing for his impending lunch, he had nodded amiably to his right-hand man and asked the wrong question entirely.

'Well, then,' he said. 'We're pretty much done here, aren't we? Unless you've got something to add before we get on with a bit of good, old-fashioned police work?'

'A couple of things,' Annika Carlsson said. 'Both a bit odd.'

'I'm listening,' Bäckström said, nodding in encouragement. As yet, of course, he was in a state of blissful ignorance.

'Okay,' Annika Carlsson said, and for some reason she shrugged her broad shoulders. 'The first case involves a rabbit. To start with, at least, if I can put it like that.'

'A rabbit,' Bäckström said. What the hell is the woman going on about? he thought.

'A rabbit that has been taken into care by the county council, because its owner was maltreating it,' she explained.

'How the hell does anyone maltreat a rabbit?' Bäckström asked. 'Did our perpetrator put it in the microwave?' Wasn't that how budding serial killers usually started their careers? Microwaving rabbits and putting the cat in the tumble-dryer? This is getting better and better, he thought, and, evidently, he wasn't alone, judging by the expressions on the others' faces. Suddenly they were alert and interested, in contrast to their attitude when they were dealing with the human victims of crime and their various sufferings.

'No,' Annika Carlsson said, shaking her head. 'I'm afraid it's considerably more tragic than that.'

4

'Our perpetrator is a seventy-three-year-old woman. Mrs Astrid Elisabeth Linderoth, born in 1940, known as Elisabeth,' Annika Carlsson began. 'Single, no children, widowed five years ago, lives in a flat in Filmstaden in Solna. I looked her up out of curiosity. Her finances are sound, she seems to have a pretty generous pension from her late husband and she's got no criminal record. No contact with us at all. Now she's being investigated for maltreatment of an animal, plus a number of other offences that arose last week. If you ask me, that's the reason she's ended up here with us at Serious Crime.'

'What's she done, then?' Bäckström asked.

'Resisting arrest, violence against a public official, attempted bodily harm, two cases of making illegal threats.'

'Hang on a minute,' Bäckström interjected. 'I thought you said the old biddy was seventy-three?'

'I did,' Annika Carlsson said. 'She's an old lady, basically, so it's a very sad story. If you can bear to hear it, I'll give you the short version.'

'I'm all ears,' Bäckström said, making himself more comfortable in his chair.

* * *

Approximately one month earlier, Stockholm County Council had decided to take the rabbit owned by the suspect into care. The background to this was a police report filed by a female neighbour just a fortnight before the council took its decision. It didn't actually seem to be a matter of animal cruelty in any particularly active sense, more just maltreatment and neglect. Among other things, the rabbit's owner was suspected of having gone away on holiday for several days and forgetting to leave it enough food before she left. On a number of occasions the rabbit was also said to have been found in the stairwell after its owner forgot to shut the door to the flat and it took the chance to escape. On one of these occasions it was also said to have been bitten by a dachshund owned by another neighbour.

'I have an idea that the rabbit's owner might be considerably older than official records suggest,' Annika Carlsson said, for some reason making a circular gesture in the air with her right index finger close to her right temple. 'The preliminary report ended up with our colleagues in the City Police, at the new animal protection unit. They seem to have responded with unusual speed, possibly because Mrs Linderoth had already been the subject of similar allegations in January this year. The same complainant, the same decision from the council, although on that occasion the animal in question seems to have been a golden hamster.'

'Looks like the old girl was stepping things up.' Bäckström chuckled. He was leaning back comfortably, and suddenly seemed to be in an excellent mood.

'Stepping things up? How do you mean?'

'Well, a rabbit must be at least twice the size of a hamster,' Bäckström explained. 'Maybe she'll drag home an elephant next time. How the hell should I know? But what I still don't understand is why she's ended up with us.'

'I was getting to that,' Annika Carlsson said. 'On Tuesday last week – Tuesday, 21 May – when two of our colleagues from the animal protection unit of the City Police, accompanied by two officials from the council, went to enact the decision to remove the rabbit from Mrs Linderoth's flat, at first she refused to open the door. After some persuasion she eventually opened it a crack, with the security chain on, and stuck a pistol out of the gap and told them to get lost at once. Our colleagues retreated and called in back-up.'

'From the national rapid response unit?' Bäckström was staring eagerly at Annika Carlsson.

'No, sorry to disappoint you. We sent one of our own patrol cars. One of our colleagues apparently knows Mrs Linderoth – his mum's an old friend of hers – so after a bit of persuasion she opened the door and let them in. She was agitated, but at least she wasn't violent. The pistol turned out to be an eighteenth-century antique. According to our colleagues, it wasn't loaded and doesn't look as if it's been fired in the past two hundred years.'

'Okay,' Bäckström said.

'But that's not the end of it.' Annika Carlsson shook her head.

'You don't say!' Bäckström said.

'Everything was fairly calm until the female vet from the council went to put the rabbit in a cage. Then Mrs Linderoth rushed in, clutching a teapot, and threatened the vet. She was disarmed and placed on the sofa, and the officers from the City Police and the two council officials left the flat with the rabbit. Our own colleagues stayed behind to talk to her. According to the incident report, she was calm and collected when they left.'

'Good to hear,' Bäckström said. 'One question. Where do all the charges come from?'

'From our colleagues in the City Police,' Carlsson said. 'The following day. They filed the charges for their own sake, and on behalf of the two council officials: resisting arrest, violence against public officials, threatening behaviour and attempted bodily harm. A total of twelve different offences, if I've counted correctly.'

'I dare say you have,' Bäckström said. 'The old bag is clearly a threat to the entire fabric of society. High time she was locked away.'

'I hear what you're saying, I understand what you mean, I've got no problem with that. What troubles me is a report of aggravated threatening behaviour that we received on Thursday evening. Filed directly with us. The complainant came down here in person. Spoke to one of the duty officers.'

'Let me guess. Our colleagues at the rabbit and hamster unit wanted to add something they'd forgotten?'

'No,' Annika Carlsson said, again shaking her head. 'The complainant was Mrs Linderoth's neighbour. She lives in the same block, on the fourth floor. Mrs Linderoth lives at the top of the building, the seventh floor. The same person who reported Mrs Linderoth for maltreatment of animals, both the rabbit and the hamster, in case you're wondering. She's also filed complaints with the residents' association on numerous occasions, but that's a different story.'

'So who's she, then?'

'Single woman. Forty-three years old. Works part-time as a secretary for an IT company out in Kista. No criminal record. She seems to spend most of her time doing voluntary work. Among other things, she's the spokesperson for the organization Dare to Care for Our Smallest Friends. Apparently, they're a more radical splinter group of the Animal Rights movement. She used to be on the committee of that as well, by the way.'

'Who'd have thought it? Does she have a name?'

'Fridensdal, Frida Fridensdal. With an "s". The "valley of peace", in other words. She changed her name; she was born Anna Fredrika Wahlgren, in case you're wondering.'

'For God's sake,' Bäckström said, feeling his blood pressure rising. 'For God's sake, Annika, it's pretty obvious, isn't it? Frida Fridensdal with an "s", and Dare to Care for Our Smallest Friends. She's a nutter. I mean, Dare to Care for Our Smallest Friends? What's she bothered about, lice and cockroaches?'

'I hear what you're saying, I understand the way you're thinking. That was why I interviewed her myself. On Friday, at her workplace, seeing as she refused to come down to the station, if anyone's wondering. According to what she said then, she daren't live at home any more. She says she thinks her life is in danger and has moved in with a friend. But what the friend's name is and where she lives, she didn't want to say. She reckons she daren't say. Says she doesn't trust the police to protect her. Nor her friend, come to that. This friend is also supposed to have been married to a police officer who used to beat and rape her.'

'Who'd have thought it?' Bäckström snorted.

'To start with, I don't think she's making it up. Apart from the usual human exaggerations that you and I have learned to live with. She's genuinely frightened. Terrified, in fact, and when it comes to the threat she's reported, it really doesn't sound good. Aggravated illegal threats, without any doubt.'

'Really?' Bäckström said. 'So what's happened, then?' I can hardly contain myself, he thought. Say what you like about Carlsson, but she doesn't scare easily.

'I'm coming to that, but the big mystery is actually something else entirely.'

'What?'

'It's completely impossible to match what she says about the threat she's received with old Mrs Linderoth, who seems to be a rather genteel old lady. None of it makes sense, but Fridensdal swears that old Mrs Linderoth is behind the threat against her.'

'Okay,' Bäckström said. 'I'm listening.'

5

On Thursday afternoon Frida Fridensdal had left work in Kista at five o'clock and had gone down into the garage, got into her car and driven off to Solna shopping centre to get food for the weekend. When she was finished she drove home to her flat in Filmstaden to have dinner, watch a bit of television, then go to bed.

'According to what she's told us, she gets home about quarter past six. She makes dinner, eats, talks to a friend on the phone. Watches the news on television, and then someone rings on her front door. She thinks it must have been just after half past seven.

'She'd locked the front door?' Bäckström asked, already guessing what was coming next.

'Yes, it was locked. Before she opened it she looked through the peephole, seeing as she wasn't expecting anyone and as she was generally pretty cautious about opening the door to people she didn't know. The man standing outside looked like a courier of some sort; he was wearing a blue jacket and carrying a large bouquet of flowers. She assumed he was delivering flowers. And so she opened the door.'

Why don't they ever learn? Bäckström thought.

'Everything happens pretty quickly after that. He marches straight into the flat. Puts the flowers down on the hall table. Looks at her and puts his finger to his lips, tells her to be quiet, even though she isn't saying anything. Then he points to the sofa in the living room. She goes in and sits down. The way she describes it, she's suddenly feeling completely empty inside, just terrified. She daren't even scream. She can't breathe, she daren't even look at him. She's at her wits' end, poor thing.'

'So what was the message, then?'

'At first he doesn't say anything. Just stands there, and when he does eventually open his mouth he speaks very quietly, in an almost friendly way, like he's trying to be persuasive, if I can put it like that. The television is on, so she has trouble hearing what he's saying. But there are three main points. Firstly, she hasn't seen him. Secondly, she must never say anything else about Elisabeth, and if she's ever asked she must only say nice things about her, and especially Elisabeth's love of animals and how good she is at looking after them. The third thing is that he's going to leave shortly. But she must sit there for fifteen minutes after she hears the door close and not say a word about any of this.'

'Elisabeth? He calls Mrs Linderoth Elisabeth? She's quite sure about that?'

'Quite sure.' Detective Inspector Annika Carlsson nodded emphatically.

'So does he say anything else?' This doesn't sound good, Bäckström thought.

'Yes, I'm afraid he does. As soon as he's finished the preliminaries, as I've just outlined, he takes out a flick-knife or stiletto. The victim describes him as suddenly standing there with a knife in his hand. His right arm jerks, then suddenly the knife is there. Well, I think it sounds like a flick-knife or stiletto. She also says he's wearing black gloves. This is the first time she mentions the fact that he's wearing gloves and, according to what she says, this is when she starts to feel convinced that he's going to murder her, or at least rape her.'

'But he doesn't.'

'No, he just grins. Looks at her and says that if she doesn't follow his advice he'll make sure she has room for a whole pet-shop up her cunt, holding up the knife at the same time, so the message is pretty clear. Then he leaves. Picking up the flowers on the way. He shuts the door and vanishes, just like that. No witnesses. No one saw anything, no one heard anything.'

'And she's not making it up?'

'No, you should have seen and heard her. That was more than enough to convince me.'

'Then what?'

'She sits there on the sofa, shaking, until she pulls herself together enough to phone a friend, the same friend she spoke to at about seven o'clock. The time of the call, according to her mobile, is twenty-one minutes past eight in the evening. The friend comes over and picks her up, then they drive down here to file a report with us. The report is lodged at quarter past nine that evening.'

'What about this friend, then? Have you spoken to her?'

'No, the victim refuses to give her name. The friend sat in on the interview, of course, and said her name was Lisbeth Johansson, and she even gave ID and mobile phone numbers, but I'm afraid none of that turned out to be genuine. This is the friend who's supposed to have been married to the policeman who assaulted and raped her. Naturally, I've asked the victim why she, or rather both of them, are behaving like this. According to her, it's because neither of them trusts the police.'

'A description, then? Has she given us anything to go on?' They refuse to say what their names are and where they live but they still expect us to sodding well protect them, Bäckström thought. Bull-dykes, he thought.

'Yes, and it's actually pretty good. Unfortunately, it matches rather too well with rather too many men who are active in this branch. The perpetrator was dressed in dark trousers and a blue, mid-length hooded jacket in some nylon-like material. No logos or stickers on the jacket, she's quite sure of that. Black gloves, but she's not sure what he had on his feet. If she had to guess, she'd say a pair of ordinary trainers. White plimsolls, as she put it. He's about one metre ninety tall. Well-built, in good shape, looked strong. Thin face, prominent features, short black hair, dark, deep-set eyes, a large, slightly crooked nose, defined chin, three days' worth of stubble, spoke perfect Swedish with no accent, didn't smell of tobacco, sweat or aftershave. Somewhere between thirty and forty years old.'

Annika Carlsson moved her pen over her notes as she spoke.

'Well, that's about all. I was thinking of digging out some pictures for her to look at – if she's willing to be interviewed again. As soon as we've finished this meeting, I'll email you the initial report and transcript of the interview.'

'Excellent,' Bäckström said, raising his hand to avert questions or any other sort of unnecessary nonsense. 'If you take care of her, I'll deal with what our colleagues in the City Police have offloaded on to us. Which leaves the second matter,' he went on. 'You said you had two cases. What's the second one about?' Just as well to get it out of the way, he thought.

'Of course,' Annika Carlsson said, and for some reason pursed her lips. 'But I think it might be best if Jenny here went through this one for us. She's the one who's been dealing with it.'

Jenny, Bäckström thought. Jenny Rogersson, his most recent and youngest colleague, and one he had recruited all on his own. Jenny with the long blond hair, dazzling white smile and generous bust. Jenny, who these days was the only breath of fresh air in the madhouse where he was forced to spend his days. Jenny, a delight to the eye, balsam for his soul, who gave his fantasies wings and offered him the opportunity to escape to a different, better world, even on a Monday like this one.

6

'Thanks, Annika,' Jenny Rogersson said as she leaned over the bundle of papers in front of her on the table.

'I'm listening,' Bäckström said curtly. I decide who gets to speak in here, he thought.

'Thanks, boss,' Rogersson said. 'Well, I should probably start with a report we received last Monday, on the afternoon of Monday, 20 May,' Jenny went on. 'It was filed at reception here in the police station, but it's a bit unclear who reported it because there were so many people who wanted help with passports and a whole load of other things. The report's anonymous. It consists of a letter addressed to the police here in Solna, and the text at the top of the letter reads "To the Crime Department of the Police Authority in Solna". Below this there's a heading: "Report of an assault that took place in the car park in front of Drottningholm Palace on Sunday, 19 May, just after eleven o'clock in the evening". End of quote. So the event in question is supposed to have taken place the evening before we received the report. Which is pretty much all there is to say about that.'

Acting Detective Inspector Jenny Rogersson nodded to emphasize what she'd just said.

'So what does it say in the report, then?' Bäckström asked.

'It's a long story, almost two pages, in which the complainant describes what happened. It's been written on a computer, neatly printed out. Well formulated, no spelling mistakes, maybe a bit lacking in structure, and concludes with the complainant saying she wants to remain anonymous, but that she swears on her honour that everything she's written is true.'

'She? How do you know that? That it's a woman, I mean?' Bäckström asked. Sweet Jesus, look at the tits on that, he thought, and crossed his left leg over the right one just in case the super-salami decided to stir. And then there was the little black top that was stretched across everything.

'That's the impression I get. Reading between the lines, I think it's fairly clear, if I can put it like that. Among other things, she mentions in passing her dead husband. An older, well-educated woman, a widow, who also happens to live in the vicinity of the palace. I'm fairly sure about that but, if you like, boss, I could give more examples,' Jenny Rogersson said to Bäckström.

'Tell me what happened,' he said. Dear God, he thought, as the super-salami had definitely worked out what was going on and had decided to turn his beautifully fitted trousers into a circus tent.

'According to the complainant, she takes her dog out for its usual evening walk. She heads south-east, through the section of the park that's just outside the fence surrounding the palace grounds, and as she approaches the car park she hears two agitated male voices. Two men are standing on the north side of the car park, close to the tennis courts, having an argument. One of them is extremely upset and is shouting and swearing at the other.'

'I'm listening,' said Bäckström, who had now taken the

extra precaution of moving his chair closer to the table so that the super-salami was completely hidden from view.

'Well, there's also a car parked beside them, but she doesn't know what make. Only that it's black and looks expensive – a Mercedes, BMW, something like that. But, otherwise, the car park is completely deserted, and there's no one else around. When she hears them she stops and, if I've understood correctly, takes cover behind the fence surrounding the tennis courts, about thirty metres or so away from the two men. So she wouldn't be seen, basically.'

'Okay, okay,' Bäckström said, experiencing an increasing need to have something else to think about apart from the deep chasm between Jenny Rogersson's breasts. Especially as she had turned to face him and the distance between them was negligible.

'Correct me if I'm wrong,' he went on. 'Two men are arguing, and one of them is very aggressive and shouting and swearing at the other one. Then our witness comes along with her dog and hides behind a fence so as not to be seen.'

'She's actually on her own – our witness, I mean,' Rogersson replied. 'Her dog's dead. Died last autumn, apparently. It was a standard poodle, by the way. Called Sickan. She says so in her letter.'

'Hang on a minute,' Bäckström said. 'Just hang on. Are you saying the old bag is wandering about in the park outside Drottningholm Palace in the middle of the night, dragging a dead dog behind her?'

'I can see what you're thinking,' Rogersson said, cautiously firing off another smile. 'If I've understood correctly, our witness went out with her dog for exactly the same evening walk for years and, apparently, Sickan was fifteen when he died. Always the same route. South from her house, then south-east, round the car park outside Drottningholm Palace, then back again. It became something of a routine for her, and she seems to have carried on with it even after Sickan died. But on her own now, of course.'

'I still don't get it. Sickan's a he? A male dog, I mean?'

'I know, how cute is that?' Jenny Rogersson grinned, flashing her white teeth and full red lips. 'It was his nickname, apparently, and—'

'Right, I see,' Bäckström said. 'But if we could—'

'Sorry to interrupt, but is it too much to ask to hear what actually happened?' Annika Carlsson said with ice in her voice and sharp eyes that for some reason were drilling into the entirely innocent Bäckström.

'Yes, sorry, this is all getting a bit muddled,' Jenny Rogersson said, not seeming unduly upset. 'The short version is that we have a male perpetrator who is extremely upset, shouting and swearing at the other man – our victim, in other words – while he's waving something in his hand, something that our witness at first thought was a sturdy piece of pipe. Then he walks over and hits the other man in the face, knocking him to the ground, and then, as the man's crawling about the car park on all fours, he starts kicking him and hitting him with the length of pipe. Then he apparently tries to stick it between the victim's legs at the same time as he gives him one last kick in the backside. Then he simply walks away, gets in his car and drives off, wheels spinning. Simultaneously, his victim gets to his feet and runs away from the scene.'

'Did she see the car's registration number?' Annika Carlsson still sounded abrupt.

'No. She didn't have time. But she's fairly sure the last

digit was a nine, and she thinks the penultimate number might have been nine as well. Two nines at the end, and it was a big, black car that looked expensive. She's sure about that.'

'What about the length of pipe, then? The weapon. If I've understood correctly, that was left in the car park?'

'Yes, of course.' Rogersson nodded happily. 'The best thing about this is that it wasn't a length of pipe after all.'

'Not a length of pipe?' Annika Carlsson didn't sound anywhere near as happy.

'No, it was an art catalogue which the perpetrator had rolled up, which is why she thought it was a length of pipe. It's from a famous English auction house. World famous, in fact. The auction house, I mean. I googled it: it's called Sotheby's; it's in London. They sell expensive paintings and furniture and carpets and antiques, and this catalogue contains pictures of a whole load of things that were sold at auction in London in early May. Just two weeks before our perpetrator decides to use it to assault his victim. I've got it here, actually,' Jenny Rogersson said, holding up a transparent plastic folder containing a green catalogue with the Sotheby's logo on the cover. 'Our anonymous witness sent it in. She found it in the car park and realized that it must have been what she saw. The catalogue and her letter were in one of those padded envelopes you can get from the post office. There are traces of blood on it – the catalogue, I mean. Spots, and a few smears. Presumably, the victim's blood, in light of the witness's statement.'

'How do you know it's blood?'

Annika Carlsson was evidently refusing to back down. Not much sisterly love there, Bäckström thought.

'I asked Hernandez in Forensics to check it out. The

traces tested positive for blood. He also sent a sample to the National Lab for DNA testing.'

'You think our victim might be in the database?' Bäckström asked. What's the point of that? The whole thing's an open and shut case, he thought. One arse-bandit assaults another arse-bandit. Typical fag-fight – they'd probably fallen out about the price of some antique dildo belonging to a third arse-bandit. What sort of normal person would ever think of using an auction catalogue as an offensive weapon?

'Well, he isn't,' Rogersson said. 'That's what's so incredible about this report. Because our witness says she recognized the victim. He's one of her neighbours. She's known him for years, so she's quite sure. She says they only live a few blocks from each other. I've checked him out. No criminal record. Seems to be a thoroughly decent person. A friend of the king's, maybe. You never know.'

'Go on,' Bäckström said. His friend the super-salami seemed to have calmed down. Must have been the dead dog, he thought. Unless it was those anal acrobats that had made him lose his concentration.

'His name is Hans Ulrik von Comer, a baron, one of those aristocratic types, sixty-three years old. Married with two grown-up children – two daughters, both married. He lives in a house that he rents. It's only a few hundred metres from the palace, evidently owned by the Court Administration. He also seems to have a connection with the court. He's some sort of art expert, he's got a PhD in art history, looks like he helps the court take care of their art and antiques. He's also got a business that trades in works of art, provides valuations, helps people to buy and sell art, that sort of thing.'

'Has he filed a complaint?' Bäckström asked, even

though he already knew the answer. Married with two daughters, and why upset his little wife unnecessarily? Lovely!

'No, that's the funny thing,' Rogersson said. 'I can't find any complaint from him. So I called him and said we'd received an anonymous report suggesting that he'd been assaulted and asked if he had anything to say about that. He denied it emphatically. Said he hadn't even been in the area when it happened. He sounded pretty upset, actually.'

'Surprise, surprise,' Bäckström said, glancing demonstratively at his watch. 'Okay, okay,' he went on. 'If you ask me, this sounds like a typical case for no further action. Write it off as "No crime committed" so we don't mess up the statistics unnecessarily. I'll nod it through. Well, let's close the meeting there. If anyone else has anything that's troubling them, I'll be in my room until lunchtime. After that, I'm afraid I shall be at a meeting with Regional Crime, so you'll have to try to manage without me.'

7

The first thing he did when he was safely behind the closed door was press the do-not-disturb button. Then he took three deep breaths before unlocking the top drawer of his desk, taking out his office bottle and pouring himself a good stiff drink, rounded off with two throat sweets as soon as the fine Russian vodka had settled nicely in his stomach. Only then did he begin to take stock of his morning.

Something that had started with an old dear forgetting to feed her pet rabbit had spawned a dozen reports of serious offences in which the perpetrator was an old woman who was clearly well into her second childhood, and all that remained was to get them written off without them spoiling his own department's clearance rate.

Unfortunately it looked as if the old dear had got hold of a seriously unpleasant character, one that he had no intention of dealing with the way his moronic colleagues in the rabbit and hamster unit over in the City Police had. How in the name of holy hell could someone like her know someone like him? It doesn't make any sense, and she hasn't got any kids of her own either. What else have we got? he thought, sighing deeply and pouring himself another little shot for good measure, even though he usually avoided such modest indulgences before noon.

Two arse-bandits of the posher variety having a girly squabble outside His Royal Majesty's palace. Where the unknown assailant had evidently made use of an art catalogue, and where the victim, some sort of court faggot, denied all knowledge of the incident. What the fuck's wrong with a baseball bat or an old-fashioned axe? he thought, sighing again as someone knocked on his door in spite of the red light.

There's only one person in this building who ignores that, he thought. He cleared his desk and locked the drawer just seconds before Annika Carlsson marched into his room.

'Make yourself at home, Annika,' Bäckström said, without looking up from the papers he was pretending to read.

'Thanks,' she said, putting a far too large plastic folder of case-notes on his desk. She'd already sat herself down.

'The collated material concerning the travails of the animal protection unit,' she explained. 'You promised to sign them off.'

'Mostly for your sake,' Bäckström said.

'In that case, allow me to give you a piece of advice,' she said, leaning back in her chair.

Annika Carlsson had spoken to her uniformed colleagues in Solna who had finally persuaded Mrs Linderoth to open the door to the two male officers from animal protection, as well as the two female officials from the county council, and let them into the flat. They had also told her about Mrs Linderoth's next-door neighbour, who had been extremely upset on her behalf at the miscarriage of justice she believed that Mrs Linderoth had been subjected to.

'According to what our colleague Axelsson says – he's

the one whose mother is an old friend of Mrs Linderoth – neither the officers from animal protection nor the two council women were wearing uniform, or anything else that indicated who they were. According to Mrs Linderoth's neighbour, at first they rang on Linderoth's doorbell, then started banging on the door, before one of them began to shout through her letterbox, telling her to open up. After a while she opened the door slightly, with the security chain on, stuck that old pistol out, and that's what put a rocket under our colleagues and sent them running for cover.'

'So does she, this Linderoth woman, have one of those peepholes in the door?' Must be the vodka, Bäckström thought.

Annika Carlsson suddenly looked pleased.

'Good, Bäckström,' she said. 'I recognize you again now. No, she hasn't, because she had it blocked up. It looks like she's got one, but you can't see out of it, so she wouldn't have seen any ID, and no one had told her in advance that she was going to be having a visit.'

'The neighbour, how certain is she?'

'She lives on the same floor. Her door is right opposite Mrs Linderoth's, and is fitted with a working peephole, in case you're wondering, and as soon as things started to get noisy out there she stood by her door with her eye glued to the peephole. Somehow, she also managed to record them on her mobile. The picture's pretty useless, but the sound quality is good. She played it to me over the phone, and our colleagues were making a hell of a racket. Anyway, she didn't have a clue about what was going on either. Says she was thinking of calling the police. She thought they were criminals picking on pensioners and trying to get into her neighbour's flat. Two women and two men, and she'd only just read an article in the local paper saying that gangs like that usually contain both women and men.'

'You've spoken to her? The neighbour, I mean?'

'Yes, what the hell do you think? I interviewed her over the phone, to see if it was worth bringing her down here.'

Now she's back to her normal self again, Bäckström thought. Open, positive, not holding back on the aggression.

'Interesting,' Bäckström said. Play it cool, he thought.

'Yes, isn't it? So you can get all that crap dropped.' Carlsson pointed at the bundle of case-notes, then stood up abruptly. 'On a completely different subject . . . our latest recruit, little Rogersson, I don't suppose she happens to be your best friend's daughter?'

'How do you mean?' Play it cool, he thought again.

'She's still wet behind the ears. She's still a child, Bäckström. In spite of those massive tits that you and the rest of the blokes in the department can't stop drooling over the whole time.' Annika Carlsson drew big circles in the air in front of her own chest to show what she meant.

'It's hardly the end of the world.' Bäckström shrugged. 'There are considerably worse places to be dry than behind the ears,' he clarified with an innocent expression. That was a good one, he thought.

'What the hell do you mean by that? What sort of worse places?'

'Well, the mouth, for instance. When you realize you're talking complete rubbish and your mouth goes completely dry. That can't be much fun,' Bäckström said. 'What did you think I meant?'

That gave the bull-dyke something to suck on, he

thought as he discreetly moved his right hand closer to the alarm button under his desk. Just in case.

'You need to be seriously fucking careful, Bäckström,' Annika Carlsson said, looking at him with extremely narrow eyes as she pointed her hand at him.

'Thanks,' Bäckström said. 'It was good to see you too. You make sure to have a good day, Annika. Always a pleasure.'

They're crazy about you, he thought as soon as she'd marched out and slammed the door behind her. Even one like his dear colleague Carlsson, even though she played both open entry and mixed doubles.

After precisely one minute there was another knock on his door, more discreet this time. And just before he had time to take out his key and unlock the desk drawer again.

'Come in,' Bäckström yelled, seeing as there was no way – judging by the sound – that it could be Annika Carlsson deciding to pay another spontaneous visit.

Even worse, he thought when he saw who it was. Detective Inspector Rosita Andersson-Trygg, well over fifty, none of which years had passed without trace, the department's very own stormcloud, so it was a good job he already had his phone in his hand.

'You'll have to excuse me, Rosita,' Bäckström said, waving his hand apologetically. 'We'll have to deal with it tomorrow. I've just received an important call,' he went on, covering the receiver.

'Tomorrow? Can you make it first thing tomorrow? It's quite important.' Andersson-Trygg gave him a look that was simultaneously suspicious and pleading.

'By all means, by all means.' Bäckström waved again, slightly more firmly this time, as he demonstratively held the phone up to his ear.

Need to get a lock for that bloody door, he thought as soon as she'd gone. In the absence of any better options, he turned the red light back on and, to make certain, moved the visitor's chair and jammed the back up against the door, then went and sat down again and unlocked the desk drawer.

Time for a serious drink now, he decided. And it was raining. An unremitting summer drizzle that streaked the windows of the office that was his prison. What sort of life is this? he thought with a deep sigh.

8

On the evening of Monday, 27 May, Bäckström had given a lecture to pensioners out in Solna about how they could best protect themselves against the increase in violent crime. This had surprised his colleagues in the police station when it eventually came to their attention, seeing as Bäckström usually avoided anything of that sort and was also known in the station for his dislike of both pensioners and small children, for similarly demonstrable reasons. They were whiney, unreliable and generally incomprehensible, while at the same time demanding far too much attention from hard-working and entirely normal people. They also smelled bad. Both pensioners and small children were simply an unnecessary expense. Every thinking person knew that, not least Bäckström himself. But on this occasion he was making an exception.

A month earlier he had been called by one of his many acquaintances outside the police world. This particular external contact was a property developer and local magnate, and Bäckström had previously had the opportunity to help him with numerous and diverse problems, to their mutual satisfaction and, naturally, with the very greatest discretion.

'I was thinking of inviting you out to dinner, Bäckström,'

his acquaintance began when he called. 'I have a modest proposal that I think might interest you.'

'Sounds like an excellent idea,' said Bäckström, who was careful to keep on top of his personal liquidity, and just a couple of days later they had met in the back room of one of the better class of city-centre restaurants to eat and drink and discuss matters of business.

The property developer needed help with his latest project, which was aimed specifically at pensioners. A housing development with a hundred exclusive apartments, on a waterside location on the banks of the Karlberg Canal, all that sort of thing, as well as an entirely secure environment to protect residents against becoming the victims of crime. The future residents weren't just any old pensioners. They could best be described as extremely well-off senior citizens who divided their time between sailing and golf, wine-tasting, concerts, foreign cruises and long lunches in the Tuscan countryside surrounded by all their children and grandchildren.

Bäckström was still dubious, because the description didn't really match his own view of the ridiculously large group of excessively old and now utterly superfluous citizens who were nothing but a burden to ordinary, decent people. Well-off senior citizens? In his book, they were a great horde of disabled, mentally deficient old crocks with badly fitting false teeth, walking frames and hearing aids, all surrounded by a faint but unmistakable smell of urine. And they were always moaning that they wanted more money and yet another hip operation, their short-term memories resembled ramshackle fencing, and they usually managed to leave their wallets at home. Only a blind and retarded criminal would ever think of picking on them.

'If only you knew how wrong you are on this occasion, Bäckström,' his acquaintance said as he poured yet another stiff Russian vodka into Bäckström's glass.

'I'm listening.' Bäckström nodded, and downed half his drink.

His host repeated that these weren't ordinary pensioners. The ones he was talking about were the approximately one hundred thousand citizens over the age of sixty who controlled more than half the country's assets and who devoted a considerable proportion of their time to worrying about the likelihood of being the victims of crime. Assaults, muggings, burglaries or just someone scratching the paintwork of their Mercedes, and after his much publicized achievements in fighting crime and his appearances in the media, Bäckström was at the top of their wish list when it came to people who could give them sensible advice on such matters.

'And that's where you come in, Bäckström,' his acquaintance declared, emphasizing his remark by raising the glass, which contained eighteen-year-old malt whisky. 'You have no idea how popular you are. This is all about scaring them just enough, and then reassuring them by stressing how important secure accommodation is. That bit, the secure accommodation, is my responsibility. I'll make sure you receive a complete script that you can stick to – simple as that. I can assure you, Bäckström, that if anyone tries to break into that building, it can only be because he's got suicidal tendencies.'

'I hear what you're saying,' Bäckström said. 'I hear what you're saying,' he repeated, for safety's sake.

But there was still a catch, and not exactly a minor one either. According to the rules that Bäckström was governed by, he wasn't able to accept payment for this sort of activity, and because he spent pretty much the whole of his waking life working as a police officer, he was very particular about how he spent the few hours of private life that remained. The only thing his employers usually offered for someone taking on duties of this nature was some time off in lieu. And when would he be able to take that, given his already overloaded schedule?

'That's bloody ridiculous, Bäckström,' his acquaintance said with a wink. 'I have no intention of subjecting you to anything like that. Why don't we do what we've always done in the past? So as far as the practical details go, there'll be nothing for you to worry about. We're talking about a brief introduction, just fifteen, twenty minutes or so, which I was thinking I'd get our PR department to write for you, and then another fifteen minutes for questions. What do you say to that?'

'Sounds good,' Bäckström said, already visualizing the brown envelope in front of him.

'Let's agree on it then,' the property developer said. 'And I'll treat you to a better dinner once we're done.'

Then they had shaken hands and drunk a toast to the deal, and one month later the day had arrived.

9

The meeting took place in the property company's head office, right next to the National Arena out in Solna. The sweet, measured smell of money had struck Bäckström the moment he walked into the large, marble-clad foyer. The members of the audience, about a hundred of them in total, also matched his acquaintance's description fairly well. The women were wearing cashmere jumpers, pearl necklaces and colourful French silk shawls, while the men wore blue blazers, coloured trousers and shoes with little leather tassels on them. There was a lot of air-kissing, chirruping and nasal consonants, and the whole lot of them had jumped the gun with the champagne. The white-clad staff who were laying the vast buffet table in the background clearly indicated that no one was going to go short of lobster tails, vendace caviar or duck liver pâté once Bäckström had delivered his speech. When he had made them see the truth and the light and, above all, realize the importance of secure accommodation and signing up to express their interest in the new apartments on the lists that were already laid out.

Not ordinary pensioners, Bäckström thought, and really there were only two of them who spoiled the image. Two local celebrities, and not least in the police station where he worked. A pair of old friends who had featured on the periphery of a murder investigation he had worked on a few years earlier, Mario 'Godfather' Grimaldi and his brother-in-arms Roly 'Stolly' Stålhammar.

The same Mario 'Godfather' Grimaldi who was rumoured in the police station to own half the district, despite the fact that he was a notorious tax-avoider who had spent a couple of decades at the top of Economic Crime's wish list. All their efforts were in vain, however, because Godfather Grimaldi hadn't picked up so much as a parking ticket throughout the course of his long life, and they had lost interest in him years ago, seeing as he had several medical certificates stating that he was suffering from Alzheimer's and declaring that he was incapable of being interviewed. Bearing in mind his non-existent assets, it was difficult to see what he was doing there.

His health and finances may have been in a poor state, but none of this seemed to have affected his appearance. He was as suntanned and distinguished as any other mafia boss in his black suit and white linen shirt, with not the slightest hint of a tassel on his shiny black shoes.

'I recognize you,' the Godfather said, putting a well-manicured index finger on the chest of the evening's speaker. 'Hang on, don't tell me,' he continued, smiling to show teeth that were as white as the sink in Bäckström's bathroom as he wagged his finger at him. 'I've got it! Beck, Superintendent Beck, that's who you are. Superintendent Evert Beck. I knew it. I often watch that programme you're in on telly.'

You need to be seriously fucking careful, you slippery little organ-grinder, Bäckström thought, giving him the Clint Eastwood glare.

'Good to see you here, Beck,' the Godfather went on. 'Dare I hope that we might be neighbours, you and I?

Apparently, there's a one-room apartment on the ground floor available at a manageable price, if you're—'

'Bäckström's here to give a talk,' Roly Stålhammar interrupted. He had once been a detective with the crime unit in the centre of Stockholm. Swedish heavyweight boxing champion several times, renowned for his physical strength, as the several thousand crooks he had single-handedly thrown in the cells during his forty years as a cop could attest. Roly 'Stolly' Stålhammar was a man with a good reputation in both camps.

He'd been retired several years now. Born and raised in Solna, a childhood friend of Mario Grimaldi, who had arrived in Sweden with his parents as part of the first wave of workforce immigration in the fifties, and since then his faithful follower. He was also a regular at the races out at Solvalla but, seeing as he was said to be as poor as a church mouse, the only thing that could explain his presence here was that his best friend had finally taken the plunge and employed him as his assistant – in spite of the jeans, checked shirt and shabby leather jacket that marked him out from the rest of the audience.

'You look perky, Roly,' Bäckström said with an amiable smile. 'Have you stopped drinking, or what?'

'Perkier than ever,' the legend agreed, looking at Bäckström with eyes that were suddenly as narrow as the proverbial arrow-slits. 'Thanks for asking, and if you feel like going three rounds with someone just get in touch. I promise to make it quick.'

He's not right in the head – pretty lethal, in fact, Bäckström thought, and contented himself with a thoughtful nod, seeing as he had no intention of letting Roly or his ham-like fists come between him and the brown envelope that was waiting just round the corner.

Then it was time. The company's head of press and hospitality introduced the evening's speaker, and the audience applauded to welcome him, applause that was both protracted and encouraging, without ever threatening to become effusive.

Bäckström carried out his mission to the letter. He scared them all just enough by telling them a few horror stories, selected from his own wealth of personal experience on the front line of policing. And then he calmed them down by mining the same rich seam to give them his opinion of how crime could most effectively be tackled. In conclusion, he emphasized the general need for prominent members of society – those who had the necessary resources, many of whom were present in the audience – to protect themselves from becoming victims of crime. In this regard, he felt obliged to place particular stress on secure accommodation.

'You should never compromise when it comes to crooks,' he concluded, giving the audience the full Clint. 'If you give them a finger, they'll grab your whole arm, it's as simple as that,' he declared, and the final round of applause was perhaps a little too effusive in its enthusiasm for his message.

Then there were questions from the audience, which Bäckström handled with aplomb, and on the way out he was greeted with handshakes, pats on the back and words of gratitude. Even his old acquaintances Godfather Grimaldi and Roly Stolly had expressed their appreciation. Mario also happened to have female company, who would have met with the super-salami's approval if she'd shown up thirty years ago. An imposing blonde, slightly taller than Mario, who appeared to be considerably younger than her gentleman friend, but in every other respect she was exactly like her sisters who went out with the men over sixty who evidently owned Sweden.

'Allow me to introduce my beloved to you, Martin,' Mario said, flashing both rows of sparkling teeth. 'You're one of Pyttan's great favourites. She always watches you when you're on television.'

'Have you ever considered going into politics, Superintendent?' Pyttan said, holding up a slender, suntanned right hand that was weighed down with jewels the size of hazelnuts.

'No,' Bäckström said. 'I've got more than enough to do as it is.' It's as simple as that, really, he thought, as he looked at the smiling old rogue squirming at her side. Pyttan's the one wearing the trousers here. I must be sure to let my colleagues in the fraud squad know about that.

'What a shame,' Pyttan declared. 'I'm convinced you'd make an excellent minister of justice, Superintendent. God knows, in these turbulent times Mother Svea needs all the help we can give her. Promise you'll think about it,' she added, and patted him on the arm.

'I promise,' Bäckström said. Another one. There's no end of them.

'You're definitely suited to politics, Bäckström,' Roly Stålhammar agreed, winking at him and rubbing his nose with his right index finger. 'You only have to listen to you for a couple of minutes to understand that you've got natural talent. Just say the word and I'll drag myself to the ballot box. That's one vote you'll get, at any rate. And there's Pyttan here. That's two votes, if I've got my sums right.'

The man had to be a psychopath, and who really fancies standing around chatting to one of them? Bäckström thought. So he made do with nodding at Mario and Roly and planted a gentle kiss on Pyttan's already extended, extremely cool right hand. On his way out he declined another invitation to the impending buffet from the master of ceremonies. He had important work that required his urgent attention at the police station in Solna, and as he stepped out on to the street the big black limousine was already waiting for him.

'Welcome, Superintendent,' the chauffeur said, holding the back door open for him.

'Success, Bäckström,' his host declared as soon as he and Bäckström were seated at the same table they had sat at one month earlier. 'I've just spoken to one of my colleagues, and he was beside himself. But, of course, who would have doubted it?' he added, proposing an introductory toast.

'Thanks,' Bäckström said, raising his glass as he picked up the thick brown envelope that was discreetly tucked under his plate and transferred it to safe-keeping in the inside pocket of his jacket.

'There's one thing I was wondering about, actually,' he said, as Mario and Roly had just popped into his head.

'I'm all ears,' his host replied.

'I ran into an old acquaintance, Mario Grimaldi. Apparently, he's one of the speculators interested in your secure housing.'

'The Godfather,' his host said, smiling weakly and nodding. 'I understand exactly what you mean, and if you check your computer at work I'm sure it will tell you that he's both completely penniless and mentally unwell these days.'

'More or less,' Bäckström said. 'So what's the real deal?'

'The exact opposite,' Bäckström's host answered,

turning his glass. 'Besides, he's done me one or two favours over the years. The sort you can't very easily turn down.'

'Mario had a former colleague of mine, Roly Stålhammar, with him. He's always hanging around with him. What do you know about him?'

'I've never heard of him,' his host said. 'A former policeman, you say? Well, of course Mario knows absolutely everybody, and presumably that includes a number of your colleagues.'

'No matter,' Bäckström said, shrugging his shoulders. Time will tell, he thought. I wonder who those other colleagues might be?

When Bäckström went to bed a few hours later he opened the envelope and counted the contents. How the hell could anyone afford to become minister of justice? he thought, shaking his head as he tucked the envelope under his pillow. Then he fell asleep, and slept soundly and dreamlessly until he was woken by the rain drumming on the sill of his bedroom window.

10

Felicia Pettersson was twenty-eight years old. She had been a police officer for five years, and would have been working on the beat if she hadn't torn one of her ligaments during an indoor bandy match a few months earlier. It turned out to be a complicated injury, and not one that could easily be reconciled with front-line duty as a beat officer. So she had ended up on the reception desk in the police station, and had been there about a month when Bäckström caught sight of her. It was Friday afternoon, when he was already in an excellent mood, because he was on his way to Kungsholmen for an important lunch meeting.

'What the hell are you doing here?' Bäckström said in surprise, and one week later Felicia had been transferred to his serious crime unit.

Bäckström had something of a weakness for Felicia, which shouldn't have been the case, considering her background and the vicious tongues that lay behind his reputation in the force. Felicia was born in Brazil. She was in a children's home in São Paolo, and when she was just a year old she was adopted by a Swedish couple who were both in the police, and lived just outside Stockholm, on one of the islands in Lake Mälaren.

A few years ago, when she was doing her preliminary

training with the crime department in Solna, she had helped Bäckström investigate a double murder, and had won his approval by differentiating herself from her cretinous colleagues, thanks to her ability to understand what he actually meant, and always doing what he told her to. This in spite of Bäckström's conviction that a real police officer also ought to be a real man, while a real woman was better suited to considerably gentler tasks, although what the latter might consist of in more definite detail was something he was wise enough to keep to himself these days.

After Monday's meeting Felicia's immediate superior, Annika Carlsson, had decided that she and Felicia should conduct another interview with Frida Fridensdal to see if she could identify the man who had forced his way into her flat and threatened her.

As a result, Felicia had spent the rest of the day picking out potential perpetrators who matched the woman's original description. It was a dispiriting task, and by the time she had finished she had downloaded over a hundred pictures into her computer, all men in the Stockholm region who, according to police records, could very well be thought to have done precisely what the man they were looking for had done to their victim.

In the meantime, Annika Carlsson had spoken to an extremely reluctant Frida Fridensdal, and it had taken a great deal of persuasion to convince her to agree to be interviewed again.

Eventually, she agreed: nine o'clock the following morning, as long as the meeting took place in her office and lasted no more than half an hour.

11

'How about this one, then?' Felicia asked as they sat in the car on Tuesday morning.

'She's not happy,' Annika Carlsson said. 'Not happy at all, so we'll just have to hope for the best. Make the best of it, you know,' she said, nodding at her younger colleague, smiling and nudging her gently in the side.

'What do you think about me showing her the pictures while you watch her reaction?' Felicia suggested.

'Exactly what I had in mind,' Annika said. If you're lucky, you can see it in their eyes before they start shaking their head, she thought.

Quarter of an hour later they walked into Frida Fridensdal's workplace, and Annika, who had been there once before, noted that as well as the receptionist there was now a Securitas guard, who nodded and smiled at them when they went in.

'We're from the police,' Annika Carlsson said, holding out her ID. 'We're here to see Frida.'

'She's expecting you.' The receptionist nodded and smiled. 'The corridor to the left, third door,' she went on, pointing. 'Help yourselves to coffee and water, if you like.'

'Thanks,' Annika said.

* * *

None of them wanted coffee or water. Least of all their victim. She just shook her head when Annika suggested it.

'No, I just want to get this out of the way so I can be left in peace,' she said.

'Okay,' Annika said, patting her arm gently. 'We'll get it sorted,' she added.

Then they had sat down at the conference table, Felicia in front of her laptop, their victim at her side, so close that she could hear her breathing and feel the fear radiating from her body. Annika Carlsson was sitting at the side of the table so that she could see both the expression in Frida's eyes and the photograph she was looking at.

How would I describe you? Felicia thought as she unfolded the screen and turned the laptop on. Middle-aged, thin, ordinary, in both appearance and clothing. But not now, she thought. Not now, when the only thing visible is a woman who's on the brink of going completely to pieces.

'Okay,' Felicia said. 'Let's get started. Try to look as carefully as you can. There's no pressure, and all you have to do is shake your head and I'll go on. If there's anyone you recognize or want to get a closer look at, just say so.'

'Okay,' Frida said, pressing the knuckles of her left hand to her mouth.

The first pictures had been met with rapid head-shakes, but the more pictures Felicia brought up, the harder it became for their victim to look at them.

How the hell is she going to cope with a hundred and twenty? Annika Carlsson thought, but just as she was thinking it she saw it in the woman's eyes. She had also said it out loud.

'It's him!' Frida Fridensdal exclaimed, putting her hands over her face. 'Oh God, get rid of him. Get rid of him, do you hear!' she shouted, standing up and turning away from the computer, then she burst out crying so hard that her shoulders and back shook.

Number 25, Annika Carlsson thought, and because she was who she was, she didn't need Felicia's laptop to identify the man in the picture. Angel García Gomez. If this had been a lottery, he would probably have been the very worst ticket to draw.

Felicia had also recognized him. Not because she'd ever seen him in real life, but because of her work the previous day, combined with her excellent memory. Angel García Gomez. He had emigrated to Sweden from Chile with his mother as a political refugee in the seventies, and he was known as El Loco, the Madman, in the circles in which he moved.

Wonder why he's called that? she had thought as she added him to her laptop, because there was no obvious explanation in their database. Besides, he was good-looking, and was even smiling slightly in the pictures they had taken of him. Compared to the others, he didn't have much of a criminal record, in a purely formal sense. Almost every charge against him had been dropped.

It had taken them half an hour, numerous paper handkerchiefs, some sisterly sympathy and a lot of soothing words to get anywhere close to sorting their victim out. As soon as they had managed that, they realized that their investigation had just come to an end.

Frida Fridensdal had taken a few deep breaths. Then she had looked at Annika Carlsson, right in the eyes, and nodded to emphasize what she was about to say.

'I want to withdraw my complaint,' she said. 'I don't want anything to do with this any more. I want to be left in peace.'

'There's no need to be frightened,' Annika Carlsson said. She crouched down in front of Frida Fridensdal and took her hands, squeezing them between her own. As if the woman were a little child.

'I don't give a damn. I want to be left in peace. I'm not doing this, not for a second longer. I've talked to a lawyer. He says you can't force me to cooperate.'

Then she had started crying again. Sobbing hopelessly this time, shaking her head the way someone does when they've already made up their mind.

12

At roughly the same time as his colleagues Carlsson and Pettersson were trying to instil fresh courage into their victim, Bäckström had arrived at his office after eight hours of reinvigorating sleep and a nutritious breakfast. Even the taxi-driver who had driven him to work had behaved. He hadn't said a word throughout the entire journey. Not until he stopped outside the police station in Solna and Bäckström started digging through his pockets to find the money to pay him.

'You're Detective Superintendent Bäckström, aren't you? You're the one who shot those bastard Iranians. I'm right, aren't I?'

'Who are you, then?' Bäckström asked. To judge by his accent and appearance, he was pretty much your standard-issue Arab, he thought. If he had any funny business in mind, he could always make little Siggy's acquaintance.

'I'm from Iraq, so you can have this trip on me, Superintendent,' the driver replied with a broad grin, saluting Bäckström with a clenched fist before driving off.

At least Tuesdays were better than Mondays, Bäckström thought as he settled down behind his desk with the red light switched on and a cup of freshly brewed coffee in his hand. And he had something to deal with, and it was high time he got to grips with it if he wasn't to jeopardize the lunch he was already looking forward to.

So he had called the head of the animal welfare unit, Superintendent Love Lindström. To judge by his name and job title, he was another one of the old women who, gender notwithstanding, were undermining the force and its sacred mission.

'Bäckström,' Bäckström said, seeing as that was more than enough of an introduction when you were the country's most famous and respected police officer.

'Good to hear from you, Bäckström,' Lindström replied. He sounded genuinely pleased. 'I understand why you're calling. How can we help you? That really was a terrible business, what my colleagues here at animal welfare were subjected to.'

'Well,' Bäckström said. 'The question is more what I can do for you.'

'How do you mean?'

'I'll give you the short version,' said Bäckström. Not sounding quite so pleased any more, he thought.

First, he had described their perpetrator. An old lady who lived on her own, a confused old dear who already had one foot in the grave, and then he had gone on to describe the actions of Lindström's two colleagues and their two friends from the council.

'Four young people, not even half her age, shouting and banging on her door. None of them in uniform, all in plain clothes, not one of them who even tries to show her their ID. Perhaps it's not so strange that she thinks they're a gang targeting old people and trying to force their way into her flat. Because that's what she thought was happening.'

'But hang on a moment. Of course they showed their IDs. My officers would have identified themselves as police. That goes without saying.'

'So you say,' Bäckström said. 'How can you be sure?'

'Can you hold on a minute?' Lindström replied, sounding worried.

'Of course,' Bäckström said. This is just getting better and better, he thought.

'Sorry it took so long,' Lindström said five minutes later. 'I've just spoken to the two officers who were there, and they both say that they identified themselves. So if Mrs Linderoth is claiming anything different, I'm afraid she's lying.'

'So you say,' Bäckström responded. 'Tell me, how did they do it? When they identified themselves, I mean.'

'According to Borgström, Thomas Borgström, he held his police ID up in front of the peephole in her door while he loudly and clearly explained that they were from the police, and why they were there. The other officer, who also works here with us – Bodström, Claes Bodström – confirms that that's exactly what happened.'

'Through the peephole in the door? Borgström showed his ID through the peephole in Mrs Linderoth's door? And Officer Bodström confirms that this is what happened?'

'Yes. You know, these days they're fitted as standard in all new buildings. And the place she lives in is only a few years old.'

'In that case, I'm afraid we have a problem,' Bäckström said.

'A problem? What do you mean?'

'Mrs Linderoth doesn't have a peephole in her door. Not one that works, anyway. When the housing association wanted to put one in, she said no, and when they went against her wishes and refused to remove it she had it blocked up. She didn't want anyone to be able to see into her flat. Like I said, she's starting to go a bit funny, the way old people often go.'

'Really. You've been there? To the scene, I mean?'

'Yes, I'm afraid that's the lie of the land,' Bäckström declared, without going into specifics. 'There's also a witness. A witness who lives on the same floor and saw the whole of this so-called intervention, and for some reason her account matches Mrs Linderoth's exactly.'

'Their word against my officers'. That's what you're really saying. That it's their word against my officers'.'

'I'm sorry,' Bäckström said, 'but this time it isn't quite that straightforward. I don't want to pre-empt any eventual preliminary investigation into your officers for misuse of office, but I'm afraid I can only conclude that things are rather worse than that. Much worse, actually, if you get my meaning? Did I mention that I'm calling you on my mobile? They're not bad these days. This one's got a video camera and a microphone and can make sound-recordings, if you understand what I mean?' That gave you something to think about, you silly little poof, he thought.

'Yes, I hear what you're saying, but—'

'I have two suggestions,' Bäckström interrupted. Before you really crap yourself, he thought.

'Okay, I'm listening, I hear you.'

'Obviously, the simplest thing would be for me to get your officers over here with the other two and interview them.'

'Oh, surely that won't be necessary?'

'I hope not. Because I'm thinking of dropping the investigation. The whole investigation, in case you're wondering. Your officers, that pair from the council, our witness, and even Mrs Linderoth.'

The sort who crumbles instantly, Bäckström thought as he ended the call. Just as he put his hand in his pocket to take out his key and open his special desk-drawer to pour himself a few well-earned drops, there was a knock on his door. Not a feeble knock, either – it sounded more like a fist banging on the door. It was just as well he hadn't had time to put the key in the lock, because she'd probably have kicked the door in.

'Please, have a seat, Annika,' Bäckström said, gesturing to the visitor's chair.

'Shit!' Annika Carlsson said, throwing her arms out. 'Shit, shit, shit!'

'Tell me,' Bäckström said, even though he had already worked out what had happened with their complainant, Frida Fridensdal, and the report which would have been a shoo-in for a guilty verdict for making unlawful threats if she had the energy to pursue it all the way to court.

13

'Our victim is out of the picture.' Annika Carlsson sighed, shrugging her shoulders in resignation. 'But before she backed out, at least she identified him. That was when it all fell apart.'

'So who was it, then?' Bäckström asked.

'Angel García Gomez.'

Oh, he thought, that lunatic. Bearing in mind the connection to old Mrs Linderoth – Elisabeth, as he ought to call her – it all seemed extremely unlikely.

'How sure is she about that, then?'

'No doubt at all. You should have seen the way she reacted when she saw his picture. You'd have believed her on the spot.'

Angel García Gomez, Bäckström thought. Not exactly the sort you'd choose to ask in for a cup of tea.

'And now she doesn't want to play any more?'

'Refused point blank and, just to make sure, her lawyer called a little while ago and demanded that the preliminary investigation be dropped immediately.'

'Well,' Bäckström said, 'that isn't down to him, of course.'

'What do we do?'

'We find out what the connection is between our old dear and someone like García Gomez.'

'Well, I haven't found anything.' Annika Carlsson sighed. 'It's unbelievable.'

'Yes, and that's what makes this profession so appealing,' Bäckström replied philosophically.

'The easiest thing would be to ask her – Mrs Linderoth.'

'Nope,' Bäckström said, shaking his head. 'First, we need to figure it out. Then we might be able to talk to her. Have you spoken to our colleague, Axelsson? Wasn't it his mother who knew the old bag?'

'Yes, I just have. He had no idea. Just as bemused as us.'

'Strange,' Bäckström said. This is completely fucking unbelievable, he thought.

'Okay. How are you getting on with those complaints, by the way?' Annika Carlsson asked, nodding towards the plastic folder on Bäckström's desk.

'Done and dusted,' he said. 'A simple misunderstanding, that's all. That sort of thing happens. What did you expect?'

'You're not all bad, Bäckström,' Annika Carlsson said with a smile, then got to her feet.

They're crazy about you, Bäckström thought as she disappeared through the doorway. It must be high time for lunch. Or it would have been, if it weren't for all the idiots who kept knocking on his door.

'Come in,' he shouted.

14

In spite of a restorative lunch, in spite of the fact that he had fended off the threat of dehydration and made sure his blood-sugar levels were okay, Bäckström still felt so out of sorts that he couldn't even manage to sign out of work and go home for a few hours of life-enhancing sleep.

What sort of life are we living? he thought as he returned to his office and all the colleagues seeking help and advice who were constantly cluttering up his doorway. Even the thugs seemed to have lost their impetus and had stopped contributing to crime-reduction programmes by conducting regular purges of their own ranks. It was almost six months since he had had a proper murder to investigate, and what had he been given instead? A mad old dear who had forgotten to feed her rabbit, and an anal acrobat who had tried to kill another bum-bandit with an auction catalogue. It was also raining, for the third day in a row, and he'd evidently forgotten to switch off his phone, because it had started to ring.

'Bäckström,' he said. Dear old Sweden's heading straight down the dumper, he thought.

It was Felicia Pettersson. 'Hello, boss, I hope I'm not disturbing you. Have you got five minutes?'

'Sure,' he answered. 'As long as you bring a double latte with you.' Same colour as you, he thought.

'Yes, boss. Coming right up.'

Where does she get the energy to sound like that? he thought. Even if she was from Brazil, and presumably had it in her blood.

Felicia didn't really want anything in particular. At least, nothing to do with work. She mainly just wanted to thank him.

'I spoke to Annika, boss,' Felicia said. 'I heard that you'd written off those silly complaints against Mrs Linderoth.'

'Oh, it was nothing,' Bäckström said. Quite sweet really, he thought. But far too suntanned for his taste.

'That sad business with Mrs Linderoth reminded me of my old granddad. He was very fond of animals as well, even if he wasn't always completely clear up top. If you've got five minutes, boss?'

'Sure,' he said. Wonder what the old bastard did? Probably managed to flush his puppy down the toilet. Or he tried to wipe his backside on it. There were several promising possibilities, and Bäckström felt instantly much brighter.

For the past few years, Felicia's old grandfather had been in an old people's home on one of the islands out in Lake Mälaren. She usually visited him a couple of times a week, but over the past year, unfortunately, he had been getting more and more depressed.

'No, it can't be easy for him.' Bäckström sighed. Surprise, surprise, he thought.

'But for the past couple of months he's been like a different person. Happy and cheerful. Just like he was before. He even remembers my name when I go to see him.'

'How lovely,' Bäckström said. 'How come?' What the fuck am I supposed to say? he thought.

'He's a completely different person since they got a care dog for the home he's in.'

'A care dog?' What the fuck's she going on about? In his mind's eye at that moment he could see a big St Bernard waving its tail, with a huge barrel of cognac round its neck.

A couple of months ago the staff at the home had bought a care dog for the old people who lived there. A suitably sized dog with a soft coat that ran round the wards while the residents patted him and scratched his neck.

'It's completely brilliant,' Felicia Pettersson said. 'When I was there on Sunday he jumped up on Granddad's bed while he was in it, and just lay there while my grandfather stroked his coat. You should have seen the look on Granddad's face, boss. He was like a little kid. It was wonderful.'

Sweet Jesus, Bäckström thought. Is she trying to kill me? When that day eventually came, he was planning to take matters into his own hands with a final conversation with little Siggy. Not try to get help from a mutt that left hair all over his silk pyjamas and drooled on his face as he lay there breathing his last with no chance of defending himself.

'It does sound wonderful,' he said. What the fuck am I supposed to say? he thought.

'That was what made me think of old Mrs Linderoth,' Felicia said. 'When we checked her out, I saw that she's an outpatient at a clinic specializing in patients suffering from dementia and showing signs of early onset Alzheimer's. It's here in Solna – seems to be a private clinic, but they haven't got any animals there. I called to check. I thought I might call them again and suggest that they buy some. A dog, maybe, or a cat, or a couple of rabbits would probably work too. Considering old Mrs Linderoth and the other old people who go there, I mean. And she wouldn't have the responsibility of looking after them on her own.'

What the fuck's going on? Bäckström thought. I thought I worked at a police station. Unless I've ended up in a vet's instead. Pretty little darkie's obviously completely mad.

'Do you know what, Felicia?' he said, smiling benevolently and glancing at his watch, just to be on the safe side. 'That sounds like a wonderful idea. Like I just said.'

'Thanks, boss,' Felicia said. 'Thanks, I knew you'd understand what I meant, boss.'

As soon as she closed the door behind her Bäckström leapt up from his desk, threw his coat on and made a run for it. In the nick of time, clearly, seeing as Rosita Andersson-Trygg was already on her way towards his office.

'Bäckström, I need to talk to you! You did promise.'

'Tomorrow,' Bäckström said. 'It'll have to be tomorrow,' he repeated. He shook his head and waved his hand to fend her off.

Emerging on to the street, he managed to grab a free taxi that was about to pull away.

'Where do you want to go?' the driver asked, switching on the meter.

'Give me a minute, just get me out of here,' Bäckström said, shaking his head in despair. What's happening to dear old Sweden? he thought. Where are we heading?

15

On Wednesday, 29 May, Detective Superintendent Evert Bäckström managed to stay away from work almost all day. This was thanks to some careful planning the previous evening, when he judiciously used his mobile phone to announce that he would be 'working from home' until eleven o'clock, and then 'attending a meeting of the National Police Board' from one o'clock in the afternoon. Which meant that pretty much all he had to do was show up at the office then turn round at once, and take his time enjoying a nice long sleep in the morning, before having a long lunch and letting his food settle afterwards. If it hadn't been for Rosita Andersson-Trygg, that is, who had evidently been standing around waiting for him all morning and more or less forced herself into his office the moment he opened the door.

So now she was sitting there on his visitor's chair. Watery eyes, skinny, boring and grey.

'I'm listening, Rosita,' Bäckström said with a nod of encouragement. 'I understand that you must want to get something very important off your chest.'

Detective Inspector Rosita Andersson-Trygg had come to express her dissatisfaction at the way Bäckström led the department's work, and, to back her up, she had brought a sheet of notes which she used to help her get through what she wanted to say.

To begin with, she deeply disliked the patronizing attitude towards their colleagues in the animal welfare unit and the important work they did which she considered Bäckström had displayed during the meeting on Monday. She also wished to make clear her own opinion. The police devoted far too much attention to human beings and all of their so-called problems, which in turn harmed all the innocent animals, which were always, both as individuals and as a collective, being subjected to incomprehensible suffering.

'I'm listening, I'm listening,' Bäckström said. 'Go on, go on.' He nodded encouragingly again. He smiled amiably and waved his right hand invitingly. Time for the Bäckström confusion strategy, he thought. This is going to be easy.

Rosita Andersson-Trygg had trouble concealing her surprise at first, but took a deep breath and carried on. Secondly . . .

The actions taken by their colleagues in the animal welfare unit as a result of the decisions of the council were, in her firm opinion, well founded. Mrs Linderoth was clearly unsuitable to care for animals. Unlike her boss, she had taken the trouble to immerse herself in the material on which the council had based its decision, and had carefully read the six complaints that their witness, Frida Fridensdal, had filed with the police and the council over the past six months. Including the horrifying occasion on which the rabbit could have been attacked and killed by a dachshund that lived in the same building if the dog's owner hadn't had the good sense to intervene and rescue the situation.

* * *

'Yes, I hear what you're saying,' Bäckström said, shaking his head sadly. 'Terrible. Simply terrible.'

'Right, okay, but I don't really understand why—'

'You should know that I share your opinion entirely,' Bäckström interrupted, nodding emphatically now. 'You're saying that it was Fridensdal's dachshund that almost killed the little rabbit.'

'No, that's certainly not what I'm saying. Fridensdal hasn't got a dachshund. That's why she left the Animal Rights movement. Because of their almost unhealthy interest in cats and dogs and horses and all the other four-legged furry creatures that only exist to fulfil the peculiar needs of their owners. That's why she and a few of the other members founded Dare to Care for Our Smallest Friends.'

'That's good to hear,' Bäckström said with a deep sigh of relief. 'Good to hear. I got it into my head that it was Fridensdal's dachshund.'

'I don't understand . . .'

'I share her attitude, as I'm sure you realize,' Bäckström said. 'As a child, I grew up with both dogs and cats, but as soon as I left home and got pets of my own, I found it was different animals altogether that I took to my heart.'

'Such as?' Rosita Andersson-Trygg was glaring at him suspiciously.

'All sorts of things,' he said vaguely. 'I've had lots over the years. I had a goldfish called Egon, for instance. He was an excellent little rascal. Bloody good at swimming. Right now I've got a parrot called Isak. We can spend whole weekends talking, him and me. Yes, I've had lots of little friends over the years. I've got a stick insect as well.'

'A stick insect?'

'Yes, they're such strange creatures. I call him Sticky. What do you think of that?'

'Sticky?'

'Yes,' Bäckström said. 'Sticky. You know what? I'm convinced he understands what I'm saying when I talk to him. It looks like he pays more attention when I call him Sticky. I usually put him on the table when I'm having breakfast each morning. He lives in one of those little glass cases, you know. So there are three of us sharing the flat, Isak, Sticky and me.'

At first she sat in silence for almost a minute. Then she started to flap her hands in front of her face. She cleared her throat several times, as if to get her breath back before going on.

'I understand, Bäckström. It's not that I think you're lying to my face, it's just that I can't make it fit with what you said at the meeting the day before yesterday.'

'How do you mean?' he asked innocently.

'Well, if I remember correctly, you called our witness, Frida Fridensdal, a nutter. At the meeting on Monday.'

'Yes, but that was all a misunderstanding,' Bäckström said, looking affronted. 'I'd got completely the wrong idea of her organization. Dare to Care for Our Smallest Friends. I thought she'd given up on animal welfare in order to protect a load of shitty little brats. That that was why she'd left the Animal Rights group. Not because of their unhealthy obsession with dogs and cats.'

'What do you mean? What brats?'

'Oh, those little bastards who spray graffiti all over tube trains and pull the legs off Jiminy Cricket. If you know what I mean?'

Evidently, she was having some difficulty. Her head looked like a bird-box, and if he piled it on just a bit more there was a chance he'd experience a miracle. For the first time in the history of humanity, he might be able to see someone's eyes fall out of their head in sheer surprise.

'Do you know what?' he said, raising his hand in an almost inviting gesture but to stop her before she had time to gather her thoughts. 'You know Cajsa, don't you? Our Chief of Police, Cajsa with the rat?'

'Yes, we're part of the same network, Female Police Officers for Animals.'

'I can imagine. I've always been a great admirer of Cajsa. I'd even go so far as to say that when she set up our new animal welfare unit, it was the most significant reform in the history of the Swedish police.'

'Really? Well, we're in complete agreement on that.'

'Of course. And our dear chief of police has an interest that I most certainly share. As I'm sure you do as well. Obviously, you're aware of her deep love of rats?'

Rosita Andersson-Trygg simply nodded.

'Just like me,' he continued, leaning back in his chair and raising his hands towards the ceiling as if he wanted to embrace the whole world. 'I've loved rats all my life. Rats and mice. Big rats, little rats, naked Japanese rats – those ones with no fur, as I'm sure you know. Not to mention mice, fieldmice, shrews, dancing mice, and the ordinary house mouse, of course.'

Bäckström lowered his hands and smiled broadly at his visitor. Even shaved rats, he thought. Nothing to complain about there when it comes to dining out in lady gardens, and on various other delicacies that you and your chum Cajsa have no idea about, he thought.

'Well, enough of that,' he said, stressing every syllable as he folded his hands on his lap and nodded piously.

'Now that I've got you here, there's something I've been

thinking about for some time. As you're no doubt aware, there are plans to appoint a dedicated animal welfare officer here in the Western District. Someone who would liaise and cooperate with our colleagues in the City Police. And do you know what, Rosita? I think you'd be perfect for the role.'

'That's good to hear, Bäckström. I was thinking of applying for the post.'

'Then I'll have a word with our chief of police. That's the first thing I'll do. I promise.'

'Thanks, Bäckström. Thank you. I owe you an apology. Clearly, I misunderstood completely . . .'

'Oh, forget it,' he said. 'Anna Holt can be a bit tricky, but I know for a fact that she listens to me. Not long ago, she told me she was thinking of getting a cat. Her bloke works in National Crime, so I suppose she spends a lot of time alone. Probably needed the company.'

'What advice did you give her?'

'Obviously, I advised against it. How can you doubt that? Considering what cats do with rats and mice?'

'Thanks, Bäckström, thanks very much indeed.' Rosita Andersson-Trygg nodded and looked at him with sparkling eyes.

As soon as the biggest lunatic in his department had left, he called his superior officer, Anna Holt, and asked to see her as soon as possible.

'What about?' Anna Holt asked.

'It's not something I can tell you over the phone,' he replied. 'But it's something that's vitally important if I'm going to get my department to work properly.'

'Okay, then. See you in five minutes. You can have ten minutes.'

* * *

'It's about the post of animal welfare officer here in the Western District,' Bäckström said as soon as he walked into Police Chief Anna Holt's room, so as not to waste any more time, bearing in mind his impending lunch.

'Oh God,' Anna Holt said, and looked as if she really meant it. 'I'm about as enthusiastic about it as you are, but the decision has already been taken at the regional level, by our commanding officers, so, regardless of what I might think—'

'What do you think of our colleague Andersson-Trygg?' Bäckström interrupted.

'So you could imagine doing without her services?' Holt said with a faint smile.

'Yes,' Bäckström said.

'That's what we'll do then,' Anna Holt said. 'I'd been thinking the same thing myself. You're not all bad, Bäckström.'

16

On Thursday, 30 May it finally stopped raining. You could even see a tiny, pale, early summer sun peering out shyly behind the veils of cloud up in the sky. There was also supposed to be a big city up there, according to what Bäckström had learned in Sunday school as a small boy. But you couldn't see that at the moment, of course. It was far too high up. His Sunday school teacher had told him that.

The day had got off to a bad start – he had barely sat down behind his desk before his phone rang – but as soon as he heard who it was, things immediately took a turn for the better. Much better, and possibly even a sign that this wretched week was approaching its conclusion. It was his latest recruit, Sergeant Jenny Rogersson, who wanted a bit of help from her boss with her investigation into the alleged assault in the car park at Drottningholm Palace.

'I think I could do with some good advice,' she said. 'So if you could spare five minutes, boss, I'd really appreciate it.'

'Of course, Jenny,' Bäckström said. 'My door is always open to you, you know that.' Not only my door, he thought as he hung up, then checked to make sure he hadn't forgotten to fasten his flies.

* * *

About a month earlier Bäckström had received a call from his old compadre and colleague Detective Inspector Jan Rogersson, from the murder squad at National Crime, who was calling on behalf of his daughter. Rogersson had heard a rumour that there might be a vacant post in Bäckström's serious crime unit.

'Where's she working at the moment?' Bäckström asked as a diversionary tactic. He had no intention of hiring any of Rogersson's many offspring. He must have at least half a dozen, distributed among a similar number of feeble-minded mothers, and, according to the rumour mill, at least half of them had joined the police. They couldn't be very bright, and were bound to be ugly as sin. They were probably the spitting image of their father, he thought.

'She's in crime prevention over on Södermalm,' Rogersson said, 'with those morons in their neatly pressed uniforms, and she's had enough of all the pensioners and snotty little brats she has to pretend to be nice to all day long.'

'I'm afraid there could be a problem,' Bäckström said. 'You know what it's like if you want to hire someone. It's not like it used to be, when you could—'

'For fuck's sake, Bäckström,' Rogersson interrupted. 'It's me you're talking to. Rog, your best friend – your only friend, if we're being honest, your only friend since we were at the Academy together.'

'Yeah, yeah. I hear what you're saying,' Bäckström said. What did he mean, best friend? A proper bloke like him looked after himself, so what did he want friends for? Least of all in the world he lived in, where everyone was out to get you.

'Good.'

'Okay, I promise I'll talk to her.' Didn't the bastard ever give up? thought Bäckström.

'Just fix it,' Rogersson said. And with that he had hung up.

A week later he had met her for the first time. She had come over to see him, and when she walked into his office she lit up the room with her smile as she held out her hand and introduced herself.

'Jenny Rogersson,' Jenny Rogersson said. 'It's good to meet Dad's best friend at last.'

'Please, take a seat,' he said, pointing at his visitor's chair. There's no way you're related to that hideous bastard, he thought. Must be candid camera, someone taking the piss, he thought.

Now she was sitting there again, with her skirt halfway up her thighs, leaning forward slightly, with her long blond hair, her red lips, white teeth and the deep cleavage between her pendulous breasts. A whole box of delights within easy reach, and all he had to do was lean forward and grab hold of her.

'What can I do for you, Jenny?' Bäckström asked. He leaned back in his chair and gave her his Clint smile. Just a half-Clint to start with, so she didn't do the splits there and then, he reasoned.

Jenny had come for some advice about the assault case out at Drottningholm Palace. Unfortunately, the investigation seemed to have ground to a halt. An anonymous tip-off, a victim who refused point-blank to admit that anything had happened, and when she spoke to the National Forensics Lab the previous day she had been told that it would be at least a month before she'd get the DNA analysis back.

'Whatever I want it for,' she said with a resigned sigh. 'Seeing as I haven't even got a victim who's prepared to talk to me.'

'Write it off,' Bäckström said. Do something worthwhile with your life, he thought.

'That's just what I was thinking,' Jenny agreed. 'Then I wondered about sending the whole case over to the Security Police, just so they know about it.'

'To the Security Police?' Bäckström said, struggling to conceal his surprise. 'What for?'

'Well, considering the special regulations that apply to us here in the Western District. With the Security Police wanting copies of everything that happens in the district that might have any connection to the court, to the king and his family. The usual security precautions, I suppose. Both Drottningholm and Haga are in our district, of course, and, if I've read the regulations correctly, the Security Police want to hear about any case that has a geographic link or any other connection to the head of state and his family. Even if it's just a bicycle getting stolen out near Drottningholm, they want to know about it.'

'Yes, I don't suppose they've got anything better to do,' Bäckström said, then gave a deep sigh. Bloody pansies, tiptoeing about. Although the king seemed to be a real man. No shadow over him. Completely normal, to judge by everything he'd read in the papers over the past year.

'Okay,' Jenny said with another smile. 'Glad we agree, boss. That we think the same, I mean.'

If only you knew, Bäckström thought.

'Is there anything else I can help you with?' he asked, nodding his head heavily in a very masculine way.

'Mainly just a question out of curiosity, really. If you promise that it'll stay between us?'

'I'm listening,' Bäckström said. He leaned forward, rested his elbows on the desk and steepled his fingers.

'I was thinking about the Anchor, our colleague Annika Carlsson,' she said, also leaning forward, and lowering her voice. 'She's not . . . that way inclined, if I can put it like that?' Jenny used her left hand to indicate what she meant.

'Has she tried to hit on you?' Bäckström asked. Attack dyke flying low, he thought.

'I think so,' Jenny said with yet another smile. 'Not that I mind at all, but I'm straight. Really straight.'

'Good to hear,' Bäckström said, smiling back. A full Clint this time, seeing as it was perfectly obvious that it would soon be time to get the super-salami out.

17

It was Friday before he heard the chimes of freedom ring out, faintly to start with, but stronger and stronger as the day wore on, and, as usual, he had spent the day at a conference. It was vital not to get too set in your ways as a boss, to make sure you were always developing if you wanted to be an aware and fully functional police officer, a public servant worthy of the title, and he himself never missed an opportunity to point out this self-evident fact to his colleagues.

Even within the organization to which he belonged it had become obvious that this lay right at the heart of fighting crime. Conferences and other forms of in-house training were without a shadow of a doubt the fastest growing area of activity within the police. The thirst for knowledge within the force appeared to be almost unquenchable, and Bäckström himself was keen to set a shining example to those around him.

One contributing factor to this was that he was extremely picky when it came to choosing which of all these courses and conferences he would attend. This itself was far from a simple task, given that the choice on offer was practically infinite and covered all manner of subjects and areas of competency. He himself preferred Friday courses which took place outside the everyday police environment, which of course could have a stultifying effect on both discussion and thought. Preferably, they should also take place within walking distance of his apartment on Kungsholmen.

They mustn't start too early, nor finish too late in the day, because this would have an adverse effect on both his preparations in advance of the learning opportunity and his need to evaluate the process he had just partaken of afterwards. It was also particularly important that the whole thing concluded with participants being given the opportunity to socialize and air the ideas that had been raised during the day. Working in small groups, on the other hand, particularly when you had to solve and give presentations about a number of written tasks, was an abomination that could seriously impede the participants' creativity in more than one way.

In light of these important considerations, that day's conference looked singularly promising. A large conference hotel in the city centre, within comfortable walking distance from his home – and it was glorious early summer weather as well – where the whole affair kicked off with coffee and socializing at nine o'clock in the morning and concluded with a general discussion that was expected to end at three o'clock in the afternoon, so participants who'd travelled a long way wouldn't have to worry about not getting home to their loved ones until the middle of the night.

Even the subject for the day was interesting – Truth, Lies and Body Language – seeing as it was aimed at detectives from the crime-solving units, and especially those who worked as lead interviewers in cases of serious violent crime.

Like a hand in a glove, Bäckström thought happily as

he stepped into the foyer of the big conference room at quarter past nine, in time to prepare himself for the pursuit of knowledge with a cup of strong coffee and a couple of Danish pastries.

The opening talk had been given by a professor of forensic psychology, who had arranged the whole conference and who also happened to have written a thesis with the same title.

The professor opened his presentation by going straight to the heart of his argument, specifically that, when it came to telling the difference between truth and lies, body language was far more useful than the purely verbal messages that the person being questioned gave out. With the aid of his computer, PowerPoint, various charts, images, short video clips and a ceaseless torrent of words, the lecturer went on to demonstrate what he meant for the best part of an hour.

People who entirely avoided eye-contact and preferred to stare down at their own laps were therefore just as suspicious as those who looked their interviewer straight in the eye and began each reply by nodding and smiling, regardless of whether they were sitting stock still or trying to wear out the seat and back of their chair.

There's not much wrong with a pair of flickering brown eyes and two little feet tapping at the floor like drumsticks either, Bäckström thought, making himself more comfortable in his chair.

After this introductory declaration of intent, the professor had really gone for it, all the way from test subjects with ordinary facial expressions and spasms to some who seemed completely catatonic, and most of the time he concentrated on physical signs and the gestures contained within them. People clearing their throats and humming as they tugged at their ear lobes, rubbed their noses, massaged their foreheads or scratched their heads.

When it came to the sort of body language that could give you away and reveal your evil deeds, not even someone in a state of total paralysis would have survived a scientific examination by the professor. A slight tremor of the eyelid was grounds enough for serious suspicion, and an enlarged pupil a complete catastrophe for your credibility.

There were also interesting connections between the test subjects' verbal utterances and their body language. People who began practically everything they said with phrases like 'to be honest', 'really', 'with my hand on my heart' and 'just between us', while simultaneously tugging at their ear lobes and rubbing their noses with their index fingers, counted among the most unambiguous liars. In the professor's world, this 'combined behaviour' was as good as a full confession.

If we can actually believe what you're saying, Bäckström thought. Their lecturer was himself making a singularly suspect impression. He was a thin, moth-eaten character in creased jeans and an ill-fitting jacket who spent a lot of time moving his thick glasses between his nose and his hairline, when he wasn't tugging his ear lobes or rubbing his nose with his index finger.

The little poof's making a hell of a racket with all that throat clearing and humming, Bäckström thought. If you were in my custody, I'd give your face a good scrub with carbolic soap, then chuck you in a cell.

* * *

After a five-minute pause for people to stretch their legs, it was time for the concluding question-and-answer session, and once the participants had returned twenty minutes later the great silence had descended.

'No questions?' their lecturer repeated for the third time as he gazed out at his audience.

'From the list of participants, I noted that I have the pleasure of having some of the country's most experienced interviewers here today. Among others, I saw that Superintendent Evert Bäckström is here.' The professor nodded amiably at Bäckström, who was sitting right at the back of the room.

Wonder who the others could be? Bäckström thought, simply nodding back. What the hell's happened to lunch? He wasn't alone in wondering, to judge by the expressions on the other participants' faces.

'It would be interesting if you could share your experiences – from the field, I mean – when it comes to body language as a way of differentiating between truth and lies.'

'Well, it isn't always easy,' Bäckström said, nodding deeply. 'So on that point we're in complete agreement. But I dare say I've learned one or two things over the years. Things that show they're lying, I mean.' He nodded again. Even more deeply this time, to underline the im portance of what he'd just said.

'Any tips? Could you give us any tips, Superintendent?'

'Well, I use a form of body language that's completely infallible. Absolute proof that they're sitting there lying, I mean.'

'That's extremely interesting,' the professor said, looking at Bäckström almost greedily. 'I don't suppose we could—'

'By all means,' Bäckström interrupted, raising his hand to make a point. 'On one condition, however: that it goes no further than this room.'

The professor nodded eagerly and from the silence in the room, he wasn't alone.

'Their noses,' Bäckström said, pointing at his own to avoid any misunderstanding. 'Their noses grow when they're lying.'

'Their noses? Like Pinocchio? Pinocchio's nose grew when he told lies.'

'Exactly,' Bäckström said emphatically. 'It's rock solid. The only sure sign we have, if you ask me. You must have thought about it yourself?'

'I'm afraid—'

'Their noses get longer when they tell lies,' Bäckström interrupted again. 'I've seen it many times, with my own eyes. I remember one interview in particular, a man who'd beaten his beloved wife to death and buried her in an old fertilizer bag as a final farewell. I suppose he wanted to save on funeral costs. Either way, he told so many damn lies that I remember thinking that it was lucky he didn't have a cold, or he'd have needed a sheet to blow his nose.'

'You're making fun of me, Bäckström,' the professor said, looking affronted. 'You're making fun of me, aren't you?'

'I don't know how you can think that,' Bäckström replied, shaking his head. 'Take a look at my nose if you don't believe me. It hasn't grown a millimetre since I answered your question.'

That gave the stupid little poof something to think about, Bäckström thought as he stepped out on to the street and set off towards his lunch. Pinocchio, that was his name, the little faggot in the old story, the one whose nose grew whenever he told a lie. Peter Pan must have been the other one. The one with wings sticking out of his back.

18

After that, he spent the afternoon in the usual way. First, a restorative lunch, then an appointment with his Polish masseuse, Little Miss Friday, whom he had first encountered by chance some months earlier. The building where she conducted her activities happened to be in the same block that he lived in, and when he noticed the red-haired bombshell unlocking the door and going inside the premises twice in the same week, he had quickly worked out what was going on.

Bäckström was a cautious general and, obviously, he had conducted the necessary checks. After a bunch of moronic politicians, aided and abetted by all the other old women – those in trousers as well as skirts – had criminalized the only true love to be found in a wretched world and a wretched epoch, a love where those involved paid their dues at the outset, and in hard cash, he had spoken to an old friend who worked in the City Police's prostitution unit. Within the force, he was known as Dirty Pelle, and he was certainly the right man to approach when Bäckström wanted to make sure his prospective masseuse wasn't on their list of prostitutes. And that her premises weren't on a list of suspect addresses and kept under regular observation.

Dirty Pelle had given the green light. There was

nothing at all in his records, and if anything cropped up to suggest the opposite he promised to get in touch at once. Bäckström had thanked him for his help and sent him the customary bottle of malt whisky.

Only then had he called to book a personal appointment. Aching shoulders and joints, the sort that could afflict a prominent businessman like him, a fully booked diary and therefore as late as possible before closing on a Friday afternoon, if that was feasible? A chirruping masseuse at the other end of the line: of course it was absolutely fine if Director Bäckström was the last customer of the day.

Little Miss Friday's real name was Ludmila, she had an hourglass figure and was a genuine redhead, which it took Bäckström only three visits to find out. Even if, from her side, it was surely love at first sight, though she had done her best to hide the fact.

On his first visit, Bäckström's treatment had begun with him lying on his stomach, covered by nothing but a towel, while Little Ludmila set to work on his stiff muscles and joints. She kneaded, pushed and pulled, and all the stiffness in his muscles and joints vanished straight into the super-salami, and in the end Bäckström was forced to lie like a set square until he rolled over and removed the tent canvas round his waist.

'Goodness!' Ludmila said, wide-eyed, when she saw the result at the front of a perfectly ordinary massage at the back.

'Indeed,' Bäckström said, giving her a half-Clint. 'You've got your work cut out there.'

Love at first sight, he thought as he pulled on his trousers after the end of his session. Even if it had begun with simple manual work, albeit requiring two hands in this instance, the job had been accomplished in a very satisfactory way.

The following week, his very own Little Miss Friday had started with a hug and a peck on the cheek the moment he walked in and concluded with a first-class blowjob that Bäckström was able to reciprocate with interest the following Friday. First, he had offered her a light picnic in the lady-garden, confirming that she was a genuine redhead, as well as a real woman, before allowing her to conclude with a quick ride on the super-salami.

Youthful infatuation, he had thought as he pulled down his trousers for the third time in three weeks in the same premises. His very own Little Miss Friday and, over the course of the next few months, she had become the way in which he always rounded off another week of hard work in the service of justice.

19

It may have been a week full of hard work, but now it was Saturday at last, and time for a simple warrior like Bäckström to slide the sword of justice back in its scabbard and enjoy some well-deserved rest. It was also high time to investigate the issue of little Jenny's origins, so as to forestall any unpleasant surprises of an incestuous nature. If he was going to allow her to ascend the super-salami, he wanted to reassure himself in good time that her supposed father, Detective Inspector Jan Rogersson, wasn't going to get anywhere close to it, not even through the agency of his daughter.

The very thought of that was enough for horrifying images to come into his head. Even though it was only eleven o'clock in the morning, he had been forced to suppress them with the help of an emergency dram, before summoning the strength to call Rogersson and suggest that they meet up for a bite to eat.

'I'll get the first round, you can get the second,' Bäckström added generously, just to make sure that the notorious skinflint didn't get any ideas.

Rogersson thought it sounded like an excellent plan, and had even suggested that they go to his own local restaurant over on Södermalm. It was run by a couple of Serbs, Marko and Janko. They served excellent fried meat, the prices were pretty reasonable and, because they knew what line of work Rogersson was in, he and his guests could always count on the odd drink or two that didn't end up on the bill.

'They're good blokes,' Rogersson said. 'If you order a short you can be sure of getting a double. All above board, some decent birds at the bar, no need to worry about any of those arty faggots. If anyone shows up who's obviously there by mistake, Janko usually chucks them out at once.'

They've been sitting there for half an hour now. They're already on their second free lager and a generously sized chaser, because the manager was practically beside himself that his humble establishment was being honoured by the legendary Evert Bäckström.

'Cheers, Bäckström,' Rogersson said. 'So, how's my daughter getting on?'

'Fine,' Bäckström said. 'I think things could turn out very well in the long term,' he added cautiously. Just not the way you imagine, he thought.

'She's a chip off the old block,' Rogersson said proudly. 'A chip off the old block,' he repeated, raising his glass and taking a couple of long swigs.

'Maybe, but you don't look terribly similar.' The ugly bastard ought to get himself a mirror.

'She's got the same head as me.' Rogersson tapped his right temple with his forefinger to show what he meant. 'That girl's like you and me, Bäckström. Daddy's little Jenny's got a proper cop's head on her shoulders. You know she changed her name to mine when she started at Police Academy?'

'I seem to remember you mentioning it, yes,' Bäckström nodded.

'She gets her looks from her mum, if that's what you're

wondering. They're like peas in a pod. Gun – that's her mum's name – she's a good girl, works as a hairdresser down in Jönköping. That's where she's from. Forty-five, but you wouldn't think it to look at her. Looks more like thirty, at most. She's not that bright, but she's definitely one of the best shags I've had in my life. That's often the way with birds who are a bit thick. They make up for it once they're in the sack, if I can put it like that. She's still got it, if you're wondering. I happened to be passing Jönköping a few months back, and we had a repeat performance.' Rogersson nodded happily, apparently mostly to himself.

'Really?' Bäckström said. This is sounding better and better. Who knows, maybe it'll end up as a double sandwich?

'How did you meet her? Jenny's mum, I mean?'

'I just happened to be passing,' Rogersson said with a grin. 'It was back in the eighties, around the time when our as yet unidentified perpetrator took down the sign with Palme's name on it. I was seconded from the drug squad in Stockholm to National Crime, because they were seriously fucking short of people, as you know. Then they got a murder down in Jönköping. The manager of a petrol station got stabbed and killed. A robbery that got out of hand, and the backwoods cops got interested in one of Gun's old boyfriends. She was a bit wild in those days. Not that surprising, really, given the way she looked.'

'Was it him, then? The boyfriend?' A bit wild, that sounds pretty good, thought Bäckström. There was a good chance that some local benefit-scrounger with shiny white teeth had got Gun up the duff and left Rogersson to take the blame.

'No,' Rogersson said, shaking his head. 'It turned out to

be another local talent. No one who knew little Gun, anyway. It only took us a week to sort it out. So things had to move pretty quickly with Gun, if you get my meaning. She'd only just turned eighteen,' Rogersson said with a sigh. 'Those were the days, Bäckström. There was never any question of us getting together properly. I had my life up in Stockholm. Both my work, and a fiancée. And the first kid, must have been a couple of years old then, and another on the way.'

Imagine, Bäckström thought, but contented himself with a nod.

'But we stayed in contact over all these years. Jenny and me mainly, but Gun as well. They've never gone short. Things turned out well for Gun, really well. She runs a couple of her own beauty salons now. Earns more than either of us.'

Really? Speak for yourself.

'Well, here's to Jenny. Cheers!' Rogersson said, and raised his glass. 'And to her old mum as well.'

'Cheers,' Bäckström responded. This sounds really promising, he thought. Mother and daughter. Could definitely turn out to be a memorable double.

After that, they dropped the subject and enjoyed a very good meal, before moving to the bar and letting the evening degenerate in the traditional pleasant way, as befitted two no-nonsense officers of the law. In fact, things had gone so well that the precise details were shrouded in mist, but, at least when Bäckström came round, he discovered that he was lying in his Hästens bed at home.

He stayed there for most of the day then pulled himself together enough to take a stroll to his local bar and have an early Sunday dinner.

It had turned into a properly lazy Sunday, and when he

got back home he sat down at his secret computer, the one whose IP address couldn't be traced back to him, and did some work on his own online fan club, with the help of the profiles 'Little Red Riding Hood' and 'Curious Blonde', who shared the fact that they each seemed to have experienced both the super-salami and a downstairs picnic. That would give the other ladies something to think about, he thought as he turned off the computer, once he'd let Little Red Riding Hood reveal in confidence the true extent of their idol's assets.

It was still early when he went to bed with a couple of measures of malt whisky to help him prepare for Monday. He nodded off and slept the sleep of the righteous for all of five hours before the phone woke him up to a new day. To Monday, 3 June, which would turn out to be the best day of his life, and proof that the age of miracles wasn't yet over.

III

The investigation into the murder of Thomas Eriksson the lawyer. Preliminary phase

20

When Bäckström stepped into the hall of his latest victim's home, Annika Carlsson was standing waiting for him. She handed him a pair of shoe-covers and gloves and nodded towards the broad staircase leading to the upper floor.

'Upstairs,' she said. 'That's where it all seems to have happened. He was found on the landing. It's big, something like fifty, sixty square metres, and he seems to have used it as a mixture of an office and a living room. There's a large terrace outside.'

'The body's still there?' Bäckström interrupted.

'Of course, I assumed you'd want to see it *in situ*. But our medical officer has been and gone, he left quarter of an hour ago. Niemi and Hernandez are still up there, but they're done with the stairs so you can go ahead.'

'What did he say, then? Our nice old doctor?' Bäckström wanted it clarified.

'Murder,' Carlsson said. 'Hit over the head with a blunt instrument, but you don't have to be a doctor to see that. The back of his head has been smashed in, his skull's completely flattened. He looks bloody awful, frankly.'

Bäckström restricted himself to a nod. Then he sat down on a chair and slipped the shoe-covers on, with some difficulty, before standing up and putting on the plastic gloves.

'I can hardly contain myself,' he said.

'One more thing,' Annika Carlsson said, lowering her voice.

'I'm listening,' Bäckström said. What's she come up with now? he thought.

'Eriksson's got a computer up there,' she said, nodding towards the ceiling. 'On his desk. When I was up there a little while ago Niemi told me that it was switched on, and that the security lock wasn't activated.'

'And?'

'I suggested that he take the opportunity to copy the hard drive, but—'

'So what's the problem?'

'There's a sticker on it, saying it belongs to the law firm Eriksson and Partners, so Niemi wanted to check with the prosecutor first.'

'Fucking coward,' Bäckström snorted.

'So I did it instead,' Annika Carlsson said, handing a small red memory stick to Bäckström.

'What did Niemi have to say about that?'

'Nothing,' Annika Carlsson said with a smile. 'He and Hernandez went off to get coffee.'

'Very wise,' Bäckström said, putting the stick in his pocket. The best day of my life, he thought. The sort of day when everything goes like clockwork and there's nothing that can get in your way.

Bäckström had stopped at the top of the stairs and looked around at the landing that was now his crime scene. In the middle of the room was a big, old-fashioned, English-style desk made of polished hardwood, a sort that Bäckström didn't recognize, with a green leather top. The desk chair was in the same style. A wooden chair with arms, its seat and back upholstered in leather, the same colour as the desktop.

On the floor between the stairs and the desk lay Bäckström's murder victim. He was on his back, parallel to the desk, arms by his sides, wearing black slippers, loose grey trousers and a white linen shirt with the collar undone and the sleeves rolled up. Comfortably and casually dressed for the final meeting of his life, with the grim reaper, and in all essential respects matching Annika Carlsson's description. His face was covered in blood. Blood had run down through his hair to his chin and neck, and a fair amount had soaked into the front of his white shirt, while his smashed-in skull rested flatly on the floor.

'Well, then,' Bäckström said, nodding towards Niemi, who was standing on the other side of the desk and seemed fully occupied taking prints from a black mobile phone. 'What do you think, Peter? Is this an unfortunate accident or just an ordinary suicide?'

'Well,' Peter Niemi said with a weak smile. 'I don't think you need have any concerns there. According to the medical officer who was here to take a look at him, it's a textbook example of how to kill someone with the classic blunt object. In this case, to the victim's head and neck. The back of his head has been beaten in with at least three or four blows, and his neck's broken.'

'Murder weapon?'

'Nothing we've found in the house, even though there are plenty of pokers and candlesticks. If you ask me, I'd guess it was a piece of metal pipe or a baseball bat, the more compact sort. Something rounded, hard, oblong, thick enough to hold comfortably, something that would do serious damage when you set to work. You can probably rule out axes, hammers, anything else with a sharp edge.'

'Was he lying like that when we found him? On his back, I mean?' Bäckström nodded down towards the dead body.

'No. He was lying on his stomach with his right arm under his chest. Left arm curved up over his head. But otherwise his head was in the same position as now, and the body was at the same angle as now, parallel to the desk. One of our uniformed colleagues who was first on the scene took a picture of him on his mobile phone while his partner confirmed the victim was dead. Apparently he used to work as a paramedic before joining the police. When Hernandez and I got here an hour later he was still lying the way he was when they found him. We turned him over when the medical officer was here. That's when we found the mobile,' Niemi said, holding up the black phone. 'It was lying under the body, but it wasn't in his hand. I suppose he must have dropped it when he went down for the count.'

'Strange,' Bäckström said. Strange, he thought.

'What are you thinking?'

'No splatters,' Bäckström said, gesturing towards the polished parquet floor around the dead body and nodding up towards the white ceiling above his head. 'Considering the blows to the back of his head, there ought to be blood everywhere. An explosion of blood. The floor in here ought to be spattered with it, the ceiling too, if you ask me, but all I can see is the pool under his head.'

'You're not the only person to be bothered by that,' Niemi said. 'Hernandez and I both noticed it when we arrived.' He indicated his white-clad colleague at the other end of the room, who was busy moving a large sofa that was set against the wall.

'He couldn't just have been attacked somewhere else, and that was where his head was smashed in, and then his body was moved here?'

'That was our first theory,' Niemi said with a nod. 'The problem is that we can't find anywhere else in the house where it could have happened. Nor any sign that the body has been moved. No drag-marks, no drops of blood along the way – if he was carried, I mean. Another possibility is of course that someone put a bag over his head before he was hit, so the blood ended up in the bag, which the perpetrator took with them when they left.'

'Sounds a bit far-fetched,' Bäckström said.

'Well, I dare say the truth will out,' Niemi added with a shrug.

'Strange,' Bäckström said. Strange, he thought.

'I'm afraid that isn't the only thing that's strange about this case,' Niemi said with a wry smile.

'Okay, I'm listening.' Bäckström gave him an encouraging nod.

'There's a bullet in the ceiling, right above the desk.' Niemi pointed up at the white ceiling.

'Is there, now?' Bäckström said, leaning forward to see better.

'Judging by the angle, it was fired straight up at the ceiling. It's a few centimetres into the plaster. I've seen it – it's visible when I shine a light into the hole – but I haven't pulled it out yet.'

'Bingo! I've just found bullet number two,' Hernandez announced. 'Over here in the sofa.'

Hernandez indicated a hole in the back of the sofa, fringed with white fluff where the stuffing had spilled out.

'Damn, this is starting to look like a gang war,' Bäckström said with feeling. This is getting better and better, he thought.

'Yes, but we've still saved the best till last,' Niemi said with an innocent expression.

'What's that?' Even better? Surely that's impossible? Bäckström thought.

'We've found another body, out on the terrace,' Niemi said, gesturing towards the glazed double doors that led out to the large wooden deck with the waves of Lake Mälaren in the background, sparkling in the sun.

'Another dead body,' Bäckström said. 'Are you having me on?'

'No.' Peter Niemi shook his head. 'He seems pretty dead.'

'Murdered?' Bäckström was looking warily at Niemi.

'Definitely,' Niemi nodded.

'No doubt about it,' Hernandez confirmed. 'But this one's had his throat cut.'

No question about it, easily the best day of my life, Evert Bäckström thought when he walked out of the victim's home a quarter of an hour later, heading for the taxi that was already waiting for him a little further along the street.

21

At roughly the same time as Detective Superintendent Evert Bäckström left the crime scene on Ålstensgatan in Bromma, heading for the police station in Solna to prepare for the first meeting of his investigative team, acting Chief Prosecutor Lisa Lamm received a phone call in her office from her ultimate superior, the Director of the Stockholm Public Prosecution Authority, who informed her that he was putting her in charge of the preliminary investigation into a murder that had in all likelihood occurred during the last day or so.

'The victim isn't just anyone, if I can put it like that,' the director said, clearing his throat gently. 'We're talking about the lawyer Thomas Eriksson, who by all accounts was murdered in his home out in Bromma sometime on Sunday evening or early this morning. So our victim isn't exactly unknown to the media, as you're no doubt aware,' he said, then cleared his throat again.

'Thomas Eriksson, the one the evening papers call the Muslim mafia's favourite lawyer?' Lisa Lamm was having trouble concealing her surprise.

'Exactly, that's the one,' the director said. 'As I'm sure you realize, this could be very complicated and rather unpleasant, depending on the end result. So if you have any doubts at all, I want you to let me know now. I'd just have to appoint someone else.' The director cleared his throat for a third time.

'No,' Lisa Lamm said. 'I'm looking forward to it.'

'Excellent,' the director said. 'If there are any problems, I want you to contact me directly. I'd also like you to keep me informed of your progress.'

'Of course,' Lisa Lamm said.

Thomas Eriksson the lawyer. Bloody hell, she thought as she hung up.

The Western District, Lisa Lamm reflected. At least there's one person there that I know and like. Then she called her old friend Commissioner Toivonen, who was head of the crime unit in the Western District.

'That's a coincidence,' Toivonen said. 'I was just thinking about you. I've just put your investigative team together, and I can give you the good news that you're going to be up to full strength, according to the National Police Committee's recommendations for the investigation of serious offences. Their first meeting is due to take place in three hours. At noon, out here in Solna. I've organized a passcard for you. It's at reception.'

'Thanks. And with me leading the investigation, if I'm allowed to express a preference.'

'On that point, I'm afraid I'm going to have to disappoint you,' Toivonen said. 'This time we've wheeled out the really heavy artillery.'

'Who's that, then?'

'Our very own Evert Bäckström. It's high time that you got to meet the man, the myth, the legend, even if I'm always a bit dubious about the first part of that description.'

'What's he like?'

'You can probably expect a fair bit of bullshit,' Toivonen said, sounding pretty pleased with himself. 'If he gets too awful you'll just have to tell me, and I'll beat some sense into him. I've done it before, so I've got no problem with that.'

Evert Bäckström. Just as well to take the bull by the horns right away, Lisa Lamm thought. Then she called Anna Holt, who was Chief of Police of the Western District, and Bäckström's ultimate boss.

'I had a feeling you were going to call, and I've already worked out what you want to talk about,' Anna Holt said as soon as Lisa Lamm said her name. 'Can I suggest that you and I have a short meeting here, quarter of an hour before you meet Bäckström and the others?'

'Quarter to twelve in your office, that suits me fine,' Lisa Lamm said.

'Excellent,' Holt said. 'Well, thanks for the call.'

Then she had simply hung up. They don't hang around, Lisa Lamm thought, shaking her head.

22

'Please, sit down, Lisa,' Holt said, gesturing to one of the three visitor's chairs that were ranged on the other side of her large desk.

'Thanks,' Lisa Lamm said, and sat down.

'You'll have to correct me if I'm wrong,' Holt went on as she opened one of the files on the desk, 'but I got the impression that you wanted to talk to me about my colleague Evert Bäckström heading up your investigation, and if you're wondering how that happened, it was my decision. Bäckström's worked for me for four years now as the head of the serious crime unit, and that's the department that's responsible for murders here. I couldn't see any reason to go against that.'

'How has it been, then?' Lisa Lamm said, smiling amiably.

'In the time he's been working for me, he's been head of the preliminary investigation in twelve murder cases, and he's cleared up eleven of them. The most recent just a week ago, so there's nothing for you to worry about there.'

'No, I understand that he's supposed to be very effective. What worries me, however, is that he's had previous dealings with our murder victim that might be regarded as affecting his impartiality. Thomas Eriksson defended Afsan Ibrahim when he and his older brother Farshad, and that heavy whose name I've forgotten, were charged with trying to murder Bäckström in his own flat—'

'Hassan Talib,' Holt interjected. 'You're thinking of Hassan Talib, the Ibrahim brothers' cousin, and their very own family thug, to use the language of the evening papers.'

'That's the one,' Lamm said. 'If I'm not mistaken, it took place in early summer . . . four years ago?'

'The evening of 29 May,' Holt confirmed. 'The trial took place in September the same year, and the only one who ended up being charged was Afsan Ibrahim. As you no doubt already know, his older brother Farshad died trying to escape from the Karolinska Hospital where he was being treated for a gunshot wound he picked up during the attempt to kill Bäckström. He lost his grip and fell six floors when he was trying to climb out of the window using a rope-ladder that had been smuggled in. That was one week after the attack on Bäckström. The same day Farshad tried to escape, Hassan Talib died on the operating table as a result of injuries he suffered during the attack on Bäckström. The only survivor was Afsan, who had driven the other two to Bäckström's flat on Kungsholmen. He didn't go into the flat with them but was arrested while he was sitting in the car waiting for them outside the door to Bäckström's building. That happened more or less at the same time as the shooting started up in the flat. As you also probably know, we already had them under surveillance, so the officers who intervened were inside Bäckström's flat just a couple of minutes later. Talib was lying unconscious on the floor of Bäckström's living room. When he tried to shoot Bäckström, Bäckström shoved him back, and he managed to crack his skull against Bäckström's coffee table. Bäckström shot Farshad in the shin when he was trying to stab Bäckström with a knife. The details are all in this file. Including the two inquiries conducted by Internal Investigations. In which, as you're again doubtless already aware, Bäckström was cleared on all counts. Everything he did was strictly by the book.'

'Yes, I've heard about all that,' Lisa Lamm said, pushing away the document folder that Holt had put in front of her. 'What worries me is what happened in conjunction with the trial. Afsan claimed that they had gone to Bäckström's to give him money. Not to kill him. Bäckström was being bribed – he was on the Ibrahim brothers' list of bent cops.'

'An explanation that the court dismissed as lacking credibility,' Holt said. 'And no money was ever found, even though our officers rushed in more or less at the same time everything happened.'

'Yes, I know,' said Lisa Lamm. 'The court rejected Afsan's story, but at the same time he was cleared of the charge of attempted murder. Apparently, it couldn't be ruled out that Afsan genuinely believed that was what was going on. That they were there to bribe Bäckström, not kill him. He was found guilty only on minor charges and got a total of eighteen months in prison. Mainly because he was found to be in possession of ten grams of heroin when he was arrested out in the street. On all other points, the case against him was rejected. If he'd been found guilty, he could have been sentenced to life.'

'Well,' Holt said, 'what the court said when he was found not guilty of attempted murder was that it couldn't be proved beyond reasonable doubt that he was aware that their intention was actually to murder Bäckström. But sure, Thomas Eriksson did a good job. In the way that became something of a trademark for him when he defended people like Afsan and his friends. Questioning and casting as much doubt on the victim as he possibly could. I've been in court and heard him do it, if you're wondering.'

'I understand that it was something of a noisy trial. I wasn't there myself, but—'

'I was there, as I just said,' Holt interrupted. 'And Bäckström was subjected to a whole load of unnecessary crap. He really was. And he was made to go through another internal investigation, where once again he was cleared on all points. I went round to see Bäckström just an hour or so after it had all happened. Forensics were going through his flat, and I have great difficulty believing that he could have hidden a couple of hundred thousand kronor in cash, as Eriksson and his client claimed.'

'Well, he could hardly have been particularly fond of Thomas Eriksson.' Lisa Lamm smiled as she said that.

'No, and he's not alone in that in the force. If that's the criterion, then we probably won't manage to put together an investigating team at all. Practically every officer you talk to believes that Thomas Eriksson was an even bigger crook than the people he defended.'

'I couldn't have put it better myself,' Lisa Lamm said. 'The problem of partiality in a nutshell.'

'Certainly, that's one side of it. The other side is that Bäckström will get this cleared up. Given that he's already convinced that it was the victim's own criminal activities that led to him being murdered, and that he'll soon be able to prove it. The last thing you need to worry about is that he might try to turn this into an unsolved case. In Bäckström's world, this is a gangland killing.'

'Which hardly makes it less of a problem.'

'No,' Holt said. 'But it's a mild westerly breeze compared

to the shit-storm we'll get if you try to have Bäckström replaced by a different lead investigator. Think about it, Lisa,' Holt said. 'Bäckström's a legend, and if you pull him off the case you'll have the whole force against you. Not to mention the public. The Swedish people's very own Clint Eastwood,' Holt concluded with a gentle smile.

'Okay, that doesn't sound great.' Lisa Lamm nodded. 'Do you know what?' Lisa Lamm smiled at Holt.

'What?'

'I'm almost looking forward to working with him. The person, the man, the legend.'

'Good luck,' Holt said with a wry smile.

23

The first meeting of the investigating team, and at twelve o'clock precisely Detective Superintendent Evert Bäckström had walked into the large meeting room, sat down at the end of the table, welcomed them all and handed over to Annika Carlsson, as his acting lead detective.

'All yours, Annika,' Bäckström said, leaning back in his chair and making himself comfortable, folding his hands over his stomach as he looked round the group. As usual, they were mainly lazy, mentally deficient dullards, but in spite of that this was going to be the best day of his life, he thought. The only light in the darkness around him was probably his very own little Jenny, who had swapped her black top for a red one.

'Thanks,' Annika Carlsson said with a nod. 'We're dealing with a murder here, and this is what we know so far. Our victim is the lawyer Thomas Eriksson, forty-eight years old, single, no children, and not exactly unknown to anyone sitting round this table. He was murdered in his home at Ålstensgatan 127 out in Bromma, probably yesterday evening. Cause of death appears to be a blow to the back of the head with a blunt object, according to the preliminary report from the medical officer. The motive is unknown, but so far there's nothing to suggest that it was a burglary or break-in that went wrong. The identity of the culprit or culprits remains to be discovered. And that's why you're sitting here, in case anyone was wondering.'

Annika Carlsson looked up from her papers and nodded to the group.

'As far as the more precise details are concerned, I was thinking that Peter could go through them for you,' Annika Carlsson said as Anna Holt opened the door and stepped in, accompanied by the prosecutor in charge of the preliminary investigation, Lisa Lamm.

'I don't want to interrupt,' Holt said. 'I just wanted to introduce the head of the preliminary investigation, Lisa, or rather Chief Prosecutor Lisa Lamm, to be more formal. I've got to run. But I'm counting on you to sort this out.'

Good-looking girl, Annika Carlsson thought. Petite, short blond hair, smartly and correctly dressed in a skirt, blouse and jacket in matching shades of white and blue. Forty years old at most, to judge by her appearance, bright eyes and, according to rumour, she was unmarried and had no children. Might be a chance here, she thought.

'Welcome, Lisa,' Annika Carlsson said, nodding and smiling. 'Sit down and make yourself at home,' she went on, gesturing towards an empty chair at the other end of the table.

'Thanks,' said Lisa Lamm, sitting down. 'I'm sorry I'm late. Don't let me interrupt,' she went on. She smiled and nodded to the group. 'Please, go on . . .'

'Good,' Bäckström said curtly. 'You're very welcome.' Ten minutes fucked because she can't get here on time, Bäckström thought, and Anchor Carlsson, the unit's very own attack dyke, was evidently already on a mission. Little

Lamm's going to have to watch herself if she wants to avoid getting caught in her clutches.

'Peter Niemi is head of Forensics here in Solna,' Bäckström said, waving his whole hand towards the man in question. 'Give us the usual about when, where and how.'

'Sure,' Niemi said. 'But there'll be a few reservations, seeing as my colleague Hernandez and I have only been on the case for eight hours, but this is how it looks so far. The estimated time of the crime is approximately quarter to ten yesterday evening. The scene of the crime is most probably the upstairs landing of the victim's home on Ålstensgatan. The cause of death, according to the medical officer's preliminary report, is trauma to the head and neck caused by a blunt instrument, which probably knocked him unconscious immediately and caused death within a minute or so.'

'And why do we think that?' Bäckström said, sinking even deeper into his chair.

For various reasons, according to Peter Niemi. Four main reasons, to be specific, and he began to explain them in order of occurrence.

Their victim appeared to be someone who was very conscious of his personal security. The house was fitted with motion sensors, cameras and an emergency alarm, and all the doors and windows were alarmed.

'This is the main entrance to the house,' Niemi said, and tapped at his computer to bring up a picture of the victim's front door on the large screen at one end of the room. 'There are no signs of a break-in, and the perimeter alarms were active throughout the whole of Sunday, until two minutes to nine that evening, when someone, most probably Eriksson himself, if you're wondering, switched off the alarm on the front door and let in one or more visitors.

'Two minutes to nine,' Niemi repeated. 'That's when someone arrives at the house, so that's our first fixed time.'

At twenty minutes to ten the emergency control room received a call from the victim's mobile phone. The call was cut off a minute later without any contact from whoever made the call.

'Emergency control doesn't do anything about the call, for the simple reason that about half of all calls they receive are made by mistake, and another twenty per cent are what they call silent calls, where they never have any contact with whoever makes the call. They only respond if there's reason to suspect that the person calling is in an emergency situation but for some reason is unable to speak. So in this instance they don't do anything. But there's reason to suspect that Eriksson is ringing for help but is beaten to death before he has time to say anything. Twenty to ten, forty-two minutes after admitting one, two or more visitors,' Niemi said.

At six o'clock in the morning, some eight hours later, the medical officer arrived at the scene of the crime to conduct a preliminary examination of the body. The victim's face and neck already exhibited full rigor mortis, and, bearing in mind the temperature inside the house, the medical officer concluded that death had occurred at least six hours earlier, sometime during Sunday evening, before midnight.

'When he was at the scene we didn't know about Eriksson's alarm call, of course, made at twenty to ten, so I called him an hour or so ago and told him about it,'

Niemi explained. 'He had no difficulty accepting that as the likely time. For when Eriksson was killed, I mean.'

'Twenty to ten on Sunday evening,' Bäckström summarized. Niemi's not totally thick, even though he must be at least half-Finnish, to judge by his name, he thought.

'Anything else?' he asked.

'Yes. There seem to have been a lot of calls yesterday evening, to the emergency control room, I mean. Between quarter past ten and five past eleven, three of Eriksson's neighbours called to complain that his dog was running around on the terrace of his house, barking like mad. So Eriksson had a dog. A Rottweiler, a vicious beast, in case anyone's not sure.'

'So what did they do then?' Bäckström asked, although he had already guessed the answer.

'Nothing,' Niemi said. 'We didn't have a car available, simple as that. Then things seem to have calmed down until just after two o'clock at night, when the dog kicks up a hell of a racket. Howling and barking, and when neighbour number four calls and refuses to back down, and also happens to mention to the officer in emergency control the identity of the person who lives in the house with the barking dog, finally things start to move. The officer sends a car that gets there twelve minutes later. Our colleagues ring the doorbell, try the handle and the door's unlocked, so they go in and soon enough find Eriksson dead on the upstairs landing, as you can see here,' Niemi said, clicking to bring up a picture of their blood-soaked murder victim lying on his stomach in front of the desk.

'And then things start to follow the usual path. Hernandez and I were on the scene about an hour later, at half past three in the morning, and that's pretty much that. I'm happy to answer any questions if there are any,' he concluded, clicking to switch off the picture of their victim.

'I've got a question,' Detective Sergeant Rosita Andersson-Trygg said, waving her hand in the air. 'I find what you've just said very, very strange. A complete mystery, if you ask me.'

And who would ever think of asking you? Bäckström thought.

'Go on,' Bäckström said silkily. 'How do you mean, Rosita?'

'The dog's behaviour,' Andersson-Trygg replied. 'Why doesn't the dog bark?'

'Correct me if I'm wrong,' Bäckström said. 'But if I've understood correctly, it was barking like crazy half the night.' The old bag's clearly completely mad. High time to have a serious word with Holt about that promise to get rid of her, he thought.

'Permit me to correct you then,' Andersson-Trygg said tartly. 'The dog's actually completely silent for all of three hours, from eleven o'clock to two o'clock, and that certainly isn't normal behaviour for a Rottweiler whose owner has been murdered.'

'Do you know what?' Bäckström said, smiling gently. 'I'd like you to take an extra good look at this business with the dog, and we'll come back to it. It feels good to know that we have an expert at our disposal.

'Niemi,' Bäckström went on. 'The crime scene. What do we know about it?'

In all likelihood, the victim was murdered where he was found. Close to his desk on the landing.

There were a number of things that still weren't clear, but they were going to have to wait on those until the medical officer had concluded his examination.

'When can we expect his full report, then?' Annika Carlsson asked.

'He promised to do the post-mortem this evening, so hopefully we'll have the preliminary results sometime tomorrow,' Niemi said. 'The final report will probably take a week or so.'

'We'll just have to live with that,' Bäckström said generously. 'To round this off, Peter, what do we know about the cause of death?'

There were still a number of question marks that meant that a conclusive answer was probably best left for the medical officer's report.

'But hit in the head with a blunt instrument, if you're asking me now,' Niemi said. 'Most of the evidence points to that.'

'Good,' Bäckström said. 'So, to sum up what we've got, we're dealing with a murder that took place at about quarter to ten yesterday evening, on the upstairs landing of the victim's home, and the victim was murdered by being hit in the head with a blunt instrument. Annika, can you make sure that our colleagues conducting door-to-door inquiries in the area are given that information at once? Preferably without them ramming it down the throats of everyone they talk to.'

'By all means,' Annika Carlsson said. 'I'll make sure—'

'Don't forget to tell them to ask about the dog as well, and why it was quiet for three hours. I mean, if he was quiet, he could have been whining and whimpering,' Andersson-Trygg interrupted.

'Of course,' Annika Carlsson said with a sigh. 'I hear what you're saying, Rosita.'

'Splendid,' Bäckström said smoothly. 'Well, I suggest a

five-minute break to stretch our legs before you, Peter, tell us about the second body you found out on the terrace.' That gave the animal-rights fascist something to think about, Bäckström thought. And evidently not just her, to judge from the expressions of the rest of the group.

24

Must be a new record for a five-minute break, Bäckström thought as he sat down in his seat at the end of the allotted time, the last one back into the room.

'Well, then,' he said, smiling broadly. 'High time for victim number two, Peter.'

'Yes,' Peter Niemi said. 'Not a pretty sight, I'm afraid.'

Then he had clicked to bring up a picture of a dead Rottweiler lying on the terrace outside the upstairs landing, ten metres from the spot where his owner had in all likelihood been murdered.

'The dog's throat appears to have been cut,' Niemi declared, showing them the gaping wound in its throat and the semicircular pool of blood that had gushed out on to the pale wooden boards of the terrace.

'When?' Bäckström asked.

'If the call to the emergency control room was right, then it must have happened at about two o'clock in the morning . . .'

'Four hours after his owner breathed his last. Strange,' Bäckström said.

'Yes,' Niemi agreed. 'This case doesn't seem to be entirely straightforward. We've sent the dog to the veterinary medicine lab, if anyone's wondering. We also found fragments of fabric in his mouth. Threads, and a larger scrap of cloth that I'd guess came from a pair of jeans.'

'So he probably bit our culprit in the leg,' Bäckström said, resting his elbows on the table and putting his fingers together. 'Anything else interesting you can tell us?'

More oddities, according to Niemi. A lawyer whose head was smashed in with a blunt object, a dog whose throat was cut more than four hours later, and also – as if that weren't already more than enough – at least two shots had been fired on the landing.

Niemi brought up more pictures, showing the bullet holes in the ceiling above the desk and in the back of the sofa. He concluded with a close-up of two flattened bullets lying on a sheet of white paper on the victim's desk, to show them off as well as possible.

'Those are the bullets,' Niemi said. 'I think they came from the same weapon. They're the same calibre, anyway, .22, and they're the same type. Unjacketed lead bullets. We haven't found any casings, which suggests a revolver, and it was probably fired by the victim, as we found traces of powder on his right hand and the lower part of his shirtsleeve. He also had a licence for a .22 revolver. For hunting and finishing off animals caught in traps. He had licences for a total of six different hunting weapons. Two sports rifles and three shotguns, as well as the aforementioned revolver. He's got a gun cabinet down in the basement, but it's locked, so we haven't been in there yet.'

'But you haven't found a revolver?' Bäckström asked.

'Not yet,' Niemi said, shaking his head. 'We've only just started looking, and it's probably going to take the rest of the week. The house is pretty massive. The ground floor is something like two hundred and fifty square metres, the first floor one hundred and fifty, plus a hundred square metres of terrace. Down in the cellar there's a large garage, a gym, sauna, billiard room, wine-cellar, laundry and storeroom. We've barely started the forensic examination so far.'

No blunt instrument and no revolver. But, according to Niemi, they had found quite a few other things. In the top drawer of the desk was a thick brown envelope that turned out to contain 962,000 kronor in thousand-kronor notes, divided into ten bundles, each fastened with a rubber band. On top of the desk was an old-fashioned and well-used handkerchief containing traces of both blood and snot. There was also a crystal carafe that was half full of whisky, and an almost empty glass with just a bit left at the bottom. Niemi hadn't yet had a chance to think about the wider implications of this. Because a number of other things had demanded his attention instead.

'There was another glass,' Niemi said, showing them another picture. 'It was on the coffee table in front of the sofa in the corner, the one with a bullet in the back. If you draw a straight line between the glass and carafe on the desk and the bullet in the back of the sofa . . . then the glass on the table is right on that line . . . just a metre or so further forward, in front of the bullet-hole in the sofa, I mean. And if we assume that the person drinking from that glass is sitting the way people usually do when they're engaged in that sort of activity . . . then there ought to have been a considerable risk that he or she would have been hit in the upper body or head . . . which doesn't appear to have happened, judging from the evidence.'

'The person on the sofa was no longer sitting there,' Annika Carlsson suggested. 'He or she had already moved.'

'No, I'm fairly sure that he . . . or she . . . was still sitting on the sofa, but without being hit. The reason I think that is the evidence we found on this sofa cushion,' Niemi said, showing them a picture of it.

'Look at the dark patch, more or less where the backside of someone sitting on the sofa ought to be,' Niemi said, pointing at the picture.

'The person sitting there shat themselves when the bullet whistled past their ear,' Bäckström concluded. What's going on with today's bad guys? he thought. Crapping themselves as soon as a faggy little lawyer starts shooting at them. If it had been him, he'd have whipped little Siggy out and sent the bullet back with interest.

'Traces of both excrement and urine,' Niemi agreed with a nod. 'Not the first time it's happened, in my experience.' He smiled amiably and closed the picture.

'Any questions?' he added.

'We can do that when we know a bit more,' Bäckström interrupted, to forestall a load of unnecessary chat.

'Annika, if I understood you correctly, we've got more pressing questions to deal with?' he went on, for some reason looking at their prosecutor and the head of their preliminary investigation, Lisa Lamm.

'Authorization to search Eriksson's home isn't a problem at all,' Lisa Lamm said, shaking her head. 'Nor his computer either, seeing as it was in the house and was switched on. Which leaves the law firm, and that could be rather more complicated, as I'm sure you appreciate. For the time being I've decided to have Eriksson's office sealed. In two hours' time I'm going to be meeting his partners to discuss how to handle any further action.'

Bloody hell, Bäckström thought.

'Any other questions, anyone?' he said with a slight sigh.

Then things had gone the way they usually did – questions, speculation, all the usual nonsense – until he'd had enough, raised his hand and put an end to the first meeting of his latest investigative team.

'That's enough talk,' Bäckström said. 'Get to work. Make sure we catch the bastard who did this. We can talk a load of bollocks once he's locked away.'

25

I've got to have some food, Bäckström thought. A proper lunch, a generous drink and at least one large and very cold lager. Then I need to be left in peace to think too. As it was already half past two in the afternoon and his blood-sugar levels were at roughly the same height as his handmade Italian shoes, he decided it was about time.

His right-hand man, Annika Carlsson, was sitting behind her desk in the office, demonstrating her renowned ability to multitask by eating salad from a plastic container at the same time as typing on her computer and nodding to Bäckström.

'Let me guess, our lead detective is thinking of going out to have some lunch,' she said with a smile.

'I was thinking of going for a walk,' Bäckström replied. 'So I can have a bit of peace and quiet to think.'

'You're thinking of going for a walk? Okay, I'm starting to get worried. You're not coming down with something, are you?'

'No,' Bäckström said, shaking his head. 'I just need to do a bit of thinking on my own.'

The first real day of summer, Bäckström thought as he stepped out into the street. Before leaving the police station he had returned to his room to get his sunglasses. His very own surveillance sunglasses, which he always got out when summer arrived and the sun's rays were strong enough to liberate enough female flesh to make it worth the bother. The steel-framed surveillance sunglasses whose black reflective glass protected him from being confused with all the cruising faggots who came out of the woodwork at this time of year looking for raw material for their sick fantasies.

Not like Evert Bäckström in his yellow linen suit and dark glasses, who, elevated above any suspicion of such base motives, calmly strolled down the street from the police station, cut through Solna shopping centre and walked past Råsunda football stadium, and found himself stepping into one of his favourite bars out in Filmstaden half an hour later.

There had been a fair amount to look at along the way, and he hadn't given his latest case any thought at all. All in good time, he thought. He may have been both a mover and a shaker, well known from all his appearances on crime shows on television and with his own internet fanclub, as well as the answer to every woman's secret dreams, but all this, his lot in life, was still only one side of his character. He was also an observer who stood above the human mud-wrestling to which the simpler creatures around him seemed to devote most of their lives. All in good time. You're something of a philosopher as well, Bäckström, he thought as he sat down at his usual table and the bar owner bestowed his usual attentive service on him and immediately brought him an acceptably large and very cold lager.

'Welcome, Bäckström,' he said. 'Can I interest you in a nice piece of grilled steak with Béarnaise sauce and fried potatoes, Superintendent? Without salad.'

'Sounds splendid,' Bäckström said. 'Plus the usual, a

little glass of water and a nice, visible carafe of proper water alongside.'

'Of course, by all means,' his host replied, nodding complicitly.

Then he had eaten in peace and quiet and slowly come back to life. Now he was starting to feel more like his usual self again. Towards the end of the meeting, when his colleagues were banging on about all the ideas and suggestions bouncing around in their little heads, he had actually felt rather flat, and in serious need of a bit of privacy and reflection. The same sort of feeling he usually got when the super-salami had done its thing and he just wanted to be left alone without some completely unknown little lady lying next to him and pawing at him in his big Hästens bed.

Coming back to life, Bäckström thought, raising the little glass and draining the last drops.

As he was drinking his coffee the bar's owner came over and sat down. He was an enthusiastic AIK supporter, just like Bäckström was the moment he entered his bar, and the rumours had evidently already reached him. That Solna's very own legendary detective was investigating the murder of one of the club's arch-enemies.

'You know the bastard was on the board of Djurgården? Talk about a motive.'

'I know,' Bäckström said. 'I know, it sounds like grounds for dropping all charges against whoever did it, if you ask me.'

Then he had taken a taxi back to work, stopping on the way to buy some extra-strong throat sweets to forestall any unfortunate gossip, and he had barely had time to settle into his chair and put his weary feet up on his desk before there was a knock on the door. His very own little Jenny, complete with a tight red top and a very wide smile, asking for a confidential meeting between the two of them.

'If you've got five minutes, that is, boss?'

'By all means. Of course. Sit yourself down,' Bäckström said, gesturing towards his visitor's chair.

Life has returned, he thought, and for a fleeting moment he even considered putting his sunglasses back on again.

26

'What can I do for you, Jenny?' Bäckström asked, crossing his right leg over the left, just in case the super-salami decided to make a move.

'I've got an idea I wanted to try out on you, boss,' Jenny said. She smiled again, leaned forward and held out a sheet of paper.

'I see,' Bäckström replied. He took the sheet and read. Three rows of handwriting, a neat, rounded schoolgirl style – just what he had hoped for when it came to that little detail – and the super-salami had evidently already woken up.

'Read it, boss.' Jenny pointed at the sheet of paper and nodded eagerly.

'Sunday, 19 May. Courtier assaulted with auction catalogue. Tuesday, 21 May. Rabbit taken into care after being neglected. Sunday, 2 June. Lawyer murdered,' Bäckström read out loud, with growing surprise. What the fuck is this? he thought.

'Are you thinking what I'm thinking, boss?' Jenny asked, leaning forward even more. More than slightly excited, apparently, given the way her bosoms were heaving.

'I'm not sure that I am,' Bäckström replied, shaking his head. 'Tell me, I'm listening.'

'It was just an idea I got while I was sitting in the meeting. All of a sudden, I mean, and how often does that happen in cases like this? And I found myself thinking of the three golden rules that apply to the investigation of any murder . . . to start with, you have to make the most of what you've got . . . secondly, you don't make things more complicated than they need to be . . . and thirdly . . . and this is what struck me in the meeting . . . you have to hate coincidence.'

'I see,' Bäckström said. 'You'll have to forgive me, but. . .'

'What I mean is, how common is it to have three cases like this in little more than a week? In the same police district? I mean, the idea that it might be sheer coincidence is a statistical impossibility, considering how unusual it must be. I had a look on the internet. Do you know how long it's been since anyone murdered a lawyer in Sweden, boss?'

'No,' Bäckström said, 'I'm afraid not, but I don't suppose it's the sort of thing that happens every day . . .'

'It's been over fifty years since the last time. That was up in Norrland, by the way, and took place during negotiations in court. One of the parties shot the other party's lawyer. Lawyers must be among the rarest murder victims in the country . . . then there's that business of the rabbit being taken into care . . . I've never heard of a case like that before . . . and then that assault with an auction catalogue as well.'

'I'm listening,' Bäckström said. What the holy fuck is she going on about? he thought.

'You've spent your whole life investigating crime, boss,' Jenny said. 'How many times have you had a case in which a courtier has been assaulted with an auction catalogue? Outside the palace where the king lives too?'

'Never,' Bäckström said emphatically, shaking his head. 'If you ask me, it's probably the first time it's ever happened in Swedish criminal history.'

'Exactly,' Jenny said. 'That's exactly what I thought.'

'I hear what you're saying, Jenny, but I still don't see—'

'It can't be coincidence,' Jenny interrupted, looking at him seriously.

'Can't be coincidence?'

'No.' Jenny nodded. 'It can't be coincidence. There has to be some sort of connection between these three events. That's the only possibility I can see. That one leads to the second, which leads to the third. If we can identify that connection, we also find the solution to the whole thing. Who murdered Eriksson, and all the rest of it for that matter, both the rabbit and the auction catalogue.'

'I see,' Bäckström said. 'I see,' he repeated, his thoughts already having moved on. Say what you like about Rogersson, Bäckström thought, but at least he was a fully functioning police officer who'd never dream of thinking with his tits, so there's no way he could be the father of this little private detective. Not with his looks and her brain – which is just as well, considering Rogersson's non-existent tits, he thought.

'I knew you'd see exactly what I was thinking, boss. That's why I thought it best to come straight to you and not say a word to any of the others.'

'Very wise,' Bäckström said. 'Very wise,' he repeated. 'Let me just check to see if I've understood correctly.'

'Is it okay if I take notes?' Jenny asked, leaning forward and taking back the sheet of paper she had given him.

'Of course,' Bäckström said. 'If I've understood you correctly, you're saying that, to start with, we've got an unknown perpetrator who beats up an aristocratic arse-bandit with an auction catalogue, which leads to a rabbit being taken into care two days later from an elderly woman with dementia issues – if I can put it like that – which finally leads to one or more unknown assailants murdering Eriksson the lawyer less than a fortnight later.'

'Yes, pretty much. I know it sounds a bit weird, but I'm a hundred per cent convinced there has to be a connection. In this case, it really is all about hating coincidence.'

'Interesting,' Bäckström said. 'Worth investigating more thoroughly.' Little Jenny must be the most incredible fuck-wit, he thought. Compared to little Jenny's brain, Little Miss Friday was practically a Nobel Prize winner, as well as being a clear seven-pointer when it came to making the beast with two backs.

'I knew you'd understand how I was thinking, boss . . .'

'Of course, of course,' Bäckström said dismissively. 'Do you know what, Jenny?'

'What, boss?'

'You're to report to me alone. Not a word about this to any of the others.'

'Thanks, boss,' Jenny said. 'I promise I won't disappoint you, boss.'

'Splendid,' Bäckström said, smiling warmly. That way I won't have to watch Anchor Carlsson drag you down to reception to sort out the post, he thought.

27

Door-to-door inquiries in the neighbourhood had started at seven o'clock that morning. They had gone on all day, but the most useful results came in the morning and evening, the way they always did when you went door to door in residential areas. Mornings and evenings were best. When the people living there weren't at work and their children weren't at school, not that you needed to be a police officer to work that out.

The area where Thomas Eriksson the lawyer lived also offered one major advantage for every serious door-knocking police officer. The majority of the murder victim's neighbours happened to be dog owners, which meant that they spent considerably more time outdoors than those citizens who didn't have dogs, and they were more likely to move in places and at times that were often of interest when it came to investigating crimes. Not least the sort of crime that had struck their neighbour Thomas Eriksson.

A neighbourhood with so many dog owners was a goldmine when it came to door-to-door inquiries, thought Detective Inspector Jan Stigson, the 32-year-old son of a farmer in Dalarna, who still thought like that even though it was now more than ten years since he had moved to Stockholm to join the police.

He had been working for Bäckström for four years and during that time had been responsible for a number of similar operations. He and four younger officers, borrowed from the district's beat squad, were going from house to house, from one door to the next, and when he had knocked on his second door he hit the first jackpot, even though it was no more than half past eight in the morning. He was also lucky with the weather. It was the first real summer's day, pretty much the ideal weather for the job, he thought.

A pleasant middle-aged woman had come to the door, with a black Labrador standing behind her wagging its tail. She had lived in the house with her husband for the past twenty years. These days, the children were long gone. Her husband had travelled to Spain to play golf, and for the past few days she had been responsible for taking the dog out for his 'evening wee'. Usually, her husband dealt with that while she took care of the morning walk.

'We have different daily rhythms, my husband and I,' she explained. 'I'm best in the mornings and usually go to bed at ten o'clock or so, and my husband's the opposite. He can sit up half the night, but he's hardly worth talking to in the morning. But goodness, come in, so we can have a proper chat. Nalle and I have already been out for our morning walk, and I was about to have some coffee. You do drink coffee, don't you, Detective Inspector?'

'Thanks, I'd love a cup,' Stigson said. Nice, he thought. She seemed alert as well, as she'd evidently noted his rank when he showed her his ID.

He ended up sitting in her kitchen for almost an hour while she told him what she'd seen the previous evening when she was out walking Nalle. She always took the same route. First up the street, past the first few side roads, then she swung right and headed back home again. In simple terms, she had just walked round the block, as she demonstrated to Stigson on the map he had with him.

'It can't be more than a couple of kilometres at most, but when you've got the company of this little fellow, it can take the best part of an hour. There's lots to smell and so many people to say hello to, other dogs and their owners too,' his witness said, smiling at Stigson.

'You wouldn't be able to give me a few names, and preferably times as well, if you can remember? As I'm sure you can appreciate, we're trying to locate anyone who was moving around the area yesterday evening. And, of course, anything you say will be treated confidentially.'

There had been no problem with that at all. She had met the same neighbours and dog-walkers she usually met. She had given him half a dozen names, and everything had been the same as usual. Nothing strange, and she certainly hadn't bumped into anyone mysterious. In fact, she'd met only one person she didn't already know by name, or at least by appearance. When she passed Eriksson's house, a hundred metres down the street, she had seen a man standing on the other side of the road, loading a couple of big boxes into the boot of a car, and at roughly the same time as she put her key in her front door she had heard the car start up and drive away.

'It must have been the same car,' she said. 'I'm sure it was.'

'Do you remember what time that was?' Here we go, Stigson thought.

'I know I left the house at ten minutes to nine, more or less. I'd been watching television, and the programme I was watching – one of those docusoaps, I think they're called – finished at quarter to nine. Then I did the usual circuit, so it must have been about half past nine or so. I remember turning on the evening news on TV4, and it had just started. It starts at ten o'clock, but before that I'd wiped Nalle's paws and filled his bowl with water, and tidied up in the kitchen.'

'The man you saw loading boxes into the car. You couldn't describe him?' Getting warmer, Stigson thought.

'No,' she said, shaking her head, suddenly very serious. 'Obviously, I heard what had happened on the eight o'clock news this morning, so I know why you're here. When I went past him he was leaning into the boot, so I never saw his face. But from the little I did see, he seemed perfectly normal. He looked like most people who live out here. Middle-aged, nicely dressed – a blazer, I think, possibly just a smart jacket, blue or black, and dark trousers. Maybe there was something . . .'

'What's that?' Stigson said, smiling encouragingly.

'I got the impression he was big, well-built. He seemed in fairly good shape somehow. I mean, I saw the way he picked the box up when he put it in the car. Not that I know what was in it, how much it weighed, I mean, but it was one of those big removal boxes, and it didn't seem to be a problem at all . . . picking it up like that, I suppose.'

'Could you give any idea of how tall he was?'

'Definitely taller than average. If I had to guess, I'd say he was closer to one metre ninety than one eighty. He was a big man. My husband's fairly tall, one metre eighty-six, even if he still insists he's one eighty-nine like he was when we first met, but he always forgets that that's almost forty years ago now.'

'You said middle-aged,' Stigson said, determined to keep going. 'Forty-five, fifty, sixty . . . ?'

'Definitely not sixty,' his witness said, shaking her head firmly. 'Fifty, or rather, fifty at the most. There was something about the way he moved. It was easy, untroubled, and age snatches that from you, no matter how often you go to the gym. Like I said, he was in good shape.'

'Was there anything else that struck you?'

'The car. It was a silver Mercedes, one of those big ones, that low, sporty model, not an estate. Definitely not the sort of car a burglar would drive around in.'

'A silver Mercedes. You're sure about that?'

'Yes, quite sure. My husband and I each have a Mercedes. I've got a small one, and his is a bit bigger, to have room for all his golf clubs and so on, but this one was considerably bigger than my husband's, and probably more expensive than both of ours combined.'

'You didn't notice anything else about the car? The registration number? Or if there were any stickers or labels on it?'

'No. I didn't even think to look at the registration number. I didn't see any stickers or labels either. It wasn't that sort of car, so I'd probably have noticed that. But I can see why you're asking. It's terrible, what's happened. It's the last thing you expect in an area like this. We haven't even had that many break-ins out here. The only thing that's happened to my husband and me was when our boat was stolen – we've got a berth in the marina next to Eriksson's house – but that must be ten years ago now.'

'I hope you got it back?'

'Oh yes, there was a perfectly simple explanation. It turned out to be our youngest son and his friends, who'd taken it without permission and run aground, and he didn't dare tell his mum and dad. But of course it all came out in the end.'

'But he's kept his nose clean since then?' Stigson said with a smile.

'These days he's married with two children and works as a lawyer for the SE Bank, so we'd better hope he has,' the lad's mum said, returning the smile.

Ten minutes later Stigson had thanked her for her time and finished by giving her his card. If there was anything else she thought of, she only had to call. Big or small, important or not important, no matter what it was, all she had to do was call, no matter what time of day it was.

So close, so close, but a miss is as good as a mile, he thought as he stepped out into the street and set off towards the next house on his list.

28

On Monday afternoon – at about the same time as Jenny Rogersson was explaining her theories to an increasingly incredulous Evert Bäckström – Lisa Lamm and Annika Carlsson had met Thomas Eriksson's colleagues in the offices of his law firm, Eriksson and Partners, on Karlavägen in Stockholm.

Before they set off, Lisa Lamm had checked the firm's website so they knew what to expect. The meeting was unlikely to be entirely straightforward, and at worst might deteriorate into a legal jousting match, in which case it was important that she knew as much as possible about her opponents.

The law firm Eriksson and Partners had been established fifteen years earlier, by Thomas Eriksson. It specialized in criminal and family law cases, and until less than twenty-four hours ago there had been sixteen people working there: five equal partners, all of them lawyers, five legal associates, an accountant who looked after the finances, personnel issues and other administration, two female paralegals and three secretaries. In terms of staff and services, it was far from being a giant in the business, but at the same time it was considerably larger than Lisa Lamm had expected. On the few occasions she had encountered Thomas Eriksson in court, he had struck her as a typical lone wolf. Certainly not as someone who would establish a law firm of this size and stay on as its longest-serving partner.

Tell me who you socialize with and I'll tell you who you are, Lisa Lamm thought, and, considering Eriksson's reputation, four lawyers and five legal associates said all that needed saying. She shook her head anxiously and switched her computer off.

Annika Carlsson also seemed aware of the potential difficulties that awaited them, and before they had even left the garage at the police station she had asked the question:

'Trying to get a search warrant for a law firm isn't exactly straightforward, is it?' she said, more as a statement than a question.

'No, it certainly isn't,' Lisa Lamm agreed, with more feeling in her voice than she had intended.

'Give me the short version. Preferably the simple one as well,' Annika Carlsson said with a smile.

'Okay. Firstly, the kind of business lawyers are engaged in makes it tricky. Their clients' interests mustn't be harmed, and the confidentiality regulations are considerably more extensive than usual. If they want to make things difficult for us, then . . .' Lisa Lamm shrugged her shoulders.

'And secondly?'

'Well, secondly, Thomas Eriksson is the victim and isn't suspected of any crime, and besides . . . thirdly . . . he was murdered in his home and not at work. When you put all that together, it becomes something of a hurdle.' Lisa Lamm sighed.

'And you haven't even mentioned the most important factor,' Annika Carlsson said.

'What's that?' Lisa Lamm asked, although she already knew the answer.

'Eriksson was a gangster,' Annika Carlsson said bluntly, flexing her broad shoulders. 'I was thinking about his colleagues. What sort of people would want to work with a gangster? Other gangsters.'

'Yes, that thought occurred to me too. And it worries me.'

'Not me,' Annika Carlsson said, shaking her head. 'If they start fucking with us, I suppose I can always twist their arms.'

'Thanks, and I really mean that, but I think maybe I'll take a different approach to begin with,' Lisa Lamm replied.

'You're welcome,' Annika Carlsson said. 'Let me know if you change your mind.' I'm sure the pair of us are going to get on just fine, she thought.

29

Nadja Högberg was fifty-two years old. Up until twenty years ago her name had been Nadjesta Ivanova, and she was born in a little farming village a short distance outside the big city of Leningrad, now known as St Petersburg. Nadjesta was a talented girl, and the chairman of the local party, who was one of her father's cousins, made sure she got into the right schools as early as possible so that she could best serve the great socialist republic in the future.

Nadjesta hadn't disappointed him. At the age of twenty-six she got her PhD in applied mathematics at Leningrad University. She had the highest grades and was employed more or less at once as a risk analyst at the regional nuclear energy authority. Only three years before 'liberation from the Communist yoke', as her old mentor, the former party chairman, would soon describe events of the final years of the eighties.

He was also the person who advised her to take the next step. If she didn't want to accept his offer and start work in the private agricultural business that he was now running, and preferred to carry on working with what she had been doing up until then, the logical step for a woman with her skills was to seek work outside the new Russia until her old employer realized the inevitable and adapted to the conditions that had to apply in any functioning economy, no matter what type of business you were in. In other words, that a highly qualified specialist like her, a nuclear physicist and doctor of mathematics, needed to be paid many times more than an ordinary doctor, teacher or police officer.

It quickly became apparent that this wasn't the only thing that her employer hadn't grasped. The first time she applied for permission to leave her homeland was in the summer of 1991, two years after 'liberation'. At the time she was working at a nuclear power station in Lithuania, not far from the Baltic Sea. She never received a reply to her request. One week later she was summoned to see her boss and told that she was being transferred to another nuclear power station a thousand kilometres to the north, just beyond Murmansk. Several taciturn men had helped her pack her belongings. They drove her to her new workplace, not leaving her alone for a minute during the forty-eight hours of the journey.

Two years later she didn't bother to ask for permission. With the help of 'new native contacts', she had made her way across the border into Finland, to be met by 'new foreign contacts', and the following morning, in the autumn of 1993, she woke up in a house somewhere in Sweden.

Nadja had never been so well looked after in her whole life, and she had spent most of the first six weeks talking to her hosts. It was a conversation where they asked questions and she answered, and where there was a specific amount of time allocated to unforced dialogue. A year later she had learned to speak fluent Swedish, been granted Swedish citizenship, had her own home in Stockholm, as well as a job and an employer who had explained with a smile that she could be prosecuted if she told anyone who she worked for.

Two years later they had gone their separate ways, on good terms. In spite of the relatively short length of her employment, Nadja had been given a generous severance package and a new job. She had spent the past fifteen years working for various departments of the Stockholm Police. For the past four years she had worked for Evert Bäckström as a civilian analyst in the department for serious crime in the Western District. She had also long been Bäckström's most trusted colleague, the only person in the world he trusted unconditionally, even if he'd rather bite his own tongue off than admit it.

Mr Högberg, on the other hand, was history. She had met him online, but divorced him after just a year, seeing as he had almost immediately shown himself to be far too Russian for Nadja's taste. She was content to keep the surname he had given her, and the future belonged to her and her new homeland. But on her terms, and she had taken Bäckström to her heart because of his many weaknesses. Possibly her own weakness too, although she'd rather bite her own tongue off than admit it, even to herself.

Now yet another murder investigation had arisen to frame her life, and her role in it had long since been determined. It was Nadja who was responsible for background detective work, and at the top of her agenda was the task of mapping the victim's life, finding out as soon as possible, and preferably immediately, what he had spent the last twenty-four hours of his life doing before he met his nemesis.

First, she had allocated different aspects of this work to her four colleagues. Then she herself had got to grips with the victim's computer and the information it contained. Just to be on the safe side, she had also checked that the contents of the hard drive matched the memory stick that Bäckström had given her. Then she'd put the stick in Bäckström's cupboard, to which only the two of them had keys. Just in case, she thought, because there had been previous cases when the prosecutor had had a change of heart when things started to get messy.

The first discovery she made was that the computer, in spite of the sticker on it, didn't belong to the law firm Eriksson and Partners but a company that went by the unenlightening name of Ålsten Management Ltd, which turned out to be a capital investment company owned by Thomas Eriksson. Its own capital amounted to approximately seven million kronor, and its annual turnover, primarily from trading in shares, to about ten million. Its only serious asset was the house at Ålstensgatan 127, which was owned by the company and rented out to Thomas Eriksson as a domestic residence and office, for an amount that matched the figure accepted by the tax office the last time they had tried to raise it.

A market value of twenty-five million, with a mortgage of fifteen million, and capital of seven million in the company that owned the house, a monthly rent of thirty thousand. Nothing remarkable so far, Nadja thought, and moved on to scan through the contents of the hard drive.

A small proportion of it seemed to be various files of a mixed and not immediately obvious character, and Nadja, true to her nature, was determined to work out exactly what they meant. But almost all the rest was considerably more straightforward, at least in terms of its basic nature.

Men, Nadja thought, sighing and shaking her head. The only consolation was probably that what she had just found would at least please her boss, Evert Bäckström. Then she had switched off their murder victim's computer and turned on her own in order to get to grips with the next item on her long list of things that she and her colleagues needed to know about the life Thomas Eriksson had lived.

30

On Friday, 31 May, two days before the murder of lawyer Thomas Eriksson, Jenny Rogersson had done as her boss Evert Bäckström had told her and concluded the investigation into the supposed assault twelve days earlier of Hans Ulrik von Comer, the courtier in the car park outside Drottningholm Palace.

Then she had put the entire file in a courier's envelope – including Bäckström's concluding statement, her own investigation into the matter, the original of the anonymous letter and the blood-stained auction catalogue – to be sent to the main police headquarters on Kungsholmen and the personal protection department of the Security Police. All of it marked 'for information', in accordance with the regulations currently governing the Western District Police, and on the morning of Monday, 3 June, the thick envelope was lying on the desk of Detective Superintendent Dan Andersson, in the pile of new post.

Dan Andersson was forty-five years old, married to a woman three years younger, who was a civilian employee of the Stockholm regional crime division. They had three children together, all boys of school age, and the whole Andersson family lived in a villa out on the islands of Lake Mälaren, some twenty kilometres outside Stockholm. The vast majority of their neighbours worked in either the police force, education, the emergency services or the health service, and thus far in this description, in bald sociological terms, Dan Andersson was a typical middle-aged police officer, working in so-called middle management in Stockholm.

In his professional capacity, that which his bosses cared about and appreciated and his colleagues observed with rather more mixed feelings, he was known for being loyal, conscientious, taciturn and both industrious and able. But, above all, taciturn.

Dan Andersson had been a police officer for almost twenty-five years, always in Stockholm, and for the past eight years he had been head of the unit within the Security Police's personal protection department that dealt with potential threats. The department which was tasked with protecting the royal family, the government and all other similarly elevated individuals who had a comparable distance to fall, and who, depending on various circumstances, might require at least temporarily the services of the personal protection department. The department was usually referred to in police headquarters as 'the bodyguards', even though most of the people working there weren't expected to shoot first or, in the worst case, block any bullet intended for their charge with their own body.

On Monday, 3 June, Dan Andersson had stepped inside his office after lunch and a morning full of meetings. When he noticed the thick envelope which the Western District Police had sent over for information, his first thought was to let his secretary deal with it, and not even bother to work out how urgent the case was.

Because he was the man he was, however, he did the exact opposite. With a wry smile, he noted his colleague

Bäckström's concluding statement, read the anonymous letter, sighed once, leafed through the auction catalogue without even considering putting on a pair of plastic gloves, and concluded by reading Detective Sergeant Jenny Rogersson's investigation into the matter. As he was doing that, he sighed more than once.

Jenny Rogersson, Dan Andersson thought. Likely to be one of that nightmare Jan Rogersson's equally stupid offspring, who had insisted on joining the police, just like Daddy, and this particular one appeared to be working for Evert Bäckström. Daughter of the same Jan Rogersson at National Crime who, regardless of who in the force you asked, was said to be Evert Bäckström's only friend in an organization that currently consisted of twenty thousand officers. That was something of a coincidence, Dan Andersson thought, then sighed one last time before starting to fill his briefcase with the various papers he needed for his next meeting.

The weeks leading up to Sweden's National Day were always busy for Superintendent Dan Andersson and his closest colleagues. On 6 June almost all of their highest ranked charges would be engaged in various public appearances, and the day itself was also critical to the conceptual and practical values that governed their work. It was an excellent opportunity to reinforce perceptions of Sweden and those who lived there. A day of great symbolic value, regardless of what those perceptions might be.

'Just say if there's anything I can do to help,' his secretary said as he walked out through the doorway of his office.

'Our colleagues in Solna have sent over an envelope containing a number of observations about some aristocrat, a von Comer, who's supposed to have been beaten up outside Drottningholm Palace a fortnight ago. He seems to have some sort of vague connection to the court, so I suppose we should run the usual checks on him. The envelope's in the pile on my desk,' Dan Andersson said, then nodded and smiled.

'I'll sort it out at once,' his secretary said.

'I'm not sure there's any great rush,' Dan Andersson replied. 'It's probably just nonsense,' he added.

Just one week later he would be wondering if he ought to have said something else entirely, and what the consequences of that would have been on what had already happened.

31

Lisa Lamm had opened their meeting at the law firm Eriksson and Partners in exactly the way she had told Annika Carlsson she would.

She had started with friendly introductions and expressions of sympathy for the personal loss they had suffered. Then she had moved to persuasion and explaining the practical problems that an event of this sort unfortunately also gave rise to. Problems that she hoped they might be able to solve together, in the shortest possible time and without any unnecessary disruption to the rest of the business.

Five minutes later everything had gone precisely as she had feared. First, there had been an increasingly animated discussion of various judicial difficulties, which had developed into an undisguised slanging match. On a practical level, there had been four specific issues and, just for once, everyone at Eriksson and Partners disagreed fundamentally with the prosecutor on absolutely every point.

Four issues. The computer and mobile phone that had been found in Eriksson's home were both the property of the company, and therefore couldn't be subjected to the procedures that the prosecutor evidently intended to implement. The same thing applied to the search of

Eriksson's own office which the prosecutor had authorized. Not to mention the remainder of the company's premises, if the prosecutor were to get it into her head to expand the scope of her and the police's investigations.

'It can't be that hard to understand,' her immaculately tailored opponent declared. 'There are no grounds whatsoever either for seizures or for search warrants in this case. That much is obvious in the Penal Code. Chapters twenty-seven and twenty-eight – particularly chapter twenty-eight, paragraph one, as there's no trace of the specific justifications in the current situation. We're talking about a law firm, after all, not some bog-standard drug-den. In case you weren't sure, Prosecutor,' he added with a sardonic smile as he gently adjusted his neat parting with his left hand.

The man who had leapt in as soon as Lisa Lamm had stopped talking was a lawyer, Peter Danielsson, ten years younger than Thomas Eriksson, his first partner, formerly his number two in the office, and nowadays – to judge by his body language, choice of words and the nods of agreement from his colleagues – the man who had already taken his place.

Lisa Lamm had encountered him before. They had met in court on several occasions over the past two years. And she was also well aware that he was working hard to acquire the same sort of reputation as his erstwhile boss, and in that respect he seemed to have succeeded, considering the type of person he usually represented.

'Well, to take things in order, I certainly don't share that interpretation,' Lisa Lamm said.

'Just as I and my colleagues feared,' Danielsson said.

'If you'll just let me finish,' Lisa Lamm interrupted, leafing through her papers and suddenly looking exactly like the clever little girl her Supreme Court judge father had tried to turn her into.

'As far as the computer that was found at the crime scene is concerned, it's very simple,' Lisa Lamm declared. 'It's Eriksson's private property. In spite of the sticker attached to it. He was using it just before he was murdered and, as far as the contents are concerned, I don't believe it has anything at all to do with your activities here in this office. I'm under the impression that its contents are of a highly personal nature, if you were wondering.'

'You couldn't be more specific?'

'No,' Lisa Lamm said, shaking her head. 'I couldn't, and nor do I want to be. As far as the mobile is concerned, the same thing applies there. Even though the contract is registered to the company. Any conversations he may have had on it are of considerable relevance to our investigation.'

'But you're refusing to tell us what you're basing that conclusion on?'

'You can always appeal against my decisions,' Lisa Lamm said, shrugging her shoulders.

'That process is already underway,' the lawyer said, making a move to stand up.

'I haven't finished yet,' Lisa Lamm said. 'My decisions stand, as far as Eriksson's computer and mobile are concerned. I'm prepared to hold back on the search of his office until the court has had its say but, obviously, it will be sealed for the time being, and I assume you'll be lodging any objections you may have to that decision as soon as possible.'

'You needn't worry about that,' the lawyer said bitterly, and stood up.

'Regarding the possible extension of the search warrant to cover the rest of the office, I'll get in touch if that becomes necessary. Is there anything you'd like to add, Annika?' Lisa Lamm said, looking at Annika Carlsson, who hadn't said a word all the way through.

'Yes,' Annika Carlsson said, looking around the table. 'Obviously, we're going to have to question everyone who works here.'

Her short, concluding nod left no doubt as to her intentions, and she had already worked out where to push hardest. Nine of the fifteen people currently employed in the law firm were in the room. Another was off sick, and the remaining five were either in court or working away from the office.

One of the people in the room seemed to be considerably more upset than the others. She also happened to be the youngest and most beautiful of them. You're the one he was fucking, Annika Carlsson thought.

32

After his conversation with Jenny, at first Bäckström thought he might go for a stroll among his colleagues and see how things were going but, because his lunch and the fact that he had had to get up in the middle of the night were starting to make themselves felt, he wanted to get home to his Hästens bed, and on the way there it was about time he paid another visit to the crime scene and saw that he got something done.

He took out the briefcase he had inherited from his old boss in the crime division in Stockholm, Superintendent Fylking, who had been something of a legend in the force. Feared, loved and renowned among his colleagues as the force's very own Superintendent Pisshead. It was a sturdy affair in brown leather and, according to one classic police story, Pisshead himself had used it to liberate twelve litres of vodka after a raid on an illegal drinking den in Gamla stan. Roomy and very handy to have if you happened to encounter anything useful. Then he had put his laptop and some assorted papers concerning the new investigation inside it, in case any of his inquisitive colleagues wondered why he was dragging it about with him.

On his way out from the office he had stopped in the doorway of the room where most of his colleagues were sitting, talking on the phone, reading their files or fiddling with their computers, clapped his hands to get their attention, and asked a question of all of them. Had anything happened that demanded his immediate attention? Going by the headshakes and muttering, the answer was no.

'Okay,' Bäckström said. 'Well, make sure that changes. I'm heading back to our crime scene to have another look round in peace and quiet. See you first thing tomorrow.'

'In that case you can have a lift with me, boss,' Felicia Pettersson said. She was heading out to relieve Stigson and lead the evening shift going door to door.

33

A Sunday evening at the start of June, unremarkable weather, not much to do, and even before midnight Ara Dosti was thinking of giving up on his nightshift and heading home to Kista to get some sleep instead. That was before he suddenly got a customer who wanted to go to Nyköping, one hundred kilometres south of Stockholm and, by the time he got back, it was already half past one.

One last circuit of the bars down in the city centre, Ara decided, and, as he drove past Stureplan, a customer had waved him down in the street and asked to be driven to his home on Alviksvägen, out in Bromma. A good customer, drunk in that Swedish way, like so many of the blokes here, but he didn't start babbling or even asking the usual questions about how he liked his new homeland and where he came from.

What was he supposed to say to that? He'd been born in a refugee camp in Småland, had spent his whole life in Sweden and had never set foot in his parents' original homeland, Iran. But there was none of that this time. Instead the bloke was just a decent customer who had given a generous tip at ten minutes past two at night, at Alviksvägen in Bromma, according to the print-out from his meter.

Ara Dosti had done a U-turn outside the building where

he had dropped the customer off and, when he reached the junction with Ålstensgatan, ready to turn left and take the shortest route home to the bed that was waiting for him in his flat out in Kista, things almost came to a sticky end, because he recognized the big house down by the water and suddenly found himself thinking of something else entirely.

He had driven a customer there only six months before. Another Swedish bloke who wanted to get home from the pub, and who had been so drunk he had fallen asleep in the back seat. As soon as Ara pulled up, the bloke had come round, stumbled out on to the road, fished out a bundle of notes from his trouser pocket and given him a thousand-kronor note. When Ara tried to explain that he didn't have enough change, he had simply shaken his head and said it was fine.

Ara had protested, saying it was far too much, seeing as the trip had cost only a few hundred, but the customer hadn't seemed to care. He just waved his hands dismissively, and as he struggled to open the gate of the drive leading up to his house he had turned round with a broad grin.

'There's no need to thank me,' the customer said. 'You should thank your old compatriots from Iran,' and it was only when he said that that Ara had recognized him from a previous occasion, when he had driven him to Stockholm City Court. The famous lawyer he had seen on television and read about in the papers.

That was who Ara was thinking about when he turned into Ålstensgatan, and that was when things could have come to a very sticky end. The man who had given him a tip of almost a thousand kronor, and without even asking seemed to assume he was from Iran.

Out of the darkness between two cars another man had walked straight out into the road, and Ara had had to slam on the brakes to avoid hitting him. A different man entirely, who had given him a quick glance with sharp eyes before heading over to a car that was parked against the flow of traffic on the other side of the street. He was limping badly on his right leg and, even though it was dark, Ara had seen enough of him to drop any thought of stopping and saying something to him, or giving him the finger in the rear-view mirror.

When Ara finished his shift at two o'clock in the afternoon of Monday, 3 June, he had already read the message from the control centre of Taxi Stockholm. That the police in Solna, in connection with a murder that had occurred at Ålstensgatan 127, wanted to contact any drivers who had taken any customers to the Alviksvägen-Ålstensgatan area on Sunday or early Monday morning or had noticed anything that might be of interest to their investigation.

Murder, Ara thought. Hope it isn't the bloke with the thousand-kronor note, that lawyer, he thought. Then he had taken out his mobile and called the police.

34

In spite of Ara's hopes, evidently it was the customer with the thousand-kronor note who had been murdered. He had realized that when he heard the news on the radio as he was driving to the police station in Solna, where it seemed they wanted to question him.

Wonder how big the reward is? he thought. If you murder someone who can afford to give a tip of a thousand kronor like that lawyer had done, the reward for anyone who helped the police to find his killer had to be big. Very big.

Detective Sergeant Lars Alm was sixty-four years and nine months old, and had been looking forward to a quiet summer. In three months he was due to retire. He was planning to use up his holiday and all the time owing he had accumulated and spend the remaining month clearing out his desk in peace and quiet.

Instead, the exact opposite had happened and, if the worst came to the worst, there was a serious risk he might end up spending half the summer helping to investigate the murder of a lawyer that neither he nor any of his colleagues had a great deal of time for. Going off sick wasn't an option, as that left a serious hole in his pay-packet these days.

And there's that fat little moron, Bäckström, Alm thought for some reason as he was leafing through the papers he had been given by the younger officer who had taken the call. Apparently, one of the many foreign taxi-drivers had called their tip-off line and given information that Annika Carlsson thought could be important enough to call the informant into the station at once and interview him in person. The bugger's punctual as well, Alm thought. He sighed and picked up the receiver of his ringing phone.

'Alm,' he said.

'You're got a visitor down at reception,' the voice at the other end responded. 'Can you come down and pick him up?'

Like I've got any sodding choice, Alm thought, and sighed once again.

No coffee, no water and no pissing about, because then you might end up here half the night, Alm thought five minutes later, once he and his witness were sitting on either side of his desk.

'Can I see your driving licence and the print-out from your meter that my colleague asked you to bring with you?' Alm said, opening his computer. Bloody hell, what a summer, he thought.

'Here you go,' Ara said. 'Have a business card as well, in case you need to call me.' Miserable sort, he thought.

'Where are you from, Ara?' Alm asked as he looked at the driving licence.

'From Gnosjö,' Ara Dosti said. 'In Småland. But I've lived in Stockholm for the past fifteen years. I wrote my address on the back of my card.' Ara nodded towards the piece of card he had just given Alm.

'I didn't mean like that,' Alm said. 'I mean where are you from originally,' he clarified.

'From Sweden,' Ara Dosti said, with affected surprise. 'Småland's in Sweden. I assumed you knew that. I was born and grew up in Småland. I went to school there and, when I was eighteen, Dad, Mum, my two elder brothers, my younger brother and my two elder sisters and I all moved to Stockholm. Eight people in total, a real exodus,' Ara Dosti said, smiling amiably at Alm.

'Okay, I understand,' Alm said, and sighed once more. 'Well, if you could tell me in your own words what you saw at two o'clock this morning, once you'd dropped your customer off in Alviksvägen out in Bromma.' Another one of all the bastards who've only come here to fuck with the police, he thought.

Ara had managed to tell his whole story in less than five minutes. How he had dropped the customer off outside his house at ten past two. How he did a U-turn and drove back to the junction with Ålstensgatan – about a minute later – and almost hit a man who stepped out into the road right in front of the house where the lawyer had been murdered. In that time, he had also managed to give a reasonable description of the man and of the car he got into.

'He was my age,' Ara said. 'Maybe a couple of years older – thirty-five, something like that. But a lot taller than me. One metre ninety, maybe. Blue jeans, dark jacket, no hat. He seemed to be limping on his right leg. He was certainly holding his right thigh with his right hand when he almost ended up on my bonnet. He looked sharp, if you know what I mean. Seriously sharp.'

'Sharp?'

'Not the sort you'd stop the car to argue with,' Ara explained.

'Don't suppose it was someone you recognized?' Alm asked. 'Someone you'd seen before?'

'Nooo . . . Why would I have seen him before?'

'You drive a taxi. Was he an immigrant, or Swedish? You must have noticed something else?'

'No,' Ara said. 'He looked the way everyone does these days. I've got a suggestion, though. If you get out some of those pictures that the cops on telly show people like me, I can have a look and see if I recognize anyone. What do you think?'

'The car he got into. Can you describe it?' I'm the one asking the questions here, Alm thought.

'Merc, silver, sporty . . . low, wide, expensive, recent model . . .'

'You're sure about that?'

'Yes. Hundred per cent. Like you said, I drive a taxi.'

'You didn't manage to see the registration number? In the rear-view mirror, I mean.'

'No.'

'You must have seen something, though. I mean, you seem to have noticed an awful lot else.'

'The man inside the car turned the headlights on as soon as I'd driven past.'

'So you're saying there were two of them? There was already someone in the car?'

'Okay,' Ara Dosti said. 'I'll go through it again. The man I almost ran over is on his way up on to the pavement as I drive off. The one sitting in the car, which is parked on the wrong side of the road, puts the headlights on as soon as I drive past. I've got no idea what he looked like. I drove straight home, got out of there as fast as I could. What would you have done?'

'I see,' Alm said. 'There's nothing else you'd like to add?'

'No. Like what?'

'Then I'm declaring this interview over,' Alm said, glancing at his watch. 'Before you leave, I need to impose a disclosure ban on you. That means you're not allowed to tell anyone what you've told me. If you break the ban, you'll be committing a crime. Is there anything you'd like to ask?'

'Photos. What about the photos?'

'We can come back to those later,' Alm said. 'It takes a while to get them sorted out, as I'm sure you can appreciate. I or one of my colleagues will be in touch if that turns out to be necessary. Anything else?'

'Is there a reward?'

'No,' Alm said, shaking his head in surprise. 'Why would there be? Surely it's reward enough that you're helping us solve a serious crime. Besides, it's a social duty to come forward and bear witness. That applies to all of us. Even people like me and my colleagues, in case you're wondering.'

'This has already taken a couple of hours of my time. I'm a working man. I've come here when I should be working. Plus the phone calls and the petrol to get here to talk to you. You're getting paid to sit here. I'm not.'

'And, naturally, we're very grateful,' Alm said. He nodded, smiled and got to his feet. That shut you up, he thought.

'In that case, I've got one more question,' Ara said.

'Yes?'

'How do you get to be a police officer? How does anyone manage it? I mean, it must be really difficult.'

Alm contented himself with a nod. Just you fucking watch yourself, lad, he thought.

* * *

Alm went down to reception with Ara Dosti, if for no other reason than to make sure he left the building.

'We'll be in touch about the photographs,' Alm said as they parted.

Ara didn't say anything. He just shrugged and disappeared out into the street.

There's something I've forgotten, Detective Sergeant Alm thought as he took the lift back up to his room again. Oh well, it'll come back to me.

Alm had spent the remainder of his working day calmly summarizing his interview with Ara Dosti. Then he asked a younger colleague who was based in the office to pull out some pictures of known criminals for Dosti to look at, based on the description he had given.

'See if you can cross-reference the description with known criminals who own or have access to a silver Mercedes,' Alm suggested.

'Anything else?' his younger colleague asked. Ever wondered why everyone here calls you Woodentop? she thought.

'Make sure he signs a non-disclosure agreement,' Alm said, having worked out what it was he had forgotten quarter of an hour earlier.

As soon as Ara got into his car, he called a friend who was also a taxi-driver. He was a Kurd named Kemal and came from roughly the same background as him. A good bloke, a white man, to use the sort of language the average Swede used. A couple of months earlier, Kemal had witnessed the robbery of a security van. He'd taken some pictures with the camera on his phone. He called the biggest evening paper straight away and was given twenty thousand kronor for his trouble, and he'd told anyone who would listen that the cops were the last people you should go to if you ever found yourself in that situation.

How stupid can you get? Ara thought, thinking about himself.

35

To save time, the interviews with Eriksson's work colleagues had been set up in the firm's offices. This had been suggested by Danielsson, the lawyer, and Lisa Lamm didn't have any objections. Annika Carlsson had called in four lead interviewers from Solna police station, while Danielsson arranged a small meeting room and three empty offices where the interviews could be held.

As soon as her colleagues arrived, Annika Carlsson had taken them aside and explained their tactics. Everyone in the firm was to be interviewed, preferably on their own, to gather information. Initially about how they had come to work at the law firm and about their relationship with Eriksson – personal as well as professional – and what they were doing on the day of Eriksson's murder. Their last contact with the victim, of course, and what the nature of this contact had been. Only then would it be time to delve into dissatisfied clients, adversaries and anyone else who, for professional or other reasons, might be thought to have a reason to assault their murder victim. She also wanted them to be interviewed in a particular order.

'Start with the partners and the legal associates, and do the others last. I want you to question Danielsson first of all,' Annika Carlsson said. 'It looks like he's the new cock on this particular pile of manure. You don't have to be unnecessarily friendly, and I'd suggest that there should be two of you questioning him. You can deal with the rest of them individually, and it would be good if you could get through them all before you leave. We'll deal with anyone who isn't here and any supplementary questions later, as soon as we can. Any questions?'

Murmuring and shaking of heads, no questions. Three hours later it was done, and Annika Carlsson had been given a preliminary report over the phone by Detective Inspector Johan Ek.

'You'll have transcripts tomorrow morning at the latest,' Ek said, 'but I can give you a brief summary, if you'd like to hear it . . .'

'I'm listening,' Annika Carlsson said.

'Eriksson seems to have been one hell of a guy,' Ek said. 'No one had a bad word to say about him. Everyone in his office is extremely upset, and one of the so-called paralegals – that's those secretaries with a bit of extra legal training, isn't it, if I've got that right? – even seems a bit too sad, to my thinking.'

'Isabella Norén,' Annika Carlsson said. 'At a guess, she'd made a move on her old boss. Or at least had the ambition to do so.'

'You're thinking along the same lines as me. Yes, that's probably what was going on. What do we do about her, then? Because I didn't ask.'

'We'll leave her to stew for a day or two before a rather more thorough interview,' Annika Carlsson suggested. 'I could even imagine joining you, as a fellow sister.'

'Exactly,' Ek said.

'Anything else?'

Nothing unexpected, according to Ek. They all had alibis for the whole weekend. The last one to speak to

Eriksson was Danielsson, who called at about twelve o'clock to discuss various things that would be happening over the coming week, but the only thing these had in common was that they were nothing to do with Eriksson's demise. Which was obviously very handy for Danielsson, because they were all covered by legal confidentiality.

'Who'd have thought it?' Annika Carlsson said.

'Yes, and, according to Danielsson, Eriksson's murder is an attack on our entire judicial system, which might be one explanation why both Eriksson's clients and their opponents were so happy with him. With one exception, however, which we had to drag out of our reluctant lawyer with pliers.'

'Who's that, then?'

'Fredrik Åkare, born Åkerström. Former chair of the Hells Angels out in Solna. Now honorary chair of the same group of middle-aged motorbike enthusiasts. In the fortunate position of being able to sit on the saddle with his hair flying around his head, because he's got a doctor's certificate stating he's got dandruff and therefore doesn't have to wear a helmet,' concluded Ek, who was a police officer with an eye for both personal and poetic details in his opponents.

'I know who you mean,' Annika Carlsson said. 'So Fredrik Åkare has expressed dissatisfaction. I didn't even know Eriksson ever had him as a client. I didn't think he took on bikers.'

'More of an opponent,' Ek said. 'Eriksson was representing the Ibrahim family when Åkare and a couple of his friends were charged with the murder of the youngest Ibrahim brother, Nasir. As I'm sure you know, there were three brothers to start with. Farshad, who was an alcoholic and died trying to escape by climbing out of the window of his room at the Karolinska Hospital, where he was being treated after our colleague Bäckström shot him in the leg. Then there's the middle brother, who's alive and kicking, and seems to have taken over from Farshad. Then there's the youngest, Nasir, who was murdered not long after a failed bank robbery. That's a few years ago now. I can email you the preliminary investigation and verdict if you like.'

'I've already got it,' Annika Carlsson said. 'I remember the case. Åkare and his friends were found not guilty, weren't they? On all counts, if I remember rightly?'

'Yes, that's right. Even though Eriksson worked harder than the prosecutor to get them put away. Either way, Åkare doesn't seem to have been terribly fond of Eriksson. Sometime after the trial he sent a postcard to Eriksson at his office, saying that, now justice had been done, all that was left was for Eriksson to go over to their clubhouse in Solna to apologize to him and his colleagues, and then he would be prepared to move on with his life.'

'Did he go?'

'No,' Ek said. 'According to Danielsson, he called Åkare and read him the riot act. Obstruction of justice, illegal threats, all that.'

'Mmh,' Annika Carlsson said. I must dig out the file and read the verdict, she thought.

But that didn't happen because, just five minutes later, she had considerably more pressing matters to think about, even though it was really high time she went home and got some sleep.

36

It was Hernandez who opened the door of the house on Ålstensgatan when Bäckström rang the bell.

'Come in, boss,' he said. 'Nadja just rang and said you'd be coming over to see if there was anything at our crime scene that spoke to you.'

'Where's Niemi?' Bäckström asked.

'He went home to get some sleep,' Hernandez said with a smile. 'His age is probably catching up with him.'

'I thought I'd have a look upstairs,' Bäckström said, nodding towards the stairs leading up to the landing above.

'Go ahead,' Hernandez said. 'We're done there. Right now we're going through the basement. Me and a couple of forensics officers from Regional Crime that we've had to bring in. It's a massive building, so we're probably going to be here all week if we're going to do it properly. Just shout if there's anything I can do to help.'

Whatever the hell that might be, Bäckström thought, but made do with a simple nod.

The large bloodstain in front of the desk was still there. It was neatly defined, almost circular, with a diameter of about thirty centimetres, on the part of the floor where the victim's head had been lying, and when he kneeled down to take a closer look, Bäckström could even make out the impression left by Eriksson's nose and forehead in the congealed blood.

But no splashes, not the slightest little drop, he thought, even though Eriksson must have fallen face first on to the floor before the perpetrator set to work smashing in the back of his skull. This doesn't make sense. None of it makes sense, he thought as he got to his feet again.

The upper floor of Eriksson's house appeared to have been his private space. There was a large landing that acted as a combination of study and living room. The desk in the centre, two sofas in separate corners of the room, built-in bookcases and various other belongings that deserved a better fate than ending up in the estate inventory of a gangster lawyer. If only Niemi and Hernandez hadn't taken so many pictures before Bäckström arrived on the scene.

To the left of the landing was the lawyer's bedroom, a large walk-in wardrobe and a bathroom that was bigger than Bäckström's own living room in his cosy apartment on Kungsholmen. To the right was a combination of television and music room, something that seemed to be a guest room, with another bathroom and a separate toilet. Tidy, clean, perfect, white walls, polished wooden floors, marble and mosaics, and how much it had all cost was something he daren't even think about.

Ingratitude is the way of the world, he thought with a deep sigh, with his own lot in mind. The only consolation in this instance was his firm conviction that the lawyer was now warming his criminal arse on Our Lord's very own barbecue, a long way below his former earthly dwelling.

There was also a large, mobile drinks cabinet on the

landing, with at least a hundred bottles on it. Whisky, gin, vodka, cognac, as well as all that other stuff – liqueurs, fortified wine, fizzy water – stuff that was best avoided unless you were a woman, a faggot or, as in Eriksson's case, a lawyer. Standard stuff, mainly, Bäckström thought, and the only thing that held any interest for a connoisseur like him was a dark wooden box with shiny metal detailing and a relief of a black double-headed eagle on the lid. Just big enough to contain a litre of malt whisky of the very finest sort. Bäckström weighed the box in his hand before opening the lid, but instead of the cut-glass carafe he had been hoping to find, it merely contained a small enamelled figurine of a boy wearing a red cap, a yellow jacket and green trousers, little bigger than an old-fashioned quarter-litre of vodka, a bit like a Christmas elf.

Just to make sure, he took it out of the box and shook it carefully in the hope of hearing the familiar glugging sound. From his wealth of experience, he knew that so-called smart folk were prone to keeping their drink in the strangest objects, such as books with old leather binding, binoculars, or even walking sticks. He himself had taken a stick of that sort when he searched a house almost thirty years ago during his early days on the violent crime squad in Stockholm, and these days it was in the umbrella stand in the hall of his flat on Kungsholmen. A treasured memory of the good old days when he was a young constable.

No treasure trove this time. The enamel elf wasn't making any glugging sound at all, even though Bäckström kept turning it over. But at the bottom of the box he found a small, handwritten note. 'Enamel music-box in the shape of a young boy. Probably of German manufacture, early twentieth century. Value approximately three thousand kronor.'

What's an old music-box doing among all the drink? Bäckström thought, shaking his head in surprise and putting the black box back. Maybe Eriksson liked listening to music when he hit the bottle? Weird fucker, he thought, as he preferred to drink alone, and preferably in complete silence.

Then he had called a taxi and, while he was standing in the hallway downstairs, he decided to get rid of the briefcase, to avoid any malicious rumours and boorish slander. He couldn't really understand why he had thought of bringing it with him to a place where a couple of control freaks like Niemi and Hernandez had obsessively photographed everything and thus wiped out any opportunity for a bit of private enterprise. The simplest solution would be to ask the little Chilean-born tango-freak to take it back to the station and leave it in his office.

Miserable business, Bäckström thought, stopping in front of the little hall table that was just inside the front door. On it was a Chinese vase that would otherwise have looked perfect on his own hall table and which would probably have fitted inside his briefcase. There was probably room for the whole bouquet of drooping tulips that Eriksson's presumably illegal cleaner had put in it the week before. What the hell's happening to the force? he thought, glancing at the briefcase that was tucked under his left arm and tentatively lifting the Chinese vase. He realized immediately that something wasn't right. He put it back down again, pulled out the flowers, and there it was, shiny and silver, like a dead bream at the bottom of the vase.

Blind bastards, Detective Superintendent Evert Bäckström

thought, especially as he'd just been deprived of a Chinese vase that he could otherwise easily have taken home on a later occasion, once everything had settled down.

37

Only an hour after talking to his friend, Ara had met the reporter who had given his friend twenty thousand for a few grainy pictures of a perfectly ordinary security van robbery. They had met in the city, finding each other on a quiet backstreet on Södermalm with the help of their mobiles, then sat in the reporter's car to negotiate the important details.

'Your friend says you've some good stuff about Eriksson the lawyer's demise,' Ara's new friend began.

'It depends on the price,' Ara said, shrugging his shoulders, wise from his experiences earlier that day.

'That shouldn't be a problem,' the reporter said, smiling. 'Tell me.'

'Okay,' Ara said. 'I'm pretty sure I saw who did it. Not as it happened, but afterwards, when he was leaving the scene of the crime. And I saw the car he and his friend made off in.'

'Was it anyone you recognized? The bloke you saw, I mean?'

'Like I said, I don't want to go into details. It depends on the price. I can give you the following. To start with, I can prove I was there. You'll get a copy of the print-out from my taxi meter, with driving times and addresses, the whole lot. Secondly, I can identify the perpetrator if I see a decent picture of him. So no, I didn't recognize him straight off. Thirdly, I can give you the car he and his mate drove off in. Not the registration number, because I never saw that, but it shouldn't be too hard to identify this particular car. It wasn't your average Volvo, if that's what you're thinking.'

'Hang on a minute,' the reporter said. 'The cops have already interviewed you. They must have shown you a load of pictures already.'

'No,' Ara said with another shrug.

'Forgive me, but that sounds really odd. They must have got you to look through a whole load of pictures?'

'No,' Ara said. 'The one I spoke to was a knackered old cop who said he'd get back to me. Just show me a decent picture.' Ara shrugged again.

'Okay, okay,' the reporter said. 'So you're saying you can give me the car they drove off in and, if you're shown the right picture, you can identify the perpetrator?'

'Yes.' Ara nodded. 'For the right price, like I said.'

'But how can you be sure it was the perpetrator you saw?'

'If you'd seen him, you wouldn't need to ask,' Ara said. 'If you want details, it's going to cost, like I—'

'Five grand,' the reporter interrupted.

'Sorry?' Ara said.

'Five grand. You can have five thousand if you tell me what happened and agree to look at some pictures and give me the car. You won't have to worry. We'll describe you as an anonymous source.'

'Five thousand? Forget it,' Ara said, shaking his head.

They didn't get any further than that. As they parted, the reporter promised to get back to Ara as soon as he'd spoken to his boss, assuming that Ara didn't speak to anyone else in the meantime. They shook hands and agreed to be in touch again soon. Not a good day, despite the fact that it had started so promisingly, Ara thought as he got behind the wheel of his own car and tapped at his computer to indicate he was available.

Not a good day – and it had, if such a thing was possible, only got worse. During his first job after the meeting with the journalist his mobile had rung and, even though the call was from an undisclosed number and he had a customer in the car, he had answered it. It was a young female police officer who had evidently taken over from Alm. She sounded friendly, and wanted to show him some pictures, so the best thing would be if he could go back to the police station in Solna as soon as possible, preferably at once.

Ara had explained that he didn't have time. He had to work if he didn't want to starve. If they wanted to compensate him for the time he'd lose, obviously, he'd be prepared to go. Otherwise, they'd have to get back to him tomorrow, when he was free all morning. It would be simplest if they could come round to his with all the pictures, so he didn't have to drag himself over to the police station. Then he had ended the call by switching his mobile off.

They weren't about to give up. When he switched it on again a couple of hours later, he had two new messages in his voicemail. The first was from the same female officer he'd already spoken to. Just as friendly as before. The second was from one of her male colleagues, and he sounded considerably more abrupt, and wanted to see him at once for a supplementary interview, to show him the pictures. Ara had sighed deeply and decided it was time he got something to eat and thought things through in peace and quiet. So he had driven to his usual café. He had ordered a kebab, a diet Coke and a cup of mint tea, and sat down to eat as he thought.

Good-looking girl, Ara thought as he was about to take the first bite of his kebab. He didn't recognize her. She was just standing there in the doorway all of a sudden. Legs apart, broad shoulders, arms dangling, the way only blokes usually did. Short dark hair, loafers, jeans and a leather jacket, checking out the people in the café.

Good-looking girl, Ara thought again, and the only problem was that she had the same look in her eyes as the person he had almost run over the night before. And that her eyes had stopped on him.

Twenty minutes later he was sitting in a room at Solna police station. His taxi was parked outside the café in the city and, before he was put in the back seat of the police car that had driven him to the station, two male officers had searched him and emptied his pockets. Then the woman who had been standing in the doorway had taken hold of his arm and nodded to him.

'Okay, Ara,' Annika Carlsson said. 'The prosecutor's decided that you need to be picked up for questioning immediately, seeing as you're evidently pissing about with me and my colleagues. So the following rules apply now. No bollocks, no games, just nice and helpful, and, if you help me, I promise I'll help you.'

'No problem,' Ara said with a nod. What choice have I got? he thought.

38

The door-to-door inquiries had far exceeded expectations, even in an area like this one. When Felicia Pettersson took over from her colleague Jan Stigson, they had sat in the police command vehicle outside the victim's house for a brief handover.

'How's it been going?' Felicia Pettersson asked.

'Like a dream,' Stigson declared. 'We've had an incredible response.'

To begin with, they had managed to get hold of practically everyone who lived in the area. They had started work at around seven in the morning. They had knocked on almost one hundred doors around the victim's home and, by the time Felicia took over ten hours later, there were fewer than half a dozen neighbours left on the list Stigson had given Pettersson.

Secondly, they had managed to talk to all four neighbours who had called SOS Alarm during the evening and night because of the barking dog: the first three, who had called between quarter past ten and five past eleven in the evening and who had been referred to the noise disturbance unit because the police had other, more important things to do, and the fourth, who had called just after two o'clock in the morning, the call which had finally resulted in a patrol car arriving at the scene ten minutes later.

'We were a bit unlucky there,' Stigson said with a wry smile. 'Nadja called and told me about that taxi-driver who almost ran over one of our perpetrators just a couple of minutes before the first patrol arrived. And there was that poor dog as well, getting its throat cut.'

'Can't be lucky all the time,' Felicia said. 'Anything else?'

'Yes, the question mark hanging over the dog,' Stigson said. 'Between ten and eleven he barks almost non-stop. Then he's quiet for almost three hours, before starting up again, at which point he makes a hell of a racket for five minutes, until someone cuts his throat. That's the collated version we've worked out from the people we've spoken to. That the dog was quiet for three hours. Bit odd, if you ask me.'

'Anything else?'

Possibly two more things, according to Knutson. They'd spoken to another witness, another dog-walker, who had made some interesting observations, even if they actually complicated the picture that was beginning to emerge. At half past nine that evening their witness and his dog had walked past the lawyer's house and had seen a man sitting on the steps, and the door standing wide open.

'An elderly, white-haired man was sitting on the steps in front of the house, and our witness says he thought about asking if he could help him with anything. But seeing as there didn't seem to be anything wrong with him, he didn't bother. The witness says he thought the man sitting there might just have gone outside for some fresh air.'

'An elderly, white-haired man?'

'Yep,' Stigson said with a nod. 'The witness was in a bit of a hurry, he needed to get home for a wee – he said that off the record and in confidence – so he didn't stop to take a close look. An elderly, white-haired man, slim, well-dressed, wearing a light summer suit. That's what he says he saw, anyway. But he didn't see the younger fit bloke who our female witness saw loading boxes into that silver Mercedes.'

'An elderly, white-haired man. How old was he, then? Sixty? Seventy? Eighty? A hundred?'

'Somewhere between seventy and eighty, if we can believe the witness,' Stigson said, pulling a face. 'That's what he reckoned when we put a bit of pressure on him. About seventy-five years old, so definitely an older man. The witness himself is around sixty, which suggests he ought to be able to make a reasonable stab at the age of the man he saw.'

Seventy-five years old, sitting on the steps with the door wide open, Felicia Pettersson thought. Doesn't sound like the sort of person who'd have smashed in Eriksson's skull. Possibly someone who'd been through something bad, she thought.

'The car,' Felicia said. 'That silver Mercedes. We've got two witnesses who've mentioned it now. That woman, and the taxi-driver. Did this witness—'

'He didn't notice any car, or see any white removal boxes,' Stigson interrupted, shaking his head. 'The fact that he didn't pay any attention to a Merc of that colour probably isn't so strange, considering the people who live here, and all their Mercs and BMWs and Lexuses and . . . well, you name it . . . It's not really that strange.'

'I hear what you're saying,' Felicia said. 'One car among a load of others, and it wouldn't have stood out here.'

'Let's drop the car for now. There are a few other things I've been wondering about,' Felicia said, looking at her notes just to be sure.

'I think I can guess,' Stigson responded with a smile. 'Shoot! I'm listening.'

'That emergency call that was made from Eriksson's mobile comes in at twenty to ten, and that's definite, because it was logged by SOS Alarm—'

'Whereas my witnesses mention a time between half past nine and just before ten.' Stigson had thought the same thing that morning when he had been speaking to his first witness. 'I can think of various explanations for that.'

'Me too,' Felicia agreed, 'but the most likely still has to be that Eriksson tried to call SOS Alarm when things kicked off, and that's when he was killed, and then the perpetrators leave the scene—'

'Taking numerous items that they've stuffed into white boxes, which would mean that our female witness got the time wrong by about a quarter of an hour. It wasn't half past nine but quarter to ten when she made her observations, and it would hardly be the first time someone's got the time wrong by fifteen minutes. But there's another explanation as well.'

'What?'

'One of them leaves the house, taking the stuff with them, while the other stays and kills Eriksson. Or they carry the stuff out first, then return to the house to finish off the lawyer.'

'What about the old man sitting on the steps, then? How do you fit him in?'

'I don't,' Stigson said with a grin. 'He doesn't feel right, so I'm hoping Bäckström can sort that bit out for us.'

'Anything else I ought to know?' Felicia went on.

'Eriksson doesn't seem to have been anyone's idea of an ideal neighbour. I can't remember ever hearing people say so many negative things about someone who's just been murdered. Not the way his neighbours have, anyway. Noisy parties in the middle of the week, strange visitors showing up at all times of the day and night, double parking on the street and slamming car doors. And Eriksson himself seems to have been a bit lacking in the charm department. And there's that dog of his, which seems to have terrorized the neighbourhood.'

'But probably not a good enough reason to smash his head in.'

'No, probably not,' Stigson said. 'But if one of them did do it, I don't suppose it's the sort of thing they'd be likely to tell us about.'

39

Annika Carlsson had decided to show Ara Dosti the pictures herself, even though it wasn't her job, and despite the fact that she'd already worked a fourteen-hour shift. Before she started she went into the bathroom, rinsed her face with cold water, did some stretches to shake off the feeling that she'd been sitting behind her desk for far too long, and took several deep breaths. Then she went and got her laptop containing the almost two hundred photographs that Nadja had loaded on to it for her.

No nonsense, no pissing about, because I'll drag you off to the cells myself, she thought as she opened the door to the interview room where Ara was waiting for her.

'It's good of you to volunteer, Ara,' Annika said. 'I promise to do my best to make sure this won't take any longer than necessary, and I'll see to it that you get compensation for the work you aren't able to do. And if you can identify the right bloke for me as well, I promise to sort out a small reward as thanks for your help.'

'Okay, no problem,' Ara said with a nod. Good-looking girl, he thought. If it weren't for those black eyes that saw straight through him.

Then they had looked at the pictures together. Photographs of a total of one hundred and eighty-five different men in the police database. Just to make sure, three of them were of the same man, Fredrik Åkare, who had of course made threats against Eriksson, and they had been taken several years apart and in different contexts. About thirty of the others were pictures of Åkare's friends in the Hells Angels, his business associates, or just criminal colleagues.

The investigating team's attention had also been drawn to Afsan Ibrahim and his circle, known locally as the Brotherhood of the Ibrahims. Eriksson may have represented the Ibrahim family and been their confidant for a number of years, but things could change quickly. Every officer worthy of the badge knew that.

That left about a hundred crooks who bore some resemblance to the descriptions that Ara Dosti and Jan Stigson's witness, the female neighbour, had given the police, and who, to judge by their previous behaviour, had what was required to murder Eriksson.

The process had taken almost three hours, and Ara Dosti had recognized about twenty of the people he had been shown. The first of them was one of the Ibrahim family's associates, the same age as Ara.

'Okay,' Ara said, pointing at the picture Annika had just brought up on her computer. 'That's Omar. We were at school together down in Gnosjö. He was a great bloke. Came here from Morocco. Head of the student council. Top of the class. How come he's in your files?'

'No idea,' Annika said, shaking her head. I ask the questions around here, she thought.

'Weird,' Ara said, apparently genuinely surprised. 'All I know is that he got into the Institute of Technology here in Stockholm. He told the rest of us he was going to be a chemical engineer.'

'But he's not the man you almost ran over in your taxi?'

A chemist? Possibly, before he got in with the wrong crowd, Annika Carlsson thought.

'Nope,' Ara said. 'But I probably wouldn't have said anything if it was him. Omar was a decent bloke. We were good mates at school.'

'I believe you,' Annika said with a smile, even though the photographs of the people she was showing him hadn't ended up on her computer by accident, and certainly not in this instance. Good mates. Great, she thought.

In several cases Ara knew the names of the other people he recognized. No more schoolmates, just people he'd had in his taxi, and several he happened to know because they did the same job. There were others he'd seen out and about, in the bars around Stureplan, and the one he recognized most clearly was Fredrik Åkare, who he identified in all three different pictures.

'That's Fredrik Åkare. He's president of the Hells Angels. Not nice. If you pick an argument with him, I mean. But he's never messed with me. Always gives a decent tip.'

'When did you meet him?'

'I've had him in the taxi several times. Mostly when he's going to the pub. That lot often hang out at Reisen, in Gamla stan. That's supposed to be where they hold their meetings with Hells Angels from other countries. Then they go and eat at that American diner up on Södermalm, where they serve those massive steaks. Once I drove him to their clubhouse out in Solna. The one out near Bromma Airport.'

'But he's never come close to your front bumper?'

'I wouldn't be sitting here if he had,' Ara said with feeling. 'That man must be lethal when he gets angry. Two metres tall, hundred and fifty kilos. Must be over fifty, but definitely not the sort of person you want to get on the wrong side of.'

An hour later they were done, and Ara had signed the non-disclosure agreement that Annika's older and considerably more weary colleague had evidently forgotten. Then he signed to acknowledge receipt of five hundred kronor that she had taken from the tip-off account and, in parting, she had given him a piece of advice.

'You need to be aware of one thing, Ara,' Annika Carlsson said. 'I don't want to alarm you unnecessarily, but the men who killed Eriksson aren't very nice people. It's important that you don't tell anyone else what you've just told me. No one in your family, no friends at work, and definitely no journalists. Understood?'

'No problem,' Ara agreed. 'I looked Eriksson up on Google. Seems to have been a proper little consigliere if you can believe the talk online.'

'Take my card,' Annika Carlsson said, getting one out. 'If anything happens, call me on my mobile, no matter what time it is, and I'll help you. If there's an emergency, call our control room. I've written the direct number on my card. Agreed?'

'Absolutely,' Ara said. 'No problem. You have my word on it.'

'We'll talk tomorrow,' Annika Carlsson said. 'I'm afraid you might have to look at a few more pictures.'

'Same compensation?' Ara said, and smiled. Now she's starting to sound human. Even if she'd only given him five hundred and not a grand.

'I promise I'll do my best. What are you going to do now? Work? Or home for some sleep?'

'Home and sleep,' Ara said. 'It's been a tough day.'

'Good,' Annika said. 'Give me a call as soon as you wake up tomorrow morning.'

'Will do,' Ara said.

40

As soon as Ara got into the car to drive home to Kista, he switched his phone on. In his voicemail he had three calls on a similar theme from the journalist he had met just a few hours before. Now he had evidently spoken to his boss, and he wanted to make Ara a new offer for a description of the man and the car he had seen, on the condition that he looked at some pictures the newspaper had picked out. Ten thousand kronor for his trouble, and he could remain anonymous. If he wanted to go a step further and agreed to be interviewed and let them publish his name and photograph, the paper would offer more – at least double – and if he could actually identify the man he had almost run over in his taxi, they could imagine doubling that again.

What the fuck do I do now? Fifty grand, cash, Ara thought. Two months in Thailand or Dubai while the cops did their job, until things calmed down enough for him to come back home again.

When Ara got back to his little flat out in Kista he had decided to make a cup of tea and then sleep on the matter. There was something about that female police officer he had met that had made a deep impression on him. She seemed the sort who knew what she was talking about, and would stand by what she said. Fifty thousand compared to five hundred, he thought, with a wry smile. Then he had filled the kettle and, just as he was pouring boiling water into his cup, someone rang on his door.

Shit, what's going on now? he thought. Then he put his hand in his pocket and took out Annika Carlsson's card and tapped the handwritten number into his mobile before padding silently over to the front door and looking at his visitor through the peephole.

His new acquaintance from the biggest evening paper evidently wasn't the sort who gave up easily, no matter what answer you gave him. Eventually, Ara let him into the flat, before his neighbours started to wonder why he had a visitor in the middle of the night, to explain to the reporter that he didn't want any more contact with either him or his paper. Not for five or ten thousand, anyway.

It didn't go terribly well, even though he started by talking about the non-disclosure agreement he had signed.

'They always try that crap,' his visitor said, shrugging his shoulders dismissively. 'At worst you'd get a fine, and I promise the paper would pay that for you. And we'll get you a lawyer if they start to make things difficult.'

'I get it,' Ara said. 'Sorry, but I'm not interested.'

'Okay,' the reporter said. 'Here's what we do. You stay anonymous, and you can be a hundred per cent certain of that, because I'd never dream of blowing one of my sources. You talk about the bloke you saw, and his car. You can have ten thousand in cash. Right now. I saw there's a cashpoint just round the corner.'

'Not interested,' Ara said.

'And if you can identify him from the pictures I've got with me, I promise you'll get fifty thousand for your trouble, and you can still be anonymous. It'll take five minutes at most, I promise. Then I swear I won't bother you again.'

'Okay,' Ara said. Fifty thousand, he thought.

The reporter from the biggest evening paper had brought about twenty pictures with him, of half a dozen different people, all of them apparently taken in connection with various stories the paper had run. Six people, compared to the almost two hundred the police had shown him. He had spread them out on Ara's kitchen table so he could look at them all at the same time, and all Ara needed was a quick glance to recognize the man he had almost run over barely twenty-four hours earlier.

He had been looking straight into the camera when the picture was taken. The same look he had given Ara in the street outside the house where the lawyer was murdered. Now he was seeing him again, for the second time in one day, and there was something in his eyes that made Ara realize what Annika Carlsson had warned him about.

'No,' Ara said. 'I'm sorry, but I don't recognize any of them. None of these ones, anyway.'

'Okay,' the reporter said, patting his shoulder. 'Let's stay in touch. Give me a call if you change your mind.'

Then he had gone at last, leaving Ara in peace.

41

From the crime scene, Bäckström had gone straight to his local bar for a well-earned dinner and no sooner had he stepped in through the door than he was welcomed by his favourite Finnish waitress, who had just got back from holiday in Thailand. Bäckström sat at the bar to study the menu in peace, as he soothed his throat with a cold lager. There weren't many customers, no one he recognized, which suited Bäckström fine, seeing as he needed to unwind – besides, he was also hoping to have a few words with the Finnish waitress. She was a busty blonde whom he'd known for several years, and she also used to clean his flat in exchange for a good seeing-to afterwards on his Hästens bed. That's probably why she's as well preserved as she is, even though she must be almost forty, he thought.

'So how was Thailand?' he asked, and took a large gulp of beer.

It had been excellent, according to his interviewee. On the third day her dear husband had fallen asleep in the sun, got sunburned and ended up in hospital in Bangkok. He had had to stay there for a week, leaving her to relax.

Then she and her husband had returned home and, as far as the cost of his stay in hospital was concerned, that was covered by their insurance, so there was nothing to worry about there.

'Bloody lucky he didn't die,' Bäckström said with feeling.

'Don't worry,' the Finnish waitress said. 'A real man like you should never have to provide for a widow. What do you want to eat?'

After further consideration, Bäckström had decided on a light evening meal, as he had to be up early, so that was what he ordered. Småland sausage, beetroot and potatoes in parsley sauce. A couple of lagers and two large shorts to aid his digestion. Then he rounded off the meal with a cup of coffee and a small cognac, paid the bill and went home.

'Call if you want any cleaning done. It must have built up while I was on holiday,' the Finnish woman said, smiling and nodding pointedly at his groin before going over and giving him a goodnight hug.

They're mad about you, more and more of them all the time, Bäckström thought as he stepped out on to the street.

Home at last, Bäckström thought, and five minutes later he was in his Japanese silk dressing-gown, sitting on his big black leather sofa in front of the television with a thirst-quenching vodka tonic, with his feet up on his antique Chinese coffee table as he looked around the room with satisfaction.

You live pretty well, he reflected happily. The only thing that really bothered him was the large gilded birdcage on the table over by the window. High time to flog that crap on the internet, he thought, seeing as the cage's former occupant had spent the past three weeks in animal hospital, where, with any luck, he was going to die. Mourned and missed by no one, least of all Bäckström. This in contrast to Egon, his beloved goldfish, who had passed away almost ten years ago as a consequence of his colleague Jan Rogersson neglecting him so shamelessly while Bäckström was away investigating a murder in the south of Sweden.

But Bäckström had never actually owned a stick insect. That was a deliberate lie he had thrown at his colleague, Detective Sergeant Rosita Andersson-Trygg, with the intention of confusing her still further and bringing the already utterly pointless discussion to a rapid conclusion.

A goldfish called Egon and a parrot he had named Isak, that was it. All those cats and dogs from his childhood were a complete fabrication. His simple-minded mother had a load of pot plants to which she devoted her tender attentions each day, watering, dusting and talking to them constantly, but he came no closer than that to anything that was actually alive. His crazy mum, who socialized with her plants. His dad, the severely alcoholic senior constable, had managed to make things even easier for himself, seeing as he had a deep dislike of people, plants and animals and never had any problem choosing between a litre of vodka and his firstborn son, Evert.

His childhood, in summary. A happy childhood, because it was long since over, and 'single is strong' only applies when you're big enough to defend yourself, he thought philosophically, nodding thoughtfully to himself. But he still missed Egon, even though it had been ten years since he slipped off this mortal coil. Egon, he thought, and raised his glass in a silent toast to absent friends.

Bäckström had been given Egon and his aquarium as a

gift from a woman he had picked up on the internet. He had replied to a contact advert, and what had prompted him to reply was partly the advertiser's description of herself but mainly the way she signed off: 'uniform a plus'.

To start with, it had all worked very well. Her description of herself as 'a liberated and broad-minded woman' hadn't been entirely unfounded. Not at the beginning, but after a couple of weeks she turned out to be remarkably similar to all the other whining women who had passed through his life. So he had sent her packing, but not Egon, who stayed on, and after a while Bäckström began to feel attached to him.

When he got home at last after a long and difficult day at work. When he sat there on the sofa in the evenings, sipping a well-earned drink and feeling a sense of well-being spread through him as he watched Egon swimming back and forth and up and down in his own little world, apparently not the slightest bit bothered about all the cruelty and misery lurking round the corner from where he and Bäckström lived.

Egon had been a real treasure, and his only friend in this life, Bäckström thought, refilling his almost empty glass. Isak, on the other hand, was a common hooligan with wings and a hooked beak. The result of an extremely unfortunate impulse purchase he had made a couple of months earlier when he happened to be passing a pet-shop on his way to work. In the window was a parrot, with an attractive mix of blue and yellow feathers, which appealed to his prospective owner for the obvious ideological reasons, and when Bäckström stopped to take a closer look at him, he tilted his head to one side and said something to him, which he had, unfortunately, been unable to hear.

Must be one of those ones you can teach to talk, Bäckström thought. Then he had gone into the shop, explained his specific requirements to the assistant, been given the usual assurances in reply and, fifteen minutes later, it was all sorted out. Bäckström was now the owner of a parrot, and had been given the cage into the bargain, but the misery he was soon to find himself in hadn't yet begun. But with a bit of luck the little fucker will soon have fluttered his last, he thought happily, turning on the television to watch the latest news on TV4.

After ten minutes he switched off, shook his weary head and was obliged to pour himself a sturdy nightcap to stop himself losing all faith in humanity. The only thing they were all going on about was the brutal murder of the renowned lawyer Thomas Eriksson. He appeared to be mourned and much missed by pretty much the whole of humankind. They had even interviewed an astonishingly skinny and stupid woman, who, to judge by the on-screen caption, was chair of the Bar Association. She had lost both a close friend and a highly gifted colleague. Eriksson's murder was also an attack on the entire justice system, and threats and violence against lawyers were a serious and rapidly growing problem which demanded immediate action from the government.

What the hell is happening to dear old Sweden? Bäckström thought. On such a joyous day as this, every right-thinking person ought to be celebrating. Then he got up, with some difficulty, went to the bathroom, brushed his teeth, put on his neatly pressed silk pyjamas and went to bed.

And just as he was about to fall asleep he had suddenly seen the truth and the light, and solved the mystery of the strange bloodstain and the way things must have happened when the as yet unknown perpetrator beat the life out of Thomas Eriksson the lawyer. A logical end for an arsehole like Eriksson, Bäckström thought. Even if it didn't match the recent eulogies. But it was a worthy conclusion to the best day of his own life, he thought. And this in spite of the fact that he had no idea that it was about to get even better still.

42

Ara Dosti didn't need to call Annika Carlsson as soon as he woke up on Tuesday morning. She was the one who woke him.

'Rise and shine, Ara,' Annika Carlsson said. 'I've got some new pictures I'd like to show you.'

An hour later he was sitting in the police station in Solna. Annika Carlsson had given him another five-hundred-kronor note from the tip-off account and told him he was a clever boy. Then she handed him over to another officer.

'This is my colleague, Johan Ek,' Annika said. 'He's found some more pictures we'd like to show you.'

Weird-looking bloke, Ara thought. He'd never seen a police officer who looked or behaved like that. Short and fat, with thick, horn-rimmed glasses, kind eyes and a permanent friendly smile. Gentle, inviting gestures, body language to try to emphasize and underline what he said.

'A pleasure to meet you, Ara,' Ek said, holding out a chubby little hand. His handshake was just firm enough, a simple marker of trust and good intentions.

'Sit down, sit down, please,' he went on, making a sweeping gesture with his left arm as he pulled out the chair in front of the computer screen with his right hand.

Must be one of those civilian employees, Ara thought. He wasn't anything like all the other cops he'd met, and when, quarter of an hour later, for the second time in eight hours, Ara was shown a picture of the man he had almost run over, he didn't have any difficulty shaking his head once more and moving on to the next picture.

Not for a five-hundred-kronor note. Not if I have to testify against him and he's the sort he looks like he is, Ara thought.

Two hours later it was over, and even though Ara had looked at another hundred or so pictures and had shaken his head at all of them, the man who had shown them to him still seemed happy.

'I'm sorry,' Ara said. 'But I don't recognize any of them. None of them clicked, if you know what I mean.'

'I understand, Ara, I understand, of course,' Ek said with a nod. 'But the way I understood it, you said you'd recognize him if you saw him again.'

'Yeees,' Ara said, nodding. 'I'm quite sure . . .I'm fairly sure I would.'

'Of course, it might well be that we just don't have any pictures of him,' Ek said, leaning forward and patting him on the arm in a friendly way. 'That sort of thing does happen, you know. It happens fairly often. If only you knew how often it happens!'

If only he weren't so nice, Ara thought, but he merely nodded. That, and the consequent guilty conscience, was probably why he said what he did next.

'Can't we do one of those photofit pictures?' Ara asked. 'The sort they always have on *Crimewatch*?'

'Funny you should mention that, Ara,' Ek said. 'That's exactly what I was about to suggest to you. We'll find a quiet corner, just the two of us, and put together a photofit picture of him.'

'Yes,' Ara said. 'I'm up for that. The only problem is that I have to start work in half an hour. But tomorrow morning would be fine. I'm off then.'

'Splendid, absolutely splendid,' Johan Ek said, beaming as if he'd just won the lottery. 'Well, let's talk on the phone first thing tomorrow.'

43

At twelve o'clock on Tuesday the investigating team met for a second time. Bäckström bade them all welcome, then, once the introductory paper-shuffling and chair-scraping had died down, he handed over to Peter Niemi.

Niemi began by telling them that the written report from the medical officer would, unfortunately, take another day or so. In conjunction with the post-mortem, a number of inconsistencies had come to light which demanded further examination and reflection. Nothing dramatic enough, however, to make him alter his preliminary finding that Eriksson had died as a result of a hard blow to the back of the head and neck with a blunt instrument.

'The only thing I can add on that score is that we've had the results back about the blood sample,' Niemi said. 'Our murder victim appears to have had a fair bit to drink. That's not to say he was really drunk when he died, but he was more than socially lubricated, seeing as he had 0.1 per cent alcohol in his blood.'

'Really?' Bäckström said, shaking his head in concern. 'What about the dog, then?' Was he on the piss as well? he thought.

As far as the murder victim's dog was concerned, everything was done and dusted. There was also no doubt that it was Eriksson's dog. The microchip that had been found under its skin also contained the dog's name.

'It appears to have been called Justice, for some reason,' Niemi said with a wry smile. 'A male Rottweiler, six years old. I got the report from the veterinary lab this morning. One cut straight across the throat, in line with the top edge of the collar he was wearing. The cut severed the carotid artery, the dog would have bled to death in less than a minute and, because the evidence suggests that our perpetrator was standing astride the dog's back and holding it by the collar, he's right-handed. He drew the knife across the dog's throat from left to right, but before he did that it looks like he hit the dog on its back. Several times, very hard. There are numerous fractures of the lower vertebrae, and its pelvis was also broken. According to the vet who carried out the post-mortem, that ought to have paralysed its back legs. Which might explain how the perpetrator was able to stand astride the dog when he cut its throat. It wasn't a small dog, after all. Weighed about fifty kilos.'

'It's appalling that anyone could do that sort of thing to an innocent animal,' Rosita Andersson-Trygg interrupted angrily. 'What sort of monster could do something like that? And why isn't there any mention of this in our opening charges? This is a clear case of aggravated animal cruelty.'

'Yes, it's extremely unpleasant,' Bäckström agreed. 'Do you have any ideas about the knife, Peter?' he went on, to shut her up as quickly as possible. Really need to talk to Holt so I can get shot of her, the old bag's utterly deranged, he thought.

'That's tricky,' Niemi said, shaking his head. 'To judge from the wound, it's sharp, extremely sharp. I also have a feeling it's double-edged, about three centimetres across and something like ten centimetres long.'

'Why do you think that?' Annika Carlsson asked in surprise. 'How could you tell that from the wound? I thought you said it was just a straight cut from left to right?'

'Supplementary evidence,' Niemi said with a faint smile. 'Not from the cut, seeing as you ask. The perpetrator wiped the knife on the dog's coat. On the right-hand side, starting at the joint on the front leg and up towards the shoulder and back, so presumably the dog was already dead by then, and lying on its left side. The way we found it. Judging from the streak of blood on its fur, the knife-blade is approximately ten centimetres long and three centimetres across. And double-edged, in case anyone's wondering, because it cut off hairs on both sides as it was pulled over the dog's coat.'

'Is that so?' Bäckström said. 'Is that so?' he repeated. The bloke can't possibly be a standard-issue Finn, Bäckström thought. Probably adopted. However the hell Finnish fuckers could be allowed to adopt Swedish children.

'Could have been a flick-knife or a stiletto,' Annika Carlsson said. 'They're popular with crims, and they're often double-edged.'

'Well, I'm not so sure about that,' Niemi said, shaking his head again and rubbing his chin thoughtfully. 'I think the blade's a bit too broad to be one of those. A double-edged, short, broad blade. Doesn't sound like the average stiletto or flick-knife. And he doesn't seem to have cut himself with it while he was using it, which in my world usually means it's got some sort of guard, or at least a solid, non-slip handle.'

'So what was the dog hit with, then?' Bäckström asked. 'Do you have any thoughts about that?' Flick-knife or stiletto? he thought. Where have I heard that? Bollocks, I'll work it out, he thought.

'Long, round and hard. Probably the same weapon that smashed in our murder victim's skull.'

Who'd have thought it? Bäckström mused, and nodded.

'Anything else?' he asked.

A fair amount of evidence had been secured at the scene and had already been sent on to the National Forensics Laboratory for the usual analysis. Shoe-prints, handprints, fingerprints, strands of hair, traces of fabrics and the other things that were always found whenever someone was murdered indoors. Generally a positive sign, but in hindsight they very rarely turned out to have anything to do with the murder.

But there were also three pieces of evidence that looked rather more promising.

An old-fashioned handkerchief containing traces of both blood and snot, a blue sofa cushion that – judging by the smell – might well turn out to contain traces of urine and excrement, and – best of all – some blood that was found on the terrace door.

'It was right on the edge of the frame, on the outside of the door,' Niemi explained. 'A streak of blood, not much, but enough for us, so we should get a DNA fingerprint from it. It was about ten centimetres below the door handle and – as I happened to read the interview with that taxi-driver – I have a feeling that it might be from someone who had been bitten in the right leg. I'd say their trousers got torn and they were bitten in the thigh, to judge from the height of the streak. About one metre up.'

'It sounds like you're talking about our perpetrator,' Annika Carlsson said, more as a statement than a question.

'If his DNA's on file, we're sorted,' Stigson said, unable to conceal his delight, seeing as he had planned to take some holiday that weekend, until Toivonen had put a stop to it.

'Let's not get carried away,' Niemi said. 'We'll soon find out. Hernandez sent the sample down to Linköping this morning, and we've asked for it to be dealt with urgently. With a bit of luck, we'll get the results back within a few days at most.'

'Is that everything?' Bäckström wondered, leaning back in his chair with an innocent expression.

'Well, there might be one more thing,' Niemi said, smiling and nodding. 'And here I would like to express my own and my colleague Hernandez's gratitude to our dear boss who, yesterday evening, when he revisited the crime scene, found the revolver that we hadn't been able to locate. It was in a vase of flowers that was standing on a table in the downstairs hall, and all we can say in our defence is that we would have found it when we got that far. And that whoever put it there put the flowers back in the vase after he'd done so, which is why we didn't find it straight away.'

'Oh, don't mention it,' Bäckström said with a grin, as he noted a number of appreciative nods and surprised looks round the table.

'From the registration number, it appears to be Eriksson's revolver, the one he had a licence for. There are six cartridges in the magazine. Two have been fired, and the calibre matches the bullets we found in the ceiling and sofa on the upstairs landing. I took the liberty of comparing them before we sent them down to the National Forensics Lab. The bullet from the back of the sofa is in very good condition and, in my humble opinion, there's no doubt that it was fired from Eriksson's revolver.'

'Excellent,' Bäckström said. 'Let's have a five-minute break, then it's time we got on with the really important stuff.'

44

Even though they had the opportunity to stretch their legs, most members of the investigating team had chosen to stay in the room, and only a couple of the most notorious smokers had needed more than the allotted five minutes. Bäckström had seen this before, and knew what the reason was. They could smell the scent of the perpetrator now, and things were hotting up. Every murder detective worth the name was taught to hate coincidence and, in this case, two witnesses had, independently of each other, and at two different times, observed a silver Mercedes in direct connection to the crime scene.

'Okay,' Bäckström said. 'Correct me if I'm wrong, but our first witness, the female neighbour, saw the vehicle in question at half past nine in the evening, which fits pretty well with the time of Eriksson's demise. Her statement is also partially supported by the other neighbour, who saw the white-haired man sitting on the steps in front of the house with the front door wide open at about the same time. Even if he didn't notice a Merc, any white removal boxes or a younger, fitter accomplice, I interpret that to mean that our perpetrators are on their way out of the house. Have I got that right?'

Bäckström nodded inquiringly at Stigson, who nodded back.

'Yes. And we mustn't forget the probability that the strong-looking individual described by the female witness and the taxi-driver might well be the same person,' Stigson said. 'I'm even prepared to buy that old bloke with white hair, even if we've only got one witness who saw him. I mean . . . who'd bother to invent an old bloke with white hair leaving the scene of a murder?'

'There's always someone,' Bäckström said with a shrug of his shoulders. 'It usually works out. If we could get back to that taxi-driver who contacted us . . . What do we know about him? Have we found out anything else?'

'Annika interviewed him yesterday, and I interviewed him again this morning,' Detective Inspector Johan Ek said, leafing through his notes.

'So what do we make of him, then?'

'The timing seems solid, given that he's got the print-out from the car to back it up. Eleven minutes past two in the morning, which is probably more than we have any right to demand. That's when he almost runs over the person crossing the road right outside Eriksson's house. I agree with Stigson, by the way. It could very well be the same man that our female witness sees at half past nine in the evening.'

'Pictures? Have we got him to look at any pictures?' Bäckström asked, for some reason glaring at his colleague Alm, who, for reasons unknown, had chosen to sit as far away from the lead investigator as possible.

'Almost three hundred so far,' Ek confirmed. 'Hasn't identified anyone yet.'

'And he's not holding anything back?' Bäckström asked.

'I don't think so,' Johan Ek said, shaking his head. 'He seems a decent bloke, no police record. I get the impression that he's keen to help.'

'In that case, we'll let him,' Bäckström said. 'Show him more pictures. Sooner or later something will click. Well, I'd like us to—'

'There's one thing I've been thinking about,' Rosita Andersson-Trygg interrupted, waving her notepad to add strength to her words.

Oh God, Bäckström thought.

'I'm listening,' he said.

Rosita Andersson-Trygg had been thinking about the poor Rottweiler that had been killed in the most bestial way and, if she was going to be completely honest, unfortunately, she seemed to be the only member of the investigating team to spare him a thought. This was probably also why none of their witnesses had recognized the man they were looking for, even though they had now looked at three hundred photographs. The man they were after was an unusually sadistic torturer of animals, and definitely not a first-time offender. But, of course, it was very sadly the case that no matter what cruelty you subjected animals to, the penalties were negligible and there was consequently a serious risk that there wasn't a single photograph of the man they were looking for in the police database.

'I hear what you're saying,' Bäckström said. 'So what do we do, then?'

'I think it's time we contacted our colleagues in animal welfare. After all, they've built up their own database of people who abuse animals, and I think that's where we might find him.'

'Excellent,' Bäckström said. 'Splendid,' he added, for emphasis, bearing in mind who he was talking to. 'Can you get on to that, Rosita?' he asked. 'Get them to pull out all the pictures they've got of the sort of people who could be thought capable of cutting a dog's throat. It would be great if you could put together a psychological profile of him as well. Talk to the perpetrator profiling unit up at National Crime. I'm sure they'll be able to help you. He certainly seems to be an unusually nasty character.'

'I've already started—'

'Splendid, absolutely splendid. It can be your special task. Drop everything else and get in touch with me at once, the minute you've got anything.' Finally shot of the old bag, he thought.

'Apart from that, I want us to prioritize the Merc,' Bäckström went on. 'And I want the identities of the people our witnesses saw. Nadja, you sort out the car, and Ek, you make sure we have IDs that we can match to it. Then I want another door-to-door session where we show pictures of the car to Eriksson's neighbours. We've got nothing to lose, seeing as the information seems to have leaked on to the internet already. Might as well do it properly. It must be possible to identify the car.'

But it seemed that wasn't altogether straightforward either, according to Nadja, who had already started thinking about the matter with the help of the databases she had access to. Within a hundred-kilometre radius of the crime scene – far enough for them to drive if they forgot something on their first visit and had to return four hours later – there were three million people and almost two million cars, of which almost thirty thousand were Mercedes.

For that reason, she had applied certain criteria, all of which could be used to search the national vehicle register, to reduce the number of possible vehicles.

'Silver, an expensive coupé, five years old at most,' Nadja summarized. 'That brings it down to a total of about four hundred vehicles within our radius. Just over half of those are hire cars, leased out or owned by businesses. And just under half are privately owned. Six of those are registered to people living within a kilometre from our victim's home.'

'Good,' Bäckström said. 'Take any safe short cuts you can. Just say if you need more people.'

'That's underway,' Nadja said. 'I've already spoken to Annika about it.'

'Okay,' Bäckström said. 'We'll stop there and get some work done, then we'll meet again tomorrow, same time, same place. I've also got something I want you to think about. I'm expecting a good answer tomorrow.'

Bäckström left a dramatic pause while he pretended to read his notes.

'Eriksson was murdered at quarter to ten in the evening. So can someone please explain to a simple officer why the perpetrators would return some four hours later to cut his dog's throat, and then smash in the skull of someone who's been dead for several hours. What is it that makes them so pissed off they're prepared to take that risk?'

That gave them something to think about, Bäckström thought. The only ones who didn't look astonished were Peter Niemi and his colleague Chico Hernandez. Neither of them said anything, just nodded in agreement.

45

Nadja handed the search for the silver Mercedes over to her colleagues. Once reinforcements had arrived, there were five of them in total, and they had each been issued with copious instructions. Purely routine, she thought, and if any problems did arise, they could always ask her. She had other things to be getting on with. Questions that couldn't be answered with the help of a simple manual and a bit of tapping at a keyboard, questions relating to what their murder victim had spent the last twenty-four hours of his life doing. Questions that required considerations of a more speculative nature, where the degree of probability had to be carefully evaluated.

Judging by the log of the alarm at Eriksson's house, he appeared to have woken up before half past ten in the morning. That's when he deactivated the alarm and opened the front door, only to reactivate it a minute later. He had probably let his dog out into the garden and fetched his morning paper from the letterbox, Nadja thought, noting her conclusions on the timeline she had drawn up on her computer.

After that, he probably read the paper and had breakfast, she thought, seeing as it wasn't until twenty to eleven that the alarm was deactivated and the front door opened again, and then the alarm was again reactivated a minute later. That's when he lets the dog back in. The dog runs round the garden while he eats breakfast and reads the paper.

To judge by the remnants in his sink, he had started the day with bacon and eggs, bread, coffee and a Fernet-Branca while reading *Svenska Dagbladet* and making a failed attempt to solve that day's difficult sudoku. He doesn't seem to have been much of a mathematician, Nadja thought, shaking her head sadly and opening the log of Eriksson's phone calls on her computer. His landline had been silent all day, but he had received three calls on his mobile and made two outgoing calls.

The first call was short, just a couple of minutes, and was from an unregistered pay-as-you-go mobile. It was made at thirteen minutes past twelve and ended at a quarter past. The identity of the caller remained to be seen, but it looked like a typical call to confirm something that he or she and Eriksson had already talked about, Nadja thought, making another note on her timeline.

The next call was more straightforward. It had been made from a mobile belonging to his colleague, the lawyer Peter Danielsson. It was received at half past one in the afternoon, and they had clearly had a lot to talk about, as the conversation lasted over half an hour, ending at seven minutes past two.

Nadja opened the transcript of the first interview with Danielsson on her computer and found the part where he said he had called Eriksson at around midday. Then she sighed and made another note on her list of contradictions and things that weren't altogether clear, things she'd have to check again just to make sure, even though she knew that, nine times out of ten, they were the result of human error and had nothing to do with anything. Memory is an unreliable companion, she thought, going back to the list of calls.

The last incoming call had been made from the offices of Eriksson and Partners at ten minutes to three in the afternoon. It lasted nine minutes, and the evidence seemed to suggest that it wasn't Danielsson calling back, as the call from his mobile which had ended only half an hour earlier had been made via a phone mast in the vicinity of Danielsson's summer cottage on Rådmansö outside Norrtälje, whereas the law firm was based in Östermalm in Stockholm.

So he was talking to someone else at work, Nadja thought, and she already had her own ideas about who that might have been. Three minutes after that call ended, Thomas Eriksson had made his first outgoing call from his mobile. He called another mobile, belonging to a young woman who worked as a legally trained secretary at the law firm and, going by the location of her phone when the call was received, she had probably called him first from the office. And he called her on her mobile three minutes later. Possibly for the simple reason that they were seeing each other, Nadja thought. She was very familiar with the pattern such calls usually followed.

Isabella Norén, twenty-four years old, employed at the law firm for the past three years, Nadja thought as she typed Norén's ID number into her computer and immediately found the interview conducted by her colleague Johan Ek late on Monday afternoon, barely twenty-four hours earlier. According to Norén herself, her last contact with Eriksson had been around lunchtime on the Friday before the murder. He had looked into her office and asked her to get out the documentation relating to a case that was due to be heard in the Court of Appeal the following week. A routine task, nothing remarkable, and, according to Norén, the short conversation had ended with them wishing each other a good weekend.

But that isn't what happened, Nadja thought, adding another note to her list of details that would require further investigation.

That just left the last phone call. Made to SOS Alarm at twenty to ten in the evening, when whoever made the call didn't say anything before the call was cut off. That was when he died, Nadja thought. He gets up just before half past nine in the morning and is killed twelve hours later. Her next task was to work out what he was doing between twenty to eleven in the morning, when he let his dog in, and thirteen minutes past twelve, when he received the first incoming call.

First, he feeds the dog, Nadja thought. Then he probably has a bath. She had the impression he was the sort who preferred baths to showers, especially on a Sunday morning, when he could do as he pleased. About half an hour in the bath, no longer, given that he had switched on his computer and logged in at quarter past eleven, and he seemed to have been sitting in front of it for the rest of the day, until almost nine o'clock that evening, when he lets his guests in.

With short breaks to let the dog out again – the alarm log indicated that the front door had been opened and closed at quarter past six and quarter to seven – and another meal, which he probably ate in front of his computer. Breadcrumbs on the keyboard, a side plate with a few olive stones on it, a cheese rind, a couple of uneaten slices of salami and an empty beer bottle. Nine hours or so in front of the computer. On the internet the whole time, and the sites he visited were pretty extreme, even for a hardened woman like her.

46

On Tuesday, Detective Inspector Jan Stigson and his colleagues had done another round of door-to-door inquiries, showing the people living in the area pictures of the silver Mercedes. It hadn't led to anything useful. But that evening they had found another witness who could provide additional information about the white boxes that Stigson's female neighbour had mentioned.

This was another neighbour who, on Thursday or Friday evening, two or three days before the murder, had seen Eriksson unloading a couple of white boxes from the back seat of his black Audi and carrying them inside the house. He was unsure which day it was – either Thursday or Friday, but he was certain it couldn't have been any other day of the week leading up to Eriksson's murder. He had been away on business for the first half of the week and returned to Stockholm only late on Wednesday evening. He had been kind enough to show his diary to one of Stigson's colleagues.

The same thing applied to the end of the week. Early on Saturday morning he had gone off to his summer house on Värmdö to play golf and see friends, and hadn't returned until Monday morning, when he went straight to his office in central Stockholm.

Which left Thursday or Friday evening, as he usually set

off to work at seven in the morning, 'to avoid the worst of the traffic, and long before someone like Eriksson would have come round after his antics the previous night', not returning before six o'clock, at the earliest, to have dinner with his wife.

Stigson's colleague had thanked him for his help and was given a few parting words from the witness.

'They say you shouldn't speak ill of the dead . . .'

'Yes, so they say,' Stigson's colleague said, then gave an encouraging nod suspecting that a confidence was on its way.

'I might be a bit more old-fashioned,' the witness began, 'and that's probably why I firmly believe that everyone should be judged according to their behaviour while they were alive. If we're to believe the papers, Eriksson was a bit of a gangster. Well, apart from the last day or so, since he was murdered. You'd hardly believe they were writing about the same man.'

'Oh?'

'As far as that's concerned, whether or not he was a bad guy in the broader sense, I probably shouldn't say anything. You can't believe everything you read in the papers, after all. But I do know what he was like on a more personal level, if I can put it like that, seeing as I've had him as a neighbour for several years.'

'What was he like, then?'

'He was a uniquely unpleasant little bastard,' Eriksson's neighbour declared, nodding emphatically.

'You couldn't give me any examples? Any concrete examples . . . ?'

'No,' the neighbour said, shaking his head firmly. 'On that point I'm afraid I must disappoint you. I'll leave the gossip to others. You'll just have to take my word for it.'

47

After Tuesday's meeting Peter Niemi had gone to see Bäckström. He nodded towards the chair in front of Bäckström's desk and asked if he could sit down.

'Sure,' Bäckström said, nodding back. If you offer one of those bark-bread munchers a finger, they try to grab your whole arm, he thought.

'I completely agree with you, Bäckström,' Niemi said. 'No trace of any splatters of blood and, considering the injuries to his head, we should be looking at a spatter pattern of several metres. The only explanation is that he had been dead for several hours by the time our perpetrator lets loose on him for the second time. Congealed blood doesn't spatter, of course. Which is something I intend to make clear to our esteemed colleagues as soon as possible in a little educational email.'

'Was that why you called the friendly old doctor this morning?' Bäckström said with a slight smile. Even a Finn like Niemi deserves a second chance, he thought.

'Partly,' Niemi said, 'and we're in complete agreement on that point, the doctor and I, in case you're wondering.'

'Partly?'

'The pool of blood he was lying in, the one he had his face in, which indicated pretty extensive bleeding through the nose and mouth. That's what was worrying me, because it suggested a serious blow from the front while he was still alive. The simple solution is that that's what actually killed him.'

'I hear what you're saying,' Bäckström said. 'I'm thinking the same as you. So what's the problem? The forensic medical problem, I mean?'

'Comprehensive injuries inflicted both before and after death. The fractures and cracks are evidently all mixed up, so the short version is that he needs more time to work out which injuries occurred at which point.'

'Bloody academics,' Bäckström said. 'Can it really be that fucking hard to work out that the bloke's dead because someone smashed his head in? Who cares about the details?'

'Each to their own, according to talent and ability,' Niemi said. 'If you ask me, it's probably also because he can't see any reason to change his preliminary statement. That Eriksson died as a result of a fatal blow to the head and neck.'

'Good to hear. Sometimes you have to be grateful for small mercies,' Bäckström grunted.

48

On Tuesday afternoon the court in Stockholm had agreed to the prosecutor's request to search the premises of the law firm Eriksson and Partners on Karlavägen in Stockholm. After some reflection, the firm had decided not to appeal against the decision: 'So that we can finally get shot of you,' as Danielsson expressed his and his colleagues' view of the matter when he spoke to Lisa Lamm on the phone. At four o'clock that afternoon two detectives and a forensics officer arrived to go through the murder victim's office in the presence of a representative of the law firm. All in accordance with the prosecutor's request, and with the approval of the court.

In Eriksson's computer, in his filing cabinets, drawers and bookshelves, the police found hundreds of thousands of documents, ninety-nine per cent of which shared the quality that they could have been acquired by other means without any great difficulty, and without the need to search the victim's office: copies of police files of preliminary investigations, court verdicts, other legal judgments and protocols, almost all of which were covered by freedom of information legislation. The impression that the victim's office gave of him as a person was simple and unambiguous. A hard-working criminal-case lawyer who had to spend all his time at work actually doing his work.

Beyond that, there was practically nothing. His diary, showing the times of his visits to the police in conjunction with his participation in interviews with clients he represented, prison visits, and the times of his appearances in court. They appeared largely to form a record upon which his invoices could be based. A few lunches and dinners were also included, but not many, and there was no indication of where they had taken place or who he was going to be dining with.

The search was conducted under the leadership of Detective Inspector Bladh, who was known among his colleagues as a practised hand when it came to looking through paperwork, and once again he lived up to his reputation. At eight o'clock that evening he called Nadja Högberg and gave his preliminary report on what he and his colleagues had found.

'Almost exclusively work-related files,' Bladh summarized.

'Oh, I see,' Nadja replied. But what else had she really expected?

'His computer,' Nadja said. 'You checked to see if anyone had been on it since he left work on Friday?'

'Yes,' Bladh said. 'There's no cause for concern. Nothing's been removed, added or altered. Presumably because they only found out what was going on when we showed up at the office and secured his room. We only found three things of a more private nature. Number one, his diary. Number two, a couple of folders in which he seems to have collected any letters or emails in which people threatened him or generally expressed disapproval. I get the impression he was very careful to monitor that sort of thing.'

'Did you find any death threats?' Nadja asked.

Considering what his house was like, Nadja thought. All those alarms, cameras and motion detectors, all of which, when it came down to it, hadn't made the slightest difference, as he had switched them off because he trusted the person who was about to kill him.

'Eleven, if I counted correctly, in which the sender promised to finish him off one way or another. But even they aren't particularly exciting. They mostly seem to be from the sort who put stamps on upside down and finish every sentence with one or more exclamation marks.'

'Number three, then,' Nadja said. 'What about that?'

'He seems to have had a number of private cases alongside his criminal caseload,' Bladh said. 'Various documents which he kept in a separate folder. Not much, but they amount to a hundred or so pages. They're quite difficult to interpret in places, so I was thinking of seizing them.'

'Good. Call me if you find anything you think it's worth waking me for. Anything else?'

'Keeping his room sealed off,' Bladh said. 'That colleague of his, Danielsson, was on my case like a polecat the whole time, so, if for that reason alone, I'm inclined to keep it sealed for an extra day, and our prosecutor seems to be of the same mind.'

'Why not?' Nadja said, with all the feeling that could only come from having grown up in the old Soviet Union. 'Say hello to him from me, and explain that this might take a bit of time if he doesn't behave and do as we say.'

49

Rosita Andersson-Trygg had begun her afternoon by contacting her colleagues in the animal welfare unit at the City Police to ask for their help in getting hold of pictures of notorious offenders who had somehow got away with terrible cruelty to animals and weren't on the usual police registers. A task which turned out to be rather complicated.

It took her five phone calls before she managed to get hold of the female civilian employee who was in charge of the unit's office, and the only one who was actually there. The other officers were hard at work out in the field. That Tuesday they were on a long-planned raid on a neglectful chicken-farmer outside Nynäshamn and didn't expect to be finished until that evening at the earliest. Unfortunately, Wednesday didn't look any better, because they were planning to visit a pig farmer in Rimbo who had been the subject of numerous complaints claiming that he was risking the lives and welfare of animals that would be sent to slaughter in the run-up to Christmas. Thursday was Sweden's National Day, and therefore a holiday, and on Friday the entire unit had decided to take a day off to reduce the mountain of time-owing that had built up over the spring.

'I'd suggest you call back on Monday,' the woman concluded.

'Okay, but the problem is that I'm working on a murder investigation,' Rosita Andersson-Trygg countered. Perhaps I should have mentioned what happened to Eriksson's poor dog at the start, she thought.

'The murder of that lawyer? The one whose entirely innocent dog was murdered, even though they can only have been after his owner?' the clerk asked, clearly better informed than she should have been.

'Yes, that's the one,' Rosita Andersson-Trygg said with feeling. 'It's a terrible business, and I thought right away that if there's anyone who can help me, it's you. You couldn't suggest to your boss that—'

'I'm afraid not,' the clerk interrupted. 'I understand your feelings, but here in the animal welfare unit we investigate thousands of murders each year, so we simply have to deal with them in order. But feel free to get in touch on Monday.'

What do I do now? Rosita Andersson-Trygg thought as she hung up. At first she felt at something of a loss, but then she decided to act on Evert Bäckström's suggestion that she put together a perpetrator profile of their unknown dog-killer. So she picked up the phone again and called the profiling unit at the National Criminal Police.

That turned out to be much more straightforward. Her first call was put through to an answerphone that informed her that all six members of the National Crime profiling unit were away on a course all week and wouldn't be back in the office until Monday 10 June.

Time to go home, Rosita Andersson-Trygg decided. Besides, she needed to buy more birdseed and a new filter for her aquarium.

50

At four o'clock on Tuesday afternoon, Annika Carlsson had decided to go home and get some sleep. Six hours' sleep in thirty-six hours, the remaining thirty of which had been devoted to investigating the murder of Thomas Eriksson. It was definitely time to recharge her batteries and reserves before the following day. If only Nadja hadn't appeared to show her the transcript of the interview with Isabella Norén and the results of her own phone calls.

'Obviously, she could just have forgotten it in the general confusion that must have arisen at the office when they found out what had happened to Eriksson,' Nadja said with a shrug. 'But it looks like she was the last person he spoke to on his mobile. We don't know who made the call to SOS Alarm, as they never said a word.'

'I agree with you,' Annika said, nodding.

'I have a feeling they might have been having a relationship,' Nadja Högberg said.

'That makes two of us,' Annika Carlsson said. 'Just as well to call her in and talk to her straight away.'

Isabella Norén didn't seem to share that opinion. She sounded calm and collected, and the expressions of grief and loss of the day before certainly weren't apparent in what she had to say over the phone.

To start with, she had a lot of work to do – more than usual, as a result of what had happened – and she didn't think she'd be able to get away for several hours. Then she needed to eat and sleep as well, so, all in all, she'd rather they met the following day. Annika Carlsson had taken the conciliatory line, expressing her sympathy but simultaneously stressing that time was the most important factor in the investigation at the moment. So that they were able to solve the murder of her boss as soon as possible.

'But I've already talked to you,' Isabella Norén objected. 'To one of your colleagues. Ek, I think his name was. Johan Ek.'

'I know,' Annika said. 'But since then we've received some more information that I need to check with you.'

'You don't think I'm a suspect, do you? That's not what you're trying to say?'

'No, definitely not,' Annika assured her. 'I just want to ask you some more questions, because I think it might be helpful. To both of us,' she added. 'How about eight o'clock? Four hours from now, here at the police station in Solna? Can you manage that? I know it's late, but I can organize a car for you if you like.'

'Okay,' Isabella Norén said. 'But I'd rather drive myself.'

'Good. Tell reception when you arrive and I'll come down and get you.'

As soon as she ended the call, Annika switched her computer off, walked straight out of the office, went home, started to take her clothes off the moment she got inside the hall, and five minutes later she was fast asleep. At five minutes to eight she walked into reception at Solna police station. Three hours' sleep, freshly showered, clean clothes, a new person, and Isabella Norén was already sitting there waiting for her. A different Isabella to the one she had seen the day before. No trace of yesterday's tears. Now there was just a welcoming smile and watchful eyes.

She's already worked out what I want to talk to her about, Annika Carlsson thought.

'Naturally, I've read the interview that my colleague conducted with you but, just to keep everything clear, I'd like us to go over the same ground,' Annika said.

'You mean how I ended up working at the firm?' Isabella Norén asked.

'Yes, a brief summary,' Annika said, smiling and nodding.

'Okay,' Isabella said, smiling back. 'I specialized in economics at high school, and graduated at eighteen. I spent a year working as an au pair in England, for some good friends of my parents, and when I came back I did a year's secretarial training, then complemented that by studying as a paralegal. And I took some economics courses at university. I started working for Thomas three years ago. It was all pretty straightforward. I replied to an advert saying they were looking for a qualified office assistant. And that was that.'

'Plans for the future?' Annika asked with a smile. A bit less watchful now, she thought.

'I've applied to study law at university this autumn. If I don't get in, I'll carry on working for the firm. In spite of what's happened, I mean.'

Annika said nothing, just nodded. Then she reached out her hand and switched off the little tape-recorder.

'I think I'll switch this off,' Annika said with a smile. 'Because what I'm about to ask you may as well stay inside this room.'

'I think I know what it's about,' Isabella Norén said. 'You want to know how long I was seeing my boss?'

'Yes, and because I don't think for a moment that you had anything to do with this, anything you say won't go beyond these four walls.' Annika nodded. If Bäckström and the others could hear you now, they'd probably have a stroke, she thought.

'Okay, then,' Isabella said, nodding back.

Then she explained.

Isabella Norén had liked Thomas Eriksson from the first time she met him. He was a dynamic person, funny, alive, with a strong personality and a genuine interest in the people and cases he got involved in. He was also a brilliant lawyer, very talented, and always knew what he was talking about.

'Thomas was nothing like that gangster lawyer the papers used to write about. It wasn't hard to fall for him, even though he was twice my age.'

'The first time,' Annika said, with a friendly nod.

'The first time we got it together, you mean?'

'Yes.'

The first time was after a year. At work they kept things low-key, remaining totally discreet despite the emotional charge they both – surely – used to feel whenever they were alone, and which had been there right from the start. The first time also depended on your interpretation, according to Isabella.

'I'd been working on the paperwork for a case in the Court of Appeal. I'd only been there for a couple of months. In terms of the amount of evidence, it was a complex case, and at his first trial our client was sentenced to life imprisonment. Then he changed lawyers, to Thomas, who appealed and got him released. I was sitting in my room, reading a load of papers, when Thomas came rushing in, waving the verdict we'd just received. He was like a little kid realizing he'd been given a really cool game console at Christmas. First, he gave me a big hug, and a kiss right on the lips. Then he held me at arm's length as he patted me on the head and called me a clever girl. When he was like that he was pretty irresistible. A grown man and a little boy, all at the same time.'

Doesn't sound much like Eriksson, Annika Carlsson thought. Not remotely like him.

'I know exactly what you mean,' Annika said. 'What about the first time, properly? When was that?'

'The first time properly,' Isabella repeated, touching the corner of her eye with her index finger. 'That was a year later. I went with Thomas down to a case in Malmö. To help carry all the files, and because he liked having company. But mainly because I think we were both starting to feel that something was happening. It was in the air, I suppose.'

The trial had gone well. That evening they had dinner in a smart restaurant. They had a bit to drink, perhaps a little too much, but not too much for what they both had in mind, then went back to the hotel and sat in the bar for a last nightcap.

'It was me who took the initiative,' Isabella said with a brief nod of confirmation. 'I just looked up at him, a bit quizzically, you know. He got up at once, and we went upstairs. To my room, if you want to know.'

'What was it like?' Annika Carlsson said. Whatever that has to do with anything, she thought the moment she'd asked the question.

'The best first night I've had,' Isabella said. 'Even though I was twenty-two and Thomas was forty-six.'

'Then what? What happened after that?'

It wasn't a big, lifelong passion. She'd never thought that, and realized as much right from the start. It had nothing in common with a normal relationship. It was a secret affair, and she was convinced that none of her workmates knew about it or had even the slightest suspicion. Neither of them had felt any need to change that. It was just a time in their lives that would last however long it lasted. As long as they both wanted it to carry on. But not a day longer. During the past two years they had had twenty or so encounters for the same reason as that first occasion, but, as so often happened, they had met up increasingly seldom. The last time they had been together was something like two months before he was murdered.

'It was beautiful, and a bit sad,' Isabella said. 'We never argued, and towards the end it was more cosy than . . . well, than anything else. We always had fun together. Even when we would sneak out to the pub and spend an hour trying to think of somewhere that no one would see us. Because of course there were plenty of people who recognized him.'

Beautiful and a bit sad, Annika Carlsson thought. It was time she pulled herself together.

'You spoke to him on Sunday afternoon,' Annika said. 'On Sunday afternoon you called him from work and spoke to him. That was at twenty minutes to three, and the conversation lasted nine minutes. Can you tell me what it was about?'

'Yes, it was about work. I was helping to prepare a case for him. It was due in court on Thursday. Not that that's going to happen now, of course. There were a few things I needed his help with. Legal technicalities, mainly. Nothing else. As soon as I'd hung up he called me back, on my mobile, and told me I was being boring. He'd been hoping I'd called to suggest a date. Our first date of the summer.'

'What did you say to that?'

'That I already had a date. Which was true, because I'd arranged to have dinner with an old friend from school. A girlfriend, although I didn't say that.'

'How did he take it?'

'He wasn't the jealous sort,' Isabella said. 'Thomas wasn't remotely jealous, and I'm sure I wasn't the only person he was seeing. He said he'd forgive me, as he had a meeting that evening as well.'

'He didn't sound worried or anything? About the meeting that evening, I mean?'

'Not at all,' Isabella said with a firm shake of the head. 'He sounded the same as usual. Maybe he sounded like he'd had a couple of glasses of wine with his lunch. If I was to say anything about him, it would be that he did drink quite a lot. He was never drunk at work – nothing like that – but he liked a bottle of wine when he was relaxing. Or a couple of bottles, if he was in the mood.'

'That meeting he was going to have. He didn't say who it was with?'

'No.' Isabella shook her head firmly. 'I didn't ask either.'

'And he didn't seem worried?'

'No.' Another shake of the head, just as firm. 'He sounded the same as usual.'

Beautiful and a bit sad, and he sounded the same as usual, Annika Carlsson thought. Then she switched the tape-recorder back on and moved on to asking questions that followed naturally from the context. Did she know of any threats against him? What was his view of that sort of thing?

'He had a number of clients who were a bit scary,' Isabella said. 'But he handled them perfectly, if you ask me. We talked about it occasionally, and he gave me some advice. Things it would be useful to know when I became a lawyer. It was all about doing a good job, the client was all that mattered, having respect for them but without losing your distance. Never promising anything that wasn't legally possible. Lots of things like that.'

'And it worked?'

'Yes, I think everyone he represented respected him.'

'What about the others, then? All his opponents, all the relatives of victims in cases where he defended the suspects?'

'He used to get a fair amount of negative stuff,' Isabella said. 'Emails and phone calls and letters. Some of them were quite entertaining. On more than one occasion he read them out when we were having a coffee break at work. But scared? No, more like amused. Thomas was respected, and he was fearless. Not remotely afraid to stand his ground. Is that what you're thinking? That someone like that killed him?'

'What do you think?' Annika countered.

'Yes,' Isabella said. 'Who else would have done it?'

Half an hour later, they had finished. Annika Carlsson had shown Isabella out of the building. She had given her her card and told her to call if she thought of anything else, if anything happened, or if she just wanted to talk to someone in general.

'Thanks,' Isabella said. 'You seem pretty all right.'

'Tough on the tough guys, and the reverse,' Annika said

with a grin, and patted her on the arm. 'Look after yourself, Isabella. Call me if there's anything. If you think of something you forgot to say, or if there's anything you're wondering about.'

Beautiful and a bit sad, not remotely jealous, and who else would have done it? she thought as she returned to her room.

51

The murder of lawyer Thomas Eriksson had been leading the news across the media for the past twenty-four hours. On Monday, after the first meeting of the investigative team, Anna Holt had tried to calm the first wave by issuing a concise press statement that at least gave them the answers to five questions. That the police in the Western District were investigating a murder, that Chief Prosecutor Lisa Lamm had been appointed head of the preliminary investigation, and Detective Superintendent Evert Bäckström lead detective. There was also a phone number and email address by means of which the detectives of the general public could get in touch and pass on any information that might help the police in their work. At three o'clock on Tuesday afternoon, after the second meeting of the investigative team, a press conference had been called at the police station in Solna.

Like trying to stop a tsunami by holding your hands up, Holt thought once she had finally switched off her constantly ringing phone.

Five minutes after Bäckström arrived at work on Tuesday morning, his boss, Chief of Police Anna Holt, had knocked on his door and asked for a short meeting.

'By all means,' Bäckström said, gesturing towards his

chair. You've got a traitor in the ranks, he thought to himself, seeing as he was well aware that it took at least three minutes to walk between their offices.

'The press conference,' Holt declared emphatically before she had even sat down. 'Is there anything I ought to know? About the state of the investigation, I mean?'

'Nothing except that I would happily abstain from participating for the sake of someone who needs it more,' Bäckström said. 'How about the Anchor? She's very diplomatic.'

'Good idea,' Holt agreed. 'I was thinking of asking Lisa and Annika and our press spokeswoman to take care of the practical details. What I'm wondering is if there's anything you'd like to have passed on?'

'No,' Bäckström said, with genuine surprise. 'To those vultures? What on earth would I want to say to them?'

'You haven't changed, Bäckström.' Holt smiled and nodded at him. 'A sturdy rock in uncertain times. Can I interpret what you've just said as an indication that an arrest is imminent?'

'Yes,' Bäckström said. 'I can't see any reason to disagree, but for the time being it might as well stay between us.'

Bäckström nodded thoughtfully, clasping his hands together on his lap and raising his eyes towards the lamp in the ceiling. Another one, he thought. And this one was scrawny, too.

'Eriksson evaded earthly justice, but divine judgement caught up with him,' Bäckström declared. 'For a simple godly soul such as myself, all that remains is to put the worldly details in place,' he added with a deep sigh.

'I'll look forward to that,' Holt said, and stood up. At best, he's no worse than mad, she thought.

* * *

In spite of Bäckström's pious hopes, the police press conference fell apart almost immediately. The largest meeting room in the station had been booked, but it was already overflowing with journalists when the female press officer for the Western District police, head of the preliminary investigation, Lisa Lamm, and acting lead detective, Annika Carlsson, entered the room. The air was pregnant with unspoken questions which the three women were expected to answer the moment they assumed their places behind the long desk at the end of the room.

The press officer began by welcoming them all and explaining that she and her colleagues were looking forward to taking their questions in an orderly fashion, and then she handed over to the head of the preliminary investigation and Chief Prosecutor Lisa Lamm. Lisa Lamm had thanked her and begun her statement by saying that, unfortunately, she didn't have much to say.

The investigation was still in its early, introductory stage. The police were working without any preconceptions and had secured various pieces of evidence at the scene, which had been sent to the National Forensics Laboratory in Linköping for analysis. According to her evaluation, the prospects were promising. The nature of the crime had been changed from suspected murder to murder, in line with the forensic medical officer's initial report – but, sadly, she was unable to go into any details. Not at the moment, for the usual reason of not wanting to jeopardize the investigation. Then she had nodded to the press officer, who took over again and asked for questions.

Annika Carlsson hadn't said a word. She was leaning forward with her elbows resting heavily on the desk, her chin on her hands as she looked at the representatives of the fourth estate through narrow eyes and with a fixed expression. Perhaps that was why she was asked the first question by a reporter from the main television news channel.

There were various contradictory accounts of how Eriksson had been murdered. He had either been shot, stabbed, strangled, beaten to death or subjected to several of these alternatives. What comment did she have on that?

'Eriksson died as a result of another person's actions, but I can't say more than that,' Annika Carlsson said, glowering at the man who had asked the question.

'When did he die?' someone in the audience wondered, kicking off the media feeding frenzy that everyone knew was coming.

'When our first patrol arrived on the scene at approximately quarter past two on Monday morning, he was found dead in his residence. He was murdered sometime between Sunday afternoon and the time we found him dead,' Annika Carlsson declared. She was unable to give them a more precise time of death. For the time being, anyway.

'Are the police following any specific line of inquiry?' one of the three journalists from the largest evening paper asked.

'No,' Annika Carlsson said. 'We're working without any preconceptions.'

'On the internet, there's considerable speculation that this was a gangland killing. Someone who was famous for being the legal representative of various people accused of being involved in organized crime – surely the most likely explanation is that one of his clients' enemies killed him?'

'No comment,' Annika said, shaking her head.

'But you have to admit,' the reporter persisted, 'there's a lot to suggest that this was basically some sort of dispute within the world of organized crime. According to police sources that are already being quoted in both the traditional media and online, there were several perpetrators, who arrived at the scene of the crime in an extremely expensive silver Mercedes, and the victim was a lawyer who, according to sources in the police, was shot several times with a pistol or automatic weapon. Classic signs of this sort of murder.

'What do you say to that?' the reporter concluded.

'Nothing,' Annika Carlsson said. 'I'm not interested in speculation. I'm investigating a murder.'

Another fifteen minutes on the theme of gangland killings followed, and Lisa Lamm had taken over from Annika Carlsson, who leaned back and stared coldly out at the audience. A lawyer murdered by gangsters who were enemies of one of his clients? Or possibly one of his own clients who felt let down? Or someone who had fallen victim to one of his seriously criminal clients? Or someone related to one of their victims? No comment, Lisa Lamm said repeatedly, losing track of how many times she did so before the whole thing was finally over.

Idiots, Annika Carlsson thought as she got abruptly to her feet. She was the first person to leave the room.

52

After the second meeting of the investigative team, Bäckström had temporarily handed the tiller to Annika Carlsson. He had to go to a long-arranged meeting with the National Police Committee but, in case of emergency, he could always be reached on his mobile, and he'd be back at his post as usual the following day.

'See you then,' Annika Carlsson said, smiling and nodding. Wonder if he actually believes that himself? she thought as Bäckström disappeared through the door.

Bäckström's afternoon had gone entirely according to plan. First, he took a taxi into the city centre and paid a visit to a discreet restaurant on Kungsholmen. It was only a couple of blocks away from the main police headquarters by Kronoberg Park, but it was still a safe bet, as the prices were aimed at a different clientele than those forced to survive on police wages. He had partaken of a fine lunch, then sat with coffee and cognac while he waited for his Finnish waitress to call him as soon as she had finished cleaning his flat on Inedalsgatan.

Seeing as Bäckström was a generous employer, he had devoted a full quarter of an hour between lunch and his afternoon nap to making sure she got properly recompensed for her efforts, before she went off to her regular job at the bar, to scrape a living for herself and her useless, alcoholic Finnish bastard of a husband. Once he was in his broad Hästens bed, he had needed only five minutes before his White Tornado from Finland arched her back and screamed out loud as he fired off the super-salami.

'*Vojne, vojne,* Bäckström,' the Finnish woman said, her moist eyes twinkling as she drew a deep breath, but Bäckström contented himself with a grunt and a short nod, so she didn't get any ideas in her pretty little head about lying there cuddling and slurping at his face.

Finally alone, Bäckström thought, hearing his domestic quietly closing the front door behind her five minutes later. He even had ten extra minutes for the restorative sleep he so badly needed. Then he made himself comfortable and did a couple of trial squeezes before letting out a resounding blast and easing the pressure in his guts after his fine lunch of stuffed cabbage leaves with cream sauce and lingonberry preserve. The little things are crazy about you, Bäckström thought, and a minute later he was fast asleep.

When he woke up after three hours he felt as splendid as he deserved to, and all that remained of the day was to follow carefully established routines. First an invigorating shower, then back in the saddle. Bearing in mind that it was already seven o'clock, it would have to be a late dinner in his local, before he spent the hour before bed possibly thinking about his current case, even though, in purely practical terms, there was nothing more to it than someone smashing in the skull of a nauseating little lawyer who had plagued Bäckström's life on far too many occasions.

It'll work itself out, Bäckström thought philosophically,

seeing as everything was running so smoothly at the moment that the days almost sorted themselves out without him having to think about it. Not just the days, in fact. Pretty much everything he did seemed to have gone like clockwork for ages. Apart from certain workaday administrative tasks, of course, which he sorted out as soon as he got out of the shower, put his dressing-gown on and mixed himself a soothing summer drink containing three parts vodka and one part grapefruit juice and plenty of crushed ice.

First, he had inspected the Finnish woman's cleaning to see if there was anything he needed to remark upon when he looked in for a bite to eat later that evening. Nothing wrong with her, Bäckström thought five minutes later. The whole of his cosy little abode was shiny and clean, the shopping list had been actioned, the fridge and larder were full of all his favourites, including assorted delicacies. Even the special toilet paper he had found online – extra thick, extra soft and embossed with pictures of famous Swedish politicians – was in place.

The account of her expenditure also appeared to be in order, Bäckström thought as he checked the receipts against the cash in the old-fashioned glass jar in which he kept his household spending money. But you mustn't forget that she's Finnish, Bäckström thought, so presumably she's too daft to try to rip you off.

Last but not least: she'd even polished the large, gilded cage to which Isak would hopefully never return. It was about time he put it up for sale online and erased the last traces of the little hooligan. Even though things had got off to such a promising start that Bäckström actually imagined he might have found himself a new companion equal to his dear, departed goldfish, Egon.

No sooner said than done, Bäckström thought, logging into his computer and putting an advert for Isak's final residence online. It had been standing there in front of his window for too long, like some caged omen, and every time he saw it he was reminded of one of the most traumatic experiences of his adult life. Far worse than the time he had been caught up in a struggle for life and death with a couple of the worst rogues in Swedish criminal history.

Time to get shot of the bastard cage, he thought, and just to make sure he altered his advert to say it was free to anyone who wanted it, then he switched the computer off and sank into gloomy contemplation. Even though things had seemed so positive at the beginning, he thought, taking a deep gulp from his glass.

During Isak's preliminary instruction he had seemed even easier to train than the shop assistant had promised. He also had a fine voice, a cackling and slightly gurgling sound that cut through the silence like a knife, and not even the deaf could miss what he was saying. Within a week Isak had learned to say both 'Bäckström' and 'Supercop', and once those were out of the way it was time to move on to more serious matters.

Because Bäckström was a man of considerable pedagogical insight – an essential quality if you wanted to be an efficient boss in the police – he had started slowly and began by teaching him the very simplest words, things like 'poof' and 'dyke', before it was time to take the momentous next step towards 'arse-bandit' and 'miserable cunt', 'anal acrobat' and 'attack dyke'. Unfortunately, that was where things got snarled up, when it turned out that Isak had got the wrong idea about pretty much everything. The disaster reached its sorry climax when Anchor

Carlsson had suddenly shown up at Bäckström's flat without warning. All of a sudden she was standing there ringing his doorbell, and because he got it into his head that it must be an urgent police matter, he had been foolish enough to open the door.

'Surprise, surprise, Bäckström,' Annika Carlsson said, smiling at her reluctant host through narrowed eyes. 'How about sharing a couple of beers?'

Bäckström simply nodded, given that he had no intention of trying to close the door again and risking ending up in A&E without a single organ worth donating to anyone else who had a chance of making it out alive.

'Good to see you, Annika,' Bäckström said with a forced smile. What fucking choice do I have? he thought as he let her in. Bäckström had gone into the kitchen to get glasses, some bottles of cold Czech lager and a litre of his Russian vodka, just to be on the safe side, and when he returned to the living room the Anchor had already stuck her hand inside the cage to tickle Isak under his chin.

Maybe everything will work out okay after all, Bäckström thought, seeing as he had almost lost a finger when he tried the same thing. But not this time. Isak merely chuckled in delight and tilted his head.

'God, he's so cute,' the Anchor said. 'What's his name?'

'Isak,' Bäckström said, without further explanation, because it was obvious to anyone with eyes in their head.

'God, what a cute name. How did you come up with that?'

'I named him after an old friend I went to school with when I was a lad,' Bäckström lied. The Anchor isn't merely stupid, he thought. She must be blind as well.

'It's one of those ones that can talk, isn't it?' Annika Carlsson asked, sitting herself down beside him on the sofa, far too close, reaching out her suntanned right arm and tensing all her muscles as she poured herself a beer.

'Er, yes, he talks non-stop about all sorts of things,' Bäckström confirmed, trying to move towards the corner of the sofa as discreetly as he could. Wonder if she'd be upset if I moved to the armchair? he thought.

'Get him to say something, then,' the Anchor said in a commanding voice.

'Okay,' Bäckström said. 'Who's a clever boy, who's a clever boy?' he repeated, seeing as the shop assistant had stressed how important it was for a well-trained parrot to have different keywords so that it said the right things on the right occasion instead of just babbling a load of nonsense.

First 'who's a clever boy, who's a clever boy?', followed by 'Bäckström', upon which Isak was expected to reply 'Bäckström Supercop', and over the past week he had delivered the goods promptly on each occasion. But not this time. All of a sudden it no longer seemed to work. Isak just sat there with his head tilted to one side, before he set about pulling the shell off a peanut he'd found among the detritus on the floor of his cage.

'He seems to be the silent type. More interested in food. Like master, like parrot,' Annika Carlsson declared, taking a deep swig of beer as she squeezed Bäckström's knee with her free hand, observing him with eyes that were even narrower than when he had let her into the home which up to now had been his castle.

What the hell do I do? Is it really that difficult to say 'Bäckström Supercop'? Bäckström thought, but at that moment Isak finally decided to speak.

'Bäckström poof, Bäckström poof,' Isak cackled, while

the Anchor gave Bäckström a look that was anything but ambiguous.

'Really?' Anchor Carlsson said, putting her glass down on the coffee table and sitting astride Bäckström's legs as she pulled her black top over her head.

'The hook-nosed little bastard's lying,' Bäckström protested, even though it was far too late, seeing as the Anchor was busy pulling the buttons off his expensive linen shirt.

'Now's your chance to prove the opposite,' Anchor Carlsson declared, changing her grip and pulling the belt from his trousers.

I should have risked slamming the door on her, Bäckström thought as he sat on the same sofa a month later, still obliged to fortify himself with a couple of deep swigs to stop his memories getting the better of him and flooring him. Creepy woman, a real psychopath, no inhibitions at all. In hindsight, considering everything that had happened, a month in intensive care would have been a picnic, he thought.

Sexual assault of the most extreme kind, he thought as he stood in his bathroom brushing his teeth one month and several hours later. A horrible crime that still demanded some extra alcoholic support whenever he thought about it. The wounds were clearly very slow to heal. And it must have been planned in advance, seeing as the evidence suggested as much. The handcuffs, for instance – she must have brought those with her – and if there was any justice in the world, his colleague Anchor Carlsson would now be sharing a cell with the former head of the Police Academy in Norrtälje Prison's special unit for particularly deviant sexual offenders.

Why does it have to be so hard to have a normal fuck? Bäckström sighed as he settled down to get some sleep after a long day, hoping at last to regain some of the detached calm that ordinarily reigned supreme inside him.

53

Sitting in front of a computer and shaking his head at all the pictures the police showed him had been easy enough, but on Wednesday morning things got rather more serious for Ara Dosti. That morning he had spent three hours in the company of the amiable Detective Inspector Ek, trying to come up with a photofit picture of the man the police were looking for, and the task had been so engaging that he soon dropped any pretence at caution and lying low and instead decided to see how close he could get to his memories.

Back at school in Småland, the artistic subjects had always interested Ara most. He was best in his class at both painting and drawing, and when he left high school and moved to Stockholm he even thought about applying to art school and taking it more seriously. Instead he had ended up at an IT business and helping out part-time at a courier firm, and ten years later he was still earning a living in much the same way. Part-time jobs, extra hours, and for the past five years he had also been working as a taxi-driver. The days piled up, and the months and years passed, and he had long since set aside any artistic ambitions. But not that morning, when he found himself in the hands of an incredibly friendly police officer who also happened to be a real virtuoso when it came to photofit pictures.

They had sat there side by side in front of the computer screen and, to start with, Ek used Ara's description of the man he had seen to draw a rough pencil sketch on a sheet of plain paper. Then he had switched the computer on, and together they worked on fitting all the details in place. The shape of the face, the ears, nose, eyes and mouth, the distance between the different parts of the face. They sorted out the hair and hairline, chin, neck and throat. When they were finished a couple of hours later, the photofit picture was identical to the police photograph he had shaken his head at the day before.

'Yes, that's him,' Ara said. Wonder what makes an artist decide to join the police, he thought.

'If you think of a scale of one to ten, where ten is a completely identical likeness, where would you put this picture?' Ek said.

'Ten,' Ara said firmly. 'It's as good as a passport photo.'

'A ten,' Ek repeated. He was still smiling amiably, but he didn't seem completely convinced.

'Okay,' Ara said. 'Maybe a nine, just to be safe. The man in the photofit looked really mean, not nice at all. Maybe it's hard to capture that particular expression. But I don't suppose he goes round looking like that the whole time.'

'No, hopefully not,' Ek said with a slight smile. 'I seem to recall you said he was tall. About one metre ninety, if I remember rightly? I'd say you're about one seventy-two yourself, at a guess?' Ek said.

'Yes,' Ara said, unable to conceal his surprise. 'How can you know that?'

'I'm one seventy-five myself,' Ek said, smiling again. 'And I looked you up in the passport register, if I'm going to be completely honest.'

'Well, I certainly got the impression that he was much taller than me,' Ara said.

Then Ek had excused himself and asked Ara to wait for fifteen minutes while he did another search of their database. When he returned fourteen minutes later he had several more photographs of the man Ara had already shaken his head at. Not just the usual police mugshot, but the sort that must have been taken when he was under surveillance. Getting out of a car, going into a doorway, even some pictures of him exercising in a gym.

'Yes,' Ara said. 'That could well be him, actually. I think I recognize him. I didn't miss him when we were sitting here yesterday, did I?' What the hell am I doing now? he thought. If the cops get it into their heads to show his picture on *Crimewatch* tonight, I won't get a single krona from that journalist.

'That sort of thing happens,' Ek said, patting him on the shoulder. 'If you ask me, it happens all the time. Sometimes the memory just needs a bit of time, that's all,' he added, because he had no intention of revealing what he thought was really going on.

'How sure are you?' he went on. 'If we use the same scale from one to ten, where ten means you're absolutely sure?' Ek said.

'I don't know,' Ara said with a hesitant shrug. 'Seven, maybe. Possibly six, even.'

'Seven, possibly six,' Ek repeated. 'Even though the photofit picture was a nine, possibly even a ten.'

'Yes,' Ara said. 'I see what you're saying, but the problem is that a lot of them look the same, if I can put it like that. It gets a lot harder. When you have to pick out one of them. This bloke actually looks pretty cool. Can I ask, who is he?'

'I'm afraid I can't tell you that,' Ek said. 'But I have to say that I agree with you. He's not a nice person at all, which makes it all the more important that none of this goes outside the police station,' he went on with a nod. For the first time without any trace of a smile.

'Don't worry,' Ara said, even though he himself suddenly felt anything but calm.

'If there's any cause for concern at all, call the number my colleague gave you,' Ek said, looking at him seriously. 'Promise.'

'Don't worry,' Ara said with a smile. 'I'll lie low, I promise.'

What are you playing at? Ara Dosti thought as he drove away from the police station a quarter of an hour later. He had spent pretty much all of the last three days working for the police, had received two five-hundred-kronor notes for his trouble, and now there was a lethal madman who wouldn't hesitate to kill him if he got the chance. Definitely time to get out of here, he thought. Dubai, Thailand, anywhere he could relax for a while until things got back to normal.

Then he had called the reporter from the big evening paper to suggest that they meet right away, at the same place in the city where they met the first time two days before. He also told him to take with him the pictures he had shown him when he showed up at his home.

'I know who it is,' Ara said. 'I'm absolutely certain.'

'Great,' the reporter said. 'Just give me fifteen minutes. See you shortly.'

'One more thing,' Ara said. 'I want fifty thousand. That's non-negotiable. And I want it all in cash, in five-hundred notes.'

'In that case I'll need at least two hours,' the reporter said. 'How about an ordinary banker's draft? That's just as anonymous as cash. Besides, I'm going to need time to check your story. If you point him out, you can have half the money. I check it out and, if it all fits, you can have the other half as soon as I'm done.'

'Cash,' Ara repeated. 'Two hours is okay. Half is okay as well, but I've got to have cash.'

'I promise,' the reporter said.

There was no way he could take on any big jobs while he was waiting. Not if he had an appointment to keep. So he had signed out on the computer and went to get something to eat at his usual café. Anxiety was starting to get the better of him, and he drove to the appointed meeting place in the same backstreet on Södermalm half an hour early. He sat in the car, thoughts racing through his head. None of them was particularly appealing, and for a while he contemplated just driving off and forgetting about it all.

Pull yourself together, he thought. In a day or two you'll be on the other side of the planet, sitting on a beach checking out the girls. I should go to Thailand, he thought. More girls, better beaches. And fewer checks on people like him who just wanted to be left alone until everything got back to normal and he could start living his usual life again.

54

At twelve o'clock on Wednesday, 5 June, the investigative team held its third meeting, and Bäckström felt he was starting to get a bit of order around him. Which was more than overdue, so he could finally ease his inhuman workload and go back to business as usual.

The door-to-door inquiries were now a closed chapter. They had gone better than usual and had resulted in one suspicious vehicle and two, possibly three, individuals who could be assumed to have something to do with the murder. Useful information that gave good grounds for hoping they might be able to find both the car and the individuals they were looking for.

The tip-off line also seemed to be working, and the initial torrent of information from the public had now dwindled to the usual more manageable trickle. It was now possible to register the calls as they came in, rather than having to transfer people from more proactive duties. As far as this particular murder victim was concerned, the task of evaluating, sorting and registering incoming information was also considerably easier than usual. The vast majority of the tip-offs concerned Eriksson's close contacts with organized crime, and they had already received the names of a hundred different perpetrators who, according to twice that number of informants, all had one thing in common: they had all killed Eriksson. Otherwise, it was much the same as usual. Good advice about the importance of taking a closer look at this or that, and the usual moronic tip-offs from the soothsayers and diviners.

They had also made good progress with other aspects of the investigation, including the mapping of the victim and his closest associates, routine checks of the usual suspects, and analysis of mobile-phone traffic around the time of the crime. But some things appeared to be taking longer. Their medical officer had been in touch again to inform them that he needed another few days so he could get a second opinion from a colleague who was regarded as one of the world's leading experts in more complicated instances of injuries inflicted with a blunt object. The only consolation was that he saw no reason 'to change my preliminary diagnosis at the present time'.

It was the usual story with the National Forensics Laboratory. They had sent in almost one hundred different samples for analysis. They would receive a response within a month at the latest, and the first results from the samples they had identified as most urgent by the beginning of next week. The search of the victim's home was also taking longer than expected and, according to Niemi, he and his colleagues would need the rest of the week at least before they could hand over the crime scene to Eriksson's colleague, Danielsson, who was named in Eriksson's will as his executor.

Despite this, Bäckström was happy. Things are happening, he thought, and the most important thing right now was to make sure he got enough food, drink and rest, then the sudden flash of decisive insight would come to him.

'Okay,' he said, leafing through the thick bundle of

papers in front of him for the sake of appearance. 'How are we getting on with the silver Merc, Nadja?'

According to Nadja, things were going as expected. After two days, she and her colleagues had managed to halve the original number to approximately two hundred possible vehicles, even though they were proceeding with caution.

'If there's any doubt at all, the information stays live until we can make more conclusive checks. So far, we've only done a rough sort-through, so you'll have to give us another week,' Nadja said. 'Although, if we get lucky, it could all be over in a matter of hours,' she added, throwing out her hands demonstratively.

'Good,' Bäckström responded, seeing as he had no intention of getting bogged down in details, certainly not when it came to Nadja's work.

'How about that character the taxi-driver almost mowed down?' he went on, nodding towards Ek.

'He and I have put together a photofit picture,' Ek said. 'If you're wondering why you haven't seen it yet, that's because there's a degree of doubt about it. Our witness says it's a six or seven on the usual scale of one to ten, and it's certainly a pretty good match for one of the men he's seen a picture of from the database. Unfortunately, that's also where the problem arises.'

'What do you mean? What sort of problem?' Hate problems, Bäckström thought.

'Well, it can't be the man who's the best match with the photofit,' Ek said, 'because he's got an alibi for the time of the crime. If we were to make public the photofit picture, I'm convinced that most of the tip-offs we received would be about him. Even though I know he had an alibi for the time when Eriksson was murdered. And, if I've understood correctly, we're fairly confident about the time of the murder.'

'Alibi,' Bäckström snorted. 'They always have alibis. Have you talked to him, then?'

'No, definitely not,' Ek said, sounding almost horrified. 'I've talked to the intelligence service, obviously in the strictest confidence, and with our colleagues in Stockholm who are working on that Nova Project, trying to keep tabs on the very worst suspects. Apparently, Regional Crime has had him and his associates under surveillance for some time.'

'So they're the ones giving him an alibi, our colleagues at Regional Crime?'

'Two of them,' Ek said with a blithe smile. 'Plus several thousand others. Maybe not your usual civic-minded citizens exactly, but a few thousand of them anyway.'

'Several thousand others? Was he live on telly then, or what?'

'Rather the opposite, actually,' Ek said with the same gentle smile. 'No, he was taking part in a martial arts competition at the Globe Arena. At ten o'clock he entered the ring, and for the next ten minutes he was fully occupied kicking the hell out of his opponent. After being applauded in the customary manner, he returned to the changing room to be patched up, by which point it was about half past ten. That's the main reason why I think we should wait before releasing the photofit picture.'

'I hear what you're saying.' Bäckström sighed. 'Does anyone else have anything that the rest of us should know about now?

'Excellent,' he went on, needing just a quick glance around the room to note an adequate number of head-shakes. 'Okay, do any of you have a good answer to my earlier question? How come one or more individuals kill Eriksson at approximately quarter to ten in the evening, and then one or more individuals give the body a new going-over some four hours later and cut his dog's throat?'

Considerably more headshakes this time, Bäckström noted.

'Okay,' he continued. 'Then I suggest we throw some ideas around. Tell me what happened on the night when Eriksson the lawyer shuffled off this mortal coil. What do you say, Peter?' he said, quickly pointing at Niemi to forestall Alm and Andersson-Trygg and all the other mentally handicapped incompetents who made up his investigating team.

'Throwing around ideas about what happened,' Peter Niemi said with a faint smile. 'Sweet music to someone like me.'

'Well, then,' Bäckström said encouragingly. 'Tell us.'

'At nine o'clock that evening he receives a visit from at least two people he already knows. The meeting has been arranged in advance and, bearing in mind its time and location, I think these people are important to our victim. I don't think Eriksson is the type to let just anyone into his home on a Sunday evening. These are people he trusts, they're important to him.'

'Quite agree with you, Peter,' Bäckström interjected. By now he was looking forward to a decent lunch and could even contemplate listening to a bastard Finn like Niemi as a way of honing his appetite.

'Then something goes wrong. Approximately half an hour later things get out of hand. I don't think this was premeditated, although of course it bothers me that we haven't found our blunt instrument. The situation spins out of control. Eriksson tries to call SOS Alarm, manages to pull out his revolver and fire off at least one shot at one of his visitors, the one sitting on the sofa a few metres away. I think the bullet in the ceiling ended up there when visitor number two wrestles the gun off him, and that's when Eriksson gets killed. I'd prefer not to speculate about the finer details surrounding the phone call, the shooting and the blunt object he gets struck with for the time being, but we're talking about a period of a few minutes around quarter to ten in the evening. The call to SOS Alarm was made at twenty to ten, after all.'

'There's one problem with that,' Annika Carlsson interrupted. 'There's our female witness who sees the well-built character loading boxes into the boot of the silver Mercedes, and there's our male witness who sees the elderly man sitting on the steps outside Eriksson's house. Their observations were made a quarter of an hour earlier. At about half past nine. That bothers me.'

'It bothers me too,' Niemi said. 'I understand exactly what you mean. First the fight, Eriksson gets killed, then they take their things and leave the scene of the crime. That would be the natural chain of events, so to speak.'

'The simplest explanation has to be that our witnesses got the time wrong,' Stigson suggested. 'That happens all the time. When they say half past nine, they could easily be talking about quarter to ten. The fight kicks off seriously when Eriksson's visitors are getting their things ready and are about to leave. That's when they start to argue, Eriksson takes out his revolver and tries to phone for help, but instead gets beaten to death and the perpetrators grab the things they came for and leave. That seems pretty straightforward, doesn't it?'

'It certainly sounds logical,' Niemi said with a nod. 'The

idea that one of his visitors would have stayed in the house while one or two others leave seems both risky and pretty far-fetched. Because it's around that time, just before ten, when Eriksson's dog is first heard barking and, according to our witnesses, it carries on for quite some time. And we haven't found any evidence in the house to suggest that anyone was there all the way through to two o'clock that night. There are no signs that anyone needed time to search the place, because why would they leave almost a million kronor in cash at the scene of the crime when all they had to do was pull out a few drawers to find the envelope it was in?'

'And while Eriksson's dog was standing out on the terrace barking,' Felicia Pettersson agreed. 'What about those shots, though?' she added. 'Wouldn't anyone passing the house have heard them?'

'No,' Peter Niemi said. 'Hernandez and I checked that with a test shot. It was a .22 calibre revolver, so it doesn't make that much noise. And Eriksson's study up on the first floor has no windows facing the street, so no noise would have reached that far.'

'What about later on, then? That's when it all gets completely unbelievable,' Annika Carlsson declared. 'Why take the risk of returning to the crime scene four hours later? And why attack someone who's already dead, and cut the dog's throat, the same dog that's now standing out on the terrace howling. That sounds like a pretty suicidal thing to do.'

'Maybe they forgot something,' Hernandez said. 'Something that was so important it was worth the risk of going back. And when they still fail to find whatever it was on the second attempt, our perpetrator loses it and attacks both the dog and its dead owner. How about that?'

A few half-hearted headshakes, a few isolated murmurs, and Rosita Andersson-Trygg's hand in the air.

'Yes, Rosita,' Bäckström said. 'The floor is all yours.'

'I don't think we should get too hung up on the gap between events,' Andersson-Trygg said. 'The worst sort of animal abusers can be extremely irrational people, very impulsive, and they're driven by entirely different motives to normal people. If you ask me, Bäckström, it could very well be the case that our perpetrator originally intended to attack Eriksson's dog, but in the commotion during which Eriksson was killed, he didn't have time to do it. He's forced to leave the scene anyway, waits somewhere nearby, then when everything has calmed down he returns to do what had been his true intention right from the start. To attack an innocent animal.'

The old bag is clearly in a class of her own within the Swedish police, Bäckström thought. Not even Alm could come up with something like that.

'Interesting,' he said with a nod. 'Well, we'll just have to think about it a bit more. Keep an open mind, don't assume anything, if I can put it like that. We'll meet up again tomorrow, same time, same place.' Andersson-Trygg is very good for working up an appetite, Bäckström thought. High time for a proper lunch and a restorative nap.

55

The reporter from the top evening paper was a punctual man. He arrived on the dot, parked in front of Ara's taxi, got into the passenger seat beside him and opened negotiations by pulling out a bundle of five-hundred-kronor notes.

'I've got the dough here,' the reporter said, showing Ara the money before tucking the bundle into his inside pocket. 'I've brought the pictures you looked at when we last met,' he went on, handing Ara a plastic folder containing the photographs.

'Okay,' Ara said. He pulled them out and quickly leafed through to the largest picture of the man he had seen. 'This is the guy,' Ara said, putting his finger on the man's forehead.

'How sure are you, then?'

'Hundred per cent,' Ara said. 'It's him. No question.'

'There's one thing I don't understand,' the reporter said. 'Why couldn't you have said that the last time we met?'

'The circumstances weren't right for a deal,' Ara said, shaking his head. 'Wrong time, wrong place, and you didn't have any money to show me. It just didn't feel right, that's all. Check out the guy in the picture and you'll see what I mean.'

'So you haven't spoken to anyone else in the meantime?' the reporter asked.

'No,' Ara said. 'I thought I'd give you a second chance first. Besides, that's not my style.'

'But you must have spoken to the cops?' the reporter persisted. 'I seem to remember you telling me that when we last met. So there's a good chance you saw a picture of this bloke then.'

'Yes,' Ara said. 'I've seen several pictures of him. I've met the local sheriff four times now, if you're wondering. Might as well move into that police station out in Solna. Have I identified him? Negative. Why haven't I identified him? No reward,' Ara said with a grin. 'And I'm not exactly keen to end up in court as a witness, like I said. But I did help them put together a photofit picture.'

'I can understand all that,' the reporter said, grinning back. 'One more question. That photofit picture, how good is it?'

'Okay,' Ara said, shrugging his shoulders. 'Your picture's much better, and there's absolutely no doubt that he's the man I saw.'

'Sounds good,' the reporter said. 'Half now, like we agreed,' and he handed over the bundle of notes.

'I've got a question as well,' Ara said, putting the money in his pocket without counting it, then nodding towards the man in the picture. 'Who is he? Should I get out of the country, or what?'

'Definitely time to lie low,' the reporter replied. 'I'm assuming you won't be talking to anyone but me. If you stick to that, there's no need to worry.'

'Who is he?' Ara repeated, nodding once more towards the picture of the man he'd identified. 'Has he got a name, or what?'

'He's a proper crazy bastard,' the reporter said with a shrug. 'What his name is doesn't matter right now. If you keep quiet and lie low, and talk to no one but me, things will be fine. He won't have any idea of how we managed to get hold of his name.'

Then they parted, with a promise from the reporter that he'd be in touch as soon as he'd completed the checks they always had to carry out in his line of work before anything ended up in the paper. Ara spent the rest of the afternoon driving his taxi, until he handed the car over to the colleague who was going to do the evening shift. Then he took the underground home to Kista, picked up some food on the way, then walked quickly back to the house where he lived.

Time to lie low, he thought, and the lowest option was actually his flat, seeing as it was a sublet and he wasn't even registered as living there. He leaned forward to key in the door code, and at that moment someone came up behind him and tapped him on the shoulder.

Shit! Ara thought, spinning round with the bag of groceries held up to his chest as protection, in the absence of anything better.

'Ara, Ara Dosti, it's been a while,' said the man who had appeared out of nowhere and practically scared the life out of him, even though his whole face was beaming. Ara recognized him at once.

'Omar!' Ara said, having trouble concealing both his surprise and his relief. 'You scared the shit out of me, man!'

'Long time, no see,' Omar said. He grinned, then gave Ara a bear hug. 'Must be ten years? More maybe, now I come to think about it.'

'For ever,' Ara agreed, even though he'd seen a picture of his old schoolmate just two days before in Solna police station.

56

After the meeting and his customary lunch, Bäckström had returned to work, closed the door and tried to come up with a suitable reason to go home for a much needed and well-deserved nap. He felt tired, a bit listless, unable to think of anything. He also felt a bit bloated, and it was when he tried to remedy this that things took a turn for the worse. When he attempted to ease the pressure by unleashing a thunderclap, he found himself the victim of a treacherous and rather loose surprise. Matters were made worse by the fact that he was wearing an ivory-coloured linen suit that day, so some sort of active intervention was now urgently required.

First, he barricaded the door with the visitor's chair, closed the blinds and pulled his trousers off so as to be able to ascertain the extent of the calamity that had befallen him. Not good, not good at all, he thought as he inspected the dark skid-marks on the pale linen at the rear of his well-tailored trousers. There was no question of attempting to sneak to the toilet in that outfit.

Seeing as he had neither water nor paper towels in his office, he was obliged to sacrifice both some of his fine Russian vodka and the silk handkerchief he'd tucked into his top pocket when he left home that morning. Fortunately, he also had a bottle of aftershave in his capacious desk and, with a little help from that, he was able to conceal the olfactory aspect of his devious assassin.

Ten minutes later he was able to pull his trousers back on and stand at his window to air them as he called for a taxi and checked that everything was in order before leaving the office. If you find yourself in an acute situation, you mustn't just rush into things, Bäckström thought, discreetly making his way sideways through the main office where most of his investigative team was based, and, as he made sure to hold his mobile close to his ear the whole time, all he had to do was nod and grunt at the colleagues he passed on the way out.

In the taxi on his way home he had attempted to restore his sense of inner calm, while his driver – who, to judge by his skin-colour and sense of direction, appeared to have arrived from Mogadishu that morning – tried to find Kungsholmen and Inedalsgatan, where Bäckström lived, and by the time he was finally able to close his front door behind him it was already half past three in the afternoon.

Once he was safe, he was at last able to get to grips with the unfortunate situation in which fate had landed him. First, he took off all his clothes and dropped them into the laundry basket, then showered and put on his dressing-gown, poured himself a stiff Fernet-Branca to settle his stomach, and sat down in front of his computer to see if he had received any serious offers for Isak's final abode.

Naturally, he hadn't. Not that he could expect anything else on a day like this, he thought, glowering malevolently at the gilded cage in front of the window, taking up unnecessary space now that its former occupant was hopefully halfway to the pet cemetery. Even though he and Isak had spent only six weeks together, from late March to early May, he had been one of the great disappointments in Bäckström's life. A very grave disappointment, to put it mildly.

Isak had not only shown himself to be largely beyond education, but was also filthy, to an almost unbelievable extent. He ate constantly, enough for a small horse, and shat like an elephant the whole time he was eating. After that, he would conclude each meal by spraying leftover seeds, nuts, shells, assorted bird treats and his own excrement all around him. Most of this ended up on the floor outside his cage, and even Bäckström's Finnish cleaner and favourite waitress, his very own White Tornado, had complained about Isak and suggested that Bäckström ought to get rid of the bastard.

'Any suggestions?' Bäckström had asked, as he had been thinking along the same lines himself, and had even considered trying to flush him down the toilet, though Isak was a bit on the large side for that sort of intervention and there was a considerable risk that he'd get caught in the U-bend on the way down. In the worst case scenario, he might be able to hack his way out using that lethal hooked beak and cause a flood in the building Bäckström lived in.

The Finnish woman had offered to wring Isak's neck with her bare hands, but Bäckström had thought better of it, rejected her offer and instead went back to the pet shop to have a serious word with the useless salesman who had landed him in this wretched situation. He had even offered the rogue the chance to buy Isak back at a drastically reduced price. His efforts failed, however, because of a downturn in the market for used parrots.

'It usually picks up over the summer,' the assistant had said, shrugging his thin shoulders apologetically. 'When people are about to go off on holiday with the kids, there's usually an increase in sales of second-hand birds – parakeets, for instance,' he explained.

Over the summer, Bäckström thought, shaking his head. I'll probably be dead by summer, he reasoned. Because Isak wasn't only filthy – he was also a noisy bastard. After just one week he had ruined Bäckström's usually untroubled sleep, even though he had done exactly as the parrot expert had told him. He turned all the lights off in the room and covered the cage with a thick blanket so that even little Isak realized it was night, time to go off to the feathered equivalent of the land of Nod, and, more specifically, time to keep his beak shut until it was morning and the blanket was removed for another day.

Isak hadn't shared this opinion, and at any moment – and preferably during the early hours of the morning – he would wake Bäckström with his hoarse cackle, which cut like a knife through an open eye, through the silence and the night and his spiritual peace. What the fuck am I going to do now? Bäckström wondered. Towards the end of their time together he was spending most of his waking hours trying to figure out a way to get rid of his tormentor.

Selling him online was out of the question after Anchor Carlsson had paid her little home visit and nearly finished off both Bäckström and his super-salami. Not just filthy and noisy, but also an unusually malicious slanderer. Rocket fuel for vicious tongues the moment Isak opened his beak in front of his new owners, who by then would be well aware of his former owner's identity. The thought of the rumours that might spread once Isak ended up with a new owner was enough to bring Bäckström out in a cold sweat. The same applied to the idea of taking him to the vet to be put down, while he and all the other pet-owners sat in the waiting room listening to Isak's final words.

Taking out his old friend Siggy and shooting his head off was out of the question as well, certainly in his own home, anyway, considering all that had happened the last time gunsmoke filled his apartment. It would be even worse to follow the Finnish woman's advice and strangle the fucker. Potentially life-threatening, Bäckström thought, seeing as he had almost lost a finger when he tried to give him a peanut and tickle his neck on the first day of their acquaintance.

Bäckström had sunk into dark rumination and had spent a whole week pondering the matter until his neighbour, little Edvin, had solved the problem for him. Even though he was only ten years old and looked like a bespectacled lizard.

57

After a restorative afternoon nap Bäckström felt considerably brighter and took the opportunity to have dinner with his tame reporter from the main evening paper. It was now more than twenty-four hours since the police press conference, and it was high time he made himself aware of how much the fourth estate knew.

They met in their usual bar over on Östermalm, where even a national celebrity like Bäckström would be left in peace, and, as soon as they had had a few drinks before eating, Bäckström's host had got straight to the point.

'How's it going?' he asked, raising his Scotch on the rocks. 'Have you found that silver Merc yet?'

'My colleagues are grappling with that,' Bäckström replied, downing half his Russian vodka and chasing it down with a few swigs of cold Czech pilsner.

'What about your witness?' the reporter went on. 'How's he doing? Has he identified that character you've shown him pictures of?'

'I don't know who you're talking about,' Bäckström said. 'We've shown pictures to lots of people.' He must have talked to that taxi-driver, he thought.

'I was thinking of the witness who saw the perpetrator jump in that Merc when he left Eriksson's house out in Bromma,' the reporter clarified.

'I still don't know who you're talking about,' Bäckström persisted. 'We've got several witnesses who saw both the car and its occupants. Tell me who you've been talking to instead. Then maybe I can help you.' That gave you something to suck on, he thought.

His host contented himself with a thoughtful murmur before beckoning the waiter over to take their order.

'What can I get you?' he asked. 'I was thinking of having the stuffed chicken breast. What do you think?'

'Don't let me stop you,' Bäckström said with a shrug. 'I'm going to have the salt beef with root vegetables, another lager and a little more vodka,' he went on, nodding to the waiter.

They spent the following hour eating, drinking and talking of other matters, and it was only over coffee and cognac that they returned to the matter in hand.

'What do you think about a bit of tit-for-tat? Regarding our deceased lawyer, Mr Eriksson, I mean,' the reporter suggested.

'You start,' Bäckström said. 'Make me an offer.'

'I've got the name of your perpetrator, the man who got into the silver Merc. At two o'clock in the morning when he'd just left Eriksson's home. What can you give me in return?'

Definitely our little taxi-driver, Bäckström thought. Who chose lots of money over Bäckström's own cretinous colleagues.

'I'll give you a piece of advice,' Bäckström said. 'Whoever tipped you off got the wrong guy. So unless you want to throw a load of money away on an unnecessary slander charge and all sorts of other crap, I'd be very careful before you publish that.'

'What makes you think that?' the reporter asked. 'I

interpret that to mean that you're saying we're on the wrong track. How can you be so sure?'

'Because it isn't him,' Bäckström said. He had a fairly good idea of who their witness, the taxi-driver, had chosen not to identify ever since he saw the photofit picture that the very same taxi-driver had helped Ek put together.

'But how can you be so sure?' the reporter persisted. 'How can you even know we're talking about the same bloke?'

'Well, I'm talking about Angel García Gomez,' Bäckström said with a shrug. 'But, naturally, if you've got another suggestion, I'd be happy to swap names.'

To judge by his expression, he didn't, Bäckström thought.

'How can you be so sure it isn't him, then?'

'Because he's got an alibi for the time of the crime and, just for once, it hasn't been provided by one of his associates in that club for middle-aged motorcycle enthusiasts.'

'You've had him under surveillance,' the reporter said, more as a statement than a question.

'I couldn't possibly comment on that point, as I'm sure you can appreciate. He's got an alibi. End of story.'

'Why is it so impossible ever to be properly happy?' his host said with a sigh.

An hour later, after another cognac and one last nightcap to welcome in the coming summer, Bäckström and his host had gone their separate ways on the best of terms. Even if no business had actually been conducted.

'Thanks, Bäckström, thanks for the tip-off, and even more so for the warning,' the reporter said, even though he hadn't managed to get anything out of Bäckström other than a well-meant warning to stay out of things that really weren't his or his colleagues' business.

'What can I do for you in return?'

'The usual,' Bäckström said, shrugging his shoulders. Many a mickle, he thought.

58

After his meeting with his tame contact within the fourth estate, Bäckström had gone straight home and to bed. He hadn't even had to mix a last little nightcap before he fell asleep. Instead he had lain down on his nice big Hästens bed with his hands folded over his stomach and, while he waited for sleep to come, he thought about little Edvin, who had helped him get rid of Isak the Terrible.

Edvin was small and skinny. Thin as dental floss, and shorter than the length Bäckström himself used each morning and night to floss the crown jewels with which he, as a result of his increasing wealth, had been able to replace his original adornment. Little Edvin had round, horn-rimmed glasses, with lenses as thick as bottle-bottoms, and he spoke like a book with very small print. A little, well-read, bespectacled lizard who had moved into the building a few years before with his mum and dad, and the only good thing about that was that he had been brought up the old-fashioned way, and was the only child both in his own family and in the building where he and Bäckström lived.

But Edvin was also very useful when it came to running small errands, such as fetching newspapers, mixers for drinks, and various titbits from the crooks who ran the delicatessen in the arcade up on Sankt Eriksgatan. But it would still be a few years before Bäckström could send him off on more serious missions to buy drink. But that time would come, and Bäckström was already rather fond of him. In fact, in his more sensitive moments, he used to think of little Edvin with the same warmth with which he still remembered his prematurely departed friend Egon.

Evert, Egon, and now little Edvin, that was how Bäckström usually thought about himself and those closest to him. That way of thinking came naturally to a good, Christian soul like him.

The fact that Edvin was called Edvin was something of a mystery, because his mother was called Dusanka and his father was called Slobodan, and they were both immigrants from Yugoslavia. In spite of their origins and the fact that they had not had the good fortune to be born Swedish, there wasn't really much wrong with either of them. Edvin's parents ran a betting shop up at Odenplan, and his dad, Slobodan, had, after only a very short acquaintance with Bäckström, been able to help him clean up his variously acquired extra income through the use of betting slips and profitable internet games hosted by mysterious foreign poker sites. In short, he was a quiet and creative member of Bäckström's growing financial network.

Mind you, there had obviously been problems during the early stages of his and Edvin's association. To start with, for instance, little Edvin had saluted every time he encountered him, until Bäckström told him to stop that nonsense. Only the gorillas of the rapid response unit and other lesser mammals did that sort of thing. Homicide detectives were governed by different rules of etiquette, and in little Edvin's case it was quite enough for him to address Bäckström by his title and call him Superintendent.

This was what happened, and the great breakthrough in their acquaintance came when little Edvin came up with a good suggestion as to how he could discreetly and effectively get rid of Isak.

One morning in early spring, when Isak had already begun to show his true nature, Bäckström and Edvin had shared a lift up to the floor where they both lived, and Edvin had told him that he was a member of a group called the Field Biologists. On his very first day he had been elected to the committee in charge of the section primarily responsible for studying the various forms of birdlife in the country.

'Field Biologists,' Bäckström said. What's wrong with surfing the internet looking at porn? The lad's ten years old, after all, he thought.

'That led me to think of your parrot, Superintendent,' Edvin went on.

'So what did you think, then?' Bäckström said.

'You must make sure he doesn't fly out through the window, Superintendent,' the lizard in glasses said. 'If he were ever allowed to fly around the apartment, I mean.'

'Why not?' Bäckström asked. Not a bad idea, he thought. Just open the window, shoo the bastard out and hope for a serious cold snap that night.

'The other birds in the yard would probably attack him,' Edvin said. 'It could end very badly.'

'Very badly? How do you mean?'

'Well, there are magpies and crows and seagulls out in the yard. And some birds of prey, even though we live in the middle of the city. I saw a sparrow-hawk catch a magpie the other day, even though it was really too large to be suitable prey for such a small hawk.'

Is that so? Bäckström thought, but made do with a nod. Is that so?

The next morning the first warm rays of spring sunlight had sought their way into Bäckström's flat, and the good Lord could hardly have sent a clearer signal. Before Bäckström went to work he had opened Isak's cage, left the balcony door wide open and, just to make certain, he had left a large pile of peanuts on the balcony table, so he was full of anticipation when he returned home after his usual long lunch.

No sooner had he walked in through the door than his hopes were dashed. Isak had returned to his cage, taking the opportunity to shit on anything he chanced upon on his way back, and of course he greeted Bäckström with the usual noise, cackling, croaking, but with some sort of synchronous descant that cut right to the core of his already hard-pressed landlord and owner.

As if that weren't already more than enough, he had also left some obvious signs of his marauding in the yard in Bäckström's absence. Two dead magpies with bloody holes in their chests made by a particularly sharp hooked beak, as well as a crow twice its size, which had evidently escaped with its life but was now staggering about on one and a half legs and with one wing dragging on the tarmac. He had also received an anonymous letter from a neighbour, advising him in the very strongest tones to keep his pet under better control. According to the letter-writer, Isak's first action that morning had been to execute a massacre of the usual visitors to the bird table that the residents' association had installed out in the courtyard.

What the fuck happened to that hawk I was promised? Bäckström wondered. Oh well, if at first you don't succeed.

He had repeated the procedure for a whole week, tossing the rapidly growing pile of anonymous letters into the rubbish chute unread and refining his tactics by keeping watch on Isak until he had flown out of the flat and then rushing over and closing the balcony door so as to render any return to the flat during the day impossible.

For the first few days, things didn't go well. As soon as it got dark Isak would return to the window sill outside Bäckström's bedroom and start making his usual unpleasant noises, as well as trying to peck a hole in the glass with his hooked beak, until Bäckström would give up in the middle of the night, open the balcony door and let him into the now tragic remains of what had once been his home.

Things had gone on in much the same vein day after day, until the seventh day, when his hopes had finally been realized. At this point in his recollections, Bäckström had fallen asleep. For the past fortnight he had been – hopefully, and if the good Lord really had heard his prayers – once again a free man and, as he dozed off just before midnight on the eve of Sweden's National Day, he knew that when he woke up it would be to a better life than before, now that his tormentor, Isak, no longer shared his abode.

59

At roughly the same time that Bäckström was sitting in the bar with his reporter, Ara and Omar took the opportunity to celebrate their own unexpected reunion by having dinner at a smart Lebanese restaurant in Kista shopping centre. Omar had offered generous amounts of food and drink, and Ara had unburdened himself and talked about the problems he had been suffering over the past few days. It was a very pleasant evening, a fine reunion. So pleasant, in fact, that Ara forgot to ask Omar how the police appeared to have a photograph of him which they had also chosen to show his old schoolmate in connection with him trying to help them solve an extremely violent crime.

'Nasty business,' Omar said, shaking his head sympathetically. 'I can understand that you're worried. Was that why you practically jumped out of your skin when I appeared behind you outside your door?'

'Yes, what do you think?' Ara said.

'In that case, you've come to the right man,' Omar said, patting his arm reassuringly. 'That bloke you recognized. Could you describe him?'

'I suppose so,' Ara said with a nod. 'He's not the sort you forget.'

'Good,' Omar said, taking a little black notebook out of

his jacket pocket. 'I don't suppose the journalist happened to mention his name?'

'No,' Ara said, shaking his head. 'No name, just that I should lie low. I was thinking of going away. Thailand or Dubai,' Ara went on. 'Until things have calmed down, I mean.'

'Wise move,' Omar agreed. 'But I think we should start by finding out who he is.'

But going abroad until everything settled down again was an excellent idea, according to Omar. He was fully in agreement, but before Ara left the country there were a few practical issues that had to be sorted out. And problems that he promised to solve for him.

'There's nothing to worry about,' Omar said, patting his arm again. 'I promise to fix this for you. Before you go away for a bit of a holiday. Not because you have to run away. Running doesn't solve anything.'

'You reckon you can fix this for me? I thought you studied to be a chemical engineer?' Wonder what they actually teach at the Institute of Technology? Ara thought.

'There's nothing to worry about,' Omar repeated with a smile. 'Knowledge is power. Surely you know that?'

Ara made do with a nod. Knowledge is power, he thought. Is that why the cops have a photo of you in their files?

60

Bäckström had spent the majority of Sweden's National Day in bed at home on Kungsholmen. His first act that morning had been to send an email to his right-hand man, Anchor Carlsson, to tell her that she would have to take command of that day's meeting of the investigative team, for three reasons.

Firstly, he needed privacy and time alone in which to be able to think about the case. A case which also – and this was the second reason – was rapidly approaching its solution, when most of the work involved sorting out the details and making sure everything was in the right order. He intended to return to this point during Friday's meeting. The third and final reason – and this was something he hoped would stay entirely between him and his most trusted colleague – was that he had sadly come down with 'some sort of stomach bollocks' and, because it would be against his nature to risk the health of his fellow workers, it would obviously be best if he were to stay at home. If anything of importance were to happen during that day's meeting, he of course assumed that the Anchor would contact him at once.

Whatever that might be, Bäckström thought, shaking his head and pouring himself a large Fernet from the bottle on his bedside table, before he once again returned to leafing through his almost magical memories of the last twenty-four hours before he and Isak had parted ways. Hopefully for good, the way things were looking.

The day before Isak had left him, Bäckström had finally worked out what to do, and when he left the police station in Solna to go home he had stopped at the shopping centre on the way and bought a large roll of plastic and a rubber hose that was long enough to reach from the gas-tap next to the cooker in the kitchen to Isak's cage.

When he got home, he fortified himself with a stiff vodka before getting to grips with the practical matters, but even as he was attempting to wrap the cage, and Isak inside it, in plastic, things had got out of hand. Using his sharp beak, Isak had ripped off the plastic as fast as Bäckström could put it in place, and there was no question of switching the gas on, as Isak had evidently decided to take Bäckström with him on his final journey.

In the end, Bäckström had given up. He sat there on the sofa with a third stiff drink and contented himself with giving Isak the evil eye as he considered other alternatives.

If gas isn't going to work, maybe electricity would do the trick, wondered Bäckström, seeing as he was a practical man by nature. The only problem with that solution was that he lacked the necessary technical skill that would be required to actually put it into practice. It would mean hiring an electrician, which was out of the question, he reasoned, with a deep sigh. How can it be so hard to murder a parrot?

Isak himself no longer seemed to care. He had gone back to ripping the shell off yet another peanut, and in the absence of any better ideas Bäckström had opened the balcony door and let him out into the yard. After sleeping on the matter, he had taken himself off to the local bar for a decent meal, during the course of which he thought matters through once more. He ended up sitting there for several hours, submerged in gloomy thoughts and with no ideas, and by the time he eventually returned home it was already dark outside.

As soon as he had shut the front door behind him, he padded silently through the darkened flat before cautiously peering out at the balcony window sill, where Isak would usually be waiting at this time of day, tapping at the window to be let in.

But not this time. No Isak as far as the eye could see, and Bäckström suddenly felt his hopes rise. Maybe he's fallen victim to an owl, he thought, seeing as little Edvin had informed him the previous week that even Isak wasn't safe during the darkest hours of night. In the middle of the great stone city where Bäckström lived, there were owls, and they hunted at night. On silent wings and with deadly precision, even if everything was utterly pitch-black around them.

When Bäckström eventually fell asleep he was in a good mood. Finally, someone up above must have heard his prayers. It wasn't until he woke up to a new day that his dreams were crushed. Going by the noise, Isak was sitting on the other side of the roller-blind and the protective window as he sharpened his beak against the glass.

Fuck it, you're going to die, Bäckström thought, and pulled Siggy from his hiding place under the mattress, pulled back the bolt and made sure there was a bullet in the chamber, before getting out of bed with some difficulty and padding over to the window to let the blind up to give him a clean shot at the little fucker. When he reached out for the cord of the blind he suddenly heard a terrible thud against the glass which made the whole window shake.

What the fuck's going on? He released the blind, opened the window and peered down at the tarmacked inner courtyard.

Isak was lying in the yard. He had evidently encountered a new friend, of a slightly tougher variety than his usual black and white colleagues. Something brown, twice his size, with a beak that was even more hooked than Isak's, was sitting there pecking holes in his chest. In the midst of the general confusion in which he found himself, Bäckström unfortunately happened to squeeze little Siggy's trigger.

Shit! He shut the window and pulled the blind down. The empty cartridge had fallen on the floor of his bedroom, which was at least some consolation, seeing as he had no desire to rush out into the courtyard in the middle of the night to look for it.

Instead he crept out into the hall, where he stood by the door and listened. Everything seemed quiet, and he padded back to his bedroom, nudged the blind aside and peered out. Isak was still lying down there, on his back, with his feet sticking up in the air, but his brown, speckled assailant seemed to have fled the field.

At last, Bäckström thought. The little fucker must be stone dead, he thought, and went back to his lovely, soft Hästens bed.

A couple of hours later he had been woken by someone evidently getting their finger stuck to his doorbell.

Edvin, Bäckström thought as he looked out through the peephole. He looked sad as well. Just like a ten-year-old young man might be expected to look when he had to pass on news of a tragic death to Isak's closest relative.

'Has something happened?' Bäckström asked.

'Don't say I didn't warn you, Superintendent,' Edvin said, nodding solemnly. 'It was the hawk that got him, just like I said last week.'

'Is Isak dead?' Bäckström said, clutching his forehead.

'Fortunately not,' Edvin said. 'I think there's a chance he might recover. We must hope for the best, Superintendent.'

What the fuck's the little lizard saying? Hope he gets better?

About an hour earlier, when little Edvin went down to the yard to get his even smaller mountain-bike and ride off to school, he had found Isak lying in the courtyard, unconscious. At first he thought he was dead, but then he discovered that he was still breathing, and could even hear his little bird-heart beating and tapping away, so he wrapped him up in his jacket. He dashed back up to the flat and his dear mother had called a taxi and gone off to the animal hospital.

'We didn't want to alarm you unnecessarily,' Edvin explained.

'What are they saying then? The animal doctors, I mean,' Bäckström clarified.

'We mustn't despair, Superintendent,' Edvin said, patting Bäckström's hand consolingly. 'While there's life, there's hope.'

* * *

As long as there's life, there's hope, and judging by the first bills that had already started to arrive, Isak was evidently determined to fuck with him for as long as he possibly could. Almost a fortnight in parrot intensive care, while ordinary people die like flies the whole time. What the hell's happening to Sweden? he thought, shaking his head disconsolately.

61

When the Thursday morning meeting of the investigative team began, Annika Carlsson had told the others present that she was temporarily taking over from their boss, but that Bäckström was expected to be back the next day. She intended to keep the reasons for his absence to herself for the time being, and handed over to Nadja.

'How are you getting on with the Mercedes, Nadja?'

'Slow but steady,' Nadja said. 'We've got about a hundred vehicles left to check. But I don't think he's slipped through the net so far.'

'When do you think we might be finished with the ones you've got left?'

'Difficult to say,' Nadja said, shaking her head. 'We're going to need another week, at least. And I'm afraid we're getting to the point where we're going to have to talk to some of the owners before we can rule them out. But we're getting there.'

'Good,' Annika Carlsson said. 'Have you got anything else to tell us?'

One more thing, according to Nadja Högberg, as she had decided to take the opportunity afforded by Bäckström's absence to talk about what she and her colleagues had found on their murder victim's computer. To save time, if nothing else, and also bearing in mind the persistent rumour within the police service that Bäckström was responsible for opening up the so-called sex angle in the investigation of the Palme murder, and was still believed to be convinced that that was the key to the prime minister's murder.

'The day Eriksson was murdered he seems to have spent over nine hours looking at online porn,' Nadja said. 'The sites he visited are rather unusual, even in this context. A lot of violent pornography, sex with animals, sex with dwarfs, and a whole load of other peculiar things that you probably wouldn't want to ask Uncle Olle about.'

'Uncle Olle? Who's that?' Detective Inspector Jan Stigson said. On the rare occasions he watched television, he seldom strayed from the sports channels.

'That psychologist who's got a sort of sexual advice programme on Channel 5,' Nadja said. 'His name's Olle. Looks a bit like a fat old lady,' she explained.

'Oh, okay,' Stigson said. 'One of those.'

'Maybe you should give it a try, Jan,' Annika said with a wry smile. 'Watch Uncle Olle and see if you can pick up some tips, I mean. So what do you think, Nadja? Is this another area for investigation, or not? Or is he just like most men?'

'Well,' Nadja said, 'in this particular instance it's possible that he was the exact opposite. That he was doing it in the course of his work, so to speak. At least, if we're to believe his associate, Danielsson. Our colleague, Bladh, has already questioned him about that. You'll get a transcript of the interview by email later today.'

'Eriksson was surfing for porn for work? Explain, before I die of curiosity,' Annika Carlsson said.

According to the other lawyer, Danielsson, his colleague Thomas Eriksson had taken on a new client just a few days before he was murdered. The client was a well-known businessman and entrepreneur who had been accused of harassing his ex-girlfriend, who was half his age, by hacking her computer and sending her vast quantities of pornography that he had downloaded from the internet.

'Her computer, her website, her Facebook page, everything,' Nadja said, shaking her head. 'But there's nothing to suggest that his legal representative, Eriksson, shared his client's special interests. It looks like he was ticking things off the list that was included in our own preliminary investigation into his client. We've been through his hard drive, and there are no traces of previous porn-surfing. And he hasn't got any software installed that would automatically erase any traces of visits to that sort of site. If you ask me, I think we should forget about this angle. The whole thing seems to be work-related – however strange that might seem.'

'Have you found anything else, then?' Annika asked.

'Various notes that are proving difficult to interpret, but they're probably financial in nature,' Nadja said. 'Plus traces of similar material on his hard drive that he seems to have deleted after a relatively short time. Eriksson appears to have been a cautious man in that regard, but I promise to get back to you if I find anything that's worth telling you about. But I don't think you should hold your breath. Eriksson seems to have been the sort of person who relied on his own memory when it came to keeping secrets.' Just like you, who picked that up with your mother's milk, she thought to herself.

Then Peter Niemi had taken over the run-through, but he didn't have much new information to add either when it came to the technical side of the investigation. He expected the search of the victim's home would be concluded early the following week, and that the first results from the National Forensics Lab concerning the DNA traces, fibres and prints they had found at the scene would be coming through at about the same time. They still hadn't been able to find the murder weapon. Which was something that concerned him a lot.

'When it comes to the classic blunt instrument, we usually find it at the crime scene, which, nine times out of ten – as in this case – is either the victim's or the perpetrator's home. They're almost always unpremeditated crimes, and when things kick off they grab whatever happens to be to hand. A hammer, a poker, a piece of piping, a frying pan, a candlestick. Anything that's solid enough, easy to hold and will do to smash someone's head in.'

'But not this time?' Annika Carlsson said.

'Not this time,' Peter Niemi confirmed. 'And that bothers me. This time I'm fairly sure the perpetrator had already decided to do away with Eriksson when he arrived and that he'd planned to make a good job of it. He brought the instrument with him, and if I had to guess I'd say we're talking about something wooden, like a baseball bat or a cudgel. I'm inclined to think it's wood rather than metal because of the way the injuries to the skull look.'

'But by the time he arrived, Eriksson was already dead,' Felicia Pettersson said.

'Exactly,' Niemi said. 'He'd been dead for several hours, there's absolutely no doubt about that. He must have seen that at once, yet this individual still attacks him and smashes his skull in, and this is where I start to have serious concerns.'

'How do you mean?' Annika said.

'Why would he do that if he knew he'd already killed him a few hours earlier? By then, surely he ought to have calmed down a bit? Why return at all?'

'To look for something he missed the first time. Because he's figured out that Eriksson tricked him,' Annika suggested. 'And that makes him so furious that he's even prepared to attack a corpse.'

'Quite possibly,' Peter Niemi said, throwing his hands out expressively. 'And nowhere near as unlikely as the idea that's got stuck in my head, even though it most definitely complicates things.'

'Go on,' Annika Carlsson said with a smile. Peter's good, she thought.

'That he had no idea that someone else had already killed Eriksson when he turned up to give him a serious going-over. But he's still furious enough to attack the body.'

'I agree with you,' Annika Carlsson said, smiling even more broadly. 'It sounds very, very unlikely. Almost as if our victim should have organized an orderly queue down in the hall for all the visitors who were planning to turn up on a perfectly ordinary Sunday evening with the express intention of beating the shit out of him.'

'I know,' Niemi said with a thin smile. 'It does sound a bit unlikely.'

'Well, we'll work it out,' Annika said with a shrug. 'There's nothing else you wanted to add?'

'One more thing. We're finished with the ballistic analysis. The two bullets we found both come from Eriksson's own gun. But of course that's what we've been assuming all along.'

'So you can't offer us any sort of breakthrough in the case, then?' Annika Carlsson concluded.

'No. No breakthrough,' Niemi conceded, shaking his head. 'Just the awareness that comes from realizing that you're only getting more confused. But I agree with you. Sooner or later everything will fall into place.'

'Does anyone else have anything?' Annika Carlsson said, looking round the room. Judging by the unanimous headshaking, it was time to draw the meeting to a close.

'Okay,' she said, getting to her feet. 'Another meeting tomorrow, Friday at ten o'clock, and our absent boss has promised to join us.'

As soon as Annika Carlsson got back to her desk she called Bäckström's mobile to give him the promised report of how things had gone in the meeting.

'We're making progress, but I haven't got anything special to tell you,' Annika Carlsson said.

'No, how could you have?' Bäckström replied.

'We're missing you already,' Annika said. 'How's your poor tummy, by the way? You don't want me to come over with some chicken soup and mineral water?'

'That's very kind of you, Annika. But to answer your question: no. I don't want any chicken soup. Nor any mineral water.'

'That's a shame,' Annika said. 'Promise you'll let me know if you change your mind.'

Bäckström refrained from making any such promises. Instead, he simply ended the call by switching off his mobile.

Creepy woman, Bäckström thought, shaking his head. Just to be on the safe side, he went out into the hall to check that he'd put the security chain on the door. However unlikely it was that a feeble little chain would be able to keep out someone like Anchor Carlsson, he thought with a shudder.

62

After his conversation with Anchor Carlsson, Bäckström had decided that it would perhaps be safest to leave the flat until he had got hold of a locksmith who could reinforce the entrance to the home that was, after all, supposed to be his castle.

After a late but substantial breakfast, he had therefore taken a walk around the city. Yellow sun, blue sky, twenty degrees in the shade, exactly what every true Swede had a right to demand on a day like today. Bäckström had walked along the shore of Norr Mälarstrand before stopping at a strategically located outdoor bar, where he quickly ordered a cooling vodka and tonic, and he remained there for a couple of hours, deploying his surveillance sunglasses to watch all the little ladies walking past as he made a note of all the ideas that popped into his head in advance of the following day's visit to Little Miss Friday.

You're a lucky man, Bäckström, he thought. You're a mover as well as something of a shaker. Women are all mad about you, more and more of them, all the time. The super-salami was in good shape before the next day's exertions, and Eriksson the lawyer had finally got what he deserved. But it was high time for him to return home for a rest before his various forthcoming evening engagements. After a quick look at his watch, he finished his fourth vodka and tonic and told the girl who had served him to order him a taxi. Naturally, he received a blinding smile in return.

That evening, as he was sitting in front of his computer, nurturing the large and growing multitude that made up his online fan club, his phone had rung. Not his usual mobile, but the one he used only to handle external contacts, and this particular call was from the man who was undoubtedly the most profitable of them all, his old friend and compadre Gustaf Gustafsson Henning. Successful art dealer, famous from antiques programmes on television and known among his closest friends by the nickname GeGurra.

GeGurra started by apologizing for not having been in touch for a while. He had been abroad on business for several weeks and had only returned to his beloved homeland and its royal capital the previous evening.

'Our National Day,' GeGurra declared emphatically. 'Every right-minded Swede knows that you have to celebrate in Sweden itself. Anything else would be unthinkable. It's an obligation. I've spent the day with a business acquaintance who has a place out in the archipelago. Herring and vodka, music by Evert Taube and Jussi Björling on a marvellous wind-up gramophone. He's even preserved the old outdoor privy in case one feels the need to experience such old-fashioned necessities.

'Sweden's National Day has to be celebrated in Sweden. That's an obligation for every right-minded Swede,' GeGurra repeated.

Evidently also an obligation for the odd gypsy, Bäckström thought, seeing as many years ago he had personally helped GeGurra to remove the last traces of his Roma origins and the reckless adolescent behaviour that had led to Juha Valentin Andersson Snygg having a file of his own in the archives of the crime division of the Stockholm Police.

'What can I do for you?' Bäckström asked. He was in a splendid mood, even though the contents of the brown envelope he had been given by his property-developer friend had diminished considerably within the space of just a few days.

'To start with, I was thinking of inviting you out for a nice meal,' GeGurra said. 'Tomorrow evening, if you can spare the time. I have a little business proposal that I'd like to discuss with you.'

'That sounds excellent,' Bäckström said. He could already see a properly old-fashioned GeGurra envelope in front of him. Of a thickness that miserly property developer would never dare to imagine. 'How can I be of assistance?' Bäckström asked.

'For once, I have a feeling that the assistance might be mutual. That we might be able to help each other,' GeGurra said. 'But I suggest we deal with that tomorrow. What do you say to Operakällaren, eight o'clock tomorrow evening?'

'Sounds good,' Bäckström said. Help each other? he thought as soon as he ended the call. In what way could GeGurra possibly help him?

63

Unlike Bäckström, Dan Andersson had spent Sweden's National Day in his office in the headquarters of the Security Police in the main police building on Kungsholmen. He had been sitting there since early that morning, making sure that the thirty or so subjects who were under his protection that day made it home in one piece. Top of the list, as usual, were the king, the queen, the crown princess and another four members of the royal family.

As on so many occasions before, it looked as though he had been worrying in vain. As the day went on, he was able to tick his charges off his list one by one, and, as far as the royal couple was concerned, he was able to do this by two o'clock in the afternoon. They had left the celebration of Sweden's National Day at the open-air museum of Skansen in order to attend a late lunch reception within the relative safety of Stockholm's Royal Palace.

By five o'clock in the afternoon most of the day's activities were over. Nothing unusual had happened, and he had decided to make his way home, go for a run, sit in the sauna and conclude the day with a light dinner in the company of his dear wife. But that wasn't how things had turned out. Instead, he had had to stay at work for another couple of hours as a result of the response he had received from the intelligence division regarding Jenny Rogersson's information about Baron Hans Ulrik von Comer, who had apparently been assaulted by an unknown assailant in the car park outside Drottningholm Palace seventeen days before.

Good grief, Dan Andersson thought, even though he very rarely thought things of that sort. Then he sent an email to his ultimate superior, Deputy Police Commissioner Lisa Mattei, requesting a meeting with her the following day.

He received a response on his mobile just five minutes later as he was stepping into the lift to go down to the garage, get in his car and drive home to his house out on the islands of Lake Mälaren. '14.00. Yrs LM'. There's really no need to say more than that, Dan Andersson thought as he acknowledged receipt of her message. Not if you were Lisa Mattei and were constantly on duty, no matter where you happened to be.

64

When Ara and Omar finally went their separate ways late on Wednesday evening, Omar had already walked home to Ara's flat with him, and before he left he had given him a hug and told him to lie low. Omar had given him a mobile number to call if anything happened. He had also suggested that they meet the next morning, and he would try to sort out a few practical details on behalf of his old friend.

'What do you think?' Omar asked. 'I'll come by and pick you up at eight o'clock tomorrow and we can start by having breakfast together?'

'Okay,' Ara said. 'I'm off tomorrow, so that'll be fine.'

Before Ara fell asleep, he switched his phone on and listened to the new messages he had received earlier that evening. All three were from the reporter from the newspaper, and each time Ara hadn't answered he sounded more and more annoyed.

The first message was left just before eleven that evening. He wanted Ara to call him immediately because 'problems had arisen regarding their earlier conversations', and the sooner they could solve them, the better it would be for both him and Ara.

When he recorded the first message he sounded more

stressed than annoyed, but when he called again half an hour later he sounded both seriously angry and more than a little drunk. Just like all the other Swedish men who bolstered their feelings by pouring drink all over them, quite regardless of whether they were happy, sad or usually just pissed off. There was something 'seriously fucked' with the tip-off that Ara had given him and, considering all the 'dough' Ara had received, it was urgent that they talked to each other at once. He could be reached at any time of the night.

The third call was made just after midnight, and the reporter's message was now loud and clear.

'Okay, Ara. I don't know what the fuck you're playing at, but if you're trying to rip me and the paper off, you need to have one thing really fucking clear. You can forget about getting any more money. Forget it, man. That's history, unless you've got a fucking good explanation. If you haven't, we want the twenty-five you've already been given back. Otherwise, things will get seriously fucked up, yeah? So, for your own sake, Ara, call me as soon as you get this.'

Trying to rip the paper off? Ara thought, then switched his phone off again, to be on the safe side. Even so, he lay awake for several hours before falling asleep. He mostly just lay there, tossing and turning, listening out for the slightest sound in the stairwell and hall outside his flat. When he did finally fall asleep he had nightmares, and in the middle of the night he sat up in bed, soaked in sweat and wide awake, because he had got it into his head that someone was trying to break his door open. He crept out into the kitchen, armed himself with the biggest kitchen knife he could find, then padded over to the front door and peered through the peephole.

The stairwell was quiet and deserted. But he still stood there for several minutes, listening and watching, just to make sure, and before he went back to bed he checked the lock and the security chain a couple more times. Even though he had phone numbers for the cops, the evening paper and his old best friend from school, all of whom he could call if he felt the slightest bit worried. Shit, man, you got to stop being paranoid, Ara told himself before he finally fell asleep.

Just after eight the next morning, Omar showed up. He seemed to be in an excellent mood and had brought both breakfast and half a dozen pictures that he spread out on the kitchen table between them.

'Take a look at these two,' Omar said with a smile. 'Do you recognize either of them?'

Knowledge is evidently power, Ara thought as he nodded, having recognized both the men in the pictures. One was the man he had almost run down a few days ago, and the other he recognized because he'd had him in his taxi on numerous occasions. Knowledge is definitely power, and Omar had always been the one who knew most and made best use of his knowledge.

'Do you recognize either of them?' Omar repeated.

'This one,' Ara said, holding up the picture of the man with the narrow eyes. 'He was the one who almost ended up on the bonnet. Who is he? What's his name?'

'He's a crazy fucking Chilean guy. Came over here with his mum when he was a kid. Angel García Gomez. He's completely mad. Known as the Madman, El Loco in Spanish. And that's what his friends call him. He's a big wheel in the Hells Angels.'

'Sounds like a great guy.' Ara sighed.

'What about this one?' Omar said, pointing at the photograph of the other man on the table.

'I know who he is, because I've had him in the taxi,' Ara said. 'Fredrik Åkare.'

'Former head of the Hells Angels out in Solna. Best mates with García Gomez. They're like Siamese twins. Only ever appear together. If you ask me, there's a good chance he was driving that Merc you saw, and that he was the one who put the lights on full beam when you were driving away.'

This just gets better and better, Ara thought, but made do with a nod.

'Pull yourself together, now, Ara,' Omar said with a wide grin, patting him on the arm. 'Omar's going to fix this. Omar's friends have nothing to worry about. Least of all if we're talking about Omar's best mate when they were nothing but a couple of shitty little schoolkids down in Småland.'

'What do we do?' Ara asked. We, he thought. Not I. What do we do?

'I've already fixed this for you. To start with, I've sorted a new place for you to crash. Somewhere you can hide up until it's time to get away from here. Just pack the essentials and I'll drive you there. And you need to call work and sign off sick until further notice. If you need a medical certificate, I can get one for you.'

'What do I do about the journalist? He keeps ringing and banging on the whole time.'

'Obviously, you're going to keep the money he gave you. After all, you kept your part of the bargain and, if he doesn't get that, that's his problem, not yours. So you can forget all about him from now on,' Omar said, putting his hand in his pocket and pulling out a new mobile phone.

'New mobile, new life, and nothing to worry about. Agreed?'

What choice have I got? Ara thought, and simply nodded.

65

Because it was Friday, Bäckström had decided to move the meeting of his investigative team back to ten o'clock in the morning, but even though he had arrived at work half an hour before the meeting, to have time to clear his head before it started, he had barely managed to sit down behind his desk before there was a knock on his door. Jenny Rogersson, with her bosom heaving, and rosy red cheeks, wearing a top the same colour, and if possible even more excited than she had been during their first meeting four days earlier.

'Sit yourself down, Jenny,' Bäckström said. 'What can I do for you?' If she could just breathe a bit deeper and lean forward a bit more, they might well pop out, he thought.

'I'm pretty sure we've made a breakthrough with the case, boss,' Jenny said, leaning forward and adjusting her top as she put a thin plastic folder of papers on his desk. 'I've put together a summary this morning, as a starting point in case you wanted to raise it with the others during the meeting. It's almost too good to be true,' she added.

'It's probably better if you explain,' Bäckström said, giving her a half-Clint, leaning back and putting his feet up on his desk. He crossed his legs, as a precaution.

'Our witness has been in touch again.'

'Which one?' Bäckström asked. There must be at least a

hundred of them by now, of whom maybe two or three might turn out to be anything other than total fantasists, he thought.

'Our anonymous witness. The woman out at Drottningholm who saw that baron being assaulted with an auction catalogue. She's sent another letter, which arrived this morning. She recognized the perpetrator when she saw his picture in the paper. She's one hundred per cent certain that it's him.'

'So who is it, then?' Bäckström asked, even though he already suspected he knew the answer.

'Thomas Eriksson, the lawyer. Our murder victim,' Jenny Rogersson said. 'I've checked with the vehicle registration database. What she said about nines at the end. It fits, so that's a hundred per cent as well,' Jenny said, tapping her forefinger on the plastic folder that she had given him.

'Nines at the end?' What the fuck's she going on about? he thought.

'The licence plate of the perpetrator's car,' Jenny explained. 'As I'm sure you remember, boss, our witness – our anonymous witness, I mean – wrote in her first letter that she couldn't remember the registration number of the car, but she was pretty sure that it ended with one, possibly two, nines.'

'So you've checked Eriksson's vehicle details?' Bäckström said.

'Sure, boss,' Jenny Rogersson replied, smiling and taking back the folder she had given him. 'We got that information on Monday. Because, of course, his cars were in the garage of his house when he was murdered. Looks like Eriksson had two vehicles at his disposal: a British 4x4, a green Range Rover, for which he's registered as the owner, and a black Audi A8 that's owned by the law firm, and the registration number of that particular vehicle just happens to be XPW 299. Am I right, or am I right?'

'I think you're right,' Bäckström said. 'Even though I'm having a hard time believing that an old antiques poof could have murdered Eriksson.' Unless he was the one who shat himself on the sofa, he thought.

'Yes,' Jenny said, nodding eagerly. 'That bit troubles me too. Admittedly, I've never met him, we've only spoken on the phone, but he doesn't feel right. Sounds mostly like one of those stuck-up types. So I think we might have been on the wrong track there. If you like, boss, I could explain my thinking now that we've found the connection between Eriksson and that von Comer bloke.'

'Yes, if you could, please,' Bäckström said. What does she mean by 'we' and 'connection'? he thought.

'At first I thought it was that old woman with the rabbit who was behind everything, Astrid Elisabeth Linderoth. Then I worked out the connection between Eriksson's murder and the fact that he was evidently the person who assaulted our baron in the car park, but then it struck me that she's also a victim, because she had her rabbit taken away from her, I mean—'

'Hang on a minute, now,' Bäckström said. 'As far as the rabbit's concerned, it was that nutter Fridensdal who saw to it that the old bag lost it. Are you saying Fridensdal is behind everything?' This is getting better and better, he thought.

'No,' Jenny said, shaking her head hard. 'Fridensdal doesn't feel right either. Besides, she was threatened by that nasty character that she didn't dare stand witness against. There has to be someone else, some unknown perpetrator that we haven't tracked down yet who's behind

Eriksson's murder, the assault in the car park and the fact that that poor old lady had her rabbit taken into care, not to mention the threats made against the animal rights activist who reported her, Fridensdal. If we can just find that person, I'm convinced all the pieces will fall into place.'

Bäckström made do with a nod. First, we've got two faggots squabbling in a car park, then a mad old bag whose rabbit is taken into care because of the actions of a common or garden nutter who is in turn threatened by a real thug and, finally, we have a lawyer who gets beaten to death and then given an extra going-over when he's already dead, just for good measure. And behind all this is evidently one single, as yet unknown perpetrator. Little Jenny's head must be the only eleven-pointer on the global ten-point fuckwit scale, he thought.

'What do we do now, boss? I mean, how do we take this forward?' Jenny asked.

'Okay, here's what I think we should do,' Bäckström said, taking his feet off the desk just in case the super-salami started to limber up. 'For the time being, what you've told me stays between us. Not a word to any of the others.'

'Sounds good,' Jenny agreed.

'Excellent, then we're in agreement,' Bäckström said. That way I won't have to watch the Anchor dragging you out by your ears, he thought.

'Just one last question, boss,' Jenny said.

'I'm listening,' Bäckström said.

'What do we do about the Security Police? They'll need to be informed of this, won't they? I mean, according to that rule, we have a duty to let them know.'

'Of course,' Bäckström said, nodding sombrely. 'Of

course we need to inform the Security Police. Goes without saying. The best idea would be for you to send them your summary at once.' That'll give those desk-jockeys something to think about over the weekend. They can probably turn that antiques poof into another royal scandal, he thought.

'My memo's already written, so that won't be a problem,' Jenny said, nodding and waving the papers in her hand. 'I'll do it straight away.'

'Do that,' Bäckström agreed. 'Now, if you'll excuse me. I've got some preparations I need to take care of before the meeting.'

Eleven points isn't enough, Bäckström thought as she closed the door behind her. Jenny is definitely a twelve-pointer. With a head like that, she's clearly utterly unique.

66

Dan Andersson was a cautious man. When he had asked for a meeting with Lisa Mattei the day before, he had also emailed her a brief explanation. Because he was also a man of few words, with an eye for the important details, he hadn't needed more than two pages to give his ultimate superior everything she needed to know. No prioritized security issue, for her eyes only, merely in case things took an unexpected and unfortunate turn for the worse.

To begin with, he had given her a brief description of the person at the centre of all this. A 63-year-old baron with a PhD in art history. Married for the past thirty years to the same woman, father of two grown-up daughters who were both married and – and this was the main point – not exactly one of the royal couple's closest friends, even if he did know them personally and had met them on numerous occasions under private circumstances. For the past twenty years or so, he and his wife had rented a villa that lay just a couple of hundred metres from Drottningholm Palace which belonged to the court's property portfolio. The reason they had ended up among this exclusive group of tenants was thanks to his wife's background in the higher nobility.

In spite of his title, Hans Ulrik von Comer had no property or estate of his own, which had been a matter of concern to his future father-in-law when he asked for his youngest daughter's hand in marriage. After some hesitation, the duke – the future father-in-law – had relented. He had four daughters and a son, who was going to be taking over the large entailed estate that the family had owned and managed for the previous three centuries, and for him that was what life was all about. The survival of the family, the fact that the eldest son would keep the line going and the land they passed on.

Things had been that way for more than three hundred years, and hopefully would continue to be so in the years to come, despite worrying signs in the modern world. Ten years ago, von Comer's father-in-law had died at the respectable age of ninety but, because his son lived according to the family motto and in the traditions of his forebears, the old duke was in good humour when he completed his earthly pilgrimage. His eldest child, his only son, had been a close friend of His Majesty the King since childhood. A close enough friend to be able to extract a small favour in the form of a house that lay in the vicinity of Drottningholm Palace for the younger sister and brother-in-law whose lot was less favourable than his.

After this description of the person at the centre of his report, Dan Andersson had moved on to the two occurrences that troubled him enough for him to feel it worth informing his boss about them. First, the incident in the car park outside the palace theatre on the evening of Sunday, 19 May, which the police in Solna had informed the Security Police about. Dan Andersson managed to condense his description of events to fifteen lines. Even though he shared his junior colleague Rogersson's belief that the baron, in spite of his claims to the contrary, had in fact been assaulted, possibly even been the victim of aggravated assault, that in itself wouldn't have been reason enough to bother Lisa Mattei. The decisive factor in the whole matter was an observation made by their own intelligence division when he had requested a check into von Comer's background and circumstances.

On Friday, 31 May, the king and queen had held a dinner at Drottningholm Palace for some fifty guests, the majority of whom were personal friends. Even though this wasn't a particularly grand affair, a number of the guests were important enough to demand the deployment of a total of eight different bodyguards. The occasion had also been more convivial than the Security Police had anticipated. The party had dragged on until past midnight, and at ten o'clock that evening the duty officer in charge of the personal protection unit had had to replace two of the bodyguards, who had been on duty since the morning and were also due back at work early the following morning.

For reasons that were unclear from the intelligence report Dan Andersson had been given, the two colleagues who had been relieved of duty so that they could go home and sleep had nonetheless decided to round the evening off with a short drive round the streets close to the palace. Presumably just to check things out seeing as they were passing, Dan Andersson thought. He appreciated officers showing initiative like that.

When they passed the house where Baron von Comer lived, they had made an observation which had prompted them to compose a report of the incident that very same evening.

Baron von Comer had received a visit from two men, the sort of men with whom someone like him would not usually be expected to associate. The baron and his two visitors were standing in the garden outside von Comer's half-open front door, and before they parted he had shaken hands with both of them, even if the surveillance photographs taken by the bodyguards seemed to suggest that it was his guests rather than von Comer himself who took the initiative on this by holding out their hands to him.

One of the two bodyguards, a recent recruit to the unit, was a female detective inspector, thirty-one years old. Her name was Sandra Kovac, and she had spent the entirety of her ten years in the force working in surveillance. When she graduated from the police academy she had been recruited directly to the Security Police, and a few years later had accompanied her boss when he moved to National Crime, where she joined the surveillance unit. She had worked in a group which focused on mapping the activities of a hundred or so of the most dangerous people in organized crime in the country.

Among her colleagues, Sandra Kovac had a very good reputation. She possessed all the qualities that characterized a first-class sur veillance officer. She had accumulated a great deal of knowledge, was known for dealing only in hard facts, and had immediately recognized both of von Comer's visitors.

'Bloody hell. Drive past and stop the car so I can get some decent pictures,' Kovac said, reaching for the camera in the footwell in front of the passenger seat.

'I didn't know you worked freelance for the gossip mags.' Her older male colleague sighed. He had been looking forward to going to bed for far too long now. But because Kovac was who she was, obviously, he had done as she asked. He pulled discreetly into a free parking space a hundred metres along the road and turned the headlights off.

'The one in the blue jacket is Baron Hans Ulrik von Comer,' her colleague said. 'If you don't believe me, just take a look in any edition of the aforementioned magazines. He's rumoured to be one of the biggest freeloaders in the country. He'll stand and grin on every page if there's a bit of free food and drink.'

'Never mind him,' Kovac said as she took the first pictures. 'It's the other two I'm interested in.'

'So who are they, then?' her colleague asked. 'I haven't got a clue, but if you asked me to judge by their appearances, I'd hazard a guess that they don't live locally. Nor do they seem to be friends of His Majesty, in spite of all the crap in the papers.'

'Hells Angels,' Kovac said. 'Laurel and Hardy on motorbikes. That massive one in the leather jacket, the one with the ponytail, he's Fredrik Åkare, and the one who's half his size and only weighs ninety kilos is his best mate. His name's Angel García Gomez. Usually known as the Madman, El Loco. And that's an affectionate nickname, if you're wondering.'

'I see what you mean,' her colleague said with a nod. 'In that case, I've just got one more wish.'

'Which is what?' Kovac said, adjusting the telephoto lens and snapping a few last pictures before putting the camera back down on the floor.

'That you write up the incident report. Because I want to get home and go to bed.'

'Don't worry,' Kovac said, taking out her mobile. 'I'll get started on that now while you tail them and see where they go.'

'I read online that the Angels are supposed to be having

some big gathering down in Skåne this weekend. So I dare say they're heading—'

'I don't think so,' Sandra Kovac interrupted. 'I reckon they're just going to cross the bridge and go back to their little clubhouse over by Bromma Airport.'

'You were right,' Kovac's colleague declared fifteen minutes later as Åkare and García Gomez unlocked the gate in the tall, barbed-wire-topped fence surrounding their clubhouse in Ulvsunda and disappeared out of view of Kovac and her camera.

'Of course I was right, and the pictures are pretty good as well,' Sandra Kovac said. She hadn't gained her reputation by accident.

'Baron Hans Ulrik von Comer's personal contacts therefore give some cause for concern,' Detective Superintendent Dan Andersson wrote in conclusion at the end of the summary that he emailed to his boss. To support his account, he attached the surveillance pictures that DI Kovac had taken, as well as the incident report she submitted the same evening.

The following morning – four hours before Detective Super intendent Dan Andersson was due to meet Deputy Police Commissioner Lisa Mattei – the Solna Police contacted him again and Dan Andersson had to postpone his lunch, as the routine information he had been planning to give his boss had just been transformed into a high-priority security issue, which in turn required more thorough investigation.

This just keeps getting worse and worse, he thought with a sigh, even though he knew he was prone to worrying about things unnecessarily.

67

The Friday meeting of the investigating team. Bäckström had begun the way he always did. The same body language, the same thoughts, the same words. He sat down at the end of the long table, made himself comfortable, leaned forward, rested his elbows on the table, hands under his chin, and surveyed the team gathered around the table. With these introductory gestures out of the way, his message was perfectly clear.

The day after Sweden's National Day the number of team members was significantly depleted, and the reasons that had been supplied as usual seemed to cover everything except the fact that they wanted to take an extra day off between the national holiday and the weekend, thus securing a break that stretched from Wednesday evening to Monday morning. You lazy, useless bastards, a whole week fucked, Bäckström thought. But seeing as the absentees included both Alm and Andersson-Trygg, he decided not to make a big deal of it.

'Okay,' Bäckström said. 'Has anything happened?'

'Yes, actually,' Peter Niemi said. 'We've had a reply from the National Forensics Lab, believe it or not. It arrived an hour ago. It concerns the DNA in the blood sample we found by the terrace door.'

'García Gomez,' Bäckström said, recalling the photofit picture.

'The very same,' Niemi concurred. 'A match for Angel García Gomez, and for once we can ignore the possibility that it might be someone else, because the chances of that are less than one against the entire population of the planet. Not that this comes as too much of a surprise, considering the photofit picture and what our taxi-driver witness told us about the limping man.'

'Okay,' Bäckström said. 'In that case I'd like some good ideas about how his blood came to be on Eriksson's terrace door.'

'I'm inclined to believe the following scenario,' Niemi said. 'García Gomez and his driver, who at a guess was one of his biker friends and, if you were to ask me, I'd put my money on Fredrik Åkare . . . Well, anyway, García Gomez and his driver appear at Eriksson's house at two o'clock in the morning. García Gomez enters the house, alone or with company. The front door is unlocked and Eriksson is already dead. García Gomez is furious. So he smashes in his skull anyway. The dog, which is outside on the terrace, starts barking like mad and García Gomez goes out to shut it up. He beats the dog over the back with the same instrument he used on Eriksson and finishes the job by cutting the dog's throat. In the process he gets bitten in the thigh. He leaves the house pretty much immediately. No sign he searched for anything.'

'That leaves a number of problems,' Bäckström said, leaning back in his chair and arching his fingers. 'Give me the usual objections that we can expect him to come up with.'

'His blood ended up there on a previous occasion when he was visiting Eriksson,' Felicia Pettersson said. 'Which is obviously a lie, but that can't be proved beyond reasonable doubt, because our DNA sample isn't date-stamped.'

'No, it isn't,' Annika Carlsson agreed. 'And there's always the possibility that we planted his DNA at the scene. I've heard worse from people like him.'

'Of course,' Bäckström said, shrugging his shoulders. 'But the biggest problem still has to be that García Gomez . . . in all likelihood, at least . . . has an alibi for the time of the crime. Any injuries that he may have, when we get the chance to take a look at them, could have been inflicted during that martial arts competition he was involved in while someone else was busy with our unfortunate murder victim.'

'Mind you, biting isn't allowed,' Stigson interjected, being something of an expert on televised martial arts contests. 'In martial arts, I mean. Maybe we could actually match the dog's teeth with a wound in García Gomez's thigh—'

'But he still has an alibi for the murder itself,' Bäckström interrupted. 'And García Gomez, if he actually admits to being inside Eriksson's house, could simply have been defending himself against a crazy dog that suddenly flew at him. What's wrong with a charge of aggravated cruelty against an animal? That it isn't enough in this case! Give me something better,' he went on, glowering at Stigson.

'If you like, I can put out a warrant for his arrest,' Lisa Lamm said, nodding amiably at Bäckström. 'If for no other reason than to give him the opportunity to express the excuses that I've just listened to. I've had to hear a fair amount of that sort of thing.'

Quite attractive, Bäckström thought. Definitely not stupid either, considering that this was practically the first thing she had said during the course of their meetings.

'I'd be grateful for that,' Bäckström said. 'If I could keep that pending for a day or two, it would be even better. I'd like to have a bit more on him before we lock him up.'

'I can see to that,' Nadja said.

'Sometimes it's important not to rush things,' Bäckström said, sighing to emphasize his point. 'And someone like García Gomez is unlikely to run away from us. Pull out everything we've got on him so we've got something to talk about when we do lock him up. By the way, does he happen to own a silver Merc?'

'Nyet,' Nadja said with a smile. 'That means "no" in Russian, if anyone wasn't sure – and we've already checked that out. He doesn't, nor does his good friend Fredrik Åkare. We looked them up when we ran the first check of potential suspects against the list of possible cars. As I'm sure you all remember, Åkare cropped up early in the investigation when we were talking to Eriksson's work colleagues, and just to be sure we checked out everyone around him who was in the intelligence service database, and Angel García Gomez was one of them. As far as the vehicles go, we've got just less than a hundred to look at, and we've switched to manual checks. We've also started to look at Eriksson's finances. Our colleague, Bladh, is dealing with that.'

'Have we got anything else?' Bäckström asked.

'Things are moving,' Annika Carlsson said. 'If you ask me, I'm fairly sure Fredrik Åkare and García Gomez know what's going on here. In spite of García Gomez's so-called alibi.'

'All the more reason to come up with something we can throw at him,' Bäckström said, by now eager to get out of there. He was keen to get on with his usual Friday routine: a restorative lunch, Little Miss Friday, then a long nap before it was time for a nice dinner with GeGurra. A worthy end to a week that had been full of hard police work – a better world, basically, he thought.

'What are we doing over the weekend?' Anchor Carlsson asked.

'How do you mean?' Bäckström said. 'I'm going to be working.' Suck on that, he thought.

'With our meetings, I mean.'

'Next meeting on Monday,' Bäckström said. 'If anything happens we can always talk on the phone and change that.'

'Monday, nine o'clock?' Annika asked. 'How about that?'

'Sure,' Bäckström said with a shrug. 'Don't let me stop you if you want to get up in the middle of the night. But there is one thing I want us to sort out right away. Our witness, the taxi-driver. Bring him in, confront him with some photographs and make sure he finally identifies García Gomez.'

'What makes you think he'd do that?' Annika Carlsson asked. 'I mean, we've already spoken to him four times.'

'Just get him to change his mind then,' Bäckström said. 'It shouldn't be too hard, bearing in mind the photofit picture he gave us. The man he saw was obviously García Gomez. He just daren't identify him, that's all. That's what the problem is.'

'There's nothing else I can do to help things along?' Lisa Lamm asked.

'You could call that medical officer and ask what the hell he's playing at,' Bäckström said.

'I've already done that, actually,' Lisa Lamm replied. 'He and his colleagues are still grappling with the issue. But his preliminary report still stands, at least for the time being. Eriksson died as a result of another person's actions, from being struck at the back of the head and neck with a blunt instrument. Because the injuries are complex, with a number of them being inflicted several hours after death occurred, he's asked for a second opinion from a colleague. That's the short version, and he's promised that we'll get a definitive report after the weekend. So, basically, no news on that front yet.'

'Okay,' Bäckström said, looking round the table. 'Well, what are you waiting for? Go and get some work done!' You lazy, useless bastards, he thought.

68

At the same time that Bäckström was leading the meeting with his investigative team, Dan Andersson was fully occupied with his own concerns. First, he had condensed Jenny Rogersson's effusive account to half a page of key points. Then he sat deep in contemplation as he compared the photofit picture of the possible suspect with the photographs taken by his colleague Kovac. Even though he wasn't a great fan of photofit pictures, he had still been struck by the obvious resemblance, and called Kovac on her mobile to ask if she had time to come and see him. Preferably immediately.

'I'm on my way in. My partner and I just need to change vehicles, then I can be with you in half an hour,' Kovac said.

While he was waiting, he called Jenny Rogersson to find out if anything new had emerged during that morning's meeting of the investigative team.

'We've had a reply from the National Forensics Lab this morning,' Rogersson said. 'About the DNA in the blood found on Eriksson's terrace door, which turns out to belong to someone in our database. His name's Angel García Gomez, and his DNA definitely links him to Eriksson's house. I can send over what we've got on him. You'll have it within an hour.'

'That's good of you,' Dan Andersson said. 'I look forward to reading it.'

'Then of course there are all the usual complications.'

'I'm listening,' Dan Andersson said.

Quarter of an hour later, he ended his call to Rogersson and, just as he started to write down what she had said, Kovac knocked on his door. Two minutes later she was on her way out again, and all she had to do in between was take a quick look at the photofit picture Dan Andersson showed her.

'That's definitely García Gomez,' Sandra Kovac confirmed. 'What's the problem?'

'The usual,' Dan Andersson said, shrugging his shoulders.

'Okay, then,' Kovac said. 'Things usually work out.'

'Let's hope so,' Dan Andersson said with a smile. 'Well, thanks for stopping by.'

'Don't mention it,' Kovac said. 'Have a good weekend.'

Dan Andersson's summary in the latest version of his memo included four points and, hopefully, he would get to see Mattei before anything else cropped up that required him to rewrite it yet again.

On Sunday, 19 May, the lawyer Thomas Eriksson had assaulted Baron Hans Ulrik von Comer. Twelve days later, around ten o'clock on the night of Friday, 31 May, Hans Ulrik von Comer met García Gomez and Åkare at his home near to Drottningholm Palace. Two days after that Eriksson was murdered in his home in Bromma. There was evidence linking García Gomez to the crime scene just hours after the crime was committed. Partly a witness, and partly through DNA. The prosecutor had decided not to issue an arrest warrant yet, for the usual investigative reasons, and the question facing Dan Andersson as a natural consequence of this required a decision, or at least an answer, that was above his own level of responsibility.

Then he had emailed his memo and asked for another fifteen minutes of her valuable time. The answer came just a minute after he sent it – 'You can come now. Yrs LM' – and five minutes later he was sitting in the visitor's chair in front of Mattei's very big desk.

69

As soon as the meeting was over, Bäckström had disappeared into his room. It was already almost noon, and it was high time he dealt with the last pieces of work before leaving the police station for a more civilized existence.

First, he rearranged the piles of paper on his desk. Then he spread out the latest bundle across the desktop in front of his chair. Bäckström nodded in contentment when this was done. Even the fifth columnists that the police hierarchy were bound to have placed in his vicinity ought to understand that this was a desk belonging to a very busy man, he thought, just as he heard the characteristic knock on his door that could mean only one thing.

'Please, take a seat, Annika,' he said, pretending to read some papers, even though she had already sat down on his visitor's chair.

'What can I do for you?' he added, pushing the papers aside and nodding amiably to her.

'Our witness, the taxi-driver,' Annika Carlsson said.

'What about him?' Bäckström said.

'We've been trying to get hold of him for two days now. We haven't heard a squeak from him even though he promised Ek he'd turn up for another interview. I'm getting bad vibes, fucking bad vibes,' Annika Carlsson concluded.

'Let's take it one piece at a time,' Bäckström suggested.

* * *

For the past two days, their colleague Ek, and other members of the interview team, had been trying to contact Ara Dosti. They'd called his mobile at least a dozen times and left the same number of messages without receiving any response at all. So they had contacted his work, where they were told that Dosti had reported in sick that day but that he had promised to get in touch after the weekend if he felt better. According to what he had told his employer, he was suffering from a bad cold and, out of consideration for his own health as well as that of his customers, he had decided to stay at home for a few days.

'What's the problem?' Bäckström said with a shrug. 'Sounds like he's alive, at least. Or was alive yesterday, anyway.' Might even be true, considering all the bastards who went round coughing and sneezing and jeopardizing his own health, he thought.

'The problem is that I've got a feeling he's done a runner,' Annika Carlsson said, glaring at him.

'I asked Stigson and his partner to pay a visit to his flat out in Kista,' she went on. 'They were there yesterday evening and got the impression that the flat's empty. Same thing when they were there this morning. No sign of Ara Dosti. His flat was quiet, no lights on.'

'Which doesn't preclude the possibility that he might have gone to stay with his dear old mum, or maybe his girlfriend, while he gets better,' Bäckström persisted.

'I don't think so,' Annika Carlsson said. 'We've already talked to his dear old mum and she hasn't heard from him for almost a month. She didn't even ask if there was any reason for her to be worried. He doesn't seem to have a girlfriend. But Stigson spoke to one of his neighbours, who says he saw Ara yesterday morning. He was getting into a car with a man the same age as him, no one the neighbour recognized. Then they drove off, and our little taxi-driver had two holdalls with him, which he put in the boot of the car. He didn't appear to be particularly ill. Not according to the neighbour, anyway. But we haven't got the registration of the car he went off in.'

'One possible explanation is that he's talked to one of the papers, got a few thousand for his trouble, has bought a last-minute ticket and gone off to warmer climes until things calm down,' Bäckström suggested.

Which would explain why his tame crime reporter had evidently known that Angel García Gomez had been seen at the scene of the crime, he thought. And also why he didn't seem to know much else.

'I don't think so,' Annika Carlsson said. 'Eriksson's murder has been all over the front pages for a week now and, if any of those bastards knew about García Gomez, they'd have run with it the moment they found out.'

'Possible,' Bäckström said. 'Perfectly possible. Unless they haven't got that far yet. Checking out the information, I mean. Unless they have checked, and came up with the same alibi that we found. The fact that García Gomez was taking part in that martial arts contest on Sunday evening. And got cold feet.'

'I hear what you're saying, Bäckström,' Annika Carlsson said. 'My problem is that I have a feeling there's a different explanation, which isn't quite as pleasant.'

'Which is what, then?'

'I've spoken to both Taxi Stockholm and the owner of the taxi Ara drives. I talked to Taxi Stockholm yesterday, our usual contact there, and she said that she had been called a couple of days before, which would have been Tuesday, by one of our colleagues, who wanted the name of the person driving one particular taxi early on Monday morning. And, for some reason, that vehicle had the same registration number as the car our witness was driving.'

'What did she say?' Bäckström asked. Not good, he thought.

'She referred them to the company that owned the taxi,' Annika Carlsson said. 'I've just spoken to them. They were called about it on Wednesday morning.'

'What did they say?'

'The same thing, as well as giving this so-called police officer the driver's name and address.'

'This police officer, does he have a name?' Bäckström asked.

'No,' Annika Carlsson said. 'Not that anyone remembers, anyway. Our contact at Taxi Stockholm is fairly sure he didn't give his name. But, otherwise, he sounded like we usually do, according to her.'

'Okay,' Bäckström said. 'It couldn't just be a mix-up, and one of our many colleagues did actually make that call? In the general confusion that followed the blessed news of the abrupt demise of lawyer Eriksson?'

'No,' Annika Carlsson said. 'I've asked everyone. They all just shake their heads. Anyway, why would they have done that? This is the witness who contacted us of his own accord, after all, and he did that on Monday afternoon. Which means that someone else is looking for him and, on this occasion, I get the feeling it isn't just some journalist sniffing about, pretending to be a police officer. I get the impression that it's considerably worse than that this time.'

'García Gomez? Åkare?' Bäckström suggested.

'Of course,' Annika said. 'I think that's more likely. If the person who was sitting in the Merc when our witness almost ran down García Gomez thought to put the headlights on full beam as he was driving away, then he probably had time to make a note of the taxi's registration number as well. Or the taxi number on the roof, even. That was probably lit up, seeing as he was free and available for a new job.'

'Bound to have been,' Bäckström said. Not good. Not good at all, he thought. Not that it had anything to do with him, seeing he would soon be having a decent lunch and then celebrating the start of the weekend in the usual way. As soon as this bull-dyke had left him, he'd be able to sneak out.

'So what do we do?' Annika Carlsson said.

'What we usually do,' Bäckström said. 'We talk to the prosecutor so we can bring our little witness in. Put a search out for him, of course, arrest the little fucker, preferably immediately. He needs to be brought in for questioning, without prior warning, and the sooner the better. Tell surveillance to check known addresses and also to keep a close eye on our two suspects and their associates. To make sure he doesn't come down with anything worse than a cold. If things start to heat up, we can always bring in Åkare and García Gomez.'

'Just what I was going to suggest,' Annika Carlsson said, now in a considerably brighter mood.

'Now, you'll have to excuse me, but I have to dash off to a meeting up at the National Police Board,' Bäckström said, glancing at his watch and shaking his round head to underline the point.

70

Wonder what she's like to live with? Detective Superintendent Dan Andersson thought, and the woman he was thinking about was sitting just a couple of metres away from him, on the other side of her big desk. Lisa Mattei wasn't the sort that he or any other man would turn round and look at if she passed them on the street but in the situation in which he now found himself, she was more tangible than any woman he had ever met.

A pale blonde, skinny, very fit, neatly dressed down to the smallest detail, in that indefinable age somewhere between thirty and forty. Then there were her blue eyes, registering interest, curiosity even – focused in a way that told you she was inside your head the moment she looked at you and that, if she was going to let you inside hers, even for the briefest moment, it would be entirely her decision.

'Thanks for the summary you sent me,' Lisa Mattei said. 'I read it with great interest. Especially the latest version.'

Which you evidently did in the two minutes it took me to walk from my office to yours, Dan Andersson thought, but because she was who she was, he made do with a nod.

'Almost all crimes involve some form of marginal activity, in the human and moral sense. We break the rules, or we stretch their boundaries, with the intention of gaining some advantage and, in the simplest cases, this involves money, sex or power. But, in your case, Dan, I think it's rather more complicated than that,' Lisa Mattei declared, and smiled at him. 'I get the impression that you came here mainly to assuage your own anxiety. Regardless of the fact that your motives are both honourable and human.'

'You'll have to forgive me, boss, but I don't quite follow,' Dan Andersson said. What's she saying? he thought.

'If we start with the purely factual aspect, we're talking about a probable connection between von Comer and two individuals who can on relatively good grounds be thought to be involved in the murder of a well-known lawyer. I'm choosing to disregard García Gomez's so-called alibi for the time being. Neither he nor Fredrik Åkerström are particularly pleasant people and I'm sure that you regard the likelihood of their committing further offences as high – as indeed do I. What concerns me, in purely concrete terms, is that our colleagues in Solna are unaware of the contact between von Comer and the other two, and because you are, in heart and soul, an honourable, old-fashioned police officer, you would like to help them clear up their murder, as well as removing the potential for further regrettable incidents. For that reason, you want me to consent to us contacting the Solna Police and telling them what we know and, up to that point, I have every understanding for your way of thinking. It's human, empathetic and perfectly correct in a purely professional sense. Unfortunately, there is a problem, even if we disregard the fact that we would be breaching our operational code if we told them what we know. No, the problem is actually quite different.'

'The fact that we don't at present know with any degree of certainty that von Comer was involved in Eriksson's murder,' Dan Andersson said. 'On that point, I'm in complete agreement with you, boss.'

'And don't forget that the lawyer's murder isn't actually our business. That notwithstanding, let us look at the cost if we were to stretch our own rules and tell our colleagues in Solna about von Comer's contact with Åkare and García Gomez, and then in hindsight were to realize that we were wrong,' Mattei said, still with the same friendly smile.

'Yes, I dare say that the risk of information leaking to the media in this particular case is somewhat greater than usual,' Dan Andersson said.

'Bearing in mind the fact that Evert Bäckström is leading the investigation, it would doubtless only be a matter of hours before the evening papers declared that the police had arrested, quote, "the king's best friend", end quote, because he had, quote, "murdered Sweden's most famous gangster lawyer", end quote. Or, to take a slightly milder version from our very own press mouthpiece, *Svenska Dagbladet*: "Close friend of king suspected of involvement in murder of famous lawyer",' Lisa Mattei concluded, indicating the quotation marks with the first two fingers of each hand.

'Which would be the worst-case scenario. I understand precisely what you mean, boss,' Dan Andersson said. A bit too creepy for my taste, in spite of the smile and gentle manner, he thought. How could anyone ever lie to Lisa Mattei, when she's already inside your head?

'Unfortunately, it's only the second from worst,' Mattei said, shaking her head. 'If you're right, and von Comer was involved in Eriksson's murder, and we help them sort it out, then we would in all likelihood be forced to tell our political masters that it's high time for them to start considering changing the constitution and abolishing the monarchy. Bearing in mind our mission, that might not be a particularly happy development.'

'No,' Dan Andersson said. You don't argue with someone holding a razor blade to your tongue. Even if she looks harmless, he thought.

'So what do we do instead, Dan?' Mattei asked, looking at him curiously.

'If I were to suggest anything, it would be to carry on as usual,' he answered. She's really enjoying this, her eyes are practically twinkling, he thought.

'Then we're in complete agreement, you and I,' Lisa Mattei declared. 'We carry on as usual. For your information, and strictly yours alone, I can also tell you that I have already dealt with the purely practical aspects.'

71

After the investigating team's Friday meeting, Detective Inspectors Jan Stigson and Felicia Pettersson had put their ears to the ground and gone out to talk to their usual contacts in the area. All their informants had been heart-warmingly unanimous. According to the word on the street, it was the Hells Angels out in Solna who had seen to it that Thomas Eriksson the lawyer had shuffled off this mortal coil. Payback for previous injustices, quite simply, and, considering the identity of the victim, it wasn't the end of the world. Various versions of the same story, but no one could deliver any hard facts. The only advantage to this was that they had been able to keep a close rein on the police authority's cashbox for paying informants.

'It was Åkare and his mate. Everyone knows that . . .'

'Those boys in the Hells Angels were behind it . . . Åkare and that crazy Chilean who's in charge of the dog-fights out in Rinkeby . . .'

'It was Bogdan and Janko who did for Eriksson. On Åkare's orders . . .'

'It's been bubbling away since that security van raid out in Bromma a few years ago. This is a Hells Angels job. I heard Grislund was driving the car, and that they took a few things with them when they left . . .'

'I don't know who did it, only that Åkare was behind it. He's had it in for Eriksson for years . . .'

And so on, and so on . . .

'If this was a vote among the lowlifes, it would be sorted by now,' Stigson sighed, after turfing the fifth grass out of the back seat of their car.

'What do we do now?' Felicia asked. 'Call it a day, or what?'

'I could do with picking up some drink,' Stigson said.

'Okay,' Felicia said with a smile. 'I'll head back to work and write the reports. Seeing as I don't drink.'

'Great, sounds like a fair deal,' Stigson agreed. She's all right, Felicia, he thought.

Fifteen minutes later Stigson was standing in the queue of the state-run alcohol shop, Systembolaget, in Solna shopping centre. Nothing excessive, six cans of beer and a quarter bottle of whisky, but in the absence of anything to celebrate it felt about right. But if there had been any justice in the world, he and his girlfriend would have been sitting on a plane heading for Spain right now, for their long-planned holiday. If only things had turned out differently, and their as yet unknown perpetrator hadn't beaten Eriksson to death. Early that morning his girlfriend had flown off with one of her friends instead. They had also spent the previous evening arguing. One thing had led to another, and neither of them knew when to stop.

Fuck the lot of them, Stigson thought. The people he had in mind were, in order of priority, Eriksson, who could have chosen a better time for his abrupt departure, Toivonen, who had put together the detectives' rota, and his own boss, that fat little bastard Bäckström, who was pretty impossible generally and had probably been sitting in the pub for the past few hours as he geared up for the weekend, leaving Stigson and the others to work their arses off.

'How's it going, son? You seem a bit low,' someone said behind his back, putting his large hand on Stigson's shoulder.

Behind him in the queue stood Roly Stålhammar. A former officer, and a legend among police and lowlifes alike.

'Stolly,' Stigson said. 'How are you? Good to see you, by the way.' Must be over seventy, two metres tall, one hundred and twenty kilos of muscle and bone, jet-black hair, Stigson thought. Mind you, that hair must be dyed.

'Buying drink on a Friday,' Roly Stålhammar said, shrugging his broad shoulders. 'This is the best place to meet police officers these days, both those who've already left the force and those like you. Still running about as if you had ants in your pants. How are you getting on with Eriksson, by the way?'

'If you're not busy, I could tell you about it over a beer,' Stigson suggested. If anyone had heard anything, it would be Roly, he thought.

Ten minutes later they were sitting in a Chinese restaurant in Solna shopping centre. More or less the same beer as in the local pub next door to Systembolaget, but empty at this time of day, which made the choice easy if you wanted to talk in confidence.

'I remember my last murder case, before I disarmed and handed in my badge and weapon,' Roly said. He had ordered a large beer and a little whisky chaser the moment he sat down at the table. 'It was a poof over on Södermalm.

Must be more than ten years ago. Miserable business.' Stålhammar shuddered and gave a crooked smile. Then he nodded and raised his glass.

'Cheers,' Stigson said, as he had evidently also been brought a whisky, however that had happened.

'We never did make any sense of it,' Roly Stålhammar said. He sighed and washed the whisky down with a few deep gulps of beer. 'Not that there was any fucking hope of that happening with that fat little bastard Evert Bäckström in charge of the investigation.'

'Things have gone pretty well for him out in Solna. Really well,' Stigson said. I don't think he's fucked up a murder since I arrived. And he is still my boss, he thought.

'Okay, I hear what you're saying. I remember the time he banged me up when he got it into his head that I'd murdered Kalle Danielsson, my best mate. That man defies all description.'

'Yes, but that got sorted out in the end. And it was Bäckström who solved it,' Stigson said.

'Okay, maybe it was. What I mean is that you should probably think twice before letting someone like Evert Bäckström investigate a murdered poof. You know what he thinks of poofs? And Eriksson, come to that. Correct me if I'm wrong, but wasn't it Eriksson who defended that little camel-jockey Afsan Ibrahim when he was accused of attempting to murder Bäckström? All that crap that came out in court about Evert taking bribes from Afsan's older brother, Farshad. There's no way in hell that Bäckström would forget something like that. Whatever happened to the old rules about bias and prejudice?'

'So what do you think, then? Who did for Eriksson?' Stigson asked, feeling a strong urge to change the subject.

'If you talk to the local lowlifes, they seem to be pretty unanimous on the subject,' Roly Stålhammar said with a smile, holding up his empty beer glass and showing it to the waitress. 'If you ask me, though, I'd say that's complete crap.'

'How do you mean?'

'The idea that Fredrik and Angel did it,' Roly Stålhammar explained. 'You know that as well as I do, anyway, because García Gomez was fighting in the Globe at the time Eriksson was murdered.'

'So you know. Just out of curiosity: how do you know?' Stigson said.

'Once a police officer, always a police officer,' Stålhammar said with an expressive shrug. 'But I'm afraid I've forgotten which of your colleagues it was who told me,' he added, raising the full glass that had just arrived. 'Christ, sitting here talking and talking, it really makes your throat dry.'

'Cheers,' Stigson said. Once a police officer, always a police officer. There's probably no more to it than that, he thought.

'No,' Roly Stålhammar said emphatically as soon as he put his glass down. 'If you're interested in what I think, I reckon you can forget Åkare and García Gomez and all their associates. Not because they lack the ambition to get rid of Eriksson. That's not what I mean.'

'What do you mean, then?'

'There's no way in hell that they'd go round his place and beat him to death where he lives. Forget it,' Roly said with a nod. 'The place was a fortress. Cameras and alarms everywhere. Åkare's not stupid, not like that. If he'd wanted Eriksson dead, it would have happened years ago.'

'As far as we know, Åkare has no alibi for the time of the

murder,' Stigson said. Good job Bäckström can't hear you, he thought.

'If he wasn't at the Globe watching García Gomez, he was probably at home with his girlfriend,' Roly said, shrugging his shoulders. 'He's got a weakness for girls, dear old Åkare. He's said to be as fond of them as they evidently are of him.'

'Regional Crime reckon they're on top of that. They're saying he didn't pay a visit to any of his women. Not that evening, anyway,' Stigson said.

'How the hell can they know that?' Roly snorted. 'According to what I've heard, he's got a new one. Danish, got to know her through his Danish colleagues. That's all there is to it.'

'What's her name, then? This new girlfriend? The Danish one?'

'No idea,' Roly said, shaking his head. 'You know that well enough, Janne. A real man doesn't talk about that sort of thing. You never talk about the women you're seeing.'

'Okay. Forget her. Who was it, then? Who did it, I mean?' Stigson asked.

'Wrong question,' Roly retorted. 'Who didn't do it? Who didn't have a reason to kill that little shit, Eriksson? There must be plenty who did. Neighbours, old girlfriends, former friends, clients, crime victims, and several hundred criminals he's rubbed up the wrong way over the years. Eriksson was a gangster. Just a gangster with a law degree.'

'Do you want another one, Roly?' Stigson said, in order to distract him, nodding at Stålhammar's almost empty glass.

'I'm good,' Roly said, shaking his head. 'Time to make a

move. I'm supposed to be having some food later with an old friend. Do you want anything else? One for the road? If you're going home, that is.'

'No,' Stigson said. 'Enough beer. Let me get these.'

'Forget it,' Roly said. 'It's on the house,' he explained, nodding to their waitress, who smiled and nodded back.

'On the house? Why?'

'I was in here the day before yesterday, after the match at the arena. The one where AIK thrashed IFK Gothenburg. Unfortunately, a few silly fuckers got lost on their way home to Gothenburg and were messing with the staff when I came in for one last beer before bed.'

'Ah, I see,' Stigson said, nodding towards the legend on the other side of the table. He must be over seventy, surely?

'So they got chucked out on their backsides,' Roly said. 'The owner let me have one beer for each one I chucked out. Valid for a week. I'm not like Bäckström, if that's what you're thinking. No bribes, no cop discounts. But I don't have a problem taking payment for a job well done.'

'In that case, thanks,' Stigson said. No, you're not much like him, Stigson thought. Someone else was bound to tell him that they'd found García Gomez's blood on Eriksson's terrace door. Once a police officer, always a police officer.

72

Friday, at last!

First, a long lunch at one of his favourite places, the tapas bar on Fleminggatan, which lay just a few blocks from the next stop on his itinerary.

Bäckström had ordered a generous selection of assorted delicacies – ham, sausage, meatballs, shellfish, cheese, little omelettes and various fried titbits – which he washed down with Spanish beer and a few sturdy vodkas, even though the owner, whom he knew well from previous visits, had tried to force a glass of dry sherry on him.

'Don't drink that sort of stuff,' Bäckström said, shaking his head. 'But you're welcome to offer me another vodka.'

'You really should try the dry sherry, Superintendent,' the bar owner said, shaking his head sadly. 'Among my countrymen, it's the custom when we eat tapas.'

'That's probably why there's such a big difference between real Spaniards and fake ones,' Bäckström said with a cheery smile. The bastard looks like a sad Andalucian dog after it's been raining, he thought. Anyway, what's wrong with adopting the traditions of your new homeland? Otherwise, you might as well move back home again.

After his meal the sun had started to shine again, and Bäckström moved outside and drank his coffee and

Spanish brandy as he put on his black surveillance sunglasses and teased his appetite before his impending visit to Little Miss Friday.

He had strolled down there and, once he was in position on the broad leather massage table, he amended his usual programme and performed it in reverse order. Probably the result of all that spicy food and those hot sauces, Bäckström thought, as he chose to begin with a salami-ride and let her conclude by softening up his muscles and joints for him. Towards the end of her ride, Little Miss Friday had begun to mutter incomprehensibly with her eyes closed, and when the moment arrived she showed the whites of her eyes and screamed out loud. Still in Polish, which was complete gobbledegook to a proper Swede like him.

She really ought to be paying me, considering all the noise I have to put up with, he thought as he tucked his note-clip back in his pocket and stepped out into the street to go home and embark upon the third part of his packed programme.

He woke up after a three-hour nap. Fresh as a daisy, his mind clear as crystal. Then he spent about an hour in the shower, anointing himself with scented potions, and concluded by dressing with the utmost care.

He checked the finished result in the hall mirror, nodded in approval at what he saw, called a taxi, had a little drink to set him up – without bothering about throat sweets – and headed off to the restaurant to have dinner with his old acquaintance GeGurra. At the stroke of eight o'clock he stepped into the foyer of Operakällaren, unquestionably the most illustrious restaurant in Sweden.

Nothing over the top, he thought. Just an ordinary, simple three-course dinner. While all his foolish and impoverished colleagues were sitting in front of the television with their miserable wives, cretinous children, pizza boxes, cheese puffs and flat beer.

IV

The true story of Pinocchio's nose. Part I

73

GeGurra was already sitting waiting for him as he stepped into the room. Elegant as ever, from the shiny black shoes you could use as a mirror, the dark blue silk suit, to the pale, cream-coloured shirt that he was wearing open at the neck, possibly as a tribute to summer, which finally seemed to have arrived after a long winter and chilly spring. The effect was perfect, like a Spanish nobleman from another age, from his shoes to his suntanned, chiselled profile and the thick white hair that crowned his head.

He had also brought his old diplomat's briefcase with him. It may have been a thin, worn affair in pale leather but it was simultaneously a sure sign that there was some good business in the offing. Bäckström knew that from previous experience. Just as much as he knew that, if things were sufficiently urgent, GeGurra's briefcase was capacious enough to contain a large brown envelope as soon as the handshakes were over and practical details agreed.

In spite of his own impeccable appearance, Bäckström always felt a pang of envy when he saw GeGurra. He wasn't remotely like your average gypsy, he thought. Who would believe he grew up in a caravan packed with all the other folk-dancers in his massive family, travelling round the country in the good old fifties, stealing chickens, tin-plating copper pans and – for good measure – robbing the occasional pensioner?

'Marvellous to see you, Bäckström. Marvellous to see you,' GeGurra repeated as he squeezed Bäckström's right hand in both of his.

'Good to see you too,' Bäckström grunted. Must remember to count my fingers afterwards, he thought.

GeGurra started their meeting by giving Bäckström a surprise. Instead of going into the large restaurant and settling down at their usual secluded table, they took the lift up one floor and walked right through the great Opera House. At the end of the corridor GeGurra stopped and tapped a code into the lock of the thick oak door, which immediately swung open with a discreet click.

In honour of the occasion, because it had been quite a while since they last met, and considering all the important things they were going to discuss, GeGurra had made sure that they would be able to eat, drink and socialize in peace.

'This is a private restaurant run by Operakällaren,' he explained, gesturing to Bäckström to go inside. 'There's only a very select number of members, and this evening there will be just the two of us.'

Hardly the sort of place where you were likely to run into the Anchor, Toivonen or any of his other impoverished colleagues, Bäckström thought as soon as he had sat down at the window table for two, which was already laid with a white linen cloth, ornately folded napkins, silver cutlery and a large array of sparkling crystal glasses. Not even Cajsa with the rat, even though she was district police chief, would be let into this little hideaway, he thought.

The staff, too, appeared to be well prepared. Without even asking, they had been brought their usual drinks. A Czech pilsner and a Russian vodka worthy of a proper superintendent, and a large dry Martini with a saucer of olives for his more refined host.

'Cheers, Bäckström,' GeGurra said, raising his glass. 'Something tells me this is going to be a particularly pleasant evening.'

'Cheers to you too,' Bäckström said. He nodded, snapped his neck back and downed half his glass in one smooth movement.

'As far as the food is concerned, I don't think you have any reason to worry,' GeGurra said, putting his glass down after a cautious sip. 'I've taken the liberty of ordering. First, a little Swedish smorgasbord, as a simple, preliminary tribute to our Swedish summer – herring, vendace caviar, smoked eel, Skagen prawn salad, butter, cheese, bread and tiny new potatoes, fresh from the rich soil of Skåne. All the usual, you know. I did, admittedly, exchange the Swedish liver pâté for French foie gras, but I don't think you'll have any reason to be disappointed. After that, we shall have grilled veal fillet, and for dessert I was going to suggest that meringue pie I know you're so fond of.'

'Sounds good,' Bäckström said. Nothing over the top. Not in these difficult times, when half of Europe is on the brink of starvation, he thought.

'I hope you won't be offended if I begin by asking a little question,' GeGurra said, leaning back in his chair and smiling at him and turning his glass in his well-manicured fingers. 'As I mentioned on the phone, I've been abroad on business for a while, but when I checked online to see what was happening at home I saw the news that Eriksson the lawyer had apparently been murdered, and that my dear friend . . . in the usual, estimable way that has become your trademark within the Swedish police service . . . had been given the task of leading the search for the perpetrator.'

'Yes,' Bäckström said, nodding. 'That's right.'

'In that case, I believe that I might for once be able to help you, my dear friend, by making a tiny contribution to the great investigative effort.'

'Sounds good,' Bäckström said. Even if the bastard talks like he's got a red rose stuck up his arse, he thought.

74

A tiny contribution to the great investigative effort, and before Bäckström leaned back to listen to GeGurra, their admirable maître d' had taken the opportunity to refill his glass. And he was quiet as well, Bäckström thought. Just appeared and topped him up, without saying a word, and without you having to tap the glass to get his attention.

On Friday, 17 May, some two weeks before he had been murdered, Thomas Eriksson had called GeGurra and asked to meet him to get help in valuing a small art collection that one of his clients had given to him to sell. Because GeGurra was due to travel to London that evening, they had met in his office in Gamla stan that same afternoon.

'He was most insistent,' GeGurra explained. 'I had a number of things to do in advance of my trip, but when he heard that I was going to be gone for almost three weeks, he wanted to meet before I left, at all costs. Because he was so persistent, I gave in. He appeared at my office that afternoon.'

'You already knew him,' Bäckström said, more as a statement of fact than a question.

'Not personally,' GeGurra said, shaking his head. 'I met him in connection to a court case some years ago. I had been called in as an expert witness. By the prosecutor, in case you were wondering. The case concerned a large art fraud in which Eriksson was defending the principal suspect. Fake pictures, supposed to be by Matisse and Chagall, lithographs, quite a catch.' GeGurra sighed, shaking his head sadly.

'You said he wanted help with a valuation.'

'A small collection, twenty objects in all, mostly paintings. All Russian, items dating from the late nineteenth and early twentieth centuries. In total, there were fifteen paintings, all of them so-called iconographic images.'

'Iconographic images,' Bäckström repeated.

'Yes, or icons, as they're also known. I assume you're familiar with the term?'

'Yes, of course,' Bäckström said, who had attended Sunday school as a child. 'They're those pictures of Christian saints? Angels and prophets and other holy figures from our biblical history?'

'Within the Orthodox Church,' GeGurra clarified with a nod. 'In a purely descriptive sense, one might say that they are illustrations to the Bible and other religious texts, but they are also part of the holy message, not least a way of transmitting and expressing it, and often, just as you say, they are portraits of people who have been significant to the history of the Christian Church.'

'Yes, I know what you mean,' Bäckström lied, nodding piously as he rubbed the bridge of his nose.

'The tradition of painting icons dates back to the sixth century AD and, during the almost fifteen hundred years that have passed since then, there have been tens of millions of icons painted,' GeGurra went on. 'Throughout history, they have been a feature of practically every Orthodox home, one or more of them, assuming of course that people had the financial wherewithal to buy an icon to put in their own home.'

'Expensive things,' Bäckström agreed, taking a fortifying gulp of the excellent vodka. 'Especially Russian icons, if I've understood correctly.'

'No, not at all,' GeGurra said, shaking his head. 'It's more a sort of religious folk art, often of mediocre or almost worthless quality. There's an awful lot of it about, and the market's full of modern copies. You can buy an average Russian icon for around a thousand kronor, and if you go into any junk-shop in St Petersburg you usually find stacks of them.'

'So why did he want you to value them, then?' Bäckström said. 'It sounds to me like it was barely worth the bother of dragging them down to your office.'

'He didn't,' GeGurra said with a faint smile. 'He brought pictures of the objects he wanted me to look at. Pictures that had been taken in connection to a previous valuation, and they were good enough for me to make a preliminary assessment. What he showed me wasn't a bad collection at all. The value of the various objects was above average for ordinary icons, even now the Russian art market has gone through the roof.'

'What sort of money are we talking about?' Bäckström said.

'Well, there were fifteen icons in total, all of them pictures of saints. I valued fourteen of them at between fifty and two hundred thousand Swedish kronor. Each, I mean, which is more than decent for an ordinary icon. An average of around one hundred thousand per painting.'

'And the fifteenth?' Bäckström said, for some reason feeling saliva building up greedily in his mouth.

'That one was worth as much as all the others put

together, even though it wasn't a real icon but more a way for the artist to make fun of his father-in-law. The artist's name was Alexander Versjagin, born in 1875. He was a young radical, a troublemaker really, not the slightest bit interested in religious painting. He was a landscape painter, active towards the end of the nineteenth century. He died on New Year's Eve, 1900. At the age of only twenty-five, in other words.'

'What did he die of?' Bäckström asked, intrigued.

'He died of the great Russian illness. Drink, basically,' GeGurra said with a gentle smile.

'Sad story,' Bäckström said. 'Sounds like the lad had reasonable expectations, from what you're saying.'

'In spite of his youth, Versjagin was an extremely talented artist. Today, his work – and here I'm talking about his landscapes – sells for between five and twenty million. Sadly, he didn't leave very many paintings behind. There are only twenty or so that are known to be his – which may possibly have been because he was a terrible rascal. Versjagin drank like a navvy, and he hated his father-in-law. The father-in-law was a wealthy man of German origin, a shipbroker in St Petersburg. He was also a good and deeply religious man, who, after much deliberation, abandoned his Lutheran faith and converted to the Russian Orthodox Church. And it was his father-in-law who made sure that Versjagin and his family had a home, food, clothing and everything else they needed. Whereas Versjagin, in contrast, devoted himself to drinking, leading a riotous life, betraying his young wife, neglecting his little children and every now and then managing to produce the occasional excellent painting.'

'Ingratitude is the way of the world,' Bäckström said with a smug sigh.

'Yes, and in this case it found expression in the fact that he painted an icon representing Saint Theodore, a fat and infamous Greek prelate from the sixteenth century who was expelled from the Orthodox Church because he kept having affairs with whores and conducting dubious financial deals in the name of the good Lord. Versjagin's icon of Saint Theodore was also an excellent work of art, not least in a technical sense. It was painted on a wooden panel that was several centuries old, using glazing techniques that dated back to the Renaissance, and it was a gift from the artist to his father-in-law on the occasion of his sixtieth birthday. The only problem with the present was that the resemblance between Saint Theodore and the artist's father-in-law was a little too striking. Because Versjagin's father-in-law also happened to be a rather corpulent man. Saint Theodore was also depicted dipping his right hand into a collection bag, which, to put it mildly, is an extremely unusual motif in this context. I'm sure you've already worked out what the father-in-law's first name was.'

'Yes, I have,' Bäckström said. 'I'm also getting an idea that you discovered that the works of art the lawyer wanted you to value were stolen.' Renowned gangster lawyer was also a big-time fence, Bäckström thought, seeing the headlines in front of him the moment he got the chance to talk to his reporter.

'No,' GeGurra, said, shaking his head. 'I'm sorry to disappoint you, but on that point I'm inclined to think that the opposite was the case. If you want to know what I think, I have a feeling that things are considerably better than that, actually.'

'You never asked Eriksson who this client of his was?'

'Of course I did,' GeGurra said, lowering his voice and

leaning forward. 'Eriksson was cold as a fish and slippery as an eel, but on this occasion I happened to believe him.'

'So what did he say, then?' Bäckström asked, leaning back in his chair.

'He said his client was keen to preserve his anonymity, and that his oath of silence as a lawyer and solicitor was absolute. He had no intention of giving any indication at all about who his client was.'

'And you bought that?' Bäckström said.

'Without the slightest hesitation,' GeGurra said. 'It's very common in situations like this for the seller to prefer to remain anonymous. If we're not dealing with an inheritance or something similar, the usual reason for the sale tends to be that the seller needs money. He or she is in financial straits, or is perhaps just a bit short, and that's not the sort of thing you want to advertise.'

'Hmm,' Bäckström grunted, making do with a deep nod. Who'd want that? he thought. It's bad enough being skint as a church mouse. Why make it even worse by talking about it?

'But Eriksson assured me that there was no need for me to worry on that score. He had known his client for many years and was familiar with the history of the collection. It had been in the family's ownership for three geneations, since they received the collection as a gift about a hundred years ago.'

'I'm guessing from what you've just said that you have an idea who Eriksson's client was.'

'Definitely,' GeGurra said, smiling happily. 'On that question I have very firm suspicions. That's also one of the main reasons I wanted to talk to you.'

'So who is it, then?' Bäckström said, leaning forward over the table.

'I'm getting to that, I'm getting to that,' GeGurra said, and indicated with a slight gesture with his left forefinger that he wanted another drink.

Bäckström merely nodded. GeGurra definitely wasn't your average gypsy, he thought. He was cold as a fish, slippery as an eel, and sharp as a razor blade. It had to be fifty years since he'd given up stealing chickens and, compared to him, Eriksson must have seemed like a complete novice.

'As far as a number of these items are concerned, I happen to know with absolute certainty that they were sold recently at auctions in Sweden and abroad,' GeGurra said, sipping cautiously at his freshly filled glass. 'I said as much to Eriksson, and that was when he began to ease the curtain up slightly.'

Ease the curtain up? Where do they get this stuff from? Why do they talk like that? Bäckström thought, conscious that he had eased up on practically everything it was possible for a human being to ease up on. But never any curtains, as far as he was aware. Whatever the hell that was supposed to mean.

'Eriksson didn't voice any doubts. Instead he confirmed that it was indeed the case. Over the course of the past year, he had in fact facilitated the sale of eight of the original twenty objects. Four of the icons, including Versjagin's painting of Saint Theodore, which went under the hammer at an auction of Russian art at Sotheby's in London about a month ago, a dinner service and two different canteens of silver cutlery. And an antique gold cigar-lighter. It was as a result of the circumstances surrounding these sales that he was so keen to meet me.'

'I'm listening,' Bäckström said, nodding encouragingly, pleased that his glass had just been refilled and he was now in a position to listen to an unusually prolix GeGurra.

'The practical arrangements regarding the sales were handled by an art expert Eriksson had originally chosen to engage, and he was also responsible for looking after the artworks, but for various reasons . . . which Eriksson was unwilling to go into . . . he wanted a second opinion regarding the value of some of the items. What this was really all about, of course, is that he was worried he was going to be cheated. Or was already standing there with great big donkey's ears.'

'So what did you say?' Bäckström asked.

'My intention was actually to reassure him on that point. So I took the opportunity to congratulate him on the sale of Versjagin's icon. Explained that it had reached a good price in the current overheated market for Russian art. That it wasn't every day that you got one and a half million kronor for a hundred-year-old icon that was originally intended as a blunt joke. A blasphemous one, at that, and one to which onlookers reacted very badly when the work was first exhibited publicly. If it had been a landscape by the same artist, then, naturally, it would have cost several million more.'

'And how did Eriksson take that?' Bäckström asked.

'He did his best to hide it, but there was no question that it came as a complete shock to him. A very unpleasant one, at that. He looked as if there had been a zero missing from the statement of account he'd already been given.'

'This expert he commissioned,' Bäckström said. 'Does he have a name?'

'Yes,' GeGurra said, nodding contentedly. 'I already knew, in fact, but if I hadn't it wouldn't have been terribly hard to find out. Not for a man with my contacts in the business. My tiny contribution to your no doubt already considerable investigative effort . . . and if you're wondering what his name is—'

'Baron Hans Ulrik von Comer,' Bäckström interrupted.

'Cheers, Bäckström,' GeGurra said, raising his glass. 'I don't mean to flatter you when I say that your incisive deduction comes as no surprise to me at all.'

'Thank you kindly,' Bäckström said, already on his third vodka and in one of his very best moods. 'I should be thanking you for confirming a suspicion that I've had for some time,' he went on as he carefully checked the length of his bulbous nose. No cause for concern, he thought.

'And you've actually made two contributions, not one,' he went on.

'Two contributions? Now I really am curious,' GeGurra said.

'I'm afraid I can't tell you what at the current time,' Bäckström said. 'For reasons relating to the investigation, as I'm sure you'll appreciate,' he added, as he now understood very well why Eriksson the lawyer had assaulted Baron von Comer in the car park outside Drottningholm Palace two days after he met GeGurra, and why he had used an auction catalogue as a weapon. He understood that as well as he understood what had been in the white boxes that Eriksson had carried into his house a couple of days before he was beaten to death and which his killers had taken with them when they left the scene of the crime.

'What do you say to a little food, Superintendent?' GeGurra asked, also in an extremely good mood. 'A little something to line our stomachs before we carry on with the story. Something tells me, even if I might be repeating myself, that this is going to be a quite splendid evening, even though we haven't yet said a word about the little business proposal I was planning to put to you towards the end of it.'

'A bit of food would be good. Yes, definitely,' Bäckström said. While you tell me who you think owned the art collection that Eriksson had been told to sell, he thought.

75

Herring and salmon and fresh Swedish potatoes, smoked eel and Skagen prawn salad, foie gras, cheese and bread and pilsner . . . and the vodkas with which Bäckström washed this divine feast down and which he had now stopped counting.

As on so many previous occasions when he had a bit to eat, he ended up in a calm, elevated and almost philosophical state, where thoughts came and went in his head, on all manner of subjects. Such as all those whining Frenchmen, for instance, constantly complaining about their hopeless economy. And they even had the gall to demand that honest, hard-working Swedes should help repay the debts they had brought upon themselves. What did those snail-eating, beret-wearing pricks have to complain about, when they could stuff themselves with as much of the foie gras that he all too seldom had the chance to taste as they wanted?

Or that mysterious Baron von Comer, who had clearly come to blows with Bäckström's murder victim, even though Bäckström was willing to bet the bill for the evening's dinner that a poof like him wouldn't have the guts to kill Eriksson the way Bäckström's perpetrator had. But he might well have sat on Eriksson's sofa and shat himself when the lunatic lawyer, who thus far had only assaulted him with an auction catalogue, took a serious step along the broad path followed by all perpetrators by pulling out a revolver and starting to shoot at him.

That shouldn't be too hard to find out, Bäckström thought, and who could be better to start with in that regard than his host for the evening, sitting opposite him on the other side of the table? About time for a bit of nice, simple police work. He finished his latest vodka, rinsed it down with a couple of gulps of beer, folded his hands over his stomach and leaned back to get a better view.

'That von Comer,' Bäckström said. 'Tell me, what's he like?'

Judging by GeGurra's description, von Comer wasn't one of his closest friends. Definitely not someone he would use as a middleman, even for lesser matters than those Eriksson had evidently been engaged in. As a connoisseur of art, he knew little more than an enthusiastic amateur, according to GeGurra. Even if he did have a degree of knowledge about Swedish painting of the nineteenth and twentieth centuries, as well as furniture and antiques of a somewhat older vintage. And he wasn't particularly pleasant as a person. Arrogant, stupid and, sadly, also indiscreet. Poor as a church mouse, of course.

'No money, no inheritance, no estate,' GeGurra said in summary. 'Just another penniless nobleman prancing about with his nose in the air, spouting a load of nonsense.'

'A fraudster, then?' Bäckström asked. 'Could he have been trying to trick someone like Eriksson?'

'I'm quite convinced he'd already done that,' GeGurra said. 'I could see it in Eriksson's eyes when I told him how much Versjagin's icon had sold for.'

'How much money are we talking about?' Bäckström said, nodding and taking a swig of beer.

'One million,' GeGurra said. 'That's how much he tricked him out of, I mean. More or less,' he said, dabbing his thin lips with his linen napkin.

'Why do you think that?' Bäckström asked. For some reason, at that moment he found himself thinking of the envelope containing almost a million in cash that his colleague Niemi had found in Eriksson's desk. Could it be the case that his old acquaintance GeGurra had just made a third contribution to his expanding investigation?

'The three icons he'd already sold,' GeGurra said. 'I checked to see what he got for them. The first one was sold in Uppsala last autumn for almost one hundred thousand kronor. The second was sold at Bukowski's in Stockholm just before Christmas for seventy thousand. The third was sold at the start of the year at a special auction of Russian art in Helsinki. I seem to recall it went for around one hundred and fifty thousand Swedish kronor, which gives us an average price of about a hundred thousand each, after deduction of the auction houses' fees. On items at that level, the standard rate is twenty per cent, in case you were wondering, excluding VAT.'

'And Saint Theodore?'

'That went for one hundred and forty-five thousand British pounds, which is equivalent to one point four million Swedish kronor at the current exchange rate. After the deduction of fees, VAT and other costs, we're down to about eleven hundred thousand Swedish kronor. If we assume that von Comer managed to forget the little detail that the sale was in pounds, and chose instead to provide accounts to Eriksson showing a sale at one hundred and fifty thousand Swedish kronor, the difference is roughly a million,' GeGurra concluded.

Straight from the horse's mouth, Bäckström thought, satisfying himself with a nod.

'No doubt, my friend, you're wondering how the accounts could be dealt with in a simple, practical way?' GeGurra said.

'Yes, tell me,' Bäckström said, making himself more comfortable on his chair. This is getting better and better, he thought.

'If I were to contemplate doing anything of a similar nature, which of course I never would, I would get the English auctioneers to email the statement of account to me. It's much easier to manipulate these things electronically, you see, and even for a man with my limited knowledge of modern computer technology, it would be a simple matter to change the pounds to kronor and print out a copy of the statement, which I would then give to Eriksson. Although it would never occur to me to do anything like that,' GeGurra declared with an expressive shrug of his immaculately tailored shoulders.

'So that's one way to earn a million,' Bäckström said.

'Yes, or nine hundred and sixty-two thousand kronor, if I remember rightly,' GeGurra said. 'Give or take the odd hundred kronor.'

'How can you know that?' Bäckström said. What the hell's he saying? he thought.

'Because I was the one who bought Versjagin's icon, so I received the same statement of account as the seller,' GeGurra said with a nod. 'The rest was just simple arithmetic.'

'You bought the painting of Saint Theodore. What for?'

'I thought I might come to that while we enjoy our veal

fillet,' GeGurra said. 'And with that in mind, I was wondering if I could tempt you with a glass or two of this establishment's rather splendid house wine. It's an excellent Italian red, made from the classic French blend of Cabernet Sauvignon, Merlot and Cabernet Franc. Except these grapes grow in Tuscany rather than Bordeaux,' GeGurra said.

'Beer and vodka's fine,' Bäckström said. This could be brilliant, he thought.

'Perhaps that's wise,' GeGurra agreed. 'One should always beware of mixing the grape with the grain. I think you have a point there, Bäckström.'

'Eriksson's client. Who's the owner of that art collection?' Bäckström prompted once more.

'We're coming to that,' GeGurra said with a friendly nod. 'We're coming to that. If I might be so bold as to offer a piece of advice while you're waiting, it might be as well for you to have another little vodka. So that you don't fall off your chair when you hear what I think about that individual.'

76

Grilled veal fillet, baked root vegetables, red-wine sauce with ox marrow, and a very content Bäckström. He drank vodka and beer while he allowed himself to think pleasant thoughts about the big brown envelope he was convinced his acquaintance would soon be getting to. But Bäckström was in no hurry. He wasn't going short of food and drink while he waited, and sometimes the business of money could take a little time.

Eventually, it looked as if his host had girded his loins. First, he cleared his throat discreetly, fortified himself with a cautious sip of his Italian red wine, before dabbing at his thin lips with his napkin and nodding, that yes, it was time.

'Are you familiar with the concept of provenance, Bäckström?' GeGurra asked, clearing his throat once more.

'Well, sort of.' Bäckström shrugged. 'But I'd be happy to hear more,' he added. Just to hedge his bets, if nothing else, seeing as he had no idea at all which province GeGurra was talking about.

'In this context, when we're talking about artistic artefacts, I mean, you could say that provenance concerns the history of the artwork. And the artist, of course, and different events connected to the origins of the work. Not least . . . especially when we consider the price a work of art might command . . . we're also talking about the people who have owned the work. The original owner, as well as those who came later. It might seem irrelevant, but it can sometimes be the case that if the owner is very well known, that can mean far more to the value of the particular piece of art or object in question than the actual work itself.'

'Of course, of course,' Bäckström concurred, as he had already received numerous anonymous online offers to buy little Siggy at a price that wildly exceeded what his employers, the National Police Authority, had paid for his service revolver. Get to the point, you long-winded bastard, he thought, checking that Siggy was still snugly nestled against his left ankle. Don't worry, lad, he thought, patting the holster reassuringly. There was no way he'd ever dream of selling his best friend.

'The best Swedish example of this occurred a few years ago when it came to the sale of the estate of Ingmar Bergman, our world-famous Swedish director,' GeGurra said, shuddering at the memory as he took another fortifying sip of red wine.

'Wasn't he the one who did that film about Fanny and Alexander?' Bäckström asked, recalling that he had accidentally happened to watch half of it on television late one evening before realizing that it wasn't a sequel to his old childhood favourite, *Fanny Hill*.

'Exactly,' GeGurra said with feeling. 'That's the chap I'm talking about, and when his estate was put up for auction, it was a very tragic business. Shabby old Dux sofas, all stained and threadbare, battered old flat-pack chests of drawers which that miserable old sod from Småland has forced on half of humanity, wonky bookcases, buckled copper pans, tatty sheepskin rugs, chipped coffee cups from Rörstrand. I could go on and on, and if you'd tried to give that lot to the Salvation Army they'd have shown you the door.'

'Everyone knows that's how people like that live,' Bäckström agreed. 'I once had to conduct a search of a famous actor's house and, if it had been an ordinary junkie's home, Social Services would have boarded it up.' Even a gypsy would have refused to live there, he thought.

'Not on this occasion, though.' GeGurra sighed, apparently not listening to his guest. 'Junk, scrap, plain old rubbish, but this time people paid millions for it. Have I ever told you about the pair of slippers he was given by Harriet Andersson – you know, the famous Swedish actress – when they were filming out on the archipelago back in the fifties?'

'No,' Bäckström said, shaking his head, as all the films he'd seen that had been made out on the archipelago certainly hadn't been directed by Ingmar Bergman. Thank God, he thought, considering what little of Bergman's work he had actually seen.

'A terrible story. It's supposed to have rained all the time they were filming, and there was a serious draught blowing across the floor of the house they were recording in, so she dashed over to the neighbour's – some old fisherman who lived out there in the habitually miserable conditions, surrounded by coffee grounds and herring scales and tatty old copies of *The Sower* – and she bought the old boy's shabby old sealskin slippers so Bergman's feet wouldn't get cold. Do you know how much they sold for? At Bukowski's, of all places?'

'No,' Bäckström said, shaking his head. How the fuck would I know that?

'Eighty thousand kronor,' GeGurra groaned. 'Eighty thousand kronor,' he repeated. 'For a couple of shabby scraps of leather held together by foot-sweat.'

'Sounds a bit steep,' Bäckström agreed.

'Now, let's imagine that Greta Garbo had given him those slippers instead. What do you think Bergman's greedy little offspring might have got for them then?'

'A lot more, no doubt,' Bäckström suggested, even though he had only the vaguest of recollections of Garbo. Wasn't she that brunette who went to Hollywood and turned into a dyke?

'Probably a million.' GeGurra sighed, shaking his head sadly.

'Forgive the question,' Bäckström said, 'but why are you telling me this?' What's happened to that brown envelope? he thought.

'So that you understand my point,' GeGurra said with feeling. 'What provenance can do to the price,' he explained.

'Okay, I get that,' Bäckström said. 'All I'm wondering about is who the previous owner that you've been talking about is. Who is it?'

'I'm getting to that,' GeGurra said. 'What put me on the trail, in case you're wondering, was one of the items that Eriksson had been instructed to sell.'

'What was it?' Bäckström asked. Presumably that portrait of the fat monk who had evidently been caught red-handed with his paw in the good Lord's honeypot, he thought.

'A hunting service for maritime use,' GeGurra said with a nod.

'A what?' Bäckström said.

77

It was a hunting service for maritime use that had put GeGurra on the trail. A complete set of twelve covers, consisting of a total of 148 pieces, produced by the royal porcelain factory in St Petersburg during the winter of 1908. Finest bone china, hand-painted with pictures of seabirds found in the Baltic, birds that were also suitable for hunting. An adornment to a table laid for participants in a hunt after the first shoot, and in this instance a wedding present from the Grand Duchess of Russia, Maria Pavlovna, to her future spouse, Prince Wilhelm of Sweden. A highly appropriate gift for a married man who was not only a Swedish prince but also an officer in the Royal Swedish Navy, a keen huntsman, and an enthusiastic fly-fisherman.

'It wasn't a bad marriage, I can assure you of that,' GeGurra said. 'A Swedish prince of the House of Bernadotte tying the knot with a grand duchess of the House of Romanov. Maria Pavlovna was a cousin of the last Tsar of Russia, Nicholas II. A close relative, in other words, of the father of all Russians, in those days known as the tsar.

'Can you imagine, Bäckström?' GeGurra went on. 'A Swedish prince marrying a Russian princess. A woman from Russia, our old arch-enemy. The House of Bernadotte has never come close to anything like it in its 200-year history. They were married on 3 May 1908 in the imperial palace in St Petersburg. The festivities went on for a whole week. But perhaps that isn't so surprising, given that there's quite some distance between St Petersburg and Ockelbo,' GeGurra declared, nodding hard and fortifying himself with a large gulp of his red wine as he reflected on his reference to the less than auspicious hometown of the current crown princess's husband.

He went on to explain that things hadn't gone well. The 24-year-old prince was a timid, feeble young man, in spite of his blue blood and gold epaulettes, whereas his eighteen-year-old wife was 'a real tearaway' who rode using a man's saddle, smoked cigarettes and used to entertain herself by sliding on a silver tray down the stairs of the large villa out on the island of Royal Djurgården where they lived.

There had never really been much matrimonial harmony. A year after the wedding they had a son, admittedly, but to all intents and purposes they lived separate lives, and by 1914 they were divorced.

'That was the first time a member of the House of Bernadotte got divorced,' GeGurra said, looking as mournful as any royal correspondent.

'What happened after that?' Bäckström asked curiously. Our own king is definitely going to turn up in this story, he thought gleefully.

Separate lives in separate worlds, according to GeGurra. Maria Pavlovna had returned to Russia at first, worked for the Red Cross during the First World War and remarried in the summer of 1917. After the revolution a few months later, she moved to Paris, and thereby avoided being murdered by the Bolsheviks, unlike so many other members of her family.

'She never returned to Russia,' GeGurra said. 'She lived in Paris to start with, and even spent a while in New York. In the mid-thirties, by which point she had divorced her second husband, she returned temporarily to Sweden. She spent the Second World War living in South America, in Buenos Aires, if I recall correctly. Towards the end of her life – she died in 1958 – she moved back to Europe. She spent her final years living by Lake Constance in Switzerland, close to her son, Lennart, and his family. He was the son she had with Prince Wilhelm. You must have heard of him? He was the one who lived at Mainau – you know, that castle with those gardens that are open to the public. For many years he was one of the most written about members of the House of Bernadotte.'

'Of course, of course,' Bäckström said. He took a deep swig of beer and wiped the drops from his lips with the back of his hand. 'Who doesn't remember little Lennart?' How the fuck can you be a prince with a name like Lennart? he thought.

'A brief summary of a life.' GeGurra sighed. 'A life full of change,' he added.

'Full of change? How do you mean?' Bäckström asked. He preferred hard facts and things that could be predicted in advance. Preferably with a decent amount of commission into the bargain.

'When she arrived in Sweden she was eighteen years old. Despite her youth, she was one of the richest women in the world. Maria was the cousin of the Tsar of Russia, after all, and he was indisputably the richest man in the world at that time. She herself was far wealthier than the entire Swedish royal family put together. When she married Wilhelm, the Russian tsar agreed to grant her an annual stipend of three and a half million kronor. At the time, that was the equivalent of the collected wages of ten thousand Swedish workers and, in today's money, it would be in the region of four billion. A year. Maria Pavlovna was rich beyond belief. Compared to her, her husband was a pauper.'

'But she seems to have given him a fair few presents,' Bäckström said. 'Like that hunting service, for instance. That must have cost a bit?'

'Yes, it certainly did,' GeGurra said. 'And it was far from the only thing she gave away while she was in Sweden. Practically everyone in her vicinity received expensive gifts, and when she moved here she brought an immense amount with her, including valuable works of art and antiquities. Not least antiquities. Almost all of it got left behind when she moved back to Russia. It looks like she just didn't care, and most of it presumably ended up in the hands of her first husband, Prince Wilhelm.'

'So what happened to him?' Bäckström asked. This could turn out to be brilliant, he thought. Four billion a year. Bergman can shove his scabby old sealskin slippers right up his arse.

'Prince Wilhelm had an artistic nature,' GeGurra said. 'He wrote books, loads of books, about anything and everything, from love poetry to ballads, lots of sea shanties, lots of travel writing. And he was very interested in film. He made films all round the world, mostly in Sweden, of course, but also in Africa, Asia and Central America. He spent the last thirty years of his life on his estate at Stenhammar in Södermanland. He died in 1965 and, if you ask me, I think he was very lonely, even though he socialized with almost all the Swedish intellectuals of note during his lifetime, painters, authors, musicians. As a patron and art lover, of course, but also as an equal. He was one of them, really, and in that respect he was fairly similar to a lot of his relatives in the House of Bernadotte. The most famous one, of course, was Prince Eugen, the painter, whom I'm sure you've heard of.'

'I've heard the name,' Bäckström lied. 'But, to go back to Prince Willy . . . the one who married the Russian with all the money . . .'

'Yes?'

'No new wife, no more kids?' Bäckström asked, seeing as he was having trouble dropping the thought of the doubtless astonishingly valuable hunting service.

'No,' GeGurra said, shaking his head. 'Towards the end of the twenties he seems to have met another woman, a French woman, but the relationship was unofficial, and she died in tragic circumstances in 1952. A car crash outside Stjärnhov in Södermanland, when they were on their way to his beloved Stenhammar. A very tragic story. The prince was driving, and he seems never to have got over it.'

'I can imagine,' Bäckström said. Dare say he'd been on the piss, he thought.

'They drove into a snowstorm,' GeGurra said, sounding as sad as if he were part of the family. 'The prince was very careful with alcohol, if that's what you're thinking,' he added.

'I'm thinking about that hunting service,' Bäckström persisted. I've heard all this other stuff before, he thought.

'I can see why,' GeGurra said. 'It definitely belonged to Prince Wilhelm, so that part of its provenance is perfectly straightforward. Nineteen of the twenty objects Eriksson was tasked with selling on behalf of his secretive client definitely – or in all likelihood, to be more correct – came from Maria Pavlovna originally, and formed part of the belongings that she brought with her to Sweden after her marriage. They were either gifts to her husband or objects that belonged to her and got left behind when she returned to Russia. I've been able to track their history that far, and most of the evidence suggests that they ended up with Prince Wilhelm after the separation.'

'Nineteen out of twenty,' Bäckström said, with a faint hint of anxiety in his voice.

'Precisely,' GeGurra said emphatically. 'But as far as one of the items is concerned, I'm quite convinced that it could never have belonged to either Maria Pavlovna or her then husband, Prince Wilhelm.'

'How can you know that? What's the problem?' Bäckström said.

'That's one of the reasons I need your assistance, my dear friend,' GeGurra said. 'I need all the help that you and your finely honed detective's mind can give me. I'm interpreting the fact that you have been given the job of investigating Eriksson's murder as a sign from above. I think it could be of great assistance to the pair of us.'

78

According to GeGurra, there were no problems working out to whom nineteen of the twenty objects had originally belonged, and who had owned them after that: first Maria Pavlovna, then her former husband, Prince Wilhelm. What confused matters was Versjagin, the young drunkard, and the 'icon' – or rather, insult – representing Saint Theodore which he painted to offend his father-in-law on his birthday. Definitely not a proper icon – in fact, the exact opposite of the work produced by true iconographers, which was intended to convey the Christian message and glorify the Lord in artistic form.

The fact that Versjagin's icon was the complete opposite of this, and that it was intended as a blunt joke at his father-in-law's expense, the man who supported both him and his family, was of secondary interest, given the broader context. Its repercussions meant that it was far worse than that. It was an almost revolutionary act that called into question both the Church and the state, blasphemous, an insult against both God and the tsar.

When the scandal was made public in the summer of 1899, during Versjagin's father-in-law's birthday celebrations, the gift was returned forthwith. Versjagin's despairing young wife took the children and moved back in with her parents, while Versjagin himself left Russia, only to pop up a week later among his radical artist friends in the Russian expatriate community in Berlin, on the run from the tsar's secret police.

He returned to St Petersburg that autumn, after several itinerant months in France, Germany and Poland. It was his wife who finally persuaded him to come home to her and their three young children. She had already forgiven him, his father-in-law never would, and just a few months later Versjagin would be dead.

On New Year's Eve in the year 1899 Versjagin drank himself to death as he celebrated the dawn of the new century at the art academy in the imperial capital. Even by then a fair amount had already been written about the events of the preceding year. Private letters exchanged within the family, with friends and enemies, newspaper articles and, eventually, also academic articles about Versjagin and the scandal he had caused.

One month before his death he had also sold his portrait of Saint Theodore, under an oath of confidentiality, and for a surprisingly good price, to one of his father-in-law's competitors. An Englishman who was the representative of a British shipping company that did a lot of business with tsarist Russia, and who chose to leave the country after the first troubles in St Petersburg in 1905 and returned home to England, where he started work in the company's head office in Plymouth.

The first time Versjagin's icon was seen in public in its new homeland was in connection with an exhibition at the Tate Gallery in London in the autumn of 1920, about art as a political statement in revolutionary Russia. And, once again, it provoked a lot of debate. The English papers wrote about the scandal the picture had caused twenty years before, and *The Times* also published a lengthy interview with the owner of the work. Now the retired director of the shipping company, Sir Albert Stanhope had for various reasons chosen to speak at greater length about Versjagin the landscape painter than the young scoundrel who had attracted international infamy by insulting his father-in-law. This despite the fact that the father-in-law had been German, and at least as fat as his Greek forerunner, but the war was over now and Sir Albert was willing to draw a line under that part of the affair.

'The war is over and it's time to let bygones be bygones. And let's not forget that Alexander Versjagin was a first-class landscape artist.'

'As far as the provenance of the portrait of Saint Theodore is concerned, it can be mapped in detail from the creation of the work in 1899 until the Second World War,' GeGurra declared. 'It was bought by Stanhope, and he owned it until his death in 1943. When the picture left Russia in 1905, Maria Pavlovna was only fifteen years old, and it's quite out of the question that anyone in the Romanov family would have touched it, even with very long tongs.'

'What about later on?' Bäckström persisted. 'What happened after the shipping agent died?'

'It was sold at auction by his descendants. At Christie's auction house in London, in the autumn of 1944. On that occasion it sold for one hundred and twenty pounds, which was a reasonable price at the time, considering the war that was raging throughout Europe. But of course it was only a fraction of the price that it reached when it went under the hammer at Sotheby's a few months ago.'

'So the picture's trail stops during the Second World War, in the autumn of 1944,' Bäckström summarized, stroking his chubby chin.

'Yes. It certainly doesn't seem to have appeared at any further exhibitions or auctions.'

'So what happened? Who bought it?' Bäckström nodded encouragingly at his host.

'No idea,' GeGurra said. 'As you've no doubt already realized, my assistants and I have conducted a fair bit of research on the matter. Among other things, my English contact has looked through Christie's records of that auction in the autumn of 1944. The buyer paid for the painting in cash. His name isn't listed. But there is a note that he wished to remain anonymous.'

'Cash? Dodgy,' Bäckström said. Fucking dodgy.

'Not really,' GeGurra said with a shrug. 'The price wasn't particularly remarkable, and plenty of buyers used to prefer it that way. Not least a considerable number of my colleagues in the art business, I can tell you.'

'Then there's a gap of seventy years until it pops up again. Here in Sweden, in the hands of Eriksson the lawyer, who's been told to sell it on behalf of an unknown client.'

'Yes, that's a pretty good summary.'

'And you haven't got any idea where it's been all this time. I mean, everything seems to suggest that it had to be owned by someone Swedish? Why else would it turn up here?'

'I'm inclined to agree with you,' GeGurra said. 'So if you could help me with that little detail, I really would be extremely grateful.'

'So our baron is the man who sells it this spring. On the orders of the lawyer. Did he sell anything else at the same auction?' That faggy little nobleman seems to be up to his ears in this crap, he thought.

'There were three items from the collection that were

sold which Eriksson wanted to have valued,' GeGurra said. 'The icon, as well as the hunting service for maritime use which appears to have made such a deep impression on you. The third was a gold cigar-lighter. That was also made in St Petersburg in the early 1900s, to judge by the hallmark. But there was no inscription, nothing that could connect it to Prince Wilhelm. If you want my opinion, I'm still fairly confident that it was given to Prince Wilhelm by Maria Pavlovna. It was also produced by the most famous jeweller in St Petersburg at that time. His name was Carl Fabergé, and he was goldsmith to the imperial court. No doubt you've heard of him.'

'So what did it cost, the cigar-lighter?'

'I don't remember exactly, around a hundred thousand at auction, I think. Nothing remarkable, and about the same as it was originally bought for, if we take into account the change in the value of money over the years. There are quite a few from that time. A cigar-lighter was pretty much an essential accoutrement to every well-equipped gentleman's room. Even if this one did cost rather more than most,' GeGurra said, and shrugged his shoulders.

'What happened to the hunting service? What did he get for that?'

'I'm not sure "service" is quite the right word, really,' GeGurra said, shaking his head. 'It's a terribly tragic business, an absolute calamity.'

'Go on.'

79

According to GeGurra, the hunting service was an absolute calamity when it was sold at auction almost one hundred years after its delivery from the imperial porcelain factory in St Petersburg. In pristine condition, it would certainly have warranted a price of more than ten million Swedish kronor, as it was made to the excellent standards of the age, and given its provenance. A gift from a Russian grand duchess to a Swedish prince. The Houses of Romanov and Bernadotte on the same plate. This, alas, was not the case, as all that remained was just a tragic fragment of what had once been a hunting service for maritime use in 148 parts.

'Certainly not a bad gift to a young prince who had just been appointed a lieutenant in the Royal Swedish Navy and commander of the torpedo boat *Castor*,' GeGurra said. He evidently had an eye for romantic details.

'But all that remained was a mere thirty-nine pieces,' he went on. 'Most of those chipped and cracked. Soup dishes, sauce boats, saucers – a right mixture. There didn't seem to have been any method in the destruction that must have taken place. So it was a very tragic business,' GeGurra declared with a deep sigh, as deep as if he had been talking about a recently deceased and much-loved relative.

'He couldn't have had it with him, then? On that

torpedo boat he went about in? I mean, he could have got caught in a storm or something,' Bäckström suggested. By now he was open to any idea that would help all the pieces to fit into place. Preferably in the ownership of the Swedish crown.

'With all due respect, I find that very hard to believe. Firstly, I doubt there would have been room for it and, secondly, Wilhelm was extremely interested in art. And a thoughtful, careful man when it came to such matters. So that thought would almost certainly never even have occurred to him.'

'I hear what you're saying. So you weren't interested in buying it in the state it was in?'

'No, I certainly wasn't. Not for half a million, anyway,' GeGurra said. 'It probably ended up in the hands of one of those Russian oligarchs who presumably aren't remotely bothered about what things cost.'

'But that icon, you bought that?'

'Yes,' GeGurra said. 'Which took on an entirely new significance when Eriksson appeared and showed me pictures of it a couple of weeks later. When I asked him who he had used to value the items, I already had a good idea who it was.'

'But if you didn't think it was one of the items Willy got from that little Russian, I don't quite understand why you still bought it?'

'As you know, my dear friend, I make my living trading in art,' GeGurra said with a conciliatory smile. 'Besides, I already had a buyer who was interested. An old friend of mine who had expressed an interest in this particular painting. He was so interested, in fact, that he contacted me, rather than the other way round. He is still thinking about it, actually, even though it can hardly be a lack of money that's stopping him, so it's still in my storage room. In case you yourself might be interested, Bäckström. And, as it's you, you could have it at a specially reduced rate. What do you say to some dessert, by the way? Oscar II's meringue pie. Perhaps I might even be able to tempt you with some fine port to accompany it?'

'Cognac will do nicely,' Bäckström said. Who does he take me for? Surely only old bags drink port. And men who are halfway to being old bags, like GeGurra, he thought.

'By the way, did you know that Oscar II, the man who lent his name to the meringue, was Prince Wilhelm's grandfather? And he was the one who contacted the Russian tsar, Nicholas II, and suggested that his grandson should marry Maria Pavlovna. As a means to strengthen the bonds between the old arch-enemies, Sweden and Russia. To break with our bad old historical traditions, once and for all. We live in a small world, my friend. A very small world.'

What's this got to do with my meringue pie? Bäckström wondered, but made do with a grunt of agreement. GeGurra has a quite phenomenal ability to talk about all manner of crap that has nothing to do with the subject, he thought.

'This collection we've been talking about. How much is it worth? In total, I mean?' Bäckström asked. He was a man who was keen on basic facts.

'Fifteen icons, two sets of silver cutlery, the cigar-lighter, the hunting service . . . a total of nineteen objects. Once the remaining paintings have been sold, I imagine the total will be somewhere in the region of four million,' GeGurra said.

'That's a lot of money,' Bäckström said.

'I suppose so,' GeGurra replied. 'But, bearing in mind the final item in the collection, I'd suggest that it's an insignificant amount.'

'So what's that, then?' Bäckström asked. The twentieth item in the collection . . .

'I thought we might get to that presently but before that . . . if you'll excuse me . . . I thought I might go to the little boys' room and wash my hands while we wait for our just desserts,' GeGurra said, gesturing with his long, slender fingers. 'And while we're enjoying them, I thought I might finally get to the real reason why I wanted to see you, my dear friend.'

About bloody time, Bäckström thought, and nodded. Time for that nice fat, brown envelope.

GeGurra's obviously pretty thorough with his personal hygiene, Bäckström thought when his host returned ten minutes later. Having a piss shouldn't take more than a minute or so. All you needed was the right amount of pressure, and he usually took care of that detail every morning and every evening, whether or not it was actually necessary. Fortunately, he wasn't left sitting in the lurch in the meantime, because he had been brought a large cognac while he was waiting. GeGurra had also taken his briefcase with him when he went to the toilet, so there was no chance of passing the time by snooping about in it.

'I assume you're familiar with the story of Pinocchio's nose, Bäckström,' GeGurra said. 'The story of the little wooden puppet whose nose grew longer and longer when he told a lie.'

'Yes, although that never actually happens at work,' Bäckström said. 'If the people I come across had noses that grew whenever they told a lie, I wouldn't have any room left in my office. That applies to the whole lot of them, in case you're wondering. The crooks, the so-called victims of crime and my so-called colleagues. They all lie the whole time, about absolutely everything. And their noses don't grow by a single millimetre,' he declared with an emphatic nod.

'Is it really that bad?' GeGurra said with a gentle smile.

'Even worse, if you ask me,' Bäckström said. He was starting to feel upset about all the lies and betrayals, all the trickery and deceit that surrounded an honest man like himself, who was just trying to do his job.

'Pinocchio in the story,' GeGurra went on, sounding largely as if he were thinking out loud. 'Pinocchio means "pine eye" – did you know that, Bäckström? The Italian story of the poor woodcarver Gepetto who carves a puppet out of pinewood in the shape of a little boy, called Pinocchio, and the puppet suddenly comes to life and his nose grows each time he tells a lie. And only when he stops telling lies does he turn into a real little boy. A story we were all told when we were small.'

'Sure,' Bäckström agreed. 'I understand what you're saying, and in my line of work it would certainly be very practical. But, sadly, I've never believed it.' Not even when I was still in short trousers, he thought.

'The writer of the story of Pinocchio was an Italian. Carlo Lorenzini. He was an author, journalist and a right-wing politician, lived in Florence, and when he wrote the story he published it under a pseudonym, Carlo Collodi. The first parts, which actually appeared as a serial in a newspaper, were published in 1881, and the final chapter of Pinocchio's story, when he stops lying and becomes a real boy, was published in 1883. A total of forty or so chapters about Pinocchio's adventures. Collodi himself died in 1890. The story of Pinocchio has been translated into—'

'I know all that,' Bäckström interrupted. Here we go again. On, and on, and on.

'Oh—'

'I know all that,' Bäckström assured him. How can I shut the fucker up?

'But the true story of Pinocchio's nose, you haven't heard that one,' GeGurra said, lowering his voice and leaning forward.

'The true story?' Is he pissed, or what? Even though he's only been sitting there sipping his red wine all evening.

'The true story of Pinocchio's nose,' GeGurra repeated. 'About the time when Pinocchio's nose came close to changing the entire history of mankind. You've never heard that, have you?'

What's the bastard going on about now? Bäckström thought. The true story of Pinocchio's nose?

80

'The true story of Pinocchio's nose, the one which could very easily have changed the entire history of mankind, had it ended differently – you've never heard that story,' GeGurra said, turning his glass of port between his long, thin fingers. 'But I'm going to tell it to you and, obviously, I'm taking it as read that what I'm about to say will stay strictly between us.'

'You've got absolutely no need to worry on that score,' Bäckström assured him, taking a large gulp of cognac, realizing from GeGurra's expression that this was likely to take a while.

The true story of Pinocchio's nose is set in the St Petersburg court of the last tsar of Russia, Nicholas II, between the autumn of 1907 and the summer of 1908. Like all good stories, it has two main protagonists. Everyone else who appears in this story plays a supporting role, and the important thing is what happens between our two main characters.

The first of these is a young Italian woman, Anna Maria Francesca di Biondi, who is twenty-four years old when our story begins. Anna Maria was born and grew up in Florence, where she has spent most of her young life, apart from short trips abroad to France, Greece, Austria,

Switzerland, Germany, Poland and Tsarist Russia. Twenty or so short trips, spread across a life of almost as many years, and in that sense not particularly remarkable for a woman of her background and family. In her thoughts, however, she is constantly travelling. Anna Maria Francesca di Biondi is an extremely talented woman, and in her mind she is free to travel wherever she chooses, and do whatever she chooses with whomsoever she chooses.

In the reality in which she lives her life, there are other, stricter barriers, however. Anna Maria Francesca di Biondi is the daughter of an Italian marquis, who lives his life according to the same rules as her, laid down by traditions born of ancestry and the blood that tied socially privileged families together. Her father is a learned man, a linguist and a professor at the University of Florence, but – in a purely relative sense – he is not a wealthy man, and it is his financial circumstances rather than free will which have led him to contribute to his own and his family's upkeep by teaching at the university. If he could have chosen, he would surely have lived the life that only his imagination could offer him. He prefers the peace and quiet of his own library to the company of his colleagues and students. At the same time, it doesn't trouble him much because the reality around him, no matter how it manifests itself, can never match up to what is going on inside his head. The fact that Anna Maria Francesca is his favourite of his six children need not perhaps be mentioned.

Anna Maria also has a mother, a good and educated woman who divides her time between taking care of the practical concerns of her family and Christian charity for the Diocese of Florence. The fact that we, after such a brief description, choose to ignore her from now on has nothing to do with her character or activities. It is simply because she is of no interest when it comes to the true story of Pinocchio's nose. But her own mother, Anna Maria Francesca's grandmother, is of more interest. She is of Russian extraction, has lived in the same house as Anna Maria throughout her childhood and is also the reason why Anna Maria speaks fluent Russian.

Anna Maria's grandmother is the daughter of a Russian nobleman and general who fought against Napoleon one hundred years before. The general had chased the French oppressor from the sacred soil of Mother Russia, following him the whole way from Moscow to Europe, killing thousands of his soldiers as they were trying to cross the Berezina River, beating him in several skirmishes and battles in both Poland and Austria. Once the usurper had been vanquished, the general remained in the Europe that had been liberated from the French oppressor. First as the tsar's ambassador in Austro-Hungary and, towards the end of his life, as his envoy to the Holy See in Rome. The general lived in Italy until his death, and when after thirty years' service abroad his body was taken home to St Petersburg from the Vatican, it was in order to be buried with every conceivable honour and in the presence of the tsar himself.

One of his many daughters had, however, stayed in Italy. She had married an Italian count, and twenty years later one of her daughters married a learned man from Florence, himself a marquis. The marquis is also a very good person, and the only criticism his wife is willing to make of him is that he perhaps devotes more time to his own thoughts than to the practical demands that life makes of a married man and father.

In the summer of 1907 the di Biondi family receives a

visit in their large house in Florence from a distant relation of Anna Maria's grandmother, and it is Anna Maria that he has come to see – at least if the letters he wrote to the marquis and man of the house before his visit are to be believed. His name is Prince Sergei, a member of the great House of Romanov, a distant relative of the tsar and, like everyone else in the family, he is also incredibly rich. He is also a bad Russian. Bad in the sense that he prefers to spend most of his time in Europe while his stewards take care of his vast estates back home in Russia, which stretch all the way from Karelia in the north to Baku on the Caspian Sea in the south.

This summer he has come to Italy, on one of his many educational tours; he has forgotten how many he has already made, because the art, music and culture keep bringing him back. The art, music and culture but, to be honest, also the women and the food. Most of all the women, and the first time he sees Anna Maria he is hopelessly smitten.

Prince Sergei is almost thirty years older than Anna Maria, and there are five thousand kilometres between Florence and his palace in St Petersburg. Judging by the expression in her eyes, he has already realized that this would not be a significant problem. The real problem is that his putative father-in-law cannot even begin to imagine that his beloved daughter might leave him for a Russian who is the same age as him, to go and live in another country. In another world, and to live a different life from the one going on inside his head – if he were to consider the matter more closely, which, fortunately, he does not.

For Prince Sergei, on the other hand, his unknowing and putative father-in-law is a human problem, and he is used to dealing with those. That's the other side of his nature. Prince Sergei is a man of many parts. A man with a genuine love of art, culture, music, food and not least women, but he is also a practical man. He cancels the rest of his tour and stays in Florence all summer while he devotes his time to courting Anna Maria secretly and, most of all, making plans for the future. Approximately one month later he is ready and can present a detailed proposal to the marquis, who eventually gives his consent, and even his approval. Entirely unaware of what is really going on.

The family's beloved maternal grandmother has expressed a strong desire to visit, one last time, the Russia where she has her roots, and it is she who has taken the initiative. But she is starting to get old, and it is worth considering that she might need the company of a close, younger relative on the journey, and, if it were up to her, she would prefer to have Anna Maria with her. Anna Maria herself is more than willing, and gives the same reason as her grandmother, that she wishes to explore her Russian roots. This leaves merely the practical arrangements, which Prince Sergei will carry out down to the last detail, and entirely in accordance with the marquis's wishes. Anything else would be unthinkable. He wouldn't dream of going against these self-evident wishes of his beloved Italian kinsfolk – family ties and nobility together are assurances of that.

He has already organized a companion for the elderly grandmother, a chaperone for Anna Maria Francesca and maids for the pair of them. As far as the rest of the company is concerned, his own exalted personage and the nature of the journey have dictated the circumstances. Sergei's adjutant, his personal secretary, three servants, two bodyguards and the usual half-dozen maids and lackeys to wash his clothes and carry heavier items of luggage. And of course Prince Sergei himself.

Towards the end of August they leave by train from Florence railway station. The journey to St Petersburg will take three weeks, because they will be taking it slowly and stopping along the way whenever they feel like doing something else. The company has three carriages for its exclusive use. One for the elderly grandmother, Anna Maria Francesca, Prince Sergei and their closest attendants. One carriage for the remainder of the staff and one for the luggage. Anna Maria Francesca has brought ten trunks for her own use, seven more than originally planned, but Sergei had spent their last week in Florence taking her round all the shops in order to procure a few extra things she would need for the journey.

It is Prince Sergei who is the instigator of this story: in a dramaturgical and narrative sense, he is what is usually known as a 'facilitator', and the reason why he 'facilitates' has nothing to do with the true story of Pinocchio's nose. His motive is extremely personal, and it is hard to conceive of a real man like him having nobler intentions than that. The parts of the story concerning his love for Anna Maria will also end happily for all concerned. For Anna Maria Francesca and for him too, for Anna Maria's grandmother and mother, for her five siblings and for her beloved father.

Not least for her beloved father. Admittedly, it will be almost a year before she returns to Florence, which is numerous months later than Sergei had indicated to her father when he gave his blessing to the trip. He will learn that they have taken the opportunity to marry in secret on the way home to Florence by way of a telegram that reaches his house only a week before they do, and it will be another month before he learns that she is already with child. But by the time they step off the train he has already forgiven them both, and he greets them with open arms.

How could he do anything else? His daughter is more beautiful than ever, and in her eyes he can see that the life she is now living is closer to her thoughts than the life she was living when she left him one year earlier.

Anna Maria Francesca di Biondi is a very beautiful young woman. Much more beautiful than all the other women Prince Sergei has met in his life. She is a highly talented woman, and speaks several languages. She is also extremely musical. She has a beautiful voice, a rich mezzosoprano that ranges with no audible effort across the scale of whatever it is she has chosen to perform. She plays a number of instruments and can when necessary – and with the greatest of ease – accompany herself on the piano, guitar or mandolin.

Because Sergei has promised to present her at the tsar's court, she had also brought with her from her homeland presents for the imperial children. Fans of the thinnest ricepaper, shawls of the finest Italian silk, artistic Venetian masks for the spring balls, gifts for the four daughters, Olga, Tatiana, Mari and Anastasia.

For their little brother, Alexei, the tsarevich, just three years old, she has brought a more personal gift. Forty issues of the Florentine weekly magazine *Giornale di Bambini*, published between 1881 and 1883. The story of Pinocchio, the entire richly illustrated tale about the little boy whose nose grew longer whenever he told a lie. A story from her own childhood, which she took to her heart when she was the same age as Alexei. In her imagination, she has already begun to read it out loud to him long before she steps off the train at the station in St Petersburg.

Alexei, the tsarevich, who is the second protagonist in the true story of Pinocchio and his nose.

81

What a uniquely long-winded bastard, Bäckström thought. The object of his ire was his host, GeGurra, who seemed utterly entranced by all the words that were flowing in a ceaseless torrent from his well-oiled lips.

Your average Polish pedlar would look autistic in comparison with this bugger, Bäckström thought. He had picked up that difficult word at one of the many police conferences he usually attended as soon as the weekend was in sight. He occasionally used it himself when he was questioning crims who just sat there and said nothing the whole time. A couple of times it had actually worked, because the crims wanted to know what sort of verbal insult their questioner was throwing at them and opened their mouths for that very reason. But GeGurra evidently suffered from the exact opposite, and there was no point even trying to say anything because it would be like pissing in the wind.

So for the past quarter of an hour he had contented himself with listening with half an ear while he nursed his cognac and tried to focus on the brown envelope that he had more or less been promised. Even though he really ought to have said thank you for the meal, then stood up and walked out. Instead, he was sitting there on the back of the lame snail that was slowly carrying him towards the goal of this particular journey, a victim of his excessive tolerance and good-natured willingness to do whatever people asked of him. By now he was starting to feel slightly aggrieved at the way GeGurra was exploiting him.

'Is there anything you're wondering about so far, Bäckström?' GeGurra asked, giving him a look that was a little too perceptive for Bäckström's taste.

'Only when you were likely to get to the point,' Bäckström replied. 'I may not have made any firm plans for the rest of the night, but—'

'I'm getting to that, my dear friend,' GeGurra interrupted, patting him cheerily on the hand. 'I shall soon be getting to the point, which is why it's important that you pay attention now that the story is starting to come together.'

82

Anna Maria and her grandmother have been installed in Prince Sergei's palace on the banks of the River Neva in St Petersburg. A five-minute ride by horse and carriage from the Alexander Palace where the tsar and his family spend most of their time at this part of the year. In short, and in summary, it can be said that they are unlikely to suffer any hardships during the ten months they will be living there. Two hundred rooms and around a hundred servants, and the suite which Anna Maria has at her disposal for herself and her maid consists of six rooms and lies directly next to Prince Sergei's own apartment. Big enough, perhaps even one room larger than she really needs, as for some time she has been spending her nights in Sergei's bedchamber.

Anna Maria's grandmother, on the other hand, lives at the other end of the house together with her staff, and if her father, the marquis, had known about these arrangements he would surely have been both surprised and concerned. But how could he have any idea about them, seeing as he was at the other end of Europe, and the letters which arrived several times a week from his daughter and her elderly grandmother had nothing to say about such trivialities?

They are instead concerned with matters raised high

above the mundane. Not least with how well they are being cared for, the generous hospitality they are enjoying, and how Anna Maria has been presented at the tsar's court after only a couple of weeks. Most of the letters are full of stories from the imperial court. Of how Anna Maria is soon spending several days each week at the Alexander Palace, as a companion to the tsar's four daughters.

Not merely as a companion, for that matter. She is also their music teacher, language tutor and storyteller from the distant land of Italy, which, especially during the autumn months, when darkness and cold close in on St Petersburg, arouses their fantasies about another life. Happier, warmer and brighter than the one that awaits them at home during the long Russian winter.

And of course she is beautiful, their very own Anna Maria Francesca, with her dark, gently curled hair, her sparkling eyes and her wide smile. She takes the lead in all their games and activities, and the fans, silk shawls and Venetian masks that she brought with her are all put to good use. They all love Anna Maria Francesca, from twelve-year-old Olga to little Anastasia, who has just turned six, and, after just one week, they receive an unexpected visit.

Their little brother, Alexei, is standing in the doorway in the company of two large, silent men in cossacks' uniforms. A little boy of three, dressed in a blue sailor-suit with long trousers. One of the cossacks is holding a small balalaika in his huge hand, while their little brother gives his sisters an imperious look. With one hand he gestures for them to leave the room, so that he can be alone with their Italian companion.

How fat he looks, even though his face is so thin, Anna Maria Francesca thinks in surprise as she stands up from the grand piano, bows her head and curtsies deeply to the tsarevich.

It is late that evening that she learns of the secret which is never mentioned outside the family.

'He suffers from haemophilia,' Sergei explains. 'He inherited it from his mother. But he isn't fat. It's his clothes, he walks around covered with padding.'

To protect him, heavy padding has been sewn into all his clothes. The slightest little scratch could kill him, because it is practically impossible to stop him bleeding.

'One fall, one bump, one blow, even as little as a scuffed knee, could kill him. The previous winter he had caught himself on a table and spent the whole spring in bed suffering from severe internal bleeding,' Sergei explains.

'*Cara mia, mia cara*, it's a very tragic business,' Sergei sighs as he strokes her cheeks and forehead with his fingertips. Now that he's lying beside her, he'd prefer to talk of other things. As full of life as he is, he doesn't want to think about death for a moment.

Alexei is three years old the first time he meets Anna Maria Francesca di Biondi. Fifty years younger than his relative, Sergei. Despite the difference in age, and the human activities that are contingent on such things, his heart is full of the same feelings as Sergei's, and just one week after their first meeting he is sitting in Anna Maria's lap with his head resting against her large breasts as she reads out loud to him about a little boy whose nose grew whenever he told a lie.

Anna Maria translates the story into Russian as she reads, leaving some Italian words in and explaining what they mean, pointing and showing him all the pictures.

When the story is finished, she carefully runs her forefinger down Alexei's own nose, while Alexei smiles and nestles closer to her warm body. The warm, soft body that smells so good.

Alexei is transformed. He stops sliding along the polished floors, stops running through the corridors and rooms without the slightest thought of what might happen if he were to fall, stops climbing the trees out in the park. All those trees, where the slenderest birch could kill both him and his guards if he were to fall.

Instead, he sits quietly in Anna Maria's lap while she reads to him, sits solemnly at her side in front of the grand piano while she helps him to find the right notes, collapsing into fits of laughter when he gets it so wrong that he himself notices. Little Alexei is transformed, and his father, Tsar Nicholas II, notes what he sees with approval. From a distance, naturally, three rooms away in the long suite facing the river. So that he can see them without them seeing him.

Each new day is not merely a gift from life but also brings with it the hope that his son might survive the childhood which constantly threatens to snatch his life away from him. One day, one moment at a time, until he is finally old enough to understand the circumstances governing his existence. Old enough to be able to take control of the Russia he will one day inherit from his father.

Is it perhaps that music, those songs and those stories that will save his beloved Russia? Nicholas thinks. That would certainly be remarkable, considering everything that has saved the Russian people over the past five hundred years. All those warriors, not least the general who was the great-grandfather of the Italian woman who is now sitting on the velvet bench in front of the grand piano in the large music room of the Alexander Palace, where she is trying to teach his young son to play the balalaika.

It is natural that he should think of her great-grandfather. The old general who served under his grandfather, Alexander I. The hero of Berezina, who rode in the vanguard of the imperial dragoon regiment on a black charger, sabre at the ready. Exactly as he does on the large painting of the battle that hangs in the gallery on the second floor.

He may well also have reflected upon the moment when he arrived home one afternoon several months before, after a ride in the park. When he entered the great marble hall on the ground floor of the palace, he immediately saw his cousin Maria Pavlovna sitting on a silver tray on the top step of the steep staircase. In her lap sat his only son, Tsarevich Alexei. And Maria pulled at the edge of the top step and sent them flying down the staircase. He can still see it, and hear it too. The sound as the tray hit each new step as it flew down, louder and louder, coming faster and faster. With Maria Pavlovna and Alexei shrieking with delight the whole way down.

That time everything had been all right. Even though Alexei's guards had stood there paralysed, hapless bystanders. Even though he himself had stood there rooted to the spot, unable to move, unable to utter a word to stop what was happening right in front of his eyes. That time everything had gone all right, even though he evidently couldn't even trust a close relative who was a grown woman, almost eighteen years old, and on the point of marrying a Swedish prince.

Only later had things changed. When music, songs and

stories became part of his child's life. Inextricably linked to their Italian companion and tutor, Anna Maria. And this is when he gets an idea of what to give Alexei as an Easter present. A logical and perfectly obvious idea, considering what is going on around him, and inside his own head. The present may well cost as much as the diamond-encrusted golden eggs he has traditionally given his wife and mother on the occasion of the greatest holiday of the year. A present which on closer reflection could be permitted to cost any amount at all, if it could secure the imperial succession and save his Russia.

'No doubt you're wondering what it was?' GeGurra asked, looking at his guest inquisitively. 'The present, I mean, the one the tsar was going to give to his haemophiliac son.'

'Yes, I can hardly contain myself.' Bäckström sighed, glancing at his watch. This will have to be my last cognac, because I'm fucked off with this now, he thought.

'A musical box,' GeGurra said. 'Not just any musical box, but the most remarkable musical box ever created in all of human history.'

A musical box. Now where have I heard that before?

83

A musical box, but not just any musical box. The most remarkable musical box ever created in all of human history. GeGurra also seemed to know everything that was worth saying about it. It had taken him quite a while, and required numerous digressions along the way before he got to the musical box itself.

Bäckström had more or less given up. He had ordered another cognac, and was now leaning back and trying not to listen. What choice did he have? Sticking his hand into GeGurra's briefcase, grabbing the brown envelope and running off was clearly no longer an option.

'I'm listening,' Bäckström said.

Carl Fabergé was a jeweller in St Petersburg, by appointment to the imperial court, and there was no doubt that his most significant customers were the tsar and his family. His company created pretty much anything that could be made with precious metals and precious stones and, as the company's customers wanted the best, most of the artefacts were made of gold and diamonds.

'All manner of jewellery, of course, but also clocks, snuff-boxes, cutlery, dinner services, photograph frames, ornaments and miniatures. Anything you can imagine made out of gold, silver and precious stones. Of course,

Fabergé is now most famous for his Easter eggs. Fifty-seven of them in total, given by the tsar as Easter presents to the tsarina and, later on, to his mother as well. Those eggs, made out of gold, jewels and enamel, are what has given Carl Fabergé a place in art history comparable to that of a latter-day Cellini,' GeGurra summarized.

'You don't say. This Cellini,' Bäckström said, having a vague notion that he had heard the name in some sort of work-related context at some point. 'What does he have to do with the story?' Must be a dago, with a name like that. Dagos are never good, he thought.

'What does Cellini have to do with this story?' GeGurra said, looking at his guest in surprise. 'Nothing at all, if you really want to know.'

'How can you be so certain?' Bäckström countered.

'Benvenuto Cellini died in 1571. He's regarded as the greatest jeweller in the history of art. He came from Florence as well. The reason I mentioned him was to help you appreciate how great Fabergé is.'

'Oh, okay,' Bäckström said. 'How about trying to stick to that musical box? Like I said, I haven't got anything planned for tonight, and of course the night is still young, but—'

'My dear friend,' GeGurra interrupted, patting him on the arm again. 'I'm getting to that.'

'The musical box,' Bäckström said. 'I want to hear about the musical box.'

'It's a remarkable story,' GeGurra said. 'Not least considering what Fabergé had produced up until then. Even though they had made all manner of objects, including clocks, both larger pieces and pocket watches, they had never made a musical box.'

'But now they did,' Bäckström said. At last, he thought.

'Yes, they did,' GeGurra confirmed. 'Even though they

later denied having done so. Which perhaps seems a little strange, given that the musical box is unequalled in the history of Western art.'

'So what was so remarkable about it, then?' Bäckström asked. Sounds pricey, he thought. Still, we seem to be getting somewhere at last.

Fabergé's musical box was unique. Unlike most conventional musical boxes, where the notes are produced with the help of combs, bells, discs, needles, strings and metal cylinders, set in motion by a spring mechanism, this one was constructed like a flute, and the man who came up with the idea was also the composer of the twenty-second-long tune of Fabergé's musical box.

'Nikolai Rimsky-Korsakov,' GeGurra said with a contented sigh. 'You'll have heard the name, no doubt. World-famous composer, conductor and professor at the St Petersburg conservatory. He was given the task by the tsar, and he knew exactly what was required. A tune played on a flute, starting and ending in a minor key. This struck him as utterly obvious, given the context that the music was supposed to illustrate.'

'A flute,' Bäckström said. 'So what was the problem?' Surely it could hardly have been much simpler? Except perhaps that triangle he was given to bash away at in primary school when all the other kids in the class were playing recorders, he thought.

The technical difficulties were enormous, according to GeGurra, but considering who the client was and the fact that it was the first musical box they had produced, Carl Fabergé hadn't wanted to leave anything to chance.

'For the purely mechanical part of the commission he had employed the finest clockmaker of the time, Anton

Hügel, who did most of his work for Patek Philippe in Geneva, and, in close collaboration with Rimsky-Korsakov, he had eventually solved the practical problems.'

'I still don't understand,' Bäckström persisted. 'A flute? Surely that couldn't have been that difficult?'

'It was,' GeGurra said. 'When you play a flute, you blow air through a tube into which the air passes over a sharp edge and through holes of different sizes and at different distances. And you produce the notes and tune by the positioning of your fingers. You open and close the holes using your fingers. But, in this instance, it was Pinocchio's nose that was going to function as a flute, and the idea that he was going to hold and keep fiddling with his nose the whole time was obviously out of the question, even if that would have been simpler to solve from a purely technical point of view. People have managed to make musical boxes with plenty of moving parts since they were first produced at the end of the eighteenth century.'

'Why?' Bäckström said. Why couldn't he just have fiddled with his nose the whole time? People do that the whole time when they're lying, he thought.

'When the tune plays, it's because Pinocchio is telling lies,' GeGurra said. 'That was the idea. And so his nose starts to grow. It gets longer and longer until he falls silent. And then it stops growing. So the nose has to function as a flute without being touched by any fingers, because that would ruin the whole conceit. That's the whole point of the story of Pinocchio. That he doesn't know that his nose grows when he tells lies.'

'So how did they solve it?' Bäckström said. A flute in the shape of a nose, he thought. Must be pretty hard to beat, for an old faggot like GeGurra.

* * *

In a number of different ways, according to GeGurra. The musical box itself, in the shape of Pinocchio, was thirty-one and a half centimetres tall. It was made of gold, but enamelled in different colours. The mechanism inside the box was driven by a powerful spring that was tightened by a key that was inserted into the base of the box, and as the spring was tightened, it sucked air into a small bladder inside the box. When the spring was tight and the bladder full of air, the box could be switched on.

The air was forced out across a metal tongue in a hole at the top, and through the holes in the underside of the growing nose, where the holes were opened and closed by a rod being moved back and forth inside the nose. That was how the tune was produced. When the tune was over and the nose had stopped growing, the last tension in the spring was used to withdraw the nose again after a four-second pause.

'Abracadabra,' GeGurra said, sounding almost as proud as Rimsky-Korsakov and Anton Hügel must have been when they completed their assignment some hundred years before.

'But when it was finished, presumably you had to wind it up again?' Bäckström asked.

'Naturally,' GeGurra said, giving his guest a look of disapproval. 'No little electric motor with a battery, if that's what you think is missing, because such things had, fortunately, not been invented at the time. Instead, there was an incredibly intricate spring mechanism which filled a bladder made out of reinforced balloon silk with air, and transformed a nose into a flute with the help of the extension of the nose. We're talking artistic craftsmanship here, my friend, and there could scarcely be a finer example of craftsmanship anywhere.'

'You said it was made of gold,' Bäckström said slowly. He was struggling somewhat with his short-term memory as the admittedly excellent cognac fought back.

'Only the best was good enough for Carl Fabergé and his most prestigious customer,' GeGurra declared. 'The box was made of gold but covered in enamel of various colours. Pinocchio has a red cap, a yellow jacket and green trousers, and the total weight of the actual box is a little less than a kilo. But if that's what we're talking about, we mustn't forget the key or the case in which the musical box was kept.'

'Tell me,' Bäckström said. Now we're getting somewhere, he thought, as the cognac had just given up and his short-term memory was suddenly working perfectly again. That little figure with the red cap clearly wasn't some ordinary whisky carafe, he thought.

'The key that was used to wind up the musical box was made of gold as well, white gold,' GeGurra said. 'It was also set with twelve diamonds, a total of thirty-two carats. As far as the case is concerned, the one the musical box was kept in, it was made of ebony and jacaranda, with gold inlays and reinforcement. There's also some onyx intarsia work on the lid, in the shape of the imperial double-headed eagle. As I said earlier, Bäckström, Carl Fabergé wasn't a man who left anything to chance.'

At last, Bäckström thought, but made do with a nod. Now he had to think quickly. Not show his cards unnecessarily. GeGurra is more than capable of stealing your fingers from you when you shake hands on a deal, he thought.

84

Fortunately for Bäckström, who needed some time to think, GeGurra didn't want to talk about money when he resumed his story.

'The musical box was ready in good time for the Easter celebrations in 1908. As usual, everyone was given their presents on Easter Saturday. Of course, Easter was the biggest festivity in those days. Alexei's mother and grandmother each received an egg. Maria Pavlovna, who of course was the tsar's cousin and had grown up in the tsar's family since she was a young girl, is said to have received a full set of jewellery for gala occasions in advance of her impending marriage – bracelet, necklace, earrings and tiara, all in white gold, set with diamonds and sapphires. There was no skimping, if I can put it like that,' GeGurra said with a contented smile.

'Perish the thought,' Bäckström said, suddenly in a quite excellent mood. Not the sort of woman you're likely to pick up on the internet, he thought.

'Happiest of all was little Alexei,' GeGurra said. 'There was no doubt that his musical box was the best present he had ever been given. Every day he would play it, and he was just as pleased each time Pinocchio's nose started to grow. I'd imagine that it was his beloved music teacher, Anna Maria, who had to wind it up for him.'

Well, he does seem to have been a bit soft in the head, Bäckström thought, but satisfied himself with a grunt of agreement. Probably not all that surprising, really, given all the inbreeding that lot got up to.

'His delight lasted until a week or so before the big wedding between Maria Pavlovna and Prince Wilhelm,' GeGurra sighed.

'What happened then?'

'A terrible accident,' GeGurra said. 'Alexei's cherished musical box almost managed to kill him.'

'What the fuck are you saying?' Bäckström for some reason found himself thinking about little Edvin. How had that happened?

'At a guess, he put Pinocchio's nose in his mouth,' GeGurra said. 'Little children do that sort of thing, of course, they try to put things in their mouths and suck on them.'

'Go on,' Bäckström said. Now we're really getting somewhere, he thought.

The accident happened eight days before the big wedding. At night, Alexei's cherished musical box was kept in a cupboard in the dressing room next to his bedchamber. That night, he must have woken up and gone to get it. The two guards who were supposed to protect him round the clock must have been fast asleep, as not even the sound of the musical box woke them.

Alexei lies in bed, playing with the musical box, and it's unclear how Pinocchio's growing nose ends up in his mouth – if he puts it there himself or if it ends up there while he was dozing. He suffers severe cuts to his gums, tongue and throat and, when his guards are finally woken by the gurgling sounds he's making, he's well on the way to choking on his own blood.

'It was the holes on the underside of the nose that injured him, the holes that made Pinocchio's nose work as a flute,' GeGurra explained. 'Their edges were very sharp, and because neither Hügel nor Rimsky-Korsakov was aware of his illness, they hadn't taken it into consideration at all. If they had, no doubt they would have constructed a more traditional musical box.'

Little Alexei had floated between life and death for several days. Tsar Nicholas was in a desperate state, and his wife, Alexandra, was unable to offer him any comfort. She was confined to her bed, and the idea that she might be able to provide him with a new heir if the worst happened was out of the question. It was also her side of the family that had introduced haemophilia into the Romanov dynasty. So everyone had set their hopes on Rasputin.

'Rasputin,' GeGurra said, shaking his head. 'You must have heard of him, Bäckström?'

'I've heard the name,' Bäckström answered with a shrug. Wasn't he some old Russian serial killer?

'Grigori Rasputin had arrived at the tsar's court three years earlier. He was the son of a peasant, a monk and religious mystic, but the reason he ended up at the imperial court was that he was also a healer and was supposed to possess miraculous powers. He had treated Alexei on several previous occasions and had managed to stem his bleeding with the help of hypnosis and the laying on of hands. Quite how is unclear, but it seemed to work, and it did so again on this occasion. Just a couple of days before the wedding, Alexei was out of danger. He remained in bed for several more weeks, which is why he doesn't appear in the family photographs of Maria Pavlovna's wedding, but he recovers, he survives, and Rasputin's power at court is greater than ever. In spite of the fact that he was, in other respects, a fairly primitive person.'

'Primitive? How do you mean?'

'The name Rasputin was adopted. His real name was Grigori Novich. In Russian, "Rasputin" means a lewd, dissolute person, and he certainly lived up to the name. There's no doubt about that. He had a terrible weakness for women and drink, and other drugs too, for that matter, a proper rake. The year before the revolution, in 1916, he was murdered by a group of noblemen from the tsar's court. They must have got fed up with him in the end. According to legend, it took a ridiculous number of bullets and knife wounds before he finally died.'

'Tragic story,' Bäckström said with a nod. Sad end to a decent bloke, he thought. Dare say the only thing he did wrong was having it off with their other halves.

'The most interesting thing about this story of Pinocchio's nose almost killing little Alexei is the political thoughts going through the tsar's mind at the time. Quite a lot has emerged from recent historical research into the Romanov family. Things that are of great political interest, I mean.'

'Is that something you could explain in more detail?' Bäckström asked. He needed more time to think, and now had no problem with GeGurra banging on while he did so.

'Of course, of course,' GeGurra assured him, scarcely able to conceal his surprise. 'It's certainly not a secret, but the point of what these historians claim is that, if Alexei had died, the tsar would probably have chosen to abdicate. The more liberal forces in Russian society at that time would have stood a good chance of taking over, and most of the evidence suggests that there wouldn't have been a revolution. The Bolsheviks would never have been able to take power the way they did in the revolution of 1917, and Lenin would have become a historical footnote. Not the founder of the greatest dictatorship in world history.'

'Is that so?' Bäckström said, nodding interestedly.

'I'm not the only one to think that,' GeGurra said. 'It's the conclusion that many notable Russian historians have reached today. I, of course, am only a simple dilettante when it comes to politics, but what I've read on the subject has left quite an impression.'

Bäckström nodded again, which was more than enough encouragement for GeGurra to carry on.

Not the usual political musings on the theme of what might have been. No, serious historical research from the past few years, and – for some reason – research which has only been possible since Russia shrugged off the Soviet yoke. 'Since the search for the truth is no longer being directed by politicians,' as GeGurra chose to sum up the situation.

At the time of his son's accident with the musical box given to him by his father, Tsar Nicholas was tormented by political doubts. The Russian people were suffering. There was great, and growing, social tension. Large parts of the middle class and many leading academics were openly opposed to him. After the failure of the war against Japan, he had also realized that he could no longer rely on his own military. There had been armed revolts in several regiments and units of the army and navy. During the 1905 revolution, the Winter Palace in St Petersburg had been stormed, in the belief that he and his family were there. The intention had been to take them captive, depose him from the throne, and perhaps even kill him and members of his family.

The things that are going on around him, things he can see with his own eyes, hear with his own ears, have little in common with what his closest advisors are telling him to do. Russian aristocrats, soldiers and the owners of estates the size of some European countries, men who are implacable, belligerent, unwilling to make even the slightest compromise, men who are unwilling to hold out a single finger to the Russian people, let alone a hand.

And then his beloved son suffers this latest accident, because of a gift he himself has given him, which very nearly kills him. Tsar Nicholas is in despair, and the night after the accident he makes a confession to his personal spiritual guide. If his son dies, this can only be a sign from God that Nicholas no longer has His support. Which would mean that he would withdraw and hand over power to the men who may have opposed him and his way of leading Russia but were, nonetheless, men who can be reasoned with.

'But of course that isn't what happened,' GeGurra said. 'Alexei survives and, according to the tsar's advisors, the good Lord couldn't give a stronger sign than that. Everything must remain as it has always been, carry on just as before, and nine years later the Russian Revolution is a political fact. And of course the whole process was only accelerated by the immense Russian losses during the First World War.' GeGurra nodded thoughtfully, as even political dilettantes are prone to doing.

'So what happened to the musical box? Once the little lad was better, I mean,' Bäckström asked. He had finished thinking and wanted to get back to the more pertinent financial matters as quickly as possible.

The tsar had given the musical box to Maria Pavlovna – on condition that she took it to Sweden so that he would never have to set eyes on it again and be reminded of what had happened.

'According to some sources, she specifically asked for it,' GeGurra said. 'If she hadn't, it would probably have been sent back to Fabergé.'

'But it wasn't,' Bäckström said. Mustn't forget that business with the province, he thought.

'No,' GeGurra confirmed. 'But it was removed from their records. The business of Alexei's illness was a state secret, of course, but people talk, and presumably they were perfectly aware that what had happened really wasn't terribly pleasant. Not least for Carl Fabergé and his jewellery company. But the fact that it was created for the tsar is beyond all doubt.'

'You're quite sure about that?' Bäckström said. 'Entirely sure?'

'Entirely sure. The Communists took over the business in 1918. Client records and stock and everything. And, of course, the client records were of particular interest to them, because they planned to reclaim what they believed Fabergé's customers had stolen from the Russian people. But Fabergé and his colleagues weren't stupid, and had already tried to remove anything that could lead back to the most sensitive of their clients. So there was no record of the tsar ever having ordered a musical box. According to the order book and their client records, anyway. When modern historians went through Fabergé's old files – and there were vast amounts when the archive was finally opened up in the early nineties – they were able to find both Hügel's designs, descriptions of the work, orders for the components and invoices. There is also a comprehensive amount of correspondence with Rimsky-Korsakov. Even his music, in various different versions that were produced as the work progressed. The fact that Carl Fabergé produced a musical box in the shape of Pinocchio is categorically beyond doubt.'

I'm inclined to agree with you, as I've held it in my hand, Bäckström thought, and nodded.

The existence of the musical box was a fact. But far more was shrouded in mystery as a result of the chaos that had followed the revolution, and not least the fact that almost all of those most closely involved had lost their lives.

'The tsar and all his family, including Alexei, who was thirteen years old by then, were murdered by the Communists in the summer of 1918. The same fate befell hundreds more members of the Russian aristocracy and the Romanov dynasty.'

'What about the Italian woman? She was the one who started it, wasn't she, if I've understood correctly? The business with Pinocchio, I mean.'

'For her and Sergei, the story actually has a happy ending. They left Russia just a couple of months after the wedding between Maria Pavlovna and Prince Wilhelm. Sergei may have been a bad Russian, but he was also a very crafty Russian, so he prepared in good time and transferred most of his fortune to Europe. They got married and moved to Italy, dividing their time between the palace in Florence and the French Riviera, where they had a magnificent villa built on Cap Ferrat, and travelled all round Europe and the rest of the world. Beautiful Anna Maria Francesca di Biondi went on to have seven children with Prince Sergei. She died in 1975 at the age of ninety-two. Her husband lived to a very respectable age as well. He may have been twenty-eight years older than her, but he's supposed to have been over ninety when he shuffled off this mortal coil.'

'Okay,' Bäckström said, throwing his hands out. 'So what can I do for you?'

'Several things,' GeGurra said with an amiable nod.

'I'm listening.'

'To start with, you can help me find eleven icons and one musical box,' GeGurra said. 'If I've understood correctly, our lawyer, Eriksson, was murdered in his home out in Ålsten.'

'Correct,' Bäckström said with a nod. 'That's no secret.'

'If I know you at all, my dear friend, by this time you will be very familiar with the situation at the crime scene.'

'There's nothing for you to worry about on that score,' Bäckström said. 'The sad thing about that is that we haven't found any icons, or a musical box.'

'Not good,' GeGurra said with a concerned shake of his head. 'Of course, he could have had them in storage somewhere. You wouldn't be able to look into that while you're investigating his affairs?'

'By all means,' Bäckström said. 'But I'm afraid to say there's information which suggests that might not have been the case, and this must stay strictly between us.'

'What?'

'Witness statements,' Bäckström said, with a heavy, sombre nod. 'According to witnesses we've spoken to, two people, probably the perpetrators, were seen carrying out some white removal boxes immediately after Eriksson was beaten to death. If there had been any old Russian paintings in the house, I dare say we would have found them. There weren't any. I can promise you that much.'

'What you've just said saddens me greatly,' GeGurra

said. From the look on his face, it wasn't the nature of Eriksson's death that was troubling him.

'It'll work out,' Bäckström said with a shrug. 'Is there anything else I can help you with?'

'Two more things, perhaps. Firstly, how that painting by Versjagin ended up among all those others. It's a complete mystery. Quite regardless of the fact that it was painted by a Russian artist, it has no business being in that collection. It was never owned by either Maria Pavlovna or Prince Wilhelm. It was bought at auction in London towards the end of the Second World War, only to pop up here in Sweden seventy years later. It just doesn't make sense.'

'And the second thing?' Bäckström said. 'What's that?' Things usually make sense, sooner or later, he thought, wise, as he was, from experience.

'The business of provenance,' said GeGurra. 'First, Maria Pavlovna, then Prince Wilhelm, that much is clear. I could do with knowing what happened to the pieces after that. The idea that Wilhelm's son, Lennart, could have inherited them doesn't seem terribly likely, as he's spent almost his whole life abroad, whereas most of the evidence suggests that the various items never left Sweden.'

'You want to know who commissioned Eriksson to sell the pieces,' Bäckström said. 'But you mentioned something about me falling off my chair when you told me who you thought it might be.'

'The evidence suggests that it ought to be a relative of Prince Wilhelm. When I asked Eriksson, all he would say was that the collection had been owned by the same family for three generations, but of course there are quite a few Bernadottes to choose from. I haven't managed to get anywhere with my own investigations, but there ought to be a power of attorney, something like that, if Eriksson was representing a client, as he claimed. A power of attorney given to Eriksson by his client, I mean.'

'What about the king himself?' Bäckström asked.

'Thinking of the provenance, that would undeniably be a true blessing,' GeGurra said with a happy smile. 'But no, to be honest I don't think we can hope for that. As far as I am aware, His Majesty has never sold anything from his private collections, and I don't believe he's under any pressing need for money. If we assume, just for the sake of it, that that was the case, I have great difficulty imagining that he would turn to Eriksson and Baron von Comer.'

'He's got quite a few kids, though,' Bäckström suggested. Might be time to check out that bloke from Ockelbo, the one who married the crown princess, he thought. Before he became a prince he used to own an old gym of some sort, and that business is crawling with jokers, he thought.

'Like I said, there are plenty of Bernadottes to choose from, and most of the evidence seems to suggest that one of them is involved in this,' GeGurra agreed. 'If I could have just one wish,' he went on, 'naturally, it would be for you to find that musical box I've told you about. It is an artistic artefact of global importance, after all. Compared to all the rest of it, which is somewhat lacking in interest.'

'Yes, of course,' Bäckström said, stroking his nose. 'Well, we shouldn't throw in the towel just yet. I promise to do what I can. I don't suppose you've got a picture of the musical box, so I know what I'm meant to be looking for?'

'Of course I have,' GeGurra said, opening his brown

briefcase and taking out two photographs, then passing them to Bäckström.

There you are, Bäckström thought. The same pointed red hat, yellow jacket and green trousers as that character he'd shaken so carefully, thinking it was an enamelled carafe containing an incredibly exclusive type of whisky. One picture with the nose retracted, like when he had held it in his hand, and one with the nose out. At full length, once Pinocchio had finished lying on that occasion.

'One question, out of curiosity,' Bäckström said. 'How much is the musical box worth?'

'It's priceless,' GeGurra said. 'Quite priceless,' he repeated, throwing his hands out.

'You couldn't be a bit more specific?' Bäckström said. You old rogue, he thought.

'If you could find the right buyer . . . ideally one of those Russian oligarchs . . . somewhere in the region of two hundred million. Swedish kronor, that is.'

What the fuck did he just say?

'Two hundred million,' GeGurra repeated, nodding once more to underline his words.

Two hundred million, Evert Bäckström thought. What the hell am I going to do now?

85

After the end of the meal, Bäckström had taken a taxi straight home to his cosy abode on Kungsholmen. He had abandoned any thought of concluding the evening by contacting one of all the yearning women who had gathered on his very own online fansite. For the time being, they would just have to join the growing queue for the super-salami and simply wait for a better opportunity. Far too much was at risk financially, and what he needed right now was a bit of seclusion, some peace and quiet so he could think.

As soon as he had walked through the door, dumped his clothes and put on his dressing-gown, he mixed himself a proper summer drink, vodka and tonic, to wash away the veils of cognac that were obscuring the view inside his head. High time for a bit of thinking – serious thinking – and to save time he didn't even bother to count the contents of the brown envelope that GeGurra had forced on him as they parted. He merely checked the denomination of the bundle of notes, squeezed it between his thumb and forefinger and made a rough estimate. Practice makes perfect: these days, he was usually within a few thousand kronor and, considering how much little Pinocchio and his nose were worth, it was like farting outside a sulphur factory. Any more accurate calculations could wait until later, he thought, once he had tucked the envelope away in his secret hiding place, where it could stay until the next departure to the quite excellent money laundry operated by little Edvin's taciturn father.

Time to do some serious thinking, he thought, having taken the precaution of lying down on his bed and getting out his little black notebook and a pen to aid his mental processes. As always when it came to thinking properly and seriously, it was basically a question of separating what mattered from what didn't matter, and, in this particular instance, of taking care of the smaller elements of his supplementary income before concentrating on Pinocchio and the really serious money.

Many a mickle, Bäckström thought with a contented sigh. The specific person he was thinking about at that moment was Baron Hans Ulrik von Comer and his extremely improbable involvement in the murder of Thomas Eriksson the lawyer. The motive was already obvious. The baron had tried to trick the lawyer out of at least a million in conjunction with the sale of a painting. The same man who had been found out, confronted and beaten up by the future murder-victim, who had also reclaimed all the other pictures and little Pinocchio. And so he decided to have his revenge. Brought in some paid muscle and made a visit to the lawyer to accomplish a fairer division of the spoils. And at that meeting everything – as so often happened – had gone straight to hell. The lawyer had started shooting wildly, the baron had crapped himself, and his hired thugs had beaten the lawyer to death while he was trying to call SOS Alarm for help. Then they had taken their haul and fled the scene of the crime. And, in the general confusion, the musical box had been left behind, and Bäckström had no intention whatsoever of making a fuss about that little detail. Just to be on the safe side, he had also made a note about it in his little black book.

That just leaves a couple of smaller practical issues, he thought. First, making sure that the baron and his accomplices got locked away, and then calling his tame journalist to give him the factual basis for another brown envelope from the larger of the two evening papers. 'Baron arrested for murder of famous gangster lawyer', and at least a five-figure sum in the brown envelope, Bäckström thought happily, taking a large mouthful of his refreshing summer drink.

On the other hand, there was reason to hope for considerably more than that, seeing as von Comer demonstrably lived next to the king in a house that was owned by the crown estate. There was also the fact that he was a baron, and quite probably one of the king's friends. Why else would the king sort out a house for him? Might even be the king's best friend, if he was going to indulge in rather more tenuous social speculation. 'King's best friend arrested for murder of famous gangster lawyer'. A shiver of excitement ran through Bäckström.

At least a six-figure sum. Definitely six figures, he thought. Plus all the other envelopes containing similar amounts he could count upon as soon as it became clear that His Majesty himself was involved in the murky business that lay behind Eriksson's murder. And in the role of innocent crime-victim as well, which left the way open for the whole of the international gossip-magazine world, and the seven-figure sums which he had come to realize were more or less standard within that sector of investigative journalism.

This could be seriously fucking good, Superintendent

Evert Bäckström thought, seeing before him the approaching summer's customary news drought being replaced by an unending torrent of media revelations and analysis linked to the Swedish head of state and those closest to him. When he reached this point in his thoughts he suddenly fell asleep, and when he woke up eight hours later he was wide awake from the moment he opened his eyes, brimming with confidence and ready to grapple with the practical problems that still remained to be solved.

86

Once Bäckström had woken up and eased the pressure from the previous day, he got in the shower. As he stood there letting the hot water pour over him, he thanked his creator for giving him a brain that worked at top speed even while he was asleep. Have to proceed with caution now, he thought. Let sleeping bears lie, while simultaneously and as quickly as possible securing the little musical box that would at a stroke, and in absolute secrecy, transform him into Sweden's wealthiest police officer of all time. Maybe even as rich as some of his Colombian and Mexican colleagues, he reasoned. Or the growing crowd of uniformed, crime-fighting millionaires on the other side of the Baltic Sea.

As he ate a fortified breakfast, he made a few more notes about all this, before getting out his secret pay-as-you-go mobile and calling his accomplice, GeGurra, to find out a few more facts before he made a decision. GeGurra sounded surprisingly alert as well, considering how little he had actually drunk. Even though any delay could be costly, he was as long-winded as usual. He started by enquiring about Bäckström's health and all that nonsense that only women and pensioners wasted time on.

'If you'll excuse me, I've got a lot to do,' Bäckström interrupted. 'But I wanted to ask a favour, and I've also got a few questions I'm hoping you can help me with.'

'I'm listening,' GeGurra said.

'Good,' Bäckström said bluntly, to avoid any further verbal digressions. 'In that case, I'd like your help with the following. Firstly, could you let me have a bit of factual background to what we discussed yesterday? Pictures of the items, when they were sold, all that?'

'Of course,' GeGurra said. 'It will be delivered within an hour, without a return address, of course. I'm assuming that everything we talked about will stay between us.'

'What do you take me for?' Bäckström snorted. 'There are no cracks in this wall,' he assured him.

'You had some questions?' GeGurra prompted.

Three, to be precise, Bäckström told him. Firstly, he was wondering if Eriksson had appeared to know how much the musical box was worth.

'According to the valuation he was given by that joker von Comer, they were talking about a few thousand.' GeGurra sighed. 'And our dear baron appears to have got it into his head that it was manufactured in Germany.' He sighed again.

'And there's no chance that Eriksson was just saying that to check your reaction?' Bäckström asked.

'No,' GeGurra said. 'Unfortunately, von Comer, as on so many previous occasions, got it completely wrong. If he had seen Fabergé's mark, no doubt he would have reacted, but I think he simply missed it altogether. It's supposed to be on the inside of the musical box, not on the outside and, if you don't know where it is, it can be a bit tricky to locate it.'

'You didn't say anything to Eriksson? About how much it was worth, I mean?'

'I said as little as possible, for very understandable

reasons,' GeGurra said. 'I offered to take a look at both the musical box and all the other pieces so I could give him a standard valuation. Because I harboured a degree of hope that I might be able to take over responsibility for the sale, I did say that I was sceptical about von Comer's valuation. That the musical box might be worth considerably more than that but that I would have to examine it before I could give a definite evaluation.'

'How did he react to that?'

'With a fair degree of interest, seeing as I had just told him what Versjagin's painting was worth.'

'But you didn't mention anything about two hundred million?'

'No, I certainly didn't,' GeGurra said forcefully. 'I'm almost insulted that you feel the need to ask.'

'That takes me to my next question,' Bäckström continued. 'You mentioned something about an old acquaintance of yours tipping you off about the painting of the fat monk. That it was going to be sold at auction, I mean.'

'In that case, you misunderstood me,' GeGurra said. 'I already knew that Sotheby's were going to be selling it in their auction. I spend something like half my time keeping an eye on the auction market. No, he called me to express an interest in the painting. That must have been a few days after I'd already seen it in the catalogue. Of course I was already aware of Versjagin's picture, and I remember being surprised that it had suddenly appeared again after all these years. But that was before my acquaintance contacted me.'

'Did he ask you to buy it for him?'

'No,' GeGurra said. 'But I realized that he was interested in it.'

'Did he have any idea of what it was worth?'

'A rough idea,' GeGurra said. 'The guide price was listed in the catalogue, of course. In the end, it reached twice that, but I remember telling him that there was a chance it could fetch considerably more.'

'So you weren't actually commissioned to buy it?'

'No,' GeGurra said. 'I'm curious – why do you ask?'

'To be honest, I'm not sure. I just thought it was an interesting coincidence,' Bäckström lied. 'I don't suppose you can tell me his name? Your acquaintance, I mean?'

'I'd rather not,' GeGurra said. 'If you want to survive in this business, you learn not to talk about things like that very early on. Anyone who doesn't learn that lesson usually ends up going hungry.'

'Okay, well, give it some thought,' Bäckström said. 'I dare say it isn't important.'

'You had one more question?' GeGurra said.

'That's right,' Bäckström said. 'I'm wondering how our current king is related to that Prince Wilhelm.'

'Let me think,' GeGurra said. 'Prince Wilhelm was the son of Gustaf V, which must mean that he was the uncle of our current king's father. Yes, that's it.'

'Okay,' Bäckström said. 'Uncle of the king's father.' That makes three generations, doesn't it? he thought. Three generations of the same family. Wasn't that what Eriksson had said?

'Was there anything else you were wondering, my dear friend?' GeGurra asked.

'No, that's the lot. Don't forget that background information you promised me,' Bäckström said. Two proper questions and one smokescreen will have to do for the time being, he thought.

'It's on its way,' GeGurra said. 'You'll have it in fifteen minutes.'

GeGurra seems to be on the ball, Bäckström thought as he ended the call. Wonder how much he thinks I'm going to give him for helping me with the sale? He can forget all about that twenty per cent, he thought.

87

Half an hour later Bäckström was sitting in a taxi on his way to the police station, leafing through the bundle of papers GeGurra's anonymous courier had delivered through his letterbox fifteen minutes earlier. On the seat beside him he had his trusty old briefcase, the one he had inherited from his mentor, Superintendent Pisshead, and in his mind he now had a detailed plan of how to proceed. All that remained was to find a suitably cretinous colleague who could accompany him as an alibi, he thought.

They're not just stupid, they're lazy too, he thought as he gazed at the meagre number of officers tapping away at their computers in the main office. With the exception of Anchor Carlsson, of course, who seemed to live there. Which was probably just as well, given the sort of thing she got up to otherwise. The moment he caught sight of her he suddenly knew how he was going to solve the last remaining detail. Who could be better than Anchor Carlsson, the Solna Police's very own law-and-order dyke?

'Bäckström,' the Anchor said, holding out her hands. 'What are you doing here? You haven't forgotten it's Saturday, have you?'

'Where's everyone else?' Bäckström said, nodding at the empty desks around them.

'The overtime ban, time owing, a few out in the field,' the Anchor said. 'What are you doing here?'

'I was thinking of picking up the keys to Eriksson's house. I've received some interesting information,' Bäckström said. 'There's something I need to check.'

'You're making me very curious,' the Anchor said, smiling at him. 'The last time you showed up at the weekend, we managed to close the case the next day.'

'I need someone to come with me.'

'In that case I'll volunteer,' the Anchor said. 'I could do with getting out and stretching my legs. I've been sitting here since seven this morning.'

'That's good of you, but I don't want to—'

'Don't try to stop me,' the Anchor said, with another smile.

'Well, it's very good of you,' Bäckström said. 'If you grab the keys to Eriksson's pad and sort out a car, I'll see you down in the garage in fifteen minutes. I just need to print out some material for us to take along.'

This is going like a dream, Bäckström thought as he printed out copies of all the interior photographs Niemi and his colleagues in Forensics had taken of the crime scene. He stuffed the bundle of pictures in his brown briefcase, then took the whole lot into his office for one last look in peace and quiet.

No messing up, he thought, taking out the list he had written before leaving for work. Absolutely no messing up, he thought five minutes later, once he'd ticked off all but two of the points on the long list in his little black book. Then he tucked it away in his desk drawer, the same drawer where he kept his finest Russian vodka, and hesitated for a moment before deciding that that would have to wait. He locked the list away, secreted the key in its usual hiding place and took the lift down to the garage.

'So, tell me,' Anchor Carlsson said as soon as he was sitting in the passenger seat.

'I've received a tip-off,' Bäckström said, opening his briefcase wide so she could get a good look, then handed her the pictures of all fifteen icons that GeGurra had sent him, while the photographs of little Pinocchio were safely tucked away in the inside pocket of his jacket.

'What's all this?' Annika Carlsson said, shaking her head.

'An anonymous source,' Bäckström said. 'But this particular one usually comes up with the goods. I have a feeling that this could be our motive.'

'A load of old paintings,' the Anchor said, shaking her head again as she leafed through the photographs. 'I haven't seen anything like this there. Are you saying that these paintings are supposed to be in Eriksson's house?'

'Doesn't harm to take another look,' Bäckström said, shrugging his shoulders expressively. 'Even if I have a feeling that they were in those white removal boxes our witnesses saw being carried out of the house. The paintings in those photographs are old Russian icons that Eriksson is supposed to have received so he could sell them on behalf of a client. Some of them are said to be very valuable. We're talking millions of kronor, according to my source,' he explained.

'You think they missed one, and that's why they went back later that night,' Annika Carlsson said, suddenly sounding considerably brighter. 'I'm with you now, boss. Some people he already knows, who themselves know that he's got these paintings, show up and rob him. They don't get everything they came for. So they come back for another go later that night. That would certainly explain a few things.'

'An extra look never does any harm,' Bäckström repeated, seeing as the attack-dyke by his side had just swallowed the bait, hook, line and sinker.

'I quite agree,' the Anchor said firmly. 'Let's get going.'

'One more thing,' Bäckström said as soon as they had pulled out into the street. 'Call in at Systembolaget in Solna shopping centre. I've just remembered that I need to buy a bottle of whisky.'

'Whisky?' the Anchor said, looking at him in surprise. 'Haven't you already got loads of alcohol at home?'

'Yes, but this is a present,' Bäckström said. 'An old colleague from National Crime who's turning fifty. I'm seeing him this afternoon. He's fond of malt whisky, so I thought I'd get him a bottle.'

'Okay,' Annika said. 'No problem.'

When he got out of the car by Systembolaget, he had taken care to leave his briefcase behind, and, if he knew the attack-dyke at all, she'd be going through its contents the moment she got a chance. Inside the shop he found a bottle of twelve-year-old malt whisky in a black presentation box. That ought to work, Bäckström thought, comparing it with the pictures his Forensics colleagues had taken of all the bottles on Eriksson's mobile bar on the upstairs landing, just to make certain. Mind you, it was undoubtedly a great pity that an honest, hard-working police officer should have to donate a bottle of whisky costing several hundred kronor to Eriksson's estate.

* * *

'All done,' Bäckström said as soon as he was back in the car again. 'Right, let's get going.'

Then he picked up the black presentation box and put it inside his briefcase. He crumpled up the green plastic bag and left it on the floor in front of his seat. He could hardly make it any more obvious.

'Expensive stuff. You're a generous man, Bäckström,' Anchor Carlsson declared. Quarter of an hour later she pulled up outside the house where Eriksson the lawyer had lived until just one week before.

88

'Okay,' Bäckström said as soon as they were inside the hall on the ground floor. 'Here's what we do. You start with the cellar and I'll take upstairs. Then we meet up back here and divide the rest.'

'Just what I was going to suggest,' Anchor Carlsson agreed. 'How are we going to report this?'

'Well, obviously, we're going to have to report it,' Bäckström said. 'We make all the notes we need and, if we find any of the items we're looking for, we'll have to call in one of our colleagues in Forensics. Niemi and Hernandez can deal with that.'

While Annika Carlsson disappeared down into the basement, he went upstairs, put his briefcase down on Eriksson's desk, then did a quick check of the other rooms to make sure everything was as it should be. No cameras on, even though he'd taken care to switch off the alarm himself. No mysterious figures tucked away and able to watch him. Just to make absolutely sure, he even checked under Eriksson's bed.

Empty, Bäckström thought with a sigh of relief as he straightened up. Only then did he do what he had actually come for. He opened his briefcase, took out the black box containing the bottle of whisky and swapped it for the more than twice as heavy wooden box containing the most valuable musical box in the world, which he put down on the floor under the desk.

As soon as the whisky was in position, he took out the Forensics pictures and went and stood in the position from which they had been taken. Perfect. Not even Peter Niemi and his magnifying glass would be able to see the slightest difference.

Then he lifted his new acquisition on to the table and opened the dark wooden case. He took out the little figure with the red pointed hat, inspected it from every angle, then put it down on the desk. He found the key pretty much by accident. While he was carefully feeling the inside of the box, the bottom opened with a discreet click, and there it was. Gold and diamonds – thirty-two carats, according to GeGurra, who usually knew what he was talking about when it came to objects like the one he had in his hand.

The music will have to wait, Bäckström thought. Then he replaced the key and put little Pinocchio back in the dark wooden box, before gently putting it inside his old brown briefcase. Welcome home, lad.

'Nothing,' Bäckström said sadly when he and Annika met up back in the hallway an hour or so later.

'Same here,' Annika said. 'Mind you, it would have been a dereliction of duty not to do an extra check,' she added, patting him consolingly on the arm.

'There's one thing that's struck me,' Annika said as they were sitting in the car on the way back to the police station.

'I'm listening,' Bäckström said.

'I noticed that most of those icons aren't framed. The majority of them are painted on wood, of course, but at least a couple were on canvas. And then I thought about that character our little taxi-driver almost ran over.'

'Angel García Gomez,' Bäckström said with a nod. This is getting better and better. He had already worked out where she was going with this.

'Well, it's obvious it was him,' Annika Carlsson said. 'I've thought that ever since I saw the photofit picture and, now that we've got his DNA from the terrace door, I'm convinced it's him. He's the one who killed both Eriksson and the dog.'

'Not Eriksson,' Bäckström said, shaking his head. 'He's got an alibi for when Eriksson was killed. When he was at that martial arts competition. But I'm fairly certain he's the one who shows up at Eriksson's later that night, smashes his skull in and cuts the dog's throat. But his good friend Fredrik Åkare could very well have been there both when Eriksson was murdered and later on.'

'When he was driving García Gomez,' Annika nodded. 'I buy that. How about this, then? Suppose García Gomez removed the painting from its frame, the one they missed the first time, rolled it up and tucked it inside his jacket. What do you think about that?'

'A definite possibility,' Bäckström agreed. 'Obviously better than running around with a painting tucked under your arm in the middle of the night.'

'What about the frame, though? The one the canvas was in. What did he do with that?'

'Smashed it, and used the pieces to roll the painting around, probably,' Bäckström said.

'Yes, that's what I think too,' Annika said with feeling. 'It would have been stupid of him to take the painting and leave the frame behind. That would even make someone like Alm wonder. A flashing red light if you find something like that at a crime scene. A broken picture frame but no picture.'

'On a completely different matter,' Bäckström said, 'I was thinking about our witness. The little taxi-driver. I don't suppose he's shown up again?'

'Afraid not,' Annika said. 'He seems to have vanished. I can't help getting bad vibes when I think about him. Another thing that bothers me is that both Åkare and García Gomez seem to have gone underground. No trace of them either, but at least we've got warrants out for them. We'll just have to hope that nothing's happened to our witness.'

Who cares? Bäckström thought, but allowed himself to be content with a nod.

89

Bäckström's weekend didn't turn out the way his weekends usually did. To start with, he kept dashing to the door to make sure it was properly locked, until he pulled himself together. He made himself a proper tray of sandwiches, poured himself a cold beer and downed a stiff drink before he'd even sat down.

Then he settled down at the kitchen table to eat and, after a couple more fortifying drinks and the usual refreshment in between them, he finally got himself back under control and managed to suppress the attack of crim's paranoia that could evidently also afflict an honest police officer like him. Switching his phone off would have to do, and he spent the evening at home watching old Clint films which he'd downloaded from the internet. Memories of the days when his own wallet used to start whining at him within a week of payday. Times have changed, he thought and, when he eventually discovered the truth lurking at the bottom of his litre bottle of vodka, he fell asleep on the sofa.

On Sunday he made a concerted effort to get his act together. He called Nadja at home and arranged to meet her at work. He ended up spending half the afternoon there while he told her what GeGurra had told him. Which wasn't altogether straightforward, as he couldn't say a word about little Pinocchio and his nose, even though his entire life seemed to revolve around him these days.

Then he returned home. He had dinner at his local and, even though his Finnish waitress was exactly the same as usual, he couldn't be bothered to listen to her.

'I'm worried about you, Bäckström,' she said, patting him on the shoulder. 'You're not coming down with something, are you?'

'Feels like I might have picked something up,' he lied, mostly as a way of changing the subject and giving him an excuse to leave.

He went to bed as soon as he got home. It took him a while to get to sleep, and when he woke up it was only six o'clock in the morning. Two hours later he was at work and, compared to the way he had felt the day before, that actually felt like something of a liberation. Must be the money, Bäckström thought. The two hundred million that had been stuck in his head like a golden nail for the past twenty-four hours or so.

V

The ongoing investigation into the murder of Thomas Eriksson the lawyer

90

Bäckström began the Monday meeting of the investigative team with a short lecture. It was high time something happened. As everyone in the room knew, or ought to know, the chances of solving a murder case diminished drastically once a week had passed and, unless he had got his maths wrong, that moment had passed the previous evening. All he had so far was a whole lot of loose threads. An as yet unidentified silver Mercedes, a witness who had suddenly vanished, two suspects who appeared to have done the same, plus a post-mortem report which had been promised for a week now but still hadn't arrived to help them with their investigation.

'Give me some good news!' he said, glaring at his colleagues.

'Well, I've got something for you,' Peter Niemi said, leafing through his papers.

Just a quarter of an hour earlier, the National Forensics Lab had called him to say that they had more information about the DNA trace they had found in the blood taken from the door to Eriksson's terrace which matched Angel García Gomez's record in the database.

'Along with García Gomez's DNA, they've found traces of different DNA, from a dog,' Niemi said. 'Eriksson's

Rottweiler, which is pretty much everything we could have wished for. He may have an alibi for the time when Eriksson is thought to have been murdered but, as far as events later that night are concerned, I believe he killed the dog and smashed in the skull of its owner.'

'Thank you very much,' Bäckström said.

'As far as the silver Mercedes is concerned, we still have approximately fifty vehicles outstanding,' Nadja Högberg said. 'I'm afraid it's going to take a few more days.'

'Okay,' Bäckström said. 'Anything else?'

'Our witness, Dosti, has been called for interview without the need for advance warning,' Lisa Lamm said. 'As soon as we locate him we can bring him straight in. And our two suspects, García Gomez and Åkare, have had arrest warrants issued against them in their absence. After what Peter has just said, I'm open to the idea of asking for them to be held in custody. If we feel like putting out an international alert for them, I mean.'

'Good, let's do that,' Bäckström said. 'Before sundown, I want those two behind bars.' Good line, he thought. Before sundown, then he could ride off into the sunset. On to the next town where the bad guys thought they were in control.

'On that point we're in complete agreement,' Lisa Lamm said, smiling warmly at him. 'Regarding the missing post-mortem results, I spoke to our medical officer before coming to this meeting.'

'What does he say?' Annika Carlsson asked. 'Are we getting it for Christmas, or what?'

'By the middle of this week at the latest, according to what he told me an hour ago. He's waiting for his colleague's report. Until then we'll just have to make do with his preliminary evaluation. If you want to know what I think,

I reckon there's something worrying him and his colleague. Seriously worrying them.'

'What the hell are they playing at?' Annika Carlsson said, unable to hide her irritation.

'Paddling round in snot,' Bäckström said, shrugging his shoulders. 'If no one has anything else to say, I've got a few things I'd like to add.

'You can't make an omelette without cracking eggs,' he went on. 'And it's about time we started cracking a few eggs. I thought I might ask Nadja to explain what I mean. But, first, we need a quick break to stretch our legs,' he concluded, and stood up.

91

The police leg-stretcher overran, as usual, and the most hardened smoker sneaked back into the room sixteen minutes later with a guilty smile on her lips. Bäckström gave her the evil eye and tapped his watch with his fore-finger to underline his message.

'I received a tip-off from one of my informants over the weekend, which I have asked Nadja to help me look into. If we're lucky, it might give us the motive for why Eriksson was beaten to death. Do you remember the case of that baron, von Comer, who was reported to have been beaten up outside the Drottningholm Palace? The anonymous report that was handed in at reception? Jenny looked into it for us a fortnight ago. The assault was supposed to have taken place on the evening of Sunday, 19 May.'

'The bloke who denied he'd been beaten up?' Annika Carlsson said, glowering sullenly at her younger female colleague Jenny Rogersson.

'That's the one,' Bäckström said. 'The same informant got in touch again before the weekend, to say that the person who beat up the baron was, in fact, Eriksson. Our anonymous witness recognized Eriksson from the pictures that were published in the press after he was murdered. You can get the details from Jenny.'

'So why did he deny it, then? Getting beaten up, I mean?' Stigson asked.

'I'm getting to that,' Bäckström said. 'According to my source, the whole business is connected to various acts of skulduggery concerning the sale of some works of art. Eriksson was commissioned by a client to sell a number of paintings and employed von Comer to take care of the practical details. The baron tried to trick Eriksson, and Eriksson found out what he was up to. He beat him up, took back the paintings and the money he had been conned out of. Nine hundred and sixty-two thousand kronor, according to my source, which is undeniably an interesting coincidence, considering that bundle of notes we found in Eriksson's desk. And the removal boxes that Eriksson carried into the house before the weekend he was murdered, and which the perpetrators carried out again a couple of days later.'

'You mean von Comer took the paintings back again?' Lisa Lamm said, nodding enthusiastically. 'So he took Åkare and one of his associates with him to save getting beaten up again. And then García Gomez enters the story later on, when they pay another visit to the crime scene. Because they forgot something the first time they were there.'

'It's not an entirely improbable hypothesis,' Bäckström said.

'Hang on a moment,' Alm said from the other end of the long table. 'Why leave so much money behind? A million – surely they should have taken that with them?'

'The simplest explanation is probably that they forgot about it in the general confusion once Eriksson started shooting all over the place and then got killed,' Bäckström replied. Suck on that, he thought. 'And the dog had kicked off as well by then. There was shooting, shouting and screaming, and the suspicion that someone might call us and that we, just for once, might actually show up certainly can't be ruled out.

'So, to answer your question,' Bäckström went on, giving Alm the evil eye, 'in situations like that, people sometimes forget one or two things.'

'I hear what you're saying, Bäckström,' Alm said, 'but I'm still having trouble believing that a man like our baron would have anything to do with a pair like Fredrik Åkare and Angel García Gomez. A great deal of trouble, actually.'

'Worse things have happened! Anyway, I had no idea that you were acquainted with von Comer,' Bäckström said, glaring at Alm.

'What do you think, Nadja?' Anchor Carlsson interrupted. They're like little kids, she thought.

'I agree with Bäckström, for three main reasons, really,' Nadja Högberg said.

Three reasons, according to Nadja. Firstly, the hypothesis explained the cryptic note that Eriksson had made on his computer a week before he was murdered.

'From what Eriksson wrote on his computer, Vom Coma – that's what he calls von Comer; a little joke, I suppose – tried to trick him out of almost a million kronor. The direct quote reads as follows: "Vom Coma has obviously tried to do me out of almost a million." End of quote. That's the first reason.'

'What about the other two?' Lisa Lamm asked.

The second reason was the calculations Eriksson had done on the same document. They showed a difference between the payment in pounds and the payment in kronor on the sale of the painting in question. The result was nine hundred and sixty-two thousand kronor, after the usual deductions for fees and VAT.

'Yesterday afternoon, after the boss and I talked about this, I called an old friend who works for our colleagues in London, specializing in art fraud,' Nadja said. 'He spoke to his contact at Sotheby's last night, and this morning he emailed a copy of the statement of account, in British pounds, that the auction firm sent to von Comer. A statement that he amended, replacing the pounds with Swedish kronor, which gives a difference of nine hundred and sixty-two thousand.'

'The statement in Swedish kronor that von Comer is supposed to have given Eriksson—'

'I found that yesterday,' Nadja interrupted, nodding to Lisa Lamm. 'It was among the files we seized from Eriksson's office.'

'Were you able to find out who Eriksson's client was?' Lisa Lamm asked.

'No,' Nadja said. 'The simplest solution is probably to conduct another interview with his colleague, Danielsson. If Eriksson was commissioned to conduct the sale, there ought to be a power of attorney at the law firm. Hopefully, a few invoices as well. For the firm's fees, if nothing else.'

'Good,' Lisa Lamm said. 'We'll have another word with Danielsson about that. And anyone else in the firm who might have known about it.'

'Noted,' Annika Carlsson said with a nod. Let's get those fuckers, she thought, squeeze them till they squeak, and preferably a bit further.

'I also agree with Bäckström about the contents of those white removal boxes,' Nadja went on. 'We're talking about a total of eleven icons out of an original collection of fifteen, and I've managed to work out their dimensions, with the boss's help. They'd need at least a couple of removal boxes if they were going to carry them about. That's the third reason why I agree with Bäckström. The collected value of these paintings is around three million. A very plausible motive,' she concluded, and for some reason she nodded in Alm's direction.

Nothing much wrong with that Russian, Bäckström thought. And she knows her vodka. Mind you, she looks terrible. The only thing missing is stainless-steel teeth. Might have to get her some next time she has a significant birthday, he thought.

'Very interesting,' Lisa Lamm said, looking as if she really meant it. 'Based on what you've already said, there seems to be a fair amount of evidence to suggest that von Comer is guilty of at least one count of attempted fraud. That ought to be enough grounds for reasonable suspicion.'

'We could do with talking to his bank,' Nadja said. 'And trying to find out if he's withdrawn a million kronor in cash recently. I'd also like us to seize his computer, so we can check if he's altered any statements of account. As well as anything else he might have got up to. Who knows? If we're lucky, maybe he's got the paintings in his house, hidden away in the cellar. That sort of thing's happened before.'

'I agree with you,' Lisa Lamm said. 'How do you want us to deal with this, Bäckström?'

'We start with the bank. Right away. Then we bring von Comer in first thing tomorrow morning, when we also conduct a search of his home. We get hold of his computer and anything else interesting, like Nadja just said. We can hold back on the suspected murder charge until we've got him in here to explain the rest of it.'

'Done,' Lisa Lamm said, now looking thoroughly delighted.

'Exactly,' Bäckström said. 'If you're going to make an omelette, you've got to crack a few eggs.' Must call my reporter so he can get some good pictures of us carrying out the search. Ideally with Drottningholm Palace in the background. This is definitely a six-figure tip-off, he thought.

The king's best friend . . .

92

That leaves one practical problem, Bäckström thought as soon as he was back in his room and had shut the door behind him. Making sure that little court faggot didn't start babbling about Pinocchio and his long nose. The easiest way to deal with that is probably to conduct the interview with him myself, and make sure we stick to the other stuff. Before I scare the shit out of him. Yes, that'll do, he thought. Upon which, inevitably, there was a knock on his door.

'What can I do for you, Rosita?' Bäckström asked. Not good. Practically a bad omen, he thought, because, although she looked like thunder, as usual, she seemed almost excited. In the happy sense, unfortunately, he thought.

'The question is more what I can do for you,' Rosita Andersson-Trygg said, smiling and waving the photofit picture of García Gomez.

'Let me guess,' Bäckström said, sinking back in his chair and folding his hands over his stomach. 'You've spent the morning showing our photofit picture of Angel García Gomez to your friends in the rabbit and hamster unit down in the city centre.'

'Yes,' Rosita Andersson-Trygg said. 'How could you know—?'

'Because his police record includes the fact that he is suspected of putting on organized dog-fights, I could have guessed that's where you were going to end up.'

'Yes, well then. So you can see why I wanted to talk to our colleagues in Animal Protection.'

'The problem is that you really should have left that the hell alone,' Bäckström said, smiling amiably. 'Because we worked that out all by ourselves as early as last week. In your absence, if you're wondering.'

'I took some time owing,' Andersson-Trygg said in an aggrieved tone. 'In case you were wondering why.'

'I don't give a damn,' Bäckström said. 'I'm assuming that you're going to make sure that the police division of the animal rights movement keep their paws off my murder investigation.'

'In purely formal terms, there's nothing to stop them opening up their own investigation into the aggravated animal cruelty that there's good reason to suspect García Gomez of committing,' Andersson-Trygg protested.

'Bollocks,' Bäckström said. 'If that idea even pops into their heads, I'll send both them and you to get dewormed.'

'I really must pro—'

'I haven't finished,' Bäckström interrupted, raising his hand. 'You can forget all about that job as animal welfare officer out here if you don't do as I say. There are three alternatives that you need to consider. Preferably sooner rather than later, because I'm planning to take care of this little detail today.'

'What do you mean, three alternatives? What are they?'

'Well, you can either help the boys down in the garage to wash the cars, or move to Lost Property over on

Kungsholmen. Or the parking office out in Vestberga. Your choice,' Bäckström said, counting to three on his fingers.

Looks like she'd rather wait a while before deciding, Bäckström thought, seeing as Rosita Andersson-Trygg had merely turned on her heel and left the room, slamming the door behind her. She may even have run straight into visitor number two, judging by the lack of delay before the next knock.

'Come in!' Bäckström roared. It never ends, he thought.

93

As soon as the Monday morning meeting of the investigative team was over, Annika Carlsson had met Commissioner Toivonen, head of crime in the Western District, and Bäckström's immediate superior.

'Please, have a seat, Annika,' Toivonen said. 'So, tell me, what's the fat little sod been up to this time?'

Apart from the fact that he was the same as ever, he hadn't been up to anything, according to Annika Carlsson. In fact, it could even be said that, in some mysterious way that neither she nor any of the others could quite understand, he was actually the person driving the investigation forward.

'So you really came to see me to suggest that he should be awarded the Grand Police Medal in gold,' Toivonen grunted. 'Unfortunately, I can still remember all too well the last time that proposal was on the table. I seem to recall that, on that occasion, the Chief of Police ended up giving him a crystal vase.'

'Which he's supposed to have either thrown in the bin or sold online. The story varies on that point,' Annika Carlsson said, shaking her head.

'Out with it then, woman,' Toivonen said. 'There's clearly something serious bothering you, and I want to know what it is.'

'Okay,' Annika said. 'I'll start with the thing that's bothering me most.'

She proceeded to tell him about their missing witness. How someone had apparently tried to find out who he was, and had, in all likelihood, succeeded. Then she told him that their two main suspects, Fredrik Åkare and his friend Angel García Gomez, had evidently gone underground at the same time that their witness had disappeared. In short, this was what was worrying her most.

'So what does Bäckström think about that?' Toivonen asked.

'That our witness told one of the papers about García Gomez. And that the paper gave him money for the information, which he's used to get out of the country until everything's calmed down. That Åkare and García Gomez have got their hands on a collection of old paintings worth several million, stolen from Eriksson. And that they've decided to lie low for a while as well.'

'That sounds like Bäckström,' Toivonen snorted. 'I remember the last time he was on the rampage. There were clouds of gunsmoke right across Solna. So what is it that's making me believe that all hell is about to break loose again?'

'What do we do?' Annika Carlsson said.

'We do the usual. I'll call in more people so we find those involved before they find each other. And, while I'm doing that, I'll be praying to Him upstairs that they haven't already done so. As far as the formalities are concerned, I understand that our prosecutor's on top of things.'

'Yes, she was even thinking of issuing arrest warrants for Åkare and García Gomez. That's under way now.'

'Okay,' Toivonen said with a crooked smile. 'Little Lisa

isn't as harmless as her name suggests. Anything else I ought to know?'

'Yes, I'm afraid so,' Annika Carlsson said. 'One more thing.'

She went on to tell him about Baron von Comer. The suspicions against him, the fact that he was going to be picked up the following morning, and his house searched. She even gave Toivonen a brief description of his character and background.

'I hear what you're saying.' Toivonen sighed. 'The problem with Bäckström is that, when it comes down to it, there's only a fifty-fifty chance at best that it's actually true. That man has absolutely no idea where to draw the line. I still remember him trying to push that so-called sex angle in the Palme murder investigation. Claiming that Palme was the member of some secret sect of sex addicts who ended up falling out with each other and that's why he got shot. That was when Bäckström ended up being sectioned. Sadly, they let the bastard out again. All I'm interested in is what you think about that story. About the baron, I mean.'

'I'm sorry, but I agree with Bäckström,' Annika Carlsson said. 'For the time being, as far as most of it goes, anyway, and the rest usually falls into place once we've stirred things up a bit.'

'God help the king,' Commissioner Toivonen said. He shook his head in resignation and let out a deep sigh.

94

'Have a seat, Jenny,' Bäckström said, gesturing towards his visitor's chair.

A blue top, just as tight as the others and, in spite of the colour, not remotely like a standard-issue uniform, he noted. As she was clearly just as excited this time as she had been during her last visit, he took out his little black notebook and put it down on the desk in front of him.

'I'm listening,' Bäckström said, tapping his pen on the notebook to underline his words.

'Was I right, or was I right? About von Comer, I mean,' Jenny said, leaning over the desk and, as usual, adjusting her neckline half a centimetre upward.

'You were right,' Bäckström said, leaning back to get a better view of what he was looking at.

Jenny had just been in touch with the National Forensics Lab, and it turned out that they hadn't discarded the sample of DNA they had found on the auction catalogue, even though the case had been dropped. After some persuasion, she had also managed to get them to examine it as a matter of urgency, which should mean that the Solna Police would soon have something they could compare any new sample against.

'As soon as we've taken a sample from von Comer,'

Jenny clarified. 'I explained to them that he was about to be brought in, and that it was urgent.'

She sounds like a proper little legal eagle, Bäckström thought, with a nod of encouragement.

'And I've been doing a bit more thinking about this whole business, now I'm completely clear about von Comer's involvement.'

'What have you been thinking, then?' Bäckström asked, with another nod. This could be good.

It was Jenny Rogersson's decided opinion that von Comer was behind Eriksson's murder. Just as he was behind everything else as well, for that matter.

'Everything else?'

'That old woman and her rabbit, and her hamster too, come to that, the one they took off her back in the winter. And the threats to that Fridensdal woman. Looks like the perpetrator in that case was the same one who killed Eriksson's dog. That nasty Chilean bloke, the one with the name like that actor. I've already spoken to the Anchor about it, actually—'

'That actor?' Bäckström said. 'What actor?'

'That Andy García, the one who was in the third *Godfather* film.'

'Oh, okay, I'm with you now.'

'Good. So, I'm convinced von Comer is behind it all. He's behind everything, absolutely everything,' Jenny concluded, nodding with enthusiasm.

'If what you're saying is true, then obviously I'm very grateful,' Bäckström said. 'That we've got our very own Lex Luthor living here in Solna, I mean. It really doesn't get any better than that for the police. The fact that the same bloke is behind absolutely everything.'

'Lex Luthor?'

'Yes, you know, the bad guy in *Superman*.'

'I'm serious,' Jenny said, adjusting her cleavage and shifting position.

'But what do you think about a motive? What's von Comer's motive for doing all this?'

'I think he's got several motives,' Jenny said. 'Partly money, the financial reward he gets from those paintings. Then there's probably an element of revenge as well. I mean, he did get beaten up.'

'Okay, but what about that old bag and all her pets? Or that lunatic Fridensdal? That doesn't sound especially profitable, if you ask me.'

'I think there's a sexual motive behind that.'

'A what?'

'I think he might have had a sexual motive in their cases. Something subconscious.'

'Money, sex, revenge,' Bäckström said. All with the same perpetrator, and all at the same time. No, it doesn't get better than that, he thought. It's odd that there isn't an echo when she talks.

'And I've got a proposal,' Jenny went on.

'A proposal. I'd be very happy to hear it.' Bäckström had been thinking along much the same lines for quite a while.

'I was going to suggest that I conduct the interview with von Comer when we bring him in tomorrow. I'm pretty sure I'm starting to get a grip on him. That I've worked out who he really is.'

'No,' Bäckström said, shaking his head. 'I'm thinking of doing that one myself. But if you promise to sit quietly and do nothing but listen, you can sit in the observation room.'

'You don't need any help, then? With me sitting in, I

mean. With all due respect, I think I'm the one who knows most about him, and I—'

'No. But thanks for the offer.'

95

Two hours before Bäckström met his investigative team, Lisa Mattei had had a meeting with the colleague who three days before had been tasked by her with doing 'all the usual stuff'. The superintendent from the Security Police's intelligence division, who was head of the section responsible for protection of the constitution, and, in this specific instance, of the head of state, His Majesty King Carl XVI Gustaf.

The report he had given her was divided into four different points, and the common thread between them was Baron Hans Ulrik von Comer. The first point concerned von Comer's apparent connection with Fredrik Åkerström and Angel García Gomez. There was no evidence of any previous contact between them. No intelligence information within either the Security Police or the regular force. Nothing had arisen from a check of von Comer's phone records, his fax and the three computers in his home and office. The only evidence of any contact was the photographs taken by Sandra Kovac the previous week.

The superintendent had given them to one of the intelligence division's experts for analysis. She was a psychologist and behavioural expert, and he wanted to know if the body language of the three men in the pictures could be used to deduce any more information about their relationship.

'What did she have to say, then?' Mattei asked. She was very fond of this sort of question.

'Most of what she said was taken up with the usual reservations and hedging,' the superintendent said with a wry smile. 'But if she had to hazard an interpretation, she would say that this was a first meeting, and that the three people in question didn't know each other before. So this would have been a first meeting, under relaxed circumstances, and it was probably about business or some other practical matter rather than anything personal or private. Definitely not something of purely emotional significance.'

'Yet they still showed up at his house, and when I look at those pictures I get the distinct impression that they're about to leave. That they're on their way out. That they've been inside his house. And that bothers me. It bothers me a great deal that someone like von Comer is standing on his doorstep shaking hands with those two.'

'Yes, it bothers me too,' her visitor agreed.

'Okay,' Lisa Mattei said. 'Is there anything to suggest that they had any contact in connection to Eriksson's murder?'

'No,' the superintendent said, shaking his head. 'Nothing simple and unambiguous, anyway. What worries me about this, and here I'm talking about information I've received from colleagues in the regular force, is that there's a witness who observed an individual at the crime scene, at the time the crime took place, who can't be ruled out as being von Comer. And there's good reason to believe that Åkerström and García Gomez have gone underground since Eriksson's murder.'

'Yes, so I understand,' Lisa Mattei said, without elaborating on how. 'Which leads us nicely to the second point on this little list you gave me.'

'That they're involved in Eriksson's murder? If I understand you correctly?'

'Yes. Affirmative,' Mattei confirmed.

'Well, that's certainly what the investigating team out in Solna currently believes. The day before yesterday arrest warrants were issued for both of them in their absence, on suspicion of murder. In Åkare's case as a potential perpetrator, or as an accessory. As for García Gomez, he has an alibi for the time of the murder, but there are both witnesses and forensic evidence linking him to the crime scene later that night. For that reason, if I've interpreted her decision correctly, the prosecutor has charged him with being an accessory to murder. There can't really be any doubt that they're at the top of the list of likely perpetrators. For the time being, at any rate.'

Lisa Mattei contented herself with a nod and put a neat tick against the second point on the document on the desk in front of her. Which brings us to the third point, she thought. The one which explained her involvement in this sordid matter.

'What do we know about von Comer's relationship with the king?' she asked.

As far as contact between the head of state and von Comer and his family was concerned, it could be divided into two different categories. Firstly, contact on an official level, and secondly, contact of a more private nature.

'As regards the official bit, we haven't found anything odd,' Mattei's colleague summarized. 'Comer appears to have had the level of contact that would be expected for someone with his involvement in the court's art collections, his interest in Drottningholm Palace Theatre, and a number of similar activities and projects. In the past five years, he and his wife have been invited to official royal dinners on two occasions, and have met the royal couple at ten other official gatherings and receptions.'

'While I've never even been to a ball at the palace. But what does that matter, who cares about a ball at the palace?' Mattei declared with a slight smile.

'That makes two of us,' her guest said. But in my case I dare say it's because I'm not smart enough, he thought.

'What about private contact, then?' Mattei asked. 'What do we know about von Comer's private contact with the king and his family?'

Even that lay within anticipated boundaries, according to Mattei's colleague. From their analysis of the king's diary, and after talking to various people close to him, they had reached the conclusion that the king had met von Comer about twenty times in the past three years. These meetings mostly occurred when they were hunting together, and during the associated lunches and dinners. In almost every instance, the explanation to their meetings was to be found in the fact that one of the king's oldest and best friends happened to be von Comer's brother-in-law.

'Without the brother-in-law, there probably wouldn't have been anywhere near as much contact,' the superintendent concluded.

'Okay,' Mattei said. 'Let's try looking at this from a different perspective for a moment. Suppose you were a journalist and knew more or less as much as you do now. Would you be able to persuade the newspaper you work for that von Comer is one of the king's so-called mates?'

'Without a doubt,' the superintendent said with a smile. 'There must be hundreds of them by now, if the papers are to be believed.'

'How about his best mate, then?'

'Possibly even that. If we ignore the facts and concentrate on the number of copies that would sell, and take into account the fact the palace spokesperson is hardly likely to enter into a debate on the subject.'

'I'm assuming that there are pictures of them together, the king and von Comer?'

'Any number of them,' the superintendent confirmed. 'Mostly from the gossip mags, of course, and the evening tabloids, but also some from the more serious papers.'

'What sort of pictures?' Mattei asked.

'There's one big article about some charity whose committee von Comer is on. A big report in *Dagens Industri*. The king and queen are in the same picture as von Comer, and the three of them seem to be getting on fine.'

'Which leads me to the last point on your little list,' Lisa Mattei said.

'Everything seems calm on the media front for the time being,' the superintendent said. 'There hasn't been a word about this in the traditional media. And, as far as the internet is concerned, von Comer is mostly notable by his absence.'

'There's nothing to suggest that that's likely to change?' Mattei asked.

'I've spoken to both the aide-de-camp and people in the press office. Everything seems calm. No one's put out any feelers, there are no papers lurking in the undergrowth, at least not right now, anyway.'

'So things are calm?' Mattei summarized.

'Yes, very calm.' The superintendent nodded emphatically.

If only it weren't for that fat little nightmare Evert Bäckström, Lisa Mattei thought, unable to feel remotely calm.

96

As Bäckström had no inkling of the thoughts inside Lisa Mattei's head, he was in an excellent mood, and, if he had known about them, sad to say, he would probably have felt even better. Bäckström had more important matters to deal with. It was high time for a decent lunch and a bit of profitable financial activity. In this instance, these two birds could be hit with the same stone, happily enough, but he was entirely unaware of the fact that this stone would also reach Lisa Mattei's desk. If he had known, he would doubtless have regarded it as a very well-deserved extra bonus.

When he called his tame reporter at the larger of the two evening papers, the journalist had initially sounded as sour as vinegar, and asked if he was calling to discuss the news that their competitors had just put up on their website. This included a photofit picture of García Gomez and information from 'a senior source inside the police' who claimed that an arrest warrant had been issued for the man in the picture, on the grounds that he was suspected of the murder of Thomas Eriksson the lawyer. All things he had decided not to publish almost a week before, on Bäckström's stern advice.

'Never mind that now,' Bäckström said. 'It was the right thing to do. Bear that in mind. Always do as I say. If we can meet up at the usual place in half an hour, I'll tell you what this is really all about.'

'It better be good,' the reporter said, still sounding bitter.

'It's even better than that. If I were you, I'd tell them to stop the presses. See you in half an hour, so make sure you're there.' That gave you something to suck on, he thought.

'Okay,' Bäckström said the moment he sat down at the table where his host was already waiting. 'Three things.' He nodded commandingly at the waiter who was standing behind his bar ten metres away, a questioning expression on his face as he held up a bottle of Russian vodka. 'Three things,' he repeated.

'Okay,' the reporter said. 'Go on.'

'Number one,' Bäckström said, holding up his first finger. 'You can forget all that crap the other rag has put online. They got it from the muppets in the rabbit division. It's complete bollocks. It wasn't García Gomez that killed Eriksson. He was there a few hours later and cut his dog's throat, but that little detail can wait.'

'Right,' the reporter said.

'Two: I'm about to tell you what this is really all about. This is a story that'll have people storming every newsagent's in the country, and you'll be able to run with it all summer, probably until Christmas if you felt like it.'

'What's the catch? Why do I get the feeling that there's bound to be one?'

'Number three,' Bäckström said. 'This information isn't free, as I'm sure you appreciate. I'm talking six figures and, if you're interested in it, I'll need at least an hour with you to make sure you can make sense of everything. Because this time all the "i"s really have to be dotted and the "t"s crossed.'

'If we're talking about a hundred thousand,' the reporter said, 'then I'm going to need a taster so I know what we're dealing with.'

'Tomorrow morning we're going to be picking up an old boy who's up to his neck in Eriksson's murder. The prosecutor has already decided to remand him in custody, and the reason he's being allowed to sleep in his own bed tonight is mostly because we need time to load our guns properly. This is no ordinary lowlife, you see.'

'Who are we talking about?' the reporter asked. 'A hundred thousand is quite a lot of money, after all, as I'm sure you're aware.'

'It is,' Bäckström said. 'But that's only the starting price.'

'Who is it, then?' his host repeated. 'Who are we dealing with here?'

'The king's best mate,' Bäckström said.

'Done,' the reporter said, holding out his hand.

During the following two hours Detective Superintendent Evert Bäckström ate ham hock with mashed root vegetables – a true classic of summertime Swedish cuisine – which he rinsed down with three glasses of beer and three shorts, while he told the entire story of Eriksson and von Comer and their murky dealings with paintings and antiques worth millions.

Oddly enough, he didn't breathe a word about Pinocchio and his nose. Even more oddly, he didn't mention who it was who had probably been tricked out of all this money. He was planning to keep shtum about Pinocchio until the end of time, if need be, and, as far as the king was concerned, he intended to save him until it was time for the next payment. Many a mickle, Bäckström thought. And for a successful entrepreneur who made his living out of other people's misfortunes, timing was everything.

97

After the meeting with his tame reporter, Bäckström had gone home so he could fit the last details into place in peace in advance of the following morning's raid. First of all, he put on his dressing-gown and mixed himself a stiff drink. Then he took out his little black book and made a list of everything that needed doing. Then he called his closest associate, Anchor Carlsson.

'About tomorrow: there are a few things I want you to sort out for me,' Bäckström said, not about to waste time on social niceties.

'Thanks for asking, I'm fine. How about you?' the Anchor replied.

'Never mind all that crap now,' Bäckström interrupted. 'I want us to bring the baron in at six o'clock tomorrow morning.'

'Sounds early,' the Anchor countered. 'Why, if you don't mind me asking? What's the rush?'

'So he has a couple of hours to sweat before we start questioning him,' Bäckström lied, seeing as he had no intention whatsoever of saying it was at the request of the paper, who needed the additional time to get an extra edition published before lunch.

'Noted,' the Anchor said with a slight sigh.

'I'm thinking of conducting the interview myself, so

you can sit in if you want. I thought we could run the old classic.'

'Which one?'

'Bad cop and even worse cop,' Bäckström clarified.

'No problem,' the Anchor said. 'Anything else?'

'I want him to be in serious need of a shit when we bring him in. Start by sending in a couple of really scary constables to drag him out of bed. And they're not to say a word to him on the way to the station, no matter how much he whines and begs. As soon as he's in the building, I want him searched and a DNA sample taken. Remove his shoelaces, belt, all that stuff. Photographs, fingerprints, DNA, the full works. You know what I mean?'

'Yes, I understand completely,' the Anchor said. 'And do you have any particular wishes regarding the search of his house, Superintendent?'

'No, except that I want them to turn the place upside down. You can sort the details out with Nadja.'

'Noted. Turn the whole house upside down. Is there anything else you'd like?'

'One more thing,' Bäckström said. 'Make sure the first officers he encounters make a careful note of everything he says, all that.'

'You don't need to worry on that score,' Annika Carlsson said. 'I thought I'd take care of the arrest myself. When are you thinking of putting in an appearance, by the way? Before or after lunch?'

'I'll be there when I get there,' Bäckström said. It was time for a little nap before dinner, he thought as he ended the call.

As soon as Bäckström woke up from a couple of hours' restorative sleep, he went and stood in the shower. Then he spoke to his tame reporter on the phone and gave him his final instructions. He put on some clean clothes and walked the perfectly comfortable distance to his beloved local hostelry, where he ate a simple evening meal served up by his very own Finnish waitress.

As he ate, he occupied himself with thinking lofty thoughts about life and the way of the world. A simple bourgeois existence, in which he had just managed to secure the health of his household finances while he waited for the serious money to arrive. Many a mickle, he thought again, with a contented sigh, and raised a toast to himself. Then he ordered coffee and cognac, asked for the bill and brought the evening to a close. Once he was home again, he changed into something more comfortable before he went to bed and mixed himself the obligatory evening drink. There's still something missing, though, he thought as he sipped it. Music, he thought. Time for a bit of evening music.

So he took out little Pinocchio from his secure hiding-place. He got him out of his wooden box, nudged the key out of its hidden compartment, wound him up, put him on the table in front of him, then leaned back on the sofa to listen.

Sounds fucking awful, he thought, shaking his head. The little haemophiliac twat must have been deaf as well.

Fortunately, the whole thing was over in about twenty seconds. The noise suddenly stopped and the nose stopped growing. Little Pinocchio had evidently made all the noise he was going to make this time. After another few seconds, just as GeGurra had promised, his nose retracted back into his head again. Leaving him with a perfectly ordinary, upturned nose, a bit like his neighbour Edvin's,

Bäckström thought as he put Pinocchio back in his black box.

Before he fell asleep, he lay in bed with his pen and notebook, trying to make sense of the province that was evidently so vital in this context.

Not an altogether simple matter, seeing as he may have drunk slightly too much over the course of the evening, and he had to keep one eye closed in order to see what he was writing.

'Province,' he wrote on the top line, then underlined it twice, just to make sure, seeing as that film director and the price of his sealskin slippers had just popped into his head.

'Previous owners,' he thought as he wrote, underlining this heading once, to be on the safe side. First Nicholas II, followed by Alexei and Maria Pavlovna. Then Prince Wilhelm. When he had done that, he numbered them from one to four and added the dates he had found on the papers GeGurra had sent him. He also made sure to add a bit of extra information for the benefit of anyone who wasn't as historically knowledgeable. 'Last Tsar of Russia' after 'Nicholas II'; 'haemophiliac, probably retarded through inbreeding' after 'Alexei'; 'the richest old bag in the world' after 'Maria Pavlovna'; and 'also commander of torpedo boat' after 'Prince Wilhelm'. So far, so good. That left a gap of almost fifty years between Prince Wilhelm's death in the summer of 1965 and his own successful expedition just a couple of days before.

Obviously, the little prince got the musical box when Prince Willy croaked. After all, he was the kid's father's uncle, or something, Bäckström reasoned, taking a large gulp of his bedtime drink as he completed his chain of ownership with the name of the most likely fifth owner: 'His Majesty the King of Sweden, Carl XVI Gustaf,' he wrote, thereby concluding the historical element of his endeavours.

Which just left his own personage. 'Current owner Detective Superintendent Evert Bäckström,' he wrote. Then he put the pen and notebook on his bedside table, let out a deep sigh of contentment at the imagined mountain of banknotes in front of him, folded his hands over his stomach and, just seconds later, fell into a deep, dreamless sleep.

98

On Tuesday morning Annika Carlsson woke up at half past four. The sun was already high in the sky, the thermometer had passed fifteen degrees, and it looked as if it was going to be a proper summer's day. Baron Hans Ulrik von Comer is lucky with the weather, at least, she thought, shaking her head.

Then her usual routines took over, the ones that gave her the security and tranquillity she required to do a job that could sometimes be so tricky to deal with. Such as on a day like today, which looked likely to fulfil all the expectations of her boss, Evert Bäckström.

First, some preliminary yoga practice, to soften up her muscles and joints, calm her mind and bring balance to body and soul. Then a shower, followed by a proper breakfast – important not to skip the first meal of the day. Clean clothes, practical clothes: in her case, jeans, a thin top, a summer jacket that stretched far enough below her waist to prevent any unnecessary flaunting of the service revolver she had brought home with her the night before. One last inspection in the hall mirror. Ready to go, high time to make the best of things, she thought with a wry smile.

When she stepped out on to the street, two uniformed colleagues were waiting for her in their patrol car, and a quarter of an hour later they pulled up outside von Comer's house, just a few hundred metres from the gates of Drottningholm Palace. Five minutes to six, with time to spare, but Nadja Högberg and her two assistants from Forensics were already there. An unmarked car, discreetly parked on the other side of the road, waiting for Annika to deal with the preliminaries.

Sadly, they weren't the only ones, Annika thought. She had already spotted the first photographer, who was crouching in the driveway three houses further along the street.

'Okay,' she said, getting out of the car. 'Make sure you keep the vultures back so we can get on with our work in peace. Call in another patrol, just to make sure.'

Then she opened the garden gate, walked straight up to the front door and rang the bell. It was four minutes earlier than planned but, as she had already counted at least two photographers and one presumed journalist, because she didn't have a camera, that was the least of her worries.

The occupant of the house took his time. Only after five minutes of ringing did von Comer open the door. He was impeccably dressed in a dressing-gown and red silk pyjamas, to judge by the trousers. His hair was neatly combed, and he had a sardonic smile on his lips, and everything he said and did went wrong right from the start. Even though he really ought to have noticed the police car parked in front of his gate.

'What do you want?' von Comer asked, looking at her with raised eyebrows and eyes that were far too wary for his own credibility.

'My name is Annika Carlsson and I work at the Crime Division of the Solna Police,' Annika said, holding up her ID. 'I'd like to speak to you. Can we go inside to talk?'

'In that case, Constable, can I suggest that you phone

and make an appointment, so that you don't go round waking people up in the middle of the night?'

'Can we go inside to talk?' Annika repeated, smiling and nodding amiably.

'No, certainly not, that isn't remotely convenient,' von Comer said and, when he made to close the door, he left her with no choice.

First, she put her foot in the way, then took a firm grip of his left arm, pushing him ahead of her into his own hall, and that's when things began to get seriously out of hand.

'What the hell are you doing, woman?' von Comer shouted, and slapped her hard across the face with his free right hand.

'Let's all calm down now, shall we?' Annika Carlsson said, even though she could taste the blood running from her nose into her mouth. Then she kicked his legs out from under him, laying him out on his front on his own hall carpet, pulled his arms behind his back and cuffed him.

'What the hell are you doing? What sort of Nazi behaviour is this?' von Comer shrieked.

'My job,' Annika said. 'I'm doing my job, and all you need to do is shut up.'

99

On Tuesday morning Lisa Mattei had planned to arrive at work at around nine o'clock. It was her turn to drop their daughter off at preschool, and as a mum with a permanently guilty conscience, this was important to her. Some time together, a morning story, girls' breakfast with just Elin and her mum. Then the walk to preschool. The sort of walk where you have plenty of time to pat sufficiently friendly dogs, look at everything and talk about whatever popped into the head of a little girl who was only three years old.

That was the plan for Tuesday, that was top of her agenda, and nothing else really mattered. At least it didn't in the morning, before she returned to her normal life and the often all too tangible fact that she was head of the Security Police.

Half past six, she thought when she was woken by her phone. Before she even answered she knew what the call was about. No suicide bomber on the underground during morning rush hour, no hijacking out at Arlanda, not even a new and immediate threat against the prime minister. Bäckström. Lisa Mattei groaned.

The call was from the duty officer of the Security Police, who wanted to inform her about one of the three cases that had been at the top of his watch list for the past few days, with instructions to call her, among others, if anything happened. One of their plain-clothes officers out at Drottningholm had contacted him fifteen minutes earlier to say that the police were conducting some sort of operation in and around von Comer's residence, close to Drottningholm Palace.

'I'm listening.' Mattei sighed. Definitely that little fat bastard, Bäckström, she thought.

A complete circus, according to the duty officer. Half a dozen journalists and photographers from the largest evening paper, judging by the logos on their vehicles. And several more hanging around outside the gates of the palace.

'I've spoken to our colleagues in Solna,' the duty officer explained. 'Evidently, they've taken von Comer in for questioning. Under arrest, apparently. And they're conducting a search of his home.'

'Under arrest? What for?' Mattei asked. For the murder of that lawyer, Eriksson, she thought, groaning silently to herself.

'For attempted fraud, or aggravated fraud,' the duty officer said, sounding as if he was leafing through his papers. 'It seems a bit odd, actually, considering that the decision was taken by Senior Prosecutor Lamm. Because she's in charge of the preliminary investigation into the murder of that lawyer.'

'Correct me if I'm wrong, but don't we have an agreement with Solna for them to give us plenty of warning if they're planning anything of this sort?'

'Yes,' the duty officer said. 'It looks like they managed to forget that this time.'

* * *

Time together and a morning story, with certain impediments. An hour later Dan Andersson called her to say that he was now out at Drottningholm Palace, and that he had also spoken to their colleagues in Solna. A suspect had been arrested and the suspect's home was being searched. If he wanted to know more than that, he would have to speak to the head of the preliminary investigation, Senior Prosecutor Lisa Lamm.

'Have they brought in anyone apart from von Comer?' Mattei asked.

'No,' Dan Andersson said. 'Apparently, they took him in an hour ago. In handcuffs, with a jacket over his head.'

'Why the hell would they do that?' Sounds like the sort of thing you see in cop shows on television, Mattei thought.

'It seems he took a swing at Anchor Carlsson, our colleague – Annika Carlsson, from Serious Crime out in Solna, you know, the one with all the muscles—'

'I know. Is there anything else that—'

'Can I suggest that we deal with that later?' Dan Andersson said.

'No,' Lisa Mattei said, shaking her head even though she was speaking to him over the phone. 'We'll deal with it now.'

'The king's press secretary has called. The hunt is evidently on. The media are quite literally hanging from the palace door-handles, if you know what I mean. And there must be at least twenty of them outside von Comer's house. TV4 and Swedish Television are there. The question they're all asking is—'

'Thanks, I get it.' Lisa Mattei had already worked it out. 'See you in my office in an hour.' What do I do now? she thought as she ended the call. I'll call Anna. Anna, as in Anna Holt, who was one of her best friends, godmother to her only child, and – fortunately enough – head of the Western District Police.

100

Eight hours of refreshing sleep, a proper breakfast and at least half an hour for personal hygiene and external appearance. You mustn't let things slip when you're going out into the field, Evert Bäckström thought as he left his home on Kungsholmen just before nine o'clock in the morning to take the waiting taxi to the police station in Solna, to have an open and honest conversation with the king's best friend.

While he was on his way in the taxi, the first voice of the choir of praise contacted him. His tame reporter, calling him on his private mobile. A happy man, a very happy man, Bäckström thought.

'Bäckström, Bäckström,' the reporter groaned. 'I don't know what to say. This could be absolutely huge.'

'Later,' Bäckström said abruptly. 'Don't call me, I'll call you.' What the fuck was he expecting?

After that, everything went smoothly. Like a knife through butter. The first person he met when he stepped into the office was his colleague Carlsson. As cheerful and positive as usual, Bäckström thought, when he noted at once how furious she was.

'Let me guess,' Bäckström said. 'When you told him you worked for the police his face went white and he asked if something awful had happened to his wife and children?'

'No,' Annika said, shaking her head. 'He wanted to know what we were doing there and, when I was reluctant to say, he tried to close the door in my face.'

'Oh dear. What an unpleasant man,' Bäckström grunted.

'Then he slapped me in the face,' she went on, pointing her finger at the swelling under her left eye.

'Excellent. So he gave you a slap? This is getting better and better. The best start we could have had.'

'If you want any more details, I suggest you look in one of the evening rags,' Annika said. 'Because, for some reason, the place was crawling with reporters when we got there.'

'What the hell are you saying?' Bäckström said in surprise. 'This building leaks like a sieve. It's an absolute disgrace, if you ask me.'

'Sure,' Annika said. 'What I'm wondering now is if you still want me to sit in on the interview?'

'Of course. Why shouldn't you?'

'The first thing he did when we got here was report me for assault. That's why I'm asking.'

'Of course you should be there.'

'Forget it,' Annika Carlsson said. 'I've already spoken to Lisa Lamm, and the pair of us are in complete agreement.'

It's a mutiny, Bäckström thought. Nonetheless, there was something in her eyes that told him that now wasn't the time to discuss the matter. Another day, perhaps, but not today, even though the sun was shining from a clear blue sky, down on Solna police station and all the officers who worked there.

101

According to the transcript of the interview which would eventually form part of the preliminary investigation into Baron Hans Ulrik von Comer, the first interview with him commenced at 9.15 in Solna police station. Lead interviewer was Detective Superintendent Evert Bäckström, assisted by Detective Inspector Johan Ek. Also present during the interview was Senior Prosecutor Lisa Lamm.

So far, so accurate, although, as far as the time was concerned, it was a slight modification of the truth, because the parties involved devoted the first ten minutes to an open and honest conversation. Perhaps it was actually more of a monologue, seeing as Bäckström made do with the occasional grunt and Ek didn't say a word the whole time. Lisa Lamm merely explained that the reason why von Comer was sitting where he was was that he was being held on suspicion of attempted fraud or aggravated fraud, and that Detective Superintendent Evert Bäckström would shortly go into the matter in more detail.

The baron, on the other hand, was furious, on the brink of being beside himself with rage. He yelled about the abuse of power, about the Swedish police state and its thugs forcing their way into his home in the middle of the night and, when he finally paused for breath, it was only to tell them that he refused to say a single word before he was allowed to talk to his lawyer in private.

'Of course,' Lisa Lamm said. 'Did you have someone in mind who you'd like me to contact?'

'Peter Danielsson,' von Comer said. 'He works for the law firm of Eriksson and Partners.'

'I'm afraid that might be a problem,' Lisa Lamm said.

'What do you mean, a problem?' von Comer snorted. 'Surely I have the right to a lawyer?'

'In this particular instance, I'm afraid he can't be regarded as impartial,' Lisa Lamm said. 'We can return to the reasons why in the interview.'

'I suppose we'll just have to find someone else,' Bäckström suggested in a gentle tone of voice, with a pious expression on his face. 'I have a suggestion, if you'd care to hear it, Baron?'

'What might that be?'

'While you're thinking about your choice of lawyer, I could explain why we're so keen to talk to you.'

'Yes, I can hardly contain myself.'

'There are three things that are troubling me and my colleagues,' Bäckström said with a sigh.

'Three things? What three things?'

'The first is that Eriksson, the lawyer, assaulted you in the car park outside Drottningholm Palace on the evening of Sunday, 19 May. Just fourteen days later he was murdered.'

'That's utterly preposterous,' von Comer protested. 'Some young woman telephoned several weeks ago, claiming to be a police officer, and I told her exactly what had happened. That my wife and I were with good friends of ours down in Södermanland. The idea that I was assaulted is a complete fantasy.'

'I'm afraid not,' Bäckström said. 'The problem is that there's a fair bit of evidence that contradicts what you've just said. But, at the same time, unfortunately, that's the least of our problems.'

'Complete fantasy,' von Comer repeated, shaking his head. 'What else do you want, then?'

'To discuss the reason why Eriksson attacked you. Because he had discovered that you had tricked him out of one million kronor in association with the sale of a painting.'

'What sort of nonsense is this? Who's tried to make you believe all this?'

'My problem is that there's a good deal of evidence suggesting that this too could be true,' Bäckström said. 'But, once again, this is of less significance compared to the third problem.'

'Given the fact that I can't believe what I've heard so far, I may as well hear that too. This is all quite absurd.'

'What really bothers me is that you seem to socialize with two of the very worst criminals that we have in this country. Two members of the Hells Angels, Fredrik Åkerström and Angel García Gomez. And the reason why we're so interested in them right now is that the prosecutor has issued warrants for their arrest on suspicion of having murdered the lawyer Thomas Eriksson.'

'Now hold on a moment,' von Comer said, raising both hands in an almost beseeching gesture. 'They were the ones who came to see me, at my home, entirely without warning. I'd never seen them before. Never in all my life.'

'Exactly,' Bäckström agreed. 'I hear what you're saying, sir, and, because I learned at a very young age that not everything is as it seems, I thought you might care to tell me what was really going on.' Who'd have thought he'd fall for that one? he thought.

'I can hardly wait,' von Comer said, looking at Bäckström. 'I can hardly wait.'

'Excellent,' Bäckström said, then pressed the button on the tape recorder. 'Interview with Baron Hans Ulrik von Comer. Lead interviewer is Detective Superintendent Evert Bäckström . . .'

He's quite remarkable, Lisa Lamm thought.

'I thought we might start by discussing that last point,' Evert Bäckström said thirty seconds later, as soon as he had finished the formalities, cleared his throat discreetly and put a throat sweet in his mouth. 'How did you come to meet Åkerström and García Gomez at your home?'

'Now just a minute—'

'I'm sorry, you really must excuse me,' Bäckström said, holding out the bag of throat pastilles towards the subject of the interview. 'I forgot to ask if—'

'No, thank you,' von Comer said. 'I might seem a little confused, but—'

'I'm happy to listen,' Bäckström said, making an almost inviting gesture as he put the bag down on the table between them.

'Well, this is what happened,' von Comer went on. 'Regarding the two men you mentioned, Superintendent . . .'

I'm all ears, Bäckström thought, giving a nod of encouragement. Even if your nose is already as long as a broomstick.

* * *

Utterly remarkable, Lisa Lamm thought. And he reminds me of someone I saw on television when I was a child. That detective who was always scratching his head and sounded like he was just thinking out loud.

102

So as not to frighten the life out of their suspect, Annika Carlsson had taken a seat in the observation room, in the same corridor as the interview room. On a television screen fixed to the wall she could listen to what was being said and watch the person saying it. Without him having the faintest idea. Baron von Comer was evidently something of an audience magnet. All the chairs in the room were already occupied when Annika walked in.

'Haven't you got more important things to be getting on with?' the Anchor asked, glowering at Jenny Rogersson, who had adopted the traditional forward-leaning position, pad and pen in her lap.

'Orders from the boss.' Jenny smiled. 'He wanted me to brief him afterwards about von Comer's body language. That's why—'

'Get another chair,' Anchor Carlsson interrupted, glaring at her. Bloody bimbo.

'No problem,' Jenny chirruped, then got up and went out into the corridor. Bloody bull-dyke.

That man defies all description, Annika Carlsson thought a quarter of an hour later as Bäckström played the amenable and absent-minded police officer who kept making his subject say the wrong thing. There isn't a single word of truth in that man. He's as fake as a three-kronor coin, Annika was thinking when she received a text message from her ultimate boss, Anna Holt, asking to see her at once. It's a good thing I've already warmed up, she thought. She had a good idea of what Holt wanted to talk about.

Anna Holt was sitting behind her big desk, and on one of the two visitor's chairs sat a pale and extremely well-dressed blonde. Thin, in good shape, and in that indefinable age between thirty and forty.

'How are you?' Holt asked with a concerned smile. 'I heard that Count Dracula of Drottningholm tried to wrestle you to the floor.'

'He gave me a slap,' Annika said with a shrug. 'The report's already written. Nothing to worry about.'

'I'm not the slightest bit worried,' Holt assured her. 'That's not why I wanted to talk to you. I don't know if you've met before, but this is Lisa, Lisa Mattei, who works with the Security Police. We're old friends and former colleagues. And I'm godmother to her young daughter.'

'I know who you are,' Annika Carlsson said, nodding towards Mattei. 'But I don't think we've ever met.' The favourite of the legendary Lars Martin Johansson, so you can't be completely useless, she thought.

'Good to meet you too, Annika,' Lisa Mattei said with a cool smile, opening the thin briefcase on the desk in front of her and taking out a sheet of paper, which she handed over.

'I've got a few questions, but I'd like you to read this through first. And sign it as soon as you've finished reading,' she went on, putting a pen down on the desk.

Not the usual disclosure ban, Annika Carlsson thought

as she read. According to Swedish law, in today's Sweden, this is utterly ridiculous.

'One question, out of curiosity,' Annika said as soon as she'd signed the document, which Lisa Mattei immediately took back and tucked away in her briefcase.

'Yes,' Lisa Mattei said. 'If I can, I'll be happy to answer it.'

'Suppose I called a newspaper and tipped them off about the document I just signed.'

'Yes . . . ?'

'What would happen? To me, I mean?'

'In that case, I'm afraid we'd have to take the measures that you've just signed to say that I've made you aware of,' Lisa Mattei said. 'But I'm fairly confident we won't find ourselves in that situation. You seem to be both sensible and honourable, which is also the reason why I'm sitting here and you're not sitting in my office.'

'What about Holt?' Annika Carlsson said, shaking her head. 'Why is she allowed to be here?'

'The only reason is because she signed the same document as you before you came in,' Mattei said.

'Which I'm also forbidden to talk about,' Anna Holt said with a delighted smile.

'This is completely absurd.' Annika Carlsson shook her head.

'I haven't come here because the Security Police have any intention of taking over the murder case that you and your colleagues are working on. I wanted to talk to you for completely different reasons. The first is that I want to find out about the suspicions against von Comer. How strong they are, basically. The second is that I'm concerned that your investigation is leaking to the media in a way that might suggest more than the usual loose talk, or because someone wants to make a bit of money on the side. The third is that I have one concrete question. Which of your colleagues is leaking information? Or is it more than one?'

'What happened to the protection of sources?' Annika Carlsson asked. 'Correct me if I'm wrong, but I thought that was written into the constitution?'

'Yes, it's there, as is the exception to that protection – specifically, crimes that threaten the security of the realm. That was also clearly explained in the document you just signed.'

'What if it's me, then? Who's been doing the leaking, I mean?'

'No,' Lisa Mattei said, shaking her head. 'It isn't you. That's why I'm sitting here talking to you now.'

'So you know that for certain, do you?'

'Yes,' Lisa Mattei said, without a trace of a smile. 'I know. And if you're wondering how I know, it's because I can see it in your eyes. Not because we've been bugging your phone or come up with some other technological gimmick.'

'Okay,' Annika Carlsson said, shrugging her shoulders. 'In that case, I'll tell you what I think.' You're probably the most unpleasant person I've ever met in my entire life, you little upper-class bitch, she thought.

Twenty minutes later she was finished. The suspicions against von Comer? It was obvious that he'd tried to defraud Eriksson over the sale of a painting. The idea that he commissioned or was otherwise involved in his murder was less certain. But it was worth pursuing, given the evidence they already had. The suggestion that he might have killed Eriksson himself was out of the question, however, in Annika Carlsson's decided opinion.

'He's too feeble, to be blunt. But I think it's all going to fall into place fairly quickly. How involved he was in the actual murder, I mean,' Annika Carlsson summarized. 'The worst case is probably that he wanted to get those paintings back, and took Åkare and another of his associates with him to help him with the practical details. That he was actually in Eriksson's house when it all happened. But that he might have smashed his skull in? Forget it. He hasn't got what it takes to do something like that. Believe me.'

'Okay,' Lisa Mattei said. 'What do you think about the leaks to the papers, then?'

'I honestly don't know,' Annika Carlsson said, shaking her head. 'As far as today's events are concerned, I haven't seen any of the media coverage – apart from the reporters who were already there when I turned up first thing this morning – but since then I've had my hands full all morning. Anyway, I know far too little about how the media work. I'm going to have to pass on that question, basically.'

'What about the photofit picture of García Gomez, then? The one you had done last week and which turned up in one of the newspapers' online editions yesterday morning. Have you given any thought to how it might have got there?'

'I'm almost one hundred per cent sure it wasn't Bäckström, anyway,' Annika Carlsson said, for some reason.

'What makes you think that?'

'Partly because he hit the roof when he found out. And partly because that's not how I think it happened.'

'How did it happen, then?'

'One of our officers, Andersson-Trygg, got it into her

head that our colleagues in the animal protection unit might be able to help us identify the man in the picture. One of them tipped off the media after she gave them the picture. Poor judgement caused by being over-ambitious, rather than anyone taking money from the paper. The sort of thing that just happens.'

'So you don't have any firm opinion about today's events?'

'If Bäckström was behind the leak, you mean?' Annika Carlsson said, looking at Mattei, her gaze not wavering for a second.

'Yes. What do you think?'

'I honestly don't know,' Annika Carlsson said. 'But, if that were the case, I'd feel very sorry for him.'

'Sorry for him? How do you mean?'

'Well, considering that piece of paper I signed,' Annika Carlsson said.

'What do you think, girls?' Anna Holt said, changing the subject. 'I don't think we're going to get much further. Can I offer you lunch, by the way?'

'I'm afraid I haven't got time,' Annika Carlsson said. 'Too much to do.'

'I'd be happy to have lunch with you,' Lisa Mattei said with a smile. 'Things were a bit stressful this morning, so I skipped breakfast. Elin says hi, by the way.'

Is this how it feels, to have met someone you haven't in fact met? Annika Carlsson thought as she returned to the observation room to watch as Bäckström, in his amiable, absent-minded way, slowly turned Baron Hans Ulrik von Comer inside out. At least no one's dared to take your chair. Always a good sign.

103

At roughly the same time as Detective Superintendent Evert Bäckström was turning 'a faggot into a marker buoy' – which was how he himself chose to describe his interview with von Comer when he spoke to his tame reporter that same evening – his colleagues Detective Inspectors Per Bladh and Lars Alm were interviewing the lawyer, Peter Danielsson, from the law firm Eriksson and Partners.

Another interview in an ever-growing sequence, another far from unconditional conversation in which the ambition was to uncover the truth, or at least some form of confirmation, but where the outcome was often the complete opposite. A dialogue in the form of questions and answers which were usually influenced by discrepancies arising from contradictions with previous statements, and in this case by information from an anonymous source whose name only Bäckström knew. If Thomas Eriksson the lawyer was commissioned to sell an art collection on behalf of an as yet unknown client, then it was not unreasonable to suspect that there might be documentation about the matter at the law firm where he worked.

According to Peter Danielsson, there was no such documentation in the office. No power of attorney, no contracts, accounts, invoices, statements of account, and Danielsson's own interpretation was that the information lacked all foundation. His former colleague had never taken on a job like that. His lead interviewer, on the other hand, was of the opposite belief, for which reason the interview soon became a discussion of the fact that the simple explanation could be that Eriksson had had a few clients 'on the side'. That this particular job had been of a more private nature.

'Naturally, that can't be ruled out,' Danielsson conceded. 'Obviously, when you're a lawyer, it can happen that you undertake to do things on behalf of good friends.

'In that regard, we're a bit like doctors,' he went on. 'You're constantly beset by friends and acquaintances who want advice and help with all manner of things.'

But, at the same time, he seemed so obviously relieved to be discussing the possibility that both Alm and Bladh noticed it. After the end of the interview, they agreed that Danielsson and his colleagues should look into the matter one more time, if only to be certain. Bladh had also taken the opportunity to give Danielsson a bit of parting advice when he and his colleague were leaving the office.

'If there's anything bothering you about Eriksson's activities, I think it would be in the best interests of both you and the firm if you told us about it.'

'Of course,' Danielsson said. 'But, to be perfectly honest, just between us, my colleagues and I never had any cause for that sort of anxiety when it came to Thomas and his work.'

Perfectly honest and just between us. Where have I heard that before? Bladh thought, but merely nodded.

Alm, however, was more direct.

'Well, my colleague and I still believe that that's the case. So I suggest you have a good think about it.'

104

After the first hour, Bäckström had suggested a short break. He had also offered von Comer coffee, mineral water, perhaps a sandwich, the chance to stretch his legs, even a visit to the nearest smoking area in the building. The full works, basically, if only to show a bit of goodwill.

Von Comer had declined the offer of smoking but accepted everything else, and while they were waiting for coffee they went out into the corridor, where Bäckström took him off to one side, with a discreet gesture to the prosecutor, who was standing a short distance away, having a whispered conversation with Ek. About time for a few confidences, man to man, and Bäckström began by suggesting that they drop the formalities. With the utmost respect, naturally, and if for no other reason than to save time, because he himself wasn't terribly impressed at having to be involved in this business.

'I'm a homicide detective,' Bäckström said with a telling shrug. 'Details of that sort, if I'm honest – strictly between us – don't really interest me at all. Unlike certain prosecutors,' Bäckström said, with another pointed nod of the head in Lisa Lamm's direction.

Of course they could set aside their titles, von Comer agreed. Not merely to save time, but also because he had realized that he had finally met a police officer who was willing to listen to him. One who hadn't prejudged him. They even shook hands on the matter.

A quarter of an hour later, the interview resumed. Coffee and mineral water for all, two ham and cheese sandwiches for von Comer.

'If I've understood you correctly, those two characters appeared at your house without warning,' Bäckström said, as soon as his victim had wiped away any evidence of his perfunctory meal with a paper napkin. 'Two men who were quite unknown to you,' he went on.

'As I said before the break, I'd never set eyes on them before.'

'So why did they want to see you?'

The explanation was that they had come to collect the paintings and other works of art which he had promised to help Eriksson sell.

'They were nice and polite, no problems of that nature at all,' von Comer said. 'They introduced themselves, and I seem to recollect that the larger of them – Åkerström, it must have been – gave me his business card while we were standing talking at the door.'

'What happened after that?'

'I invited them in, and then I explained the situation. I told them that there must be some misunderstanding, because Eriksson had himself picked up the whole collection just a few hours before.'

'As you understood it, they were there on Eriksson's behalf?'

'Yes, why else would he have sent them to my house?' von Comer said, looking at Bäckström in surprise. 'I took it to mean that they had misunderstood what each of them would be doing.'

'I understand,' Bäckström said. 'What did you say after that?'

'I went and got the receipt that Eriksson had signed. Proving, of course, that he had already collected the paintings.'

'How did they react to that?'

'Oh, there was no problem at all. I seem to recall that I even gave them a copy of the receipt. As I understood it, we were in complete agreement. About the fact there must have been some sort of misunderstanding between them and Eriksson, I mean.'

'But they didn't explicitly state that Eriksson had sent them?'

'No, but who else would have done?'

'Yes, that's certainly a good question,' Bäckström said with a friendly smile, as Nadja Högberg knocked on the door and peered cautiously into the room.

'Interview suspended at 10.31,' Bäckström said after a quick glance at his watch.

'What can I do for you, Nadja?' Bäckström said.

'Could I have a few words with you?' she asked.

'Yes,' Bäckström said. 'Just give me a minute, then we'll go on,' he said to von Comer.

'How's it going?' Nadja asked as soon as they were in the corridor and Bäckström had shut the door of the interview room.

'It's coming together,' Bäckström said with a shrug. 'How are things going for you?'

'He's certainly got plenty of paintings in the house, but none of the ones we're looking for. But we have found a receipt signed by Eriksson, saying that he acknowledges receipt of all the items. With a note of the date and place as well. Friday, 31 May, von Comer's address.'

'Anything else?'

'This business card,' Nadja said, handing over a business card in a sealed plastic sleeve. 'It looks like Åkare's. Fredrik Åkerström. Managing director of Åkerström Security. Imagine, Fredrik Åkare has his own security business.' She smiled. 'This is the receipt for the paintings,' she went on, handing Bäckström another plastic sleeve.

'Okay,' Bäckström said. 'What about his computer? And his bank?'

'We're working as hard as we can.'

'Interview resumed at 10.35,' Bäckström said, switching the tape recorder back on as soon as he had made himself comfortable on his chair.

'You mentioned that one of your visitors gave you his business card,' Bäckström said. 'Could it by any chance have been this one?'

'Yes,' von Comer said. 'Yes, that's the card. I'm quite sure of it.'

'Let it be noted for the record that I have just shown Hans Ulrik von Comer a business card with Fredrik Åkerström's name and that of his company, Åkerström Security, printed on it,' Bäckström declared.

'That's definitely the business card he gave me,' von Comer interjected.

'Excellent,' Bäckström said. 'And here we have a receipt which I thought I might show you, by which Thomas Eriksson acknowledges receipt of a total of twelve different works of art which, according to this, he collected from you on Friday, 31 May. Eleven paintings and an enamel figure. Is this the receipt that you mentioned before?'

'Definitely,' von Comer said. 'I'm quite sure of that.'

'I see,' Bäckström said, then let out a happy sigh and leaned back in his chair. He looked at Lamm and Ek.

'Well, I'm satisfied, so if no one else has any questions, I thought we might move on and talk about something else entirely: your previous relationship with the lawyer Thomas Eriksson.'

'Where would you like me to start?' von Comer said, who seemed more and more comfortable with the situation in which he found himself.

'I suggest you start at the beginning,' Bäckström said, still smiling happily. 'That's usually best. Start with the first time you met him.'

'That sounds like an excellent idea,' von Comer agreed.

That way we can save the last time till the end. When you were sitting on his sofa and shat yourself while bullets were flying past your ears, Bäckström thought.

The first time von Comer met Thomas Eriksson had been at a hunting party in Skåne organized by a mutual friend who was a property developer. He couldn't remember precisely which year it was, but it must have been about ten years ago.

And after that first meeting? A total of ten, perhaps twenty occasions. All in social situations, out in the city, in bars, at hunts and dinners arranged by mutual friends and acquaintances. That was all, according to von Comer.

'I take it that he had been to your house,' Bäckström said. 'When he collected those paintings we were talking about.'

'Yes, and on perhaps a couple of other occasions, actually. When my wife and I have held large parties. I seem to remember a lunch in the spring, if nothing else.'

'How about you? Had you ever been to Eriksson's house out in Ålsten?'

'No, never,' von Comer said. 'I believe he may have invited my wife and me to a large dinner he was hosting but we had already committed to go elsewhere. So it never happened.'

'You must excuse me if I seem to be labouring the point,' Bäckström said. 'But you have never been to the home of the lawyer Thomas Eriksson?'

'No, never,' confirmed von Comer. 'I know where he lives, but I've never set foot in his house. Why would you think I had?'

'Perhaps I've just been conditioned by previous cases,' Bäckström said, in an almost jovial tone of voice. 'I hear what you're saying, and I have no reason to mistrust you. But just for the record. And at the risk of overstating the point. You've never been inside Eriksson's house at number 127, Ålstensgatan?'

'No, never, but I have been to his office. Twice, about a year ago. That was when he asked me to sell the artworks we've talked about. On the first occasion I gave him a valuation of the various items. He had the collection in his office. There must be plenty of people there who can confirm that visit. I also have a definite recollection that Peter – Danielsson, the lawyer, I mean – also came in to look at the paintings.'

'I see,' Bäckström said. 'What about the second visit?'

'Thomas telephoned me, and we met a couple of days later, again at his office, and that was when we agreed my fee, among other things. The collection was sent to my home – I have my office in the house – but a delivery company took care of that.'

'From what you're saying, I take it to mean that you

weren't close friends, but not unknown to each other. Acquaintances, perhaps. And that on one occasion you had a business relationship. When he asked you to help him sell those paintings.'

'Yes,' von Comer said. 'That would be a perfectly correct interpretation.'

'Which leads me naturally to that little incident outside the Drottningholm Palace. I have every sympathy for the idea that one might think that the police should have nothing to do with private matters of that nature, but, considering what later happened to Eriksson, perhaps you can appreciate why we're unable to ignore it.'

'Yes,' von Comer said. 'I must admit that it was foolish of me, but my attitude was precisely as you describe. That it was a private misunderstanding that had nothing to do with the police, and which Eriksson and I had already resolved by the time the police contacted me. For Eriksson and myself, the matter was in the past.'

'Just for the record, could I ask you to explain what happened in your own words?' Bäckström said.

Eriksson had called him on his mobile when he was out taking his evening walk and, because he was already shouting and screaming, and was apparently on his way to von Comer's house, he had suggested that they meet in the car park in front of the theatre. Eriksson had been upset, shouting and waving an auction catalogue, which at one point struck von Comer in the face, making his nose bleed.

'That was when I decided it would be best to walk away,' von Comer said. 'He was impossible to reason with, actually very abusive. So I walked away.'

'Why was he so upset?' Bäckström asked.

'It was all a complete misunderstanding arising from the sale of one of the paintings. It was actually my fault in part, because I had calculated the accounts in the wrong currency and Eriksson received too little money. As soon as I was aware of this, naturally I took the necessary actions to rectify the situation. There's also a receipt that will confirm this, of course. While we were talking about this, I also made it clear to him that, in light of what had happened, I was unwilling to continue with the work I had undertaken to do for him.'

'I can quite understand that,' Bäckström said. 'How did he take it?'

'He didn't raise any objections, and actually apologized and said that he regretted what had happened and told me that he respected my decision.'

'One last question before we break for lunch,' Bäckström said. 'Did Eriksson say who had commissioned him to sell those paintings? Who the owner was?'

'No,' von Comer said. 'I certainly asked, but he explained that he was prohibited from divulging the identity of his client. That isn't at all unusual, I can tell you. He also assured me that their provenance was entirely in order. No cause for concern.'

'How about you?'

'How do you mean?' von Comer asked.

'Obviously, I've come to understand that you're regarded as a prominent art historian,' Bäckström said. 'I was just wondering if you might have recognized the items and knew who they belonged to?'

'No,' von Comer said. 'Naturally, I conducted the usual searches in various art databases and old auction catalogues, but to no avail. It wasn't that he'd asked me to help him sell a lot of rubbish, but there wasn't anything particularly special, if I can put it like that. When we're dealing with the provenance of Russian art during the twentieth century, unfortunately, things often get extremely confused. We mustn't forget that Russia had a revolution and two world wars in the last century, in which millions died and everything that they owned simply vanished.'

'I see,' Bäckström said. 'Well, I'm satisfied,' he went on, giving Lisa Lamm and Johan Ek a questioning look. They shook their heads in unison.

'Is there anything that you yourself are wondering?' he said, nodding in von Comer's direction. 'Anything you'd like to raise, anything you think we've forgotten, anything that isn't clear?'

'No,' von Comer said. 'Although I can't help wondering how long I'm going to have to sit here. I have a lot to be getting on with at home, you see.'

'I can assure you, you won't have to sit here a minute longer than is strictly necessary. Well, if no one has any more questions, I can confirm that the interview is now concluded. The time is 11.50,' Bäckström declared, switching the tape recorder off.

105

After the first interview Lisa Lamm went back with Bäckström to his office, because she had a number of things she wanted to discuss between just the two of them.

'Okay,' Bäckström said as soon as he had sat down. 'What can I do for our senior prosecutor?' Before I starve to death, he thought.

'To start with, I'd like to pay you a compliment,' Lisa Lamm said. 'I had no idea you could be so empathetic.'

'It's all about saving time,' Bäckström said, shrugging his shoulders. 'Once someone like von Comer clams up, it can take years before they're behind bars.'

'You got him to admit that Eriksson had assaulted him,' Lisa Lamm said.

'Sure, but that's not going to land him in prison. That just makes him a crime victim.'

'But it's also a potential motive, which is a good start. I think you're being too modest, Bäckström. And he's also conceded that he met both Åkare and García Gomez just a couple of days before the murder. In his own home, no less. We didn't have any idea about that.'

'Rather that than have one of his neighbours tell us, meaning we could accuse him of lying,' Bäckström said. 'The chances that one of them might have noticed Åkare and García Gomez must be pretty reasonable, to put it mildly. If you ask me, he's only said one thing that I think is of any value. But, at the same time, it worries me.'

'What's that?' Lisa Lamm asked.

'That he denies ever having been inside Eriksson's house. That he's never even set foot there. Suppose he was sitting there and shat himself on Eriksson's sofa when Eriksson tried to blow his head off and that one of his accomplices goes on to kill Eriksson.'

'Would he be so stupid as to deny ever having been inside the house? I see what you mean,' Lisa Lamm said.

'If I was in his trousers, I'd have said, sure, I was there a few days before, to celebrate the fact that we'd patched things up, and because we'd had a bit to drink – a lot, actually – I happened to let out a little fart that turned out to be considerably wetter than anticipated.' The sort of thing that can happen to the best of us, Bäckström thought.

'I agree,' Lisa Lamm said. 'If it is his DNA on that sofa, which we might know as early as tomorrow, then I promise to remand him in custody on suspicion of Eriksson's murder.'

'And what if it isn't?'

'Attempted fraud, or actual aggravated fraud,' Lisa Lamm said. 'He won't be able to wriggle out of that one.'

'I'm inclined to agree with you,' Bäckström said with a shrug. 'The problem is that I'm a homicide detective, and that's not really much comfort to me. Anyway – there are two things I wanted to ask you for.'

'Yes?'

'Firstly, that we hold him until we get the results from the National Forensics Lab, telling us if it was him trying to lay a log on Eriksson's sofa.'

'Of course,' Lisa Lamm said. 'Agreed. And the second thing?'

'That you and Ek take charge of interviewing him after lunch. You could even bring in Nadja as well, if she's got anything to contribute. Ask him about the fraud. If you're wondering why I don't want to wield the axe, it's because I've got other, more important things to do.'

'Do you think he's going to deny it?'

'Categorically,' Bäckström said. 'He'll deny it categorically. And then he'll clam up. Refuse to talk to you. Won't say another word until he's got a lawyer present. After that, we're fucked. Then you'll have to drag him all the way to the Court of Appeal. And when they shake their heads, you'll end up at the European Court.'

'Suppose you led the interview with him instead, then?'

'It wouldn't make the slightest bit of difference,' Bäckström said. 'People like him are just made that way.'

106

Lisa Lamm and Johan Ek had spoken to Nadja Högberg, and what Nadja had been able to tell them put them in a very good mood in advance of the interview they would be conducting with von Comer after lunch. According to von Comer's bank, over the course of the ten days between Monday, 20 May, and Thursday, 30 May, he had made three separate withdrawals, amounting in total to a million kronor. He had even told his contact at the bank that the reason for this was the conclusion of an art deal with a seller who wanted payment in cash, and in Swedish kronor.

The search of his computer had shown beyond any reasonable doubt that someone with access to the computer had manipulated the original invoice in pounds and actively changed it to look like the amount was in Swedish kronor. The difference was nine hundred and sixty-two thousand kronor. The same amount that had been found in Eriksson's desk. The amended invoice had then been emailed to Eriksson from the same computer, and fourteen days later an amount of approximately one hundred thousand Swedish kronor had been transferred from von Comer's business account to an account belonging to Eriksson.

The original invoice amounting to just over a million

kronor that had been sent in the post by Sotheby's in London had also been found, in one of the files in von Comer's office. The balance from Sotheby's had been paid into his business account at the SE Bank. The day after the money arrived from England, the amount on the amended invoice had been transferred to Eriksson's account. The difference – almost one million kronor – stayed in von Comer's account. An amount which stood out, seeing as it was pretty much the only payment into the account during the month in question.

'And let's not forget that, according to the notes Eriksson made on his computer, he was the one who discovered what von Comer was up to. The person who put him on to it was probably Bäckström's anonymous informant,' Nadja Högberg said.

Well armed with facts and in good spirits, Senior Prosecutor Lisa Lamm chose to lead the interview with von Comer herself. She laid her cards on the table, showing him the evidence as she set out to question their suspected perpetrator. He responded by doing exactly what Bäckström had predicted.

To begin with, he explained to Lisa Lamm that it was all a misunderstanding, discovered by him and immediately rectified. That was all there was to it. A lamentable misunderstanding, no more than that. Lisa Lamm didn't share that opinion, nor his interpretation. In her opinion, this was without doubt an attempt at aggravated fraud. What followed was again exactly what Bäckström had described.

'That's quite preposterous,' von Comer said. 'This is a completely pointless discussion, and I refuse to say another word until I'm allowed to see my lawyer.'

'That sounds to me like a very sensible decision,' Lisa Lamm agreed. 'Because I've decided to request that you be remanded in custody this afternoon on the grounds of reasonable evidence. Bearing in mind your attitude, I'm afraid this could take quite a while to sort out.' Welcome to the real world, you stuck-up arsehole, Senior Prosecutor Lisa Lamm thought.

107

Once Bäckström had left the police station, the remainder of his day had gone very well. While von Comer was sitting in his cell in the custody unit out in Solna, enjoying boiled sausage with horseradish sauce and mechanically peeled potatoes, Bäckström had partaken of a light lunch on the veranda of Operakällaren: fresh prawns with vendace caviar, grilled lamb cutlets, a raspberry parfait, as well as the drinks that formed a natural accompaniment. After a final cognac to aid his digestion, he took a taxi home to Kungsholmen for an afternoon rest.

On the way, his driver had stopped to buy a copy of the biggest evening paper in the country. Bäckström had already realized from the bellicose headlines that this was a day that would go down in Swedish media history. For the first time, investigative reporters had managed to connect His Majesty the King with the murder of a famous lawyer. The fact that there was also evidence of connections to the very worst sort of organized crime and art fraud amounting to millions was almost irrelevant in the larger context.

Bäckström began by switching off his phone, then he put on his dressing-gown, mixed the cooling summer drink that was obligatory at this time of year, lay down on the sofa and devoted a whole hour to reading the paper.

From the introductory leader column, in which the paper's political correspondent thundered against the Swedish banana monarchy and an aristocracy in a state of utter decay, to the final article, in which the newspaper's court reporter gave an account of the king's close friendship with Baron Hans Ulrik von Comer, and all the constitutional problems this could lead to.

In the middle of the paper, the editor-in-chief had expressed his own opinion. The only reason that they had chosen to publish the name of this latter-day Anckarström – harking back to Gustaf III's assassination in 1792 – was of course that he was suspected of having committed one of the worst crimes in the Swedish Penal Code. Of murdering one of the country's most famous lawyers.

Between all these principled observations they had managed to squeeze in over ten pages of news on the same theme, generously illustrated with pictures of all those involved in the story. His Majesty the King in an admiral's uniform, in a frockcoat with the blue sash of the Royal Order of the Seraphim, in a white smoking jacket holding a glass of champagne, in a green Loden hunting jacket, clutching a shotgun, Baron von Comer in similar attire, all the way down to Eriksson the lawyer in a pinstripe suit, and Åkare and García Gomez in their motorbike helmets and leather waistcoats bearing the Hells Angels emblem. All the known actors in the drama, one of whom had been lying as a corpse in the forensic medical centre out in Solna for the past week or so, one now in custody at the police station, two with arrest warrants issued in their absence and the fifth on a state visit to Turkey.

The newspaper's editorial staff had hit the bull's-eye again and again throughout the past twenty-four hours, whereas the palace press department appeared to have coped less well. They had denied any particular knowledge of the villain of the piece. In the more familiar sense – considering the context – they had even denied him. Baron Hans Ulrik von Comer was at best a superficial acquaintance of the king and his family, and that acquaintanceship rested entirely upon the fact that he had been engaged for a number of minor tasks relating to the royal art collections. This was a trifling duty, and one which was currently being both investigated and brought to a close. This in spite of the fact that, to judge by the press secretary's statement, it might have been thought that those duties consisted merely of dusting one or two old cabinets and adjusting the fringes of a few carpets along the way.

In response to this denial, the paper had published a veritable bombardment of pictures of the king and von Comer together in various social situations. In uniform and tails, smoking jackets and dark suits, scout caps, hunting jackets, golf trousers, riding boots, and – nine times out of ten – with a glass in their hands. Even pictures from the Riviera, in which both gentlemen were adorned with nothing but bathing trunks, cocktails with umbrellas in and happy smiles.

This is going to be brilliant, Bäckström thought with a sigh of contentment as he logged into his computer to take a look at the video on the newspaper's website showing 'the violent arrest of the king's best friend', in which he 'was assaulted by a female police officer'.

The paper's well-placed cameraman had managed to capture most of the action. In one take, with a shaky handheld camera, the film began with von Comer, dressed in a dressing-gown and red silk pyjamas, trying to shut the door in Anchor Carlsson's face, then she grabs him by the arm, shoves him back into the hall, he slaps her in the face, she knocks his legs out from under him and literally throws him to the floor, sits astride his back, pulls his arms back and handcuffs him. In both sound and vision, so Bäckström was able to hear shouting and yelling, insults and swearing, even the click of the handcuffs. Just to make sure, subtitles had been provided for the hard of hearing.

Quite phenomenal, Bäckström sighed, directing a devout nod of gratitude towards the chandelier, just in case. A stroke of genius to let the Anchor handle the arrest, he thought. Mind you, it was surely no more than fair for him to receive commission of just a few per cent on the millions the film had probably already earned the paper.

After a couple of hours of restorative sleep, Bäckström called Lisa Lamm and enquired about the afternoon's developments. As far as von Comer was concerned, he had done precisely as Bäckström had predicted. And she had done her duty as a prosecutor and had requested that he be remanded in custody on the grounds of reasonable suspicion of having committed either aggravated fraud or attempted aggravated fraud. She had opened a preliminary investigation into him for the assault of a public official and planned to take action on the murder as soon as they had heard back from the National Forensics Lab. No matter what those results showed, she was inclined to hold him over the weekend. Ambitious woman. She's probably trying to ingratiate herself because she's heard about the super-salami, Bäckström thought.

That left just one more work-related call to make before it was time to relax and plan the evening's activities. He took out his private mobile and called his tame reporter at the larger of the country's two evening papers to tell him about the latest developments.

'Brilliant, Bäckström,' the reporter said. 'So you're saying he's being remanded in custody on grounds of reasonable evidence and will be held over the weekend? What about his suspected involvement in the murder?'

'That's ongoing,' Bäckström said. 'I'm expecting to get results back from the National Forensics Lab tomorrow. Naturally, I'll keep you informed as and when anything happens.

'By the way, what have you lot got planned for tomorrow?'

There was any amount of material, according to the reporter. Their readers' response had been huge, and the torrent of tips that had crashed down on the newsroom was like a tsunami, so now they just had to go through everything in the right order. The problem they faced was the opposite of what was usually the case for the media, considering all the material they had at their disposal. Usually, they were trying to make mountains out of molehills, but now they suddenly had the opposite problem.

'How do you mean?' Bäckström asked. What's the fucker going on about?

'We don't want to make a molehill out of a really big mountain just so we can squeeze it in the paper,' the reporter explained.

'Okay,' Bäckström said. 'Has anything else happened that I ought to know about?'

Nothing much, according to the reporter. The newsroom was planning to dig deeper into Eriksson's murder and the comprehensive art fraud that had to be the motive behind it. And of course they were going to be investigating the close connections between the king's best friend and the leading representatives of the very worst forms of organized crime.

The paper's political desk had already mobilized fifty female MPs from various parties who intended to go public with their support of Bäckström's colleague, Detective Inspector Annika Carlsson. They were also going to run a lengthy interview with the Minister for Equality, in which she heaped praise on Carlsson the policewoman. Finally, a woman who had had enough of male violence against women and had the courage to fight back. The minister herself had joined the Republican Association the moment she saw the video. Only now had she realized the swamp of misogyny that the king and his friends inhabited.

'The old bag must be a fucking dyke,' Bäckström pronounced.

'Does Dolly Parton sleep on her back?' the reporter sighed. 'Right now, we're working on getting an interview with the queen about the king's view of women. Apparently, their press secretary is going to get back to us tomorrow. With a bit of luck, we'll be able to get it into the paper over the weekend.

'And then there's all the usual, of course. Statements and petitions and campaigns, all that stuff,' the reporter said in summary. 'It seems the sports desk is going to run some sort of special report where female boxers, wrestlers and martial arts experts give women advice on how to beat men up.'

'Okay, I hear what you're saying,' Bäckström said. How could anyone defend themselves against a woman like Anchor Carlsson?

'Actually, there was one more thing,' the reporter said, sounding like he'd just thought of something.

'Okay, I'm listening,' Bäckström said.

'Some weird woman called, claiming she'd seen one of her paintings in the paper. It was the one of that fat priest, the one I got from you. The bloke with his hand in the collection box. She reckoned it was her painting.'

'Did she give her name?' That must be the one GeGurra said he'd bought.

'Obviously, I asked, but she said she wouldn't dream of giving her name to someone like me. She sounded really stuck-up, if that wasn't already obvious.'

'So what did you say to that?'

'I suggested that she call you. If she was having such a problem talking to someone like me, I mean. If she wanted to come forward with any information.'

'And what did she say?'

'That she'd thought of doing that. But that she hadn't got time. She was about to get married and would be away on her honeymoon. But she said she'd call you as soon as she gets back.'

'She's going to call me?'

'Yes, she reckons she knows you, and as soon as she gets back from her honeymoon she's going to call you.'

Knows me? Another one, Bäckström thought. There's no end to them.

108

Anchor Carlsson had had to turn her phone off. Journalists had been calling non-stop all day, almost all of them women, or 'sisters', as a few of them called themselves, and they all wanted the same thing. That she would come forward and tell them about the sense of liberation she must have felt when she assaulted the king's best friend and put him in cuffs. It wasn't until she got in her car that evening to drive back to her little flat in Bergshamra that she discovered she had five messages from a very agitated Isabella Norén, asking her to call her back.

'Sorry I haven't called before, but my phone's been switched off,' Annika said. 'How can I help you?' She sounds wiped out, she thought. Something must have happened.

'I've been threatened,' Isabella said. 'Some really nasty blokes appeared after I got home from work. You've got to help me.'

'Okay,' Annika said. 'I'm on my way. Don't hang up . . . start by taking a deep breath . . . then we'll talk as I'm driving . . . I'm going to need the code to the front door . . . and I'll be there in ten minutes . . .'

Annika Carlsson kept her promise. Ten minutes later she stepped into the hall of Isabella's apartment in Östermalm to find a red-eyed and agitated Isabella Norén. Five minutes later they were sitting on her sofa in the living room.

'Tell me,' Annika Carlsson said. She leaned towards her, giving her a friendly nod and a sisterly smile.

Isabella had left the office just before seven that evening. She had walked home, stopping on the way to get some food and a newspaper, and got to her apartment about half an hour after leaving work.

While she was standing in the hall, one bag in her hand, another that she'd just put down, the doorbell rang, and, assuming it was her neighbour wanting to talk to her, she opened the door without checking to see who it was first.

'My neighbour's a nice old lady. Sometimes I get the feeling that she's been standing waiting for me when I get home.'

'I understand.' Annika nodded for her to go on.

'It was Afsan Ibrahim,' Isabella Norén said. 'You know who that is, don't you?'

'Yes,' Annika Carlsson said. 'All too well.'

'Thomas's most regular client,' Isabella said with a forced smile. 'Him and all his friends. He had two of them with him. In the office, we usually call them Ali and Ali. I can find out what their names are if you want to know. Two really nasty types, with dead eyes. They just stand there staring at you, if you know what I mean. Never say anything. Not even if you say hello to them.'

'So what did Afsan want?'

'He wanted to talk to me. He wasn't threatening, but it wasn't as if he was asking. So I said yes. As long as it didn't take too long, because I was going to be meeting my boyfriend for dinner in half an hour.'

'But you'd made that bit up?'

'Yes, of course. Boyfriend and dinner. So we sat down in here, to talk, while those two creeps stayed in the hall. He wanted to talk about Thomas.'

'He wanted to talk to you about Thomas? Why you in particular?'

'He told me why. It was the first thing he said. Because I used to be Thomas's girlfriend, he wanted to talk to me.'

'Why did he think that?'

'Thomas and I were in a bar a few months ago. We were having a nice time, tucked away in a corner drinking wine, then Afsan came over and said hello. Then he spoke to Thomas for a while – five minutes, maybe – about one of his friends who'd messed up and needed help, and then he left. It can't have been too difficult for him to work out what was going on.'

'Your address, then? How did he get hold of that?'

'Certainly not from me, anyway. But it's probably not that hard to find out where I live.'

'What did he want?'

Afsan Ibrahim wanted to talk about money. Money that Thomas Eriksson owed him. A lot of money. Money he wanted back.

'Because I was Thomas's girlfriend, he wanted me to help with that. I told him the truth: I said I had no idea about Thomas's finances or how much money he had and where it was. Or if he even had any.'

'How did he take that?'

'He said, if that was the case, then I'd better find out. That I and everyone else working for the firm was just as responsible for Thomas's debt as he was himself. I didn't comment on that, as you can probably appreciate.'

'I certainly can.'

'Anyway, he was up at the office yesterday, talking to

Peter. He's the executor of Thomas's estate, of course. They must have been talking for a good hour. He had Ali and Ali with him. And one other man I'd never seen before. He seemed a lot more pleasant. He actually smiled, but he didn't say what his name was. Peter must have sat with the four of them for at least an hour.'

'You don't know what they were talking about?'

'No,' Isabella Norén said, shaking her head. 'But it can't have been a particularly pleasant conversation, because I don't think I've ever seen Peter so shaken up as when they eventually left. He just went straight into his room and closed the door.'

'Afsan – did he say how much money he wanted?'

'I did ask. Then he said that if he got twenty million he was prepared to let it go.'

'Okay,' Annika Carlsson said. 'If you don't mind, I'd like to write an official report about this. For making unlawful threats.'

'Yes, that's fine. Mind you, he did say just before he left that he assumed our conversation would stay between the two of us. But I don't care about that. I don't think I've ever been so terrified in my life.'

'That's the right attitude. You need to tell your boss about this as well. Explain to him that, as your employer, he's responsible for your safety. I'm thinking of having a word with him myself. There's no need for you to worry about little Afsan. I'll make sure he's got more important things to worry about than messing you about.'

'I can imagine,' Isabella said, suddenly seeming much happier. 'We must have spent half the afternoon at work watching that video on the net. You've never considered going on that television programme? *Gladiators*?'

'No,' Annika said, shaking her head. 'Never.'

'Why not? You'd wipe the floor with them.'

'That's why,' Annika Carlsson said. 'I'm the sort of person who can't do pretend fighting.'

109

In the beginning, there were three Ibrahim brothers. Afsan's elder brother, Farshad, was five years older than him, and his little brother, Nasir, was five years younger. Now there's only Afsan himself. His older brother was murdered by the police. The police are bad people. The one who murdered his brother was the worst of the lot. He was a superintendent called Evert Bäckström. He had shot Farshad, shot him up badly, and, when he was in hospital, fighting for his life, another policeman had thrown him out of the window of his room. And Farshad had died, and the man behind everything that happened was Superintendent Bäckström. He was the one who planned it. Who had decided what was going to happen.

The Hells Angels had murdered his younger brother, Nasir. They were just as bad as the Christian crusaders who had tried to kill all righteous men like him a thousand years ago. The one who had murdered his younger brother was called Fredrik Åkare. He had murdered his little brother in such a way that not even Afsan's prayers could grant him peace. Fredrik Åkare, he was the worst of all the men who had helped to murder Nasir.

There were friends, and there were enemies, and all a real man's life was ultimately about was being able to tell the difference between them. Living life as the friend of your friends and the enemy of your enemies, and if it turned out to be the case that he was only able to destroy two of his enemies, the choice was obvious. He was willing to give his own life if he could take Bäckström's and Åkare's from them.

There were also friends. He had many friends, several of whom he was prepared to lay down his life for. All his faithful brothers, all the righteous brothers who had chosen the same path as him and had chosen to live their lives alongside him. He also had an inheritance from his elder brother, Farshad, to pass on in such a way that it honoured both his brother and him and, so far, he had managed that well. His friends respected him and his enemies feared both him and his men. The group of brothers founded by Farshad and now led by him: the Brotherhood of the Ibrahims.

There were also men who weren't like him and his soldiers but who had still chosen to do him big favours, the sort demanded by life in Sweden, and one such man who had meant a lot to him was his legal advisor, Thomas Eriksson, who, in terms of the actual work he did, was as important to him as his real brothers. Never mind that he had been handsomely rewarded for it, and that he, like all the others of his kind, had demanded their reward in money, and not in the sight of God.

Now he had been murdered, and anyone who knew anything knew that Åkare and his crusaders were responsible. The fact that the police had given Superintendent Bäckström the job of finding and punishing the murderers merely showed that they had been in league with each other right from the start.

Everything had its time. Including revenge, and now was the time. High time for revenge, before his enemies got the idea that he, Afsan Ibrahim, was as weak as a woman, and that he wasn't worthy of passing on Farshad's inheritance.

110

Ten days ago, his life had changed. He had gone to the police to tell them about a man they were looking for, because they thought the man had murdered a well-known lawyer. Now he himself was on the run, in fear of his life, and if it hadn't been for his old schoolfriend Omar, he may very well have been murdered already. At least, that was how Omar had described what had happened.

Almost a week ago, he had left his flat out in Kista, as well as his job, and he'd even thrown his mobile away. Omar had sorted out a new place for him to stay. A flat out in Flemingsberg, on the south side of Stockholm, where he was among friends and could feel safe. Omar had also given him more money than he'd ever had in his whole life – whatever use that was to him, seeing as Omar preferred him not to leave the flat, even to go shopping, sit at a café or so much as go for a walk.

Okay, so he wasn't exactly suffering. The flat he lived in with Omar was three times the size of his own place. It had everything he could want: flat-screen televisions with hundreds of channels, sound systems, big, soft leather sofas, a jacuzzi and a steam sauna in the larger of the two bathrooms. More food and drink than he could stuff himself with. Omar could sort everything out. He just had to say. Girls, drink, weed, even Swedish girls and heavier stuff, if that's what he wanted. But all Ara wanted was to get away from there.

At first he had thought of going abroad until the whole thing had calmed down. Go to Thailand for a couple of months, to get a bit of rest and have a good think about what he was going to do when he eventually returned to his old life and everything had gone back to normal. But even that was impossible now. The murderers weren't the only ones looking for him – the police were too. According to Omar, they'd put out an alert for him, and the moment he tried to board an international flight he'd find himself in a cell in Solna police station instead. So he had to wait until Omar had sorted out a new passport for him. A good passport, Swedish. Omar needed a few more days to get all the pieces in place so that Ara could get out of Sweden safely. A good Swedish passport took time, he explained. But sure, if he wanted to travel as a nigger, Omar could drive him to the airport within an hour.

Ara just nodded. There was a lot of sense in what Omar said. Which just left him with everything he had been given in place of his previous life. A large, expensive flat instead of a home with his own bed to sleep in, a life of idleness shut inside four walls instead of a job to go to. A new mobile that must have cost thousands of kronor, on which he could do everything he used to do on his computer. As long as he didn't call anyone he knew and needed to talk to. More money than he had ever had. That he couldn't use. That he didn't even need to use, seeing as Omar kept paying the whole time.

He had done a lot of thinking about his old friend Omar. How helpful he was being, and not least the fact that he seemed to know more about what had happened to him and his life than he himself knew. In the end he had asked him. How, for instance, did Omar know that he had contacted the police to tell them what he had seen that night when he almost ran over a murderer in his taxi?

According to Omar, he had been told by Kemal, and Ara needn't have bothered asking, really, seeing as Kemal had told anyone who was prepared to listen. Their old friend Kemal, who also drove a taxi, who had taken photographs of a raid on a security van with his mobile, sold the pictures to one of the evening papers and got loads of money for his trouble. More each time he told the story, Omar said with a smile. Kemal was saying that Ara had called him for advice about how to sell information the way he had done.

Omar had good answers to all his questions. Better answers than Ara himself had, even though this was supposed to be all about him. It was just like when they were at school together down in Småland: Omar was the one who knew stuff, Omar was the one who made sure things happened. Omar, who didn't even get pissed off the way normal people did. In the end, Ara had asked him about the thing he was most curious about. How come the police had pictures of him? How come Omar was in the same cop database as the lethal character he'd seen only by chance?

Omar had an answer for that as well. A good answer. It wasn't his fault that he was on the database but his dad's, and, because everyone who was at the same school as them had spent more time talking about Omar's dad than everyone else's dads put together, Ara had believed that too. Even though none of them had ever met Omar's dad. Just read about him in the papers and seen him on television, usually on *Crimewatch*, which was the show that all the tough guys down in Småland really liked. Omar's dad, Abdul ben Kader, the man who – according to rumour – was behind all the major crimes in the country at the time when Omar and Ara were at school together.

'You can imagine what the cops thought when they realized that I, Omar ben Kader, was the son of Abdul ben Kader. An ordinary bloke studying at the Institute of Technology, claiming he's going to be a chemical engineer. How many cops do you think bought that? You wouldn't believe me if I told you what they offered me to grass on my own dad.'

'How did you sort that out?' Ara asked. I only got two five-hundreds in exchange for my whole life, he thought.

'I tried to tell it how it was,' Omar said, shrugging his shoulders. 'That my dad had more kids than he was even aware of. And more wives than the Prophet. That the cops had probably spoken to my dad more times than I had. And that, if they didn't believe me, they could talk to my mum. They couldn't talk to Dad, of course. He went back to Morocco fifteen years ago. He's a big man there, a very rich and powerful man, and if the Swedish cops went down there and tried to talk to him, the local sheriff would lock them up the minute they set foot on Moroccan soil.'

'So you never got caught for anything?' Ara asked.

'Never,' Omar said, holding up both palms. 'Not even a speeding ticket. If you don't believe me, you can take a look at my criminal record. It's completely empty. Omar ben Kader is a Swedish chemical engineer with absolutely no convictions. Born and raised in Gnosjö in Småland, a graduate of the Institute of Technology in Stockholm. I never got mixed up in any of the funny business they kept going on about. On the few occasions I've got up to any business at all, there was never anything funny about it as long as I was involved.'

'You're like me then,' Ara said. His employer had asked to see his record when he applied to start driving taxis. No convictions, Ara thought. For the simple reason that he had never committed any crimes, apart from the occasional bit of speeding.

'That's just how it is,' Omar declared with a shrug. 'The fact that the cops refuse to listen to people like us is our problem, but that's probably the last thing they're worried about.'

'But all your contacts, all this money . . . You just have to snap your fingers and a load of blokes show up to sort things for you. That's what I can't get my head round,' Ara said.

'That's because I'm the son of Abdul ben Kader,' Omar said. 'Not because of what I do, but because of who I am. You've no idea how many people would give me their right hand if I could just arrange for them to meet my father.'

'I get it,' Ara said, nodding. Not who you are, but who they think you are, he thought.

The next morning he woke up to find Omar in his room with his hand on his shoulder, shaking him gently so as not to startle him. He was looking at him with the same friendly smile, to let him know that there was nothing to worry about.

'Things are starting to move,' he said with a nod. 'If everything goes to plan, you'll be able to leave first thing tomorrow.'

'First thing tomorrow?' At last, Ara thought.

'If everything goes to plan,' Omar repeated. 'But first we need to change location. I've got a place outside Nyköping that's only ten kilometres from Skavsta Airport. It'll have to be Skavsta. That's much better than Arlanda. More brothers and sisters manning the borders for Sweden, if you get my meaning,' Omar said, smiling his usual wide, friendly smile.

'I get it,' Ara said.

'The first plane to London leaves at six o'clock tomorrow morning. It's Ryanair, but you'll just have to put up with that, because it gets better. Okay?'

'Okay,' Ara said.

'You're booked on a direct flight from London to Bangkok, leaving after lunch tomorrow. Thai Air, first class. So, soon your suffering will be over, my friend,' Omar said with a smile.

111

It had turned into a late night for Detective Inspector Annika Carlsson. As soon as she left Isabella Norén she drove back to the station to prepare for the following day. First, she called Lisa Lamm and told her about Afsan Ibrahim's threatening behaviour towards Isabella and about his and his associates' visit to see Danielsson the lawyer the previous day. The conversation took fifteen minutes, and they had been heartwarmingly unanimous from the outset.

Fresh interviews with Norén and Danielsson the following morning, preferably before the daily meeting of the investigative team. Then writing up Norén's report and trying to get her boss, Danielsson, to follow suit. Then pick up Afsan and his associates as quickly as possible. Identify the latter with the help of more photographs, tell them they were under suspicion, conduct interviews with them and then – ideally – get them locked up.

While Annika Carlsson downloaded pictures of Afsan Ibrahim and thirty known members of the 'voluntary association for Muslims in Sweden', as he had once described the Brotherhood of the Ibrahims in a much remarked upon interview in a magazine, Lisa Lamm called Peter Danielsson on his mobile.

Enough squirming from this little worm, she thought,

and it's possible that the message got through, because just ten minutes later the lawyer agreed to be at the police station in Solna at eight o'clock the next morning to be interviewed about the grave threats that Afsan Ibrahim had directed against one of his female colleagues, Isabella Norén.

The interviews with Norén and Danielsson started at eight o'clock on Wednesday morning, and Annika Carlsson's interview with Isabella Norén went swimmingly. First, she identified the four men who had visited the law firm on Monday: Afsan Ibrahim, Ali Ibrahim, Ali Issa and Omar ben Kader. Three of them had shown up at her apartment the following day: Afsan Ibrahim, Ali Ibrahim and Ali Issa. But not Omar ben Kader, she was certain of that.

'I almost missed him, actually,' Isabella said, shaking her head. 'He was the only one who seemed normal when they were at the office. He seemed nice, even.'

'Yes, that what he's known for,' Annika Carlsson said. 'It's said that Omar is always polite and courteous.'

'So what's he done?' Isabella asked. 'How did he get caught up with those others?'

'Okay,' Annika said. 'If you promise this won't go any further, and because we're in the same branch, he's never been convicted of anything. Among my colleagues who work exclusively with men like this, he's believed to be Afsan's right-hand man. But there's some doubt about that, apparently.'

'How do you mean?'

'According to a number of my colleagues, Omar is the one in charge, even if his boss Afsan hasn't quite grasped that.'

* * *

The entire interview with Isabella Norén was over in less than an hour. First, the photographs and identification, then her official complaint against Afsan, Ali Ibrahim and Ali Issa and, finally, the usual friendly, concluding chat that ends most interviews that have gone smoothly. Before they parted, Isabella asked Annika for her opinion on something.

'I'm thinking of handing in my notice,' Isabella said.

'I think that sounds like a very wise decision.'

The interview with the lawyer Danielsson hadn't gone as smoothly as the one his interlocutors Detective Inspectors Bladh and Alm had conducted with him at his office two days before, and which they intended to supplement now in the presence of Senior Prosecutor Lisa Lamm because of recent events which were of significance to the investigation.

'I understand that the Senior Prosecutor has already informed you of the threats that were made against one of your employees, Isabella Norén,' Bladh said.

'Yes, it's terrible,' the lawyer agreed. 'I called her as soon as I heard about it, and I can assure you that we at the firm have already taken all the security measures at our disposal.'

'Good,' Bladh said, putting three photographs in front of Danielsson.

'She's identified these three,' Bladh said. 'Afsan Ibrahim, Ali Issa and Afsan's relative, Ali Ibrahim. She wasn't the least bit uncertain, because she's seen them on a number of occasions in your offices.'

'Yes, as soon as I get the opportunity, naturally, I will be holding discussions with the other partners to see if it will be possible for us to represent them in the future, bearing in mind—'

'That's not what interests me most,' Bladh interrupted. 'We're wondering what sort of threats they made against you, the day before they paid their home visit to Norén.'

'I have no comment to make on that point, as I'm sure you understand,' Danielsson said, shaking his head. 'That conversation is of course covered by my oath of confidentiality as a lawyer—'

'Hear what you're saying,' Bladh persisted. 'It can't have been a particularly pleasant conversation, from what we've heard. And you were also visited by one extra person. Four in total – quite a little delegation. His name is Omar ben Kader, in case you were wondering,' Bladh went on, putting a fourth photograph down in front of Danielsson.

'No comment,' Danielsson said. 'Anyway, he didn't introduce himself.'

'Indulge our curiosity,' Bladh said. 'Seeing as we appear to be in agreement that they were in your office talking to you for about an hour, give or take, according to what we've been told.'

'As I've already said, I have no comment to make, for the simple reason that it would conflict with the rules by which I am governed in my role as a lawyer.'

'It's good that you said that,' Lisa Lamm interjected. 'Because I don't share that interpretation—'

'Like I said—'

'Don't interrupt me,' Lisa Lamm said. 'We have good reason to believe that your former colleague received approximately twenty million kronor in unofficial payment from Afsan Ibrahim, for various forms of legal and other advice. Money which a lawyer really shouldn't have.'

'Like I said . . . I can't have any—'

'Think very carefully now, Danielsson,' Lisa Lamm warned.

'I have no comment to make,' Danielsson insisted, shaking his head to underline his point.

'You're not giving me any choice then, Danielsson,' Lisa Lamm said with a regretful shrug. 'I understand that you're due in court out in Attunda this morning.'

'That's right,' Danielsson said in surprise, glancing at his watch. 'I've only got thirty minutes at most before I—'

'Don't worry,' Lisa Lamm said. 'I'll call and talk to them.'

'I don't understand,' Danielsson said, looking as if he genuinely didn't.

'I've decided to remand you in custody. And, bearing in mind the circumstances, I—'

'Now hold on, just hold on,' Danielsson said, raising his hands in an almost beseeching gesture. 'Surely we can discuss this like adults?'

'Let's make one last attempt, then,' Lisa Lamm said, leaning back in her chair with her arms crossed over her chest. 'One last attempt,' she repeated with a warning nod.

How could that have been so hard to squeeze out? Lisa Lamm thought half an hour later, once Detective Inspector Bladh had concluded the interview with lawyer Peter Danielsson.

'Do you want me to order you a taxi?' Detective Inspector Alm asked as a pale, sweating Danielsson was leaving the room.

'No problem,' Danielsson said. 'I'll get one.'

'That's good,' Alm said. 'Looks like I just ran out of battery.'

'A word in your ear, Danielsson,' Bladh said as he headed down the corridor towards the exit with him. 'And it's out of consideration for both you and your family, if you're curious.'

'Yes? What do you want to say?'

'Afsan Ibrahim is capable of absolutely anything,' Bladh said, looking at him solemnly. 'Believe me. Absolutely anything.'

'Thank you,' Danielsson said. 'I understand what you're saying. I believe you.'

'Good,' Bladh said. 'Take care.'

112

The head of the crime unit at Solna Police, Commissioner Toivonen, was a man who lived his professional life through his cases and, to make the day-to-day work easier, he had got into the habit of listing them on the whiteboard on the wall behind his desk. For the past four days things had been simplified by the fact that the usually long list now consisted of just one case.

'Find Å, GG and driver', in Toivonen's simple code, because he couldn't be sure that his room wouldn't be visited by nosy individuals who had nothing to do with the case. In plain language, his current task was to find Åkare and García Gomez, arrest them and make sure they ended up behind bars in Solna police station before they found the witness that Bäckström and his team wanted to get hold of.

One case, compared to the usual half-dozen, hundreds of officers out in the field, hopefully working their backsides off so that Toivonen would soon be able to wipe the board clean and get back to normal. Four days without any new leads, even though Fredrik Åkare was two metres tall and made up of one hundred and fifty kilos of muscle and bone, as well as having a dark-blond ponytail that hung halfway down his back. Measured against the usual police scale, he had to be one of their least challenging targets.

It had been like this for four days, until his old friend Commissioner Honkamäki had called him for a confidential chat, one Finnish brother to another. Honkamäki used to be head of the rapid response unit in Stockholm, but for the past few years he had been in charge of the Intelligence and Surveillance Division at National Crime. The sort of thing one never talked about. Except perhaps to a Finnish brother who also happened to be a Swedish police officer.

'How's things?' Honkamäki asked. 'I understand that you're looking for Åkare and his underling, García Gomez, and some bastard taxi-driver who's reluctant to do his civic duty. Correct me if I'm wrong.'

'I'm listening,' Toivonen said. At last, he thought, because Honkamäki was a man who took his duties as seriously as he did and would never waste his time on sympathetic chit-chat.

'Just to be clear, I have one simple question,' Honkamäki said. 'How certain are you that Eriksson was bumped off at a quarter to ten in the evening?'

'Absolutely certain,' Toivonen said. 'I've spoken to Niemi, if that's what you were wondering, so this isn't just something Bäckström has tried to foist upon me.'

'Hit over the head with a blunt object? That was the cause of death?'

'Yes,' Toivonen said.

'In that case, you can forget about Åkare being the perpetrator,' Honkamäki said. 'You can drop him completely. He's got an alibi that's as good as García Gomez's. Even better, if you ask me.'

'What time period does it cover?'

'The whole of Sunday evening, 2 June, from eight

o'clock onwards. At least until midnight, midnight between 2 and 3 June,' Honkamäki clarified.

'In that case I think it would be a good idea for us to meet.'

'See you at the usual place in half an hour,' Honkamäki suggested.

'The usual place,' Toivonen agreed.

Which was exactly what happened. 'The usual place', among brothers, was an English pub just a few blocks from central police headquarters on Kungsholmen. Once the lunchtime rush was over it offered the requisite seclusion for confidential conversations. At that time of day there were just a few regulars squabbling at the bar with the humble bartender. If you sat in the booth at the far end of the room you were at least ten metres away from the nearest unauthorized ear. Discreet lighting, black oak panelling, wall-to-wall carpets – what more could you ask for a conversation of that sort? Possibly a couple of large glasses of beer, given that it was past two in the afternoon and that summer had finally arrived.

'Cheers,' Toivonen said, raising his glass.

'Same to you, brother,' Honkamäki said, raising his.

'So, tell me,' Toivonen said.

Unfortunately, there wasn't a great deal to tell, according to Honkamäki. Not considering the organization he was currently in charge of, but, because Toivonen was who he was, the message inherent in this – the things he wasn't saying – ought nonetheless to be clear enough. Fredrik Åkare had an alibi from eight o'clock in the evening of Sunday, 2 June, until midnight, four hours later. An alibi chiselled in stone, and, just for once, he was the person holding both hammer and chisel.

As far as Åkare and García Gomez were concerned, he could have them behind bars within an hour, if that was what was called for. The problem was that he and everyone else in the department he ran would rather have them on the loose. For the time being, at least. Åkare and his friends were planning something big, and Honkamäki and his colleagues were inclined to let them carry on until they had enough evidence to get secure convictions, at long last.

'This time we've really got our eyes on them,' Honkamäki said. 'It's got nothing to do with Bäckström's murder of that lawyer, nothing at all, but this time we're looking at over ten years for the lot of them, more for Åkare, García Gomez and a few others.'

'Okay,' Toivonen said. 'I hear what you're saying, in which case there might be something else that you ought to know.'

'Tell me,' Honkamäki said.

Toivonen went on to tell him about the tip Stigson had given him three days before, about the fact that Åkare had apparently got himself a new woman, which certainly wasn't anything that had appeared in any of the databases Toivonen had access to, and probably wasn't on any others either.

'She's said to be Danish,' Toivonen said. 'Supposed to have come highly recommended by Åkare's Danish brothers. My officer was tipped off by a former colleague who knows practically everyone who's anyone out in Solna, regardless of which side of the fence they're on.'

'Roly Stålhammar.' Honkamäki smiled. 'How is he these days? I usually see him out at the races at Solvalla, pretty much every week, but it's been a while since I last saw him.'

'Still going, as far as I know,' Toivonen said with a shrug. 'If Fredrik's latest should turn out to be one of our own, perhaps it might be time to bring her in.'

'People talk,' Honkamäki said. 'I understand what you're getting at,' he added.

'People talk,' Toivonen agreed.

'Anything I can help you with?'

One more thing, Toivonen said. Help with sorting out the question marks surrounding the fact that García Gomez had definitely shown up at their crime scene about four hours after Eriksson was murdered. During that visit he cut Eriksson's dog's throat and took the opportunity to smash in the head of the dog's dead owner on his way out. And very nearly got run over by a taxi the moment he stepped on to the street.

'García Gomez is crazy, obviously, but I had no idea he was that crazy. What the hell was he doing there? We didn't find any sign of an orderly queue outside Eriksson's door, if I can put it like that.'

'I'm afraid I can't help you with that,' Honkamäki said, shaking his head regretfully. 'I'm as curious as you are, so it will have to be a guess. I'd say he wanted to exchange a few blunt words with Eriksson and had no idea that someone had already shut him up for good a few hours before he showed up.'

'That same thought has occurred to me,' Toivonen said. 'But, considering that the likelihood of that is pretty much zero, I dropped it. But I appreciate you trying to help.'

'Don't mention it,' Honkamäki said, taking a sip of his beer. 'What I might possibly be able to help you with, however, is the registration number of that silver Mercedes you've been looking for.'

'When could you do that?' At last, Toivonen thought, with a nod.

'As soon as possible,' Honkamäki said. 'I'm still grappling with the issue, if I can put it like that.'

113

Everything that was happening to him these days wasn't really about him, but about Omar, Ara thought. For the past week his whole life had been in Omar's hands, and every time anything slightly unusual had happened, it had started the same way. One of Omar's many mobile phones would ring. It seemed like he had a different one in every pocket, all with different ringtones. Omar would answer with the usual short grunt. He would then switch to Arabic, which Ara barely understood a word of, and after a minute at most the call usually ended. And then things would start to happen. Like now.

'Okay, let's go,' Omar said with a smile. 'Looks like everything's sorted.'

Two of Omar's many assistants were standing waiting outside when they emerged on to the street. Ara had never seen these two before and, going by their manner, this would be the first and last time he met them. It wasn't that they were at all unpleasant, but there was something in their eyes that told him they hadn't come to socialize and make small-talk.

'This is Ali and Ali,' Omar said with a broad smile. 'Ali and Ali – you have to admit that's pretty practical. They're going to drive us down to our last stop before it's time for you to leave. They've also got your passport.'

They drove in two cars. Ali One went first, alone, in one car, and a kilometre or so behind was Ali Two, with Omar and Ara in the back seat.

'You could be Siamese twins,' Omar said, sounding delighted as he handed Ara his new passport. 'You have to admit, it's good. All you need to do is learn your name and a bit of background information. We'll run through that later.'

It was certainly good enough for the average Swede at passport control not to notice any difference, Ara thought, nodding.

'Samir,' Ara said, nodding again. A Swedish citizen, like him, and, judging by his surname, from Iran, like him. Ought to work.

'No need to worry, my friend,' Omar assured him. 'We didn't just pick that up off the street. He's a trustworthy brother who just wants to help us, that's all.'

'Tickets, hotel, all that sort of thing?'

'Also sorted,' Omar said with a smile. 'Nothing to worry about, man.'

An hour later they arrived at the house where he was going to be spending his last night in Sweden until things had quietened down again. A red wooden house with white windows and a glassed-in veranda and its own jetty down by a little lake just fifty metres from the gravel drive where they were standing.

'Not bad, eh?' Omar said. 'Every ordinary Swede's dream house.'

'How did you find this?' Ara asked.

'Another brother,' Omar said, holding out his hands disarmingly. 'A trustworthy brother,' he added.

The Swedish dream of a summerhouse in the country, Ara thought. Just half an hour from Skavsta Airport but at least a kilometre away from the nearest neighbour. No one could accuse Omar of not paying attention to detail. This wasn't the sort of place the police would think of looking for someone like him.

Ali and Ali carried their bags in. Then they nodded at Omar, got back into one of the cars and drove off, leaving the other car so Omar could drive Ara to the airport the next morning.

'Alone at last,' Omar said with a wide smile. 'What do you want to do? Play cards, watch television, have something to eat?'

'You decide,' Ara said with a shrug.

'How about a bit of fishing?' Omar said, nodding towards the jetty. 'You used to like fishing. Do you remember, when we were still at school? Sitting on the jetty with our little fishing rods, talking about life.'

'Sounds good,' Ara agreed. Just like when he and Omar were at school together, he thought.

Just like when they were at school together, Ara thought a couple of hours later when they were standing in the kitchen preparing a meal. Omar had caught six perch, while he had only got one roach. Just like when they were at school together twenty years ago. The only difference this time was that they hadn't had to skive off to fish for a while and talk about life.

Then Omar's phone rang. First, the initial grunt, then the big smile. The usual apologetic nod to Ara, because he was talking Arabic, which of course Ara didn't understand.

'Everything's fine, things are moving. The kid's tethered to the tree,' Omar said, smiling even more broadly. He nodded and winked at Ara, who of course couldn't understand a word he was saying.

The kid's tethered to the tree, Afsan Ibrahim thought as he put his mobile back in his pocket. Wasn't that what his older brother, Farshad, had told him Omar's father, the great Abdul ben Kader, used to say when he described his hunting expeditions in the mountains overlooking the Mediterranean when he was young? That he used to tether a kid to a tree to lure the wolves that would otherwise rip into the families' sheep and goats.

Like father, like son, Afsan thought, nodding slowly.

114

'Where is everyone?' Bäckström asked, nodding heavily towards the forlorn remnants of what just a few days before had been a full-strength squad for the investigation of a murder.

'Bladh, Alm and Lisa Lamm are interviewing our lawyer, Danielsson,' Annika Carlsson said. 'Rosita is off sick, and the rest are out looking for Åkare and García Gomez. And our taxi-driver, of course.'

'Rosita's off sick,' Bäckström said. 'Nothing serious, I hope?'

'Don't know,' Annika Carlsson said, shaking her head. 'She's off sick until further notice.' Unless that scrawny little blonde has already put her on a plane to Guantanamo Bay, Annika thought. American crew, drugged, packed and ready to go, in a red jumpsuit with her hands and feet tied.

'Well, we can only hope that it isn't anything serious,' Bäckström said with a smug smile and a concerned shake of the head.

'Quite,' Annika Carlsson agreed. You should probably watch yourself, you little fat bastard, she thought.

'Okay,' Bäckström said, nodding at Niemi. 'How are we getting on with the results from the National Forensics Lab?'

'Things finally seem to be moving down in Linköping,'

Niemi replied, leafing through his papers. 'If we start with von Comer, who of course is still in custody, the position is as follows . . .'

'I'm listening,' Bäckström said, making himself more comfortable on his chair.

'The blood on the auction catalogue is his. And he's no longer denying that, as you no doubt all know . . .'

Thank fuck for that, Bäckström thought. All thanks to me.

'But it isn't his DNA on the sofa cushion. It's someone else's. Unknown, not in the database.'

'Shame,' Bäckström said, looking like he meant it.

'I'm afraid it's even worse than that,' Niemi went on. 'We haven't found any evidence to link von Comer to Eriksson's house. That's the first thing. The second is that witness, the neighbour who says he saw an elderly man with white hair sitting on the steps in front of Eriksson's house. You remember the one I mean?' Nods of agreement from everyone, Niemi noted.

'We've shown the witness a video. It wasn't von Comer that he saw.'

'How sure is he?' Annika Carlsson asked.

'Hundred and twenty per cent,' Niemi said with a slight smile. 'The witness already knew von Comer. They belong to the same golf club out on Värmdö.'

'Who'd have thought it.' Bäckström sighed. 'He's not just helping a fellow golfer in his time of need?'

'I really don't think he is,' Niemi said. 'Because, according to this witness, von Comer is guilty of far greater crimes than boring old art fraud.'

'What?' Bäckström said.

'It seems he cheated when he and the witness were playing a round of golf,' Peter Niemi said.

'That's what his sort is like,' Bäckström said, shrugging his shoulders. 'Anything else, Peter?'

A minor detail, possibly, but one which wasn't without significance to anyone trying to make sense of the sequence of events of the crimes they were investigating.

'Our forensic medical officer appears to have found dog-hair in Eriksson's skull,' Niemi said. 'From his own dog, but – considering their location – they didn't get there as a result of him stroking the dog and then scratching his head. The dog's hairs are embedded deep in the wounds in Eriksson's skull.'

'So first García Gomez goes out on to the terrace and breaks Eriksson's dog's back, then sits astride it and cuts the dog's throat,' Bäckström suggested.

'Then he goes back inside the house and, as he passes Eriksson, he lets loose on his skull with the same instrument he used on the dog. It could simply be the case that he was furious in general because Eriksson's dog evidently had time to take a bite at his leg,' Niemi continued.

'Of course,' Bäckström said. 'The dog-hairs on the instrument end up inside Eriksson's head, I get that. But what the hell is he doing there? Why does he turn up at Eriksson's house in the middle of the night? Given their previous dealings, he should have expected Eriksson to throw himself at the alarm button the minute García Gomez showed up at his door.'

'You don't think whoever killed Eriksson earlier that evening could have called to let him know, and then García Gomez turns up, marches straight in and leaves one last message?' Stigson suggested.

'Is that a question?' Bäckström said, glaring at his younger colleague.

'Yes. What do you think?'

'No,' Bäckström said, shaking his head. 'Even García Gomez isn't that stupid.

'To change the subject,' he went on. 'What about the fraud? How are we getting on with that, Nadja?'

'Nothing for you to worry about,' Nadja said. 'Von Comer's still denying it, admittedly, but it doesn't look like that's going to help him. Lisa says she might be able to bring charges against him as early as today.'

'Okay,' Bäckström said. 'Has he got an alibi, then? For the time of Eriksson's murder, I mean?'

'None that anyone else can corroborate. Right now he's refusing to answer any questions at all. His wife says she was away from Saturday to Monday. No phone calls, nothing on the computer, nothing from a neighbour to indicate that he was at home.'

'Let's not get carried away,' Bäckström said with a sigh. 'Maybe he was just out putting his red rose in the wrong vase.'

'I don't follow,' Nadja said. 'What do you mean?'

'It's a metaphor,' Bäckström said. 'I'll explain later,' he added with a shrug. 'I suggest we interview him again. Explain the situation to him and, if he still doesn't want to tell us where he was and who with, then he'll just have to stay locked up.' That'll give the papers something to write about, he thought.

'Okay,' Annika said, staring at him. 'What else have we got? What about that handkerchief? Did they find anything on it?'

'Some of Eriksson's blood, snot and probably saliva from another unknown individual who isn't in the database,' Niemi said.

'Sorry,' Stigson said, looking like he'd just lost the thread. 'Another one? How do you mean, Peter?'

'Not the one who crapped on the sofa,' Bäckström explained. That lad's IQ is the same as his shoe size, he thought.

'Oh, okay, I get it,' Stigson said, cheering up.

'It's pretty thin, I'm afraid,' Niemi said. 'We can't tie von Comer to the crime scene. Nor Åkare. What we have got is García Gomez and these two new ones. Two unknown individuals who aren't in our database. If you ask me, I'm afraid it's starting to look as if we're back at square one.'

'I agree,' Annika Carlsson said. 'And it also rules out Afsan Ibrahim and all his friends, if we were starting to think along those lines.'

'Hold on,' said Bäckström, who had just had a thought. 'What about that Omar ben Kader?'

'You're quite right, Bäckström,' Nadja said. 'Omar ben Kader has never had to give a DNA sample. But we have got his picture in the database. I imagine someone saw fit to add his passport photograph.'

'Okay,' Bäckström said. 'Let's get a DNA sample from him, then.'

Already underway, according to Annika Carlsson. For the past hour, the search had been expanded beyond Åkare, García Gomez and their witness, Ara, to include another four men: Afsan Ibrahim, Ali Ibrahim, Ali Issa and Omar ben Kader.

'It's as if they've all gone up in smoke,' Annika concluded, shaking her head.

'Well, just make sure that changes, then,' Bäckström grunted as he stood up. 'We can't have cells standing there empty, costing honest taxpayers loads of money.'

115

After the meeting, Lisa Lamm had informed everyone by email of the latest developments in the investigation.

Baron Hans Ulrik von Comer was being remanded in custody, as the investigation into his activities was far from finished. From what had emerged during an interview with Peter Danielsson the lawyer, his former partner Thomas Eriksson had borrowed twenty million kronor from a bank in Cyprus. The person who negotiated the loan was Afsan Ibrahim, and the money was transferred five years ago, one month before Thomas Eriksson bought the house on Ålstensgatan.

Five days after Eriksson's murder, Afsan Ibrahim was instructed by the bank to call in Eriksson's debt to them. He had given Danielsson copies of the bank's instructions and the original loan agreement, and in total he was demanding almost twenty million from Eriksson's estate, plus around a million in interest.

Copies of these documents were circulated to all the detectives, for information, along with a few personal observations from Lisa Lamm:

'If you ask me, I'd say it was Ibrahim who loaned the money in the first place, with the bank acting as a front for him. Naturally, I asked Danielsson about this, and he seems prepared to accept it as a possibility. Otherwise,

I'm happy to be able to inform you that our forensic medical officer has promised to attend our meeting tomorrow. He will also be bringing a female colleague with him, who's supposed to be the world's leading expert on fatalities caused by the classic blunt instrument. The tension is almost unbearable. See you there, Lisa.'

That little lady's worth her weight in gold, Evert Bäckström thought, getting out his secret mobile to call his tame reporter and arrange a little lunchtime meeting at some discreetly secluded location where a soon-to-be multimillionaire like him wouldn't risk coming down with food poisoning into the bargain.

'Bäckström, Bäckström, you're worth your weight in gold,' the reporter sighed an hour later, when Bäckström had just concluded his opening remarks about the 'approximately twenty million kronor' that former lawyer Eriksson had received from one of the biggest organized criminal gangs in the country, while he refreshed himself with a well-earned and very cold pilsner.

'Yes, it all seems to be going well,' Bäckström agreed, nodding at today's copy of the country's leading evening paper on the table in front of him. 'How are you getting on with that interview with the queen, by the way? Is she going to do it?'

'We're working on it, but right now we haven't got room for her in the paper. As soon as I get back to the newsroom I'm going to have to pull a few things to make sure we've got room for the twenty million Eriksson got off Afsan. That'll be the lead story tomorrow.'

'Good to hear,' Bäckström said, raising his first vodka of the day. 'I think it's important that the public are kept informed. Important for democracy, I mean. That ordinary, decent people find out what people like Eriksson get up to.'

'Gold, Bäckström, pure gold,' his lunch partner sighed.

116

After his meeting with Honkamäki, Toivonen had returned to the police station in Solna, where he almost immediately sank into gloomy thoughts instead of finally getting to grips with the growing piles of paper on his desk. On the one hand: his friend Honkamäki and his secret friends, given that they had evidently managed to plant an infiltrator very close to them, knew full well where both Åkare and García Gomez were and what they were doing. On the other: he and all his officers, who had spent almost a week running themselves ragged to find Åkare and García Gomez, because they didn't have a clue about what their colleagues knew. This, even though they all shared the fact that they worked for the same Swedish police organization.

Toivonen remained seated behind his desk for far too long, mostly sighing and shaking his head, but, because he couldn't do anything about the situation in which he found himself, he decided to walk home to his row-house out in Spånga. It was almost ten kilometres away, rather more than an hour at a reasonable pace, but that didn't bother him at all. Moving his legs was a good way to make sense of the thoughts moving around inside his head.

On his way home he stopped for a bite to eat at a little Italian restaurant. His wife had gone to see her parents up in Norrland and, as cooking was one of his least favourite things, it was just as well to get food out of the way. He also took the chance to console himself with his second beer of the day.

As soon as he walked through the door, he turned the sauna on, then sat and watched the news on television, in the company of another beer. His wife called and they talked for a while, saying all the things you were expected to say when you were still married after twenty years.

'I'll be home tomorrow,' his wife said. 'Look after yourself, and don't drink too much beer while I'm gone.'

Commissioner Toivonen promised to do as she said; he was missing her, big hug, drive carefully.

Then he sat in the sauna for an hour or so, celebrating his Finnish roots. He drank another cold beer and tried to think of something other than the woman he was married to.

Just after ten o'clock he returned to the television to watch the day's V75 horse racing on one of the sports channels, and barely had time to settle on the sofa before the doorbell rang. Honkamäki, Toivonen thought. They had a special signal for when they visited each other's homes.

Honkamäki was dressed for fieldwork – overalls, boots, bulletproof vest, and out in the road was one of the rapid response unit's unmarked minibuses, which presumably contained several more officers dressed like him behind the tinted glass.

'Do you want a beer?' Toivonen said, waving the can of beer he was holding in his hand.

'No,' Honkamäki said, shaking his head. 'As the lads and I were passing, I thought I'd let you have that registration number we spoke about.'

'I suppose I can let you have five minutes,' Toivonen said, shrugging his shoulders. They went into the living room and sat down in front of the television. Toivonen turned down the sound but left the picture, as he had an accumulator that was going nicely, even though it was already time for the fifth race.

On Sunday, 2 June, Fredrik Åkare had gone round to see his latest woman for a bit of the usual, and then they spent several hours lying in her bed until his phone rang and he answered with the customary grunt people like him always used.

While he was still muttering monosyllabically into the phone, he got out of bed and started to put his clothes on. As it was almost midnight and he had promised they would have breakfast together the next morning, his lady-friend realized this had to be something that was both unplanned and impossible to ignore.

'She asked, naturally,' Honkamäki said. 'Åkare said he and Angel had some urgent business to attend to.

'She pretended to be upset, of course, and Åkare told her they had to go and talk some sense into a cunt of a lawyer who had behaved very badly towards one of his old friends earlier that evening.'

'That's what she said?'

'Yes, and she's not prone to messing things up, so we can assume it's accurate.'

'Have I got this right? García Gomez calls to tell him about Eriksson, who has evidently behaved badly towards one of Åkare's old friends?'

'Affirmative,' Honkamäki said. 'Which in turn can only mean that neither Åkare nor García Gomez, nor Åkare's old friend, had any idea that Eriksson had given up the ghost several hours earlier.'

'This person who calls García Gomez to complain about Eriksson,' Toivonen said. 'You haven't got any idea who that could have been?'

'Negative,' Honkamäki said. 'If it's any consolation, we haven't actually tried to find out. We've got other things on our plate – considerably more important things, if I can put it like that. You know how it is with people like Åkare – so many balls in the air at the same time – and we realized at once that this wasn't the ball we were interested in.'

'I get it,' Toivonen said with a nod. 'The registration number?'

'As soon as Åkare gets his trousers on, it's a quick kiss goodbye, and out in the street there's a silver Merc waiting. García Gomez gets out of the car and talks to Åkare, but obviously she didn't hear what they were saying, and then Åkare gets in behind the wheel and they drive off. It's the first time this car has showed up since we've had them under surveillance, in case you're wondering. And the only time. When Åkare came back around three in the morning, he arrived in a taxi.'

'The Merc?' Toivonen prompted.

'Of course,' Honkamäki said. 'It's one of those personalized plates, which is pretty stupid, given the circumstances, Åkare driving round showing off in a car like that. The number-plate is evidently the name of the company that owns the car, GENCO – Genco Ltd, in other words. The company's been in existence for several years now; seems to be based in Malmö. Nothing funny about it, if you were wondering. Seems to pay its taxes and all that.'

'What business are they in, then?'

'Anything and everything, including car rental, which is probably the simplest and most innocent explanation. That they just rented it. Shouldn't be too hard to find out.'

'It'll sort itself out, I'm sure,' Toivonen said. I'll ask Nadja, he thought.

Then Toivonen walked his old friend to the door, nodded in the direction of the minibus and didn't even have to ask the question to get an answer.

'We're on standby,' Honkamäki explained. 'We've received information that Åkare and his friends are about to move, so the lads and I are hovering.'

'Well, promise to look after yourself,' Toivonen said, tapping on the bulletproof vest Honkamäki was wearing under his overalls.

'If you're tempted, Commissioner, you could always pull some trousers on and come along,' Honkamäki suggested with a wry smile. 'We've got a spare seat in the van, and you could always borrow the rest of it.'

'Another time,' Toivonen said. 'I've got an accumulator I need to keep an eye on.'

He didn't win the V75, but he got six right, so – considering that the equivalent of a month's wages had just unexpectedly landed in his lap – Toivonen ended up sitting in front of the television with another couple of beers to celebrate. He even considered phoning his wife to tell her, even though it was already after midnight and in spite of the fact that he'd managed to get through six beers along the way.

He was woken at five o'clock in the morning by his mobile phone. It was Honkamäki, as he'd already worked out before he answered.

'Has something happened?' Toivonen asked, even though he already knew that the answer to his question could only be a yes.

'Yes, I'm afraid so,' Honkamäki said.

'Something bad?'

'Yes.'

'Tell me,' Toivonen said.

117

Ara had also been watching television with Omar and, despite the fact that he was going to have to get up at half past four the following morning, he ended up sitting there far too long. Omar was more sensible. In the middle of the film he let out a loud yawn, rolled his shoulders and smiled apologetically.

'I've got to go to bed,' Omar said. 'I always have trouble getting up in the morning.'

'I'll set the alarm,' Ara said. The film was good, it was still light outside, and one hour more or less didn't make much difference to someone like him, who had spent hundreds of nights in recent years driving a taxi. Anyway, it was a good film and he wanted to see the end.

'Give me a hug, my friend,' Omar said, smiling at him. 'Last night in Sweden.'

'Last night in Sweden,' Ara repeated, giving him the hug they had come up with when they were at school together and realized that even a real man could hug another man. Another real man, Ara thought.

It was past midnight before he made it to the little bathroom on the ground floor to brush his teeth. It was dark outside now, which would make it easier to sleep as soon as he was tucked under the covers.

It was pitch-black as he made his way out into the hall, and it had evidently started to rain, because he could hear it dripping on the roof of the veranda.

Tomorrow you'll be able to relax at last, he thought, and at that moment someone put their arm round his neck and squeezed until he started to lose consciousness. The man pushed him up against the wall, changed his grip, grabbed him by the hair and pulled his head back.

'You and I need to talk, Ara,' Angel García Gomez said. He flicked his right hand and was suddenly holding a knife to Ara's throat. It took no more than that for Ara to feel completely empty inside, completely empty and completely mute, unable to get a single word out, even though García Gomez was speaking quietly, his voice almost friendly. So Ara simply nodded, trying not to move his neck, because he could feel the blade of the knife against his throat.

'There's one thing bothering me,' García Gomez said. 'I understand that you talk far too much. I thought I might give you the chance to persuade me that you're going to keep quiet.'

Ara merely nodded again. He was unable to get the slightest little sound out.

'I'm listening,' García Gomez said, at the same moment that someone must have let off a flash of light in the darkness surrounding them. A flash of light and a deafening crash that made Ara's ears pop. García Gomez jerked his head, let go of Ara's neck, dropped the knife and fell backwards on to the white hall rug. He lay there on his back, his arms and legs jerking as blood streamed from his head and mouth.

'Fuck!' Ara yelled. 'Fuck! What's happening?'

'It's okay,' Omar said. He stepped out of the darkness,

where he must have been standing the whole time, even though Ara hadn't heard a sound from him.

'It's okay,' Omar repeated, smiling exactly as he always did.

'Look at me instead, don't look at him, I'll sort this. There's nothing to worry about,' he went on, taking Ara gently by the arm.

'He's fucking dead!' Ara yelled, stepping to one side, as he'd already trodden in the pool of blood that was spreading so fast he could see it growing. The whole of the white rug was now completely red and, apparently, blood had a smell as well.

'I'll sort it,' Omar said. Then he took Ara by the arm, a bit harder this time, and looked him straight in the eye.

'Listen to me, now. Listen to Omar, your best mate. I'm going to sort all this. All you have to think about is your trip. In six hours' time you'll be sitting on the plane. Everything else will be history.'

What the fuck's he saying? Ara thought.

'What the fuck are you saying? What fucking trip? After that?!' Ara yelled, pointing at the man lying on the floor. At last, at last I can speak.

Omar merely smiled at him, the same warm smile, almost disarmingly this time, as if he were trying to talk sense into a stubborn child.

'You're going to have a good trip, Ara,' Omar said. 'Have a good trip, mate,' he repeated. He patted him on the arm, smiled the same warm smile, then raised his pistol and shot his best friend from school straight through the head.

VI

The investigation into the murder of Thomas Eriksson the lawyer takes an unexpected turn

118

Bäckström began the Thursday meeting of the investigative team by turning to Annika Carlsson and asking if anything had happened. She was, after all, the person who was expected to handle the simpler practical matters so that he was able to concentrate undisturbed on the weightier and more intellectually demanding work. According to Annika, nothing in particular had happened. Still no trace of Åkare and García Gomez, or their witness. Things were no better with the four members of the Brotherhood of the Ibrahims, for whom their prosecutor had issued arrest warrants the day before.

'All seven of them seem to have gone to ground,' Annika Carlsson declared.

'Yes, well, where else would they go?' Bäckström agreed.

'What about the car, then?' he went on, nodding towards Nadja.

Not much better. There were still a few dozen vehicles they hadn't got round to checking, but, considering all the hundreds they had already discounted, things weren't really looking very hopeful.

In the absence of anything better to get their teeth into, they then moved on to discussing the possibility that they might have got everything wrong and were actually back at square one again. Alm, at least, wanted to raise that possibility, and several of the other members of the investigating team had nodded in agreement and even suggested alternative solutions. Unhappy clients, opponents, old girlfriends, the usual nutters, even the victim's neighbours.

'We mustn't forget Eriksson's neighbours,' Stigson said. 'I can't remember taking part in any previous door-to-door inquiries where the neighbours had so much shit to say about the victim as they did this time.'

'I hear what you're saying,' Bäckström interrupted. 'The problem is, how do you link the neighbours to the car, the removal boxes and that pair we haven't yet been able to identify? The one who shat himself on Eriksson's sofa and the one who left his snotty handkerchief at the crime scene.'

'One possible explanation could be that all that doesn't actually have anything to do with the murder itself,' Stigson persisted. 'That we're simply barking up the wrong tree entirely, so to speak.'

'What sort of bollocks is that?' Bäckström said, shaking his head. 'The simple reason why Eriksson's neighbours had so much shit to say about him is that he was a wanker of quite unprecedented proportions and, on top of that, happened to own a dog that was lethally dangerous. How hard is that to understand?'

'I agree with you, Bäckström,' Annika Carlsson said. 'In my eyes, this is about three things. Firstly, Eriksson and his dodgy affairs. Secondly, the fact that Åkare, García Gomez and von Comer are caught up in them. Up to their necks, if you ask me. And, thirdly, it's about getting hold of the two others who were sitting there talking to Eriksson when this mess kicked off, sometime around half past nine that evening. There's a connection between sofa-man and handkerchief-man and the other three, and if we can just find that we're home and dry.'

'Good to hear that,' Bäckström said, glancing at his watch. 'Well, as a small reward for the insights that you've just volunteered, you can have fifteen minutes to stretch your legs. Before we all finally find out about the latest flashes of genius in the field of forensic medical science.'

119

Within Solna police station the forensic medical officer responsible for the post-mortem examination of lawyer Thomas Eriksson was mostly known by his surname. Dr Lidberg was short and skinny, with thinning hair, and in the conduct of his work he was a careful and conscientious man who preferred not to leave anything to chance. He was also an excellent communicator and was able to explain what he had found to police officers and other laymen in perfectly plain Swedish.

That day he had also brought with him some very prestigious back-up, a female colleague who was a professor, head of the forensic medicine unit in Linköping and a globally renowned authority on injuries caused with blunt objects and other instances of physical force, such as kicks and punches. She was middle-aged, short and rectangular, with ruddy cheeks.

After the obligatory throat-clearing and leafing through his papers, Lidberg had begun by lamenting the fact that the forensic medical report had taken so long to compile. He would be returning to the reasons for this shortly, and had asked his secretary to email the report to the investigating team as soon as he had finished his oral present ation. Both he and his esteemed colleague preferred to do things in that order for simple, pedagogical reasons. In this particular case – regarding the violence to which Eriksson had been subjected – there were also very strong reasons for doing it this way. From a forensic medical perspective, Eriksson presented a quite remarkable case.

'If I could begin with the injuries to Eriksson's head and neck, these were inflicted on two separate occasions. Partly before he died at about ten o'clock in the evening, and partly during the night, when he had already been dead for several hours and rigor mortis had set in to both his face and neck,' Dr Lidberg said, clearing his throat discreetly.

Unravelling that process was why the examination had taken so long. It constituted a complicated puzzle, the pieces of which were the compression injuries, loose fragments of bone of various sizes, fractures of varying lengths, an overlapping pattern of injuries that needed to be matched and evaluated against blood loss, swellings, cuts, scratches and ordinary bruising. To put it in plain Swedish.

'Unfortunately, this is where things start to get really tricky, and certainly more complicated in a legal sense,' Dr Lidberg said with a sigh. 'The injuries that were inflicted after death are extremely extensive. To put it simply, we can say that someone smashed his skull in with a rounded wooden implement with a diameter of approximately ten centimetres, possibly a baseball bat of the older variety or a so-called cudgel of similar size. A dozen or so different blows in total.'

'Excuse me, but what's the legal complication?' Lisa Lamm asked with a friendly smile.

'The violence to which he was subjected while he was alive was, in all likelihood, inflicted with nothing more than a fist, and on that point my esteemed colleague and

I are in complete agreement – two, possibly three very hard punches.'

'At the risk of sounding stupid,' Lisa Lamm said, smiling even more warmly now, 'I still don't understand—'

'The problem is that those punches couldn't have killed him,' Professor Hansson interrupted, fixing her eyes on Lisa Lamm. 'One blow to his nose, then another to his right cheekbone. Nose broken, lots of blood. He'd have had a serious black eye a few hours later if he'd lived, but that didn't develop because he died within half an hour, at most. That's all we've got. In other words, not enough violence to have killed him,' said the only globally renowned authority on this specific type of cause of death in the room.

'So what did he die of, then?' Lisa Lamm said, suddenly bearing a striking resemblance to a prosecutor who has just discovered a legal complication.

'Eriksson died of a heart attack,' Dr Lidberg said, with an even deeper sigh, if such a thing were possible.

What the hell's the bastard saying? A heart attack? He was too fucking feeble, that was all, Bäckström thought.

Professor Hansson had taken over. One blow that fractured his nose, lots of blood, but not the sort of thing that would kill you. Another to the right cheek, more blood, but not even enough to have knocked him unconscious. There was also one more injury. A fracture in his right wrist, caused by someone twisting it by pulling it out and simultaneously forcing it down. Certainly very painful, but – again – not the sort of thing that would kill you.

What Eriksson actually died of was a massive heart attack which occurred shortly afterwards. The poor condition of his heart was well documented in his medical records. The problem had first been diagnosed ten years ago. His doctor had prescribed the usual medication but, like far too many patients with heart disease, he had been careless about taking it, and with the way he lived generally. He drank too much, ate the wrong things, exercised too little and put more pressure on himself than his body could cope with.

As recently as three years before he died he had suffered his first heart attack, in the middle of a trial. He ended up in A&E at the Karolinska Hospital and was admitted for several days. While he was there, extensive examinations showed that he was exhibiting all the symptoms of a typical heart-disease patient. As soon as he was discharged he had resumed the way of life that could kill him at any time.

'Certainly, the abuse he was subjected to, together with the severe stress he was presumably under, is highly likely to have triggered the heart attack that was the actual cause of death,' Professor Hansson declared. 'You're bound to have a better grasp than me of the legal complications that this gives rise to,' she went on, turning to look at Lisa Lamm.

'Assault, combined with causing another person's death,' Lisa Lamm said with a nod of agreement.

'Yes, that's where the courts usually end up in cases like this,' Hansson said. 'At least on the occasions when I've been involved.'

Five minutes later she and her colleague had thanked Lisa Lamm and her investigators for giving them the opportunity to attend the meeting. If there was anything else they could do to help, they only had to say. They also wished them luck in their hunt for the perpetrator. Hopefully, they would soon meet again in court.

* * *

'Okay, then,' Lisa Lamm said as soon as the visitors had closed the door behind them. 'Help me. What do we do now?'

'We carry on as usual,' Bäckström said with a heavy nod. 'We make sure we get hold of whoever punched Eriksson in the face. Once we're done with that little detail, we can move on to the scientific debate.'

'Good to hear that. That we agree, I mean,' Lisa Lamm said, as Toivonen walked into the room without knocking.

The price of getting rid of two lunatic doctors is evidently one standard-issue Finnish clown, Bäckström thought.

'And of course we need to get hold of Åkare, García Gomez and our witness,' Annika Carlsson said. 'If only to stop anything else bad happening.

'Welcome to the meeting, Toivonen,' she went on, smiling at their new visitor. 'You just missed today's forensic medical highlight.'

'I know,' Toivonen said. 'But that isn't why I'm here. I'm afraid it's rather worse than that,' he added, sitting down at the table beside them.

120

At 01.23:20 that morning the pilot of a Ryanair flight that was three hours late had made an emergency call to traffic control at Skavsta Airport. He and his plane were on the northern approach to the runway at a height of approximately three hundred metres and were expected to land in a couple of minutes. At a distance of almost exactly six kilometres north of the runway, he had observed two cars burning on a forest road leading to an isolated house up in the woods. He was primarily interested in making sure there was nothing going on at the airport that he ought to be keeping clear of.

The air-traffic controller had assured him that everything was fine, while his colleague called the police and fire brigade in Nyköping, and for once the fire brigade were only a few kilometres away from the two cars burning in the forest, because a couple of hours earlier they had been called to a false alarm at a signal box ten kilometres west of Skavsta, and were on their way back to the fire station in Nyköping when the new alarm came in.

Three minutes later they were on the scene. There wasn't much they could do about the two cars, which were both burning like beacons. But they were able to save the nearby house, a summer cottage of the standard Swedish variety, where the fire hadn't yet managed to take a firm hold.

If things had taken their usual course, the house would have burned to the ground, perhaps leaving the chimney standing, but this time that didn't happen. Half an hour earlier, a torrential shower of rain had fallen, and that, in conjunction with the rapid response of the fire brigade, meant they were able to extinguish the fire with most of the house still standing. Which wasn't to say that it made the ideal crime scene. The ground floor was badly fire-damaged, smoke and soot had spread to the upper floor and attic, and before they got the fire under control the firemen had to pour tons of water on to the house. The cars were in a considerably worse state, and all that remained of them were two burned-out, warped metal wrecks and some melted rubber.

Toivonen had spoken to the police officers at the scene, as well as the senior firefighter. The first body had been found ten metres from one of the wrecked cars. There were two more inside the house, and neither of them looked as if they'd died in the fire.

'The first one is Åkare – he's already been identified. He was both shot and stabbed, and, just to make sure, a metal noose was tied round his neck and he was strung up from a nearby tree. Apart from the fact that he's dead, he's in reasonable condition, and the order in which his injuries were inflicted ought to become clear once our forensic medical officer has taken a look.'

'So he was the one found near the burned-out car on the road, a hundred metres from the house?' Annika Carlsson asked.

'Yes,' Toivonen said. 'As for the others, the pair found inside the house, one of them is probably García Gomez, and, unfortunately, there's evidence to suggest that the other one might well be our witness, the taxi-driver,'

Toivonen concluded, glowering at his colleague Evert Bäckström.

'So what did they die of?' Alm asked.

'Well, certainly not natural causes,' Toivonen said. 'I spoke to Forensics half an hour ago – they've been on the scene since four o'clock this morning – it looks like they've both been shot in the head. Before the house was set alight, if anyone's wondering. The medical officer has also been to take a look, so we'll find out soon enough,' he concluded with an expressive shrug.

'This doesn't make sense,' Annika Carlsson objected, shaking her head. 'Not García Gomez and the taxi-driver, not both shot in the head at the same time and in the same place.' I warned him, she thought. If only he'd listened to me, he'd still be alive.

'I think it does,' Toivonen said. 'The problem is just that we haven't worked out how it fits together. Once we've sorted that out, no doubt it will all make sense.'

'Who's going to be responsible for the investigation?' Lisa Lamm asked.

'Not Solna, fortunately,' Toivonen said, giving Bäckström the evil eye once more. 'Regional Crime in Södermanland, with help from Stockholm and our colleagues at the National Murder Unit. According to the most recent information I have.'

'Good to hear,' Bäckström said with a cheery smile. 'This sort of turf war between organized criminal gangs can be really tricky to sort out. Something that starts with someone shooting one of our motorcycling friends can easily lead to someone finishing off half the Muslim community.'

'Don't worry,' Toivonen said. 'There's no chance of it landing on your desk. I've also got another piece of reassuring news for you.'

'That's nice,' Bäckström said. 'I can hardly contain myself.'

'It wasn't Åkare who beat up Eriksson.'

'Really? How can you be so sure?'

'I'm as sure of that as I am that it was Åkare and García Gomez who showed up later that night. When García Gomez let loose on the corpse and cut the dog's throat while Åkare was sitting outside in the street in the Merc they'd arrived in.'

'One question, out of curiosity,' Bäckström said. 'How do you know that?'

'I know,' Toivonen said. 'And, because I don't want to read about it in the papers, you'll have to make do with that.'

'I hear what you're saying,' Bäckström said with a shrug. The bastard Finn really isn't himself, he thought. Probably spent half the night in the sauna getting pissed.

121

Once Toivonen had left them, Bäckström concluded the meeting and took his closest colleagues back to his room with him to get some sort of control over the new situation. Just as well to get it over and done with before he died of starvation.

'Well, then,' Bäckström said as soon as Lisa Lamm and the Anchor had sat down on the other side of his desk. 'Would you like to start, Lisa? Explain the legalities to us simpler souls.'

As she saw things, there was no reason to think they were in any sort of crisis situation. What she planned to do now was to amend the preliminary charge of murder to include assault and causing another person's death.

'It's far too early to discount the possibility of charging them with murder or manslaughter. If they assaulted Eriksson in the knowledge that he was in poor health and just left him to die, I have every intention of testing that possibility in court,' she concluded.

'What about this idea that we can discount Åkare as our perpetrator?' Bäckström asked. 'What does our Finnish colleague know that seems to have escaped us?'

'Looks like Åkare was under surveillance on the night Eriksson was killed. By the sort of people us regular cops aren't supposed to know about,' Anchor Carlsson said.

'Who'd have thought it?' Bäckström said, who had already thought of the possibility himself.

'Okay,' Lisa Lamm said. 'So we carry on as usual. I was thinking of getting some lunch – you'd be more than welcome to join me if you like.'

'Sorry,' Bäckström said with an apologetic shake of the head. 'It would have been nice, but I've got a meeting to go to, so lunch will have to wait.'

'If you can give me fifteen minutes,' Annika Carlsson said. 'Shall we meet down in the canteen?'

On his way out of the office to the taxi that was waiting to drive him to his seriously overdue lunch, Nadja stopped him.

'This better be fucking important,' Bäckström said, feeling hunger gnawing at his insides.

'I've just spoken to Toivonen. He gave me a tip-off about the silver Mercedes we're still trying to find.'

'Anything worth having?' Bäckström asked.

'I haven't had a chance to get very far yet,' Nadja said. 'But this particular vehicle isn't in the range we've been checking. It's registered in Malmö. Belongs to a company down there, but I haven't managed to find anything odd so far.'

'You've got the licence number?'

'Yes,' Nadja said. 'That may be what's making me a little dubious. It's one of those personalized numbers. I'm having trouble believing that Åkare would drive around in one of those. And I can't find any connection at all between Åkare and the company that owns the car.'

'What was the registration?'

'Genco.'

'Genco,' Bäckström repeated, shaking his head. Where the hell have I heard that before?

122

Finally shot of the fat little bastard, Annika Carlsson thought as she watched Bäckström vanish through the door of the corridor where they had their offices. Then she went and sat down next to Nadja to talk about something that had been bothering her for the past hour or so. Ever since Toivonen had told them that their witness had been murdered.

'It's just so bloody awful,' Annika said. 'Even though I told him to lie low.'

'I'm listening,' Nadja said, patting her arm consolingly. Annika's the sort of person who really does care, she thought. In the midst of everything that both enticed and terrified her colleagues, and presumably kept a number of them awake all night for reasons that they'd never dare talk about.

'I showed him pictures about a week ago,' Annika said, 'and something he said then came as a bit of a surprise. He recognized Omar ben Kader. Not because he was the man he almost ran over outside Eriksson's house but because they were childhood friends. He said they were at school together.'

'Omar ben Kader. Correct me if I'm wrong, but isn't he Afsan Ibrahim's right-hand man, his closest advisor?'

'That's right. You couldn't check that out for me, could

you? If they really were at school together? It would have been in Gnosjö, something like fifteen, twenty years ago.'

'Of course,' Nadja said. 'Easy as pie,' she added. 'Should be able to get the answer to you today.'

'If you're wondering why—'

'I know exactly what you're thinking. That Afsan and Omar exploited Omar's old schoolfriend to lure Åkare and García Gomez into the open. If that's the case, then it would be a dereliction of duty not to tell our colleagues in Södermanland.'

'By the way, do you know who's in charge of the investigation down there?' Annika asked.

'From what I heard, Lewin from National Crime is going to be in charge of the preliminary investigation,' Nadja said. 'Apparently, that's the way the regional police commissioner in Södermanland wanted it.'

'Jan Lewin,' Annika said. 'Who just happens to be married to our boss, Anna Holt.'

'The very same,' Nadja said with a nod.

Jan Lewin, married to Anna Holt. Small world, Annika Carlsson thought, but merely nodded back.

123

Bäckström had started by preparing a sturdy lunch, to stop his blood sugar from sinking any lower – by then it was already somewhere in the vicinity of his handmade shoes. Fried pork chops with black pudding and lingonberry jam, a couple of cold pilsners and two generous vodkas. When he was finally able to settle down on his sofa with a well-earned cup of coffee and a small cognac, he began by calling his tame reporter at the larger of the evening papers to inform him of the latest developments in the murder of the country's most famous gangster lawyer, which by now was leading the news across all the media. Worth at least six figures, plus a little bonus in the form of an opportunity to teach his so-called colleague, that Finnish drunk Toivonen, a practical lesson in the conditions pertaining to the sacred protection of sources and freedom of the press in a constitutional state and democracy.

Over the course of the next hour he informed his personal press spokesman about the latest developments in the full-blown gangster war that had broken out following the murder of the lawyer who for many years had been an advisor to one of the most violent groups within organized crime in Sweden, the Brotherhood of the Ibrahims. The same organization which over the past few years alone had 'paid at least twenty million kronor to their legal advisor, the lawyer Thomas Eriksson'.

'Four murders in little more than a week,' Bäckström summarized. 'First Eriksson. Then Ibrahim and his men get revenge by executing Åkare and García Gomez, and, just to be on the safe side, get rid of a witness who could have been of decisive importance to the police investigation,' Bäckström concluded.

'Bäckström, Bäckström.' The reporter sighed, now at a complete loss for words.

'Trust me,' Bäckström said. 'This is only the beginning. Revenge nurtures revenge, as you know, and before the summer is over there'll be plenty more murdered, tortured and maimed on both sides. And we mustn't forget that entirely innocent people are going to suffer. Not just witnesses who are only trying to do their civic duty but also members of the public who just happen to be in the wrong place at the wrong time.'

'How do you want to be quoted?' the reporter asked. 'Is it okay for us to carry on with a senior source in the police hierarchy?'

'With full knowledge of the investigation,' Bäckström corrected. Such as that Finnish pisshead, who was welcome to a taste of the shit he was trying to smear Bäckström with.

'Well, speak to you again tomorrow,' the reporter concluded. He was going to have his work cut out trying to pull together the following day's paper, what with the veritable summer massacre that Sweden's organized criminal gangs had just embarked upon.

'Okay,' Bäckström said. 'Oh, there was one more thing,' he added, as he had been struck by the same thought as when Nadja told him about that Merc they were looking for. 'You don't happen to have anyone at the paper who's good with films?'

'Of course, you need to talk to one of the photographers. Is there anything—'

'Not a photographer,' Bäckström interrupted. 'Someone who knows about films, films at the cinema, I mean.'

'Film Ronny, our cinema reporter.'

'Film Ronny?'

'Yes, or Ronny the Reel. That's the name he uses on his blog and on Twitter. Where he recommends more unusual films. Ronny the Reel, as in old porn reels, basically.'

'So he's good at films?'

'Good at films? He's world class, Bäckström. If Ronny doesn't know the answer, it's because what you're asking about has never been committed to film. He can even recite the credits by heart. You've probably seen him on our TV channel. *Ronny the Reel's Best Reels*. Big guy in a Hawaiian shirt. You're fairly similar, actually. Superficially, I mean.'

'You haven't got his number?' Bäckström said. Sounds like a reliable bloke, he thought. He never missed an opportunity to dress that way as soon as the weather allowed.

'Sure,' the reporter said. 'You can have his private number if you promise not to tell him who gave it to you. What do you want him for, anyway? Anything we need to put in the paper?'

'If it is, you'll be the first to know,' Bäckström said.

As soon as Bäckström ended the call, he phoned Ronny the Reel and left a message on his answer-machine.

'My name is Bäckström,' he said. 'I'm a police officer, and there's something I think you might be able to help me with.'

Definitely time for an afternoon nap, he thought, as his favourite Finnish waitress had promised to look in and take care of the cleaning, washing-up and laundry, and generally tidy up before starting her evening shift at his local bar.

Yes, definitely time for a bit of rest, he thought, just as someone rang his doorbell.

124

At first he thought his Finnish cleaner had arrived three hours early because she was so keen she couldn't wait, but it turned out to be his neighbour, little Edvin, who was standing there with a serious expression and his neatly parted hair at the same level as the letterbox in Bäckström's door. He's come to tell me that Isak has finally fluttered off to the other side, Bäckström thought, and hurried to open the door.

'Come in, Edvin, come in. Has something happened?' Bäckström asked, making an effort to look suitably concerned.

Little Edvin was the same as usual. A serious little fellow who began by expressing a hope that he wasn't disturbing the superintendent. Before he rang the bell he had listened through the letterbox, as Bäckström had taught him, and that had told him that Bäckström was at home and up and about, but you could never be entirely sure.

'It's fine. Don't you worry about that, lad,' Bäckström said, patting him on the head. 'I dare say there's something you want to tell me.' Good job he didn't just crawl through the letterbox, he thought.

'I've got good news for you, Superintendent,' Edvin said, nodding steadily.

At last, Bäckström thought, raising his eyes towards the ceiling.

Edvin had come to tell him that Isak had recovered. He was still a little subdued, but he had been discharged from the animal hospital before the weekend, and the fact that Edvin had waited a week to share this happy news depended on two things. Firstly, he had realized from the newspapers that the superintendent was fully occupied with a serious murder investigation, and for that reason was perhaps unable to give Isak the care he required. Secondly, he had consciously chosen to wait until he was sure Isak was going to make a full recovery, so as not to raise Bäckström's hopes in vain.

'Where is he now, then?' Bäckström said quietly. What the hell's the bespectacled little lizard saying?

Isak had spent the past week of his convalescence in Edvin's bedroom. It had been a successful period of recuperation and, apart from the fact that he was still traumatized, there was good reason to hope that Isak would soon be back to his usual self. What Edvin wanted to know was whether he should hold on to Isak for a bit longer, considering Bäckström's immense burden of work.

There's still hope for the little sod, Bäckström thought, thinking of Edvin rather than Isak.

'Why don't we talk about it?' Bäckström suggested. 'Can I get you anything? A glass of juice, perhaps?'

'Thank you,' Edvin said. 'I never say no to a nice glass of juice.'

Bäckström went into the kitchen and was hunting through his fridge and cupboards when he suddenly realized that no normal adult male kept juice in his home. Instead he got out a can of Coca-Cola for Edvin and a cold pilsner for himself.

'I'm afraid I'm out of juice,' Bäckström lied. 'I hope Coca-Cola will be all right?'

His guest assured him that Coca-Cola would be absolutely fine. Both his mother, Dusanka, and his father, Slobodan, used to have large glasses of Coca-Cola when they sat to watch television in the evenings, and Edvin had realized that drinking Coca-Cola made you happy. Even if he himself preferred raspberry juice.

'What are we going to do, Superintendent?' Edvin said, looking at him through his thick glasses. 'Should I keep Isak for a bit longer, or would you prefer me to give him back straight away, Superintendent? I can write a note of all his medications. To make it easier to look after him, I mean.'

Considering Bäckström's currently incredible burden of work, he definitely preferred the first option. Even though he was of course longing to see his dear little Isak.

'A wise decision, Superintendent,' Edvin agreed. 'Let's agree that he should stay with me for the time being. You only have to let me know when things are a bit easier at work.'

Before Edvin left, Bäckström peeled a satisfactory wad of notes from his money-clip and pressed them into Edvin's hand.

'For food and so on,' Bäckström explained.

'That's far too much,' Edvin said, wide-eyed at the sight of all the money he had just been given.

'Maybe, but parrot medicine can't be entirely free of

charge,' Bäckström said, patting Edvin on the head. 'Get in touch when you need more.' He ought to be able to work out the message behind that, he thought.

Before Bäckström slid into the peaceful depths of his afternoon nap, he found himself thinking positive thoughts about his little neighbour. If he was used in the right way, someone like Edvin would be very useful within the police, he thought. Skinny as a piece of dental floss, little more than a hand-span tall and as nimble as a grass snake. If they needed someone to search confined spaces, little Edvin would be a genuine asset alongside the dogs the police used for sniffing out bombs, he was thinking as he was lulled off to the land of Nod.

When Bäckström returned from his customary dinner at his local bar that evening, GeGurra called to ask how the search for Pinocchio was going.

Bäckström expressed cautious optimism, and before the short conversation ended they agreed to meet the following evening to discuss their ongoing plans in more detail.

'What do you say to meeting at mine for a bite to eat?' GeGurra suggested. 'So we won't be disturbed, I mean. I have an excellent catering firm who usually take care of the practical details, so there's no cause for concern, my dear friend.'

Bearing in mind the fact that the work was already done and they were talking about a couple of hundred million, Bäckström didn't have any objections.

'Excellent,' GeGurra said. 'In that case, I'll expect you at my home on Norr Mälarstrand at eight o'clock.'

125

It turned into a late night, because Bäckström ended up sitting at his computer until after midnight, but he compensated for this by calling work as soon as he woke up and cancelling the morning meeting of the investigative team. When he walked into the office he bumped into Anchor Carlsson, who looked so angry that he decided he'd rather talk to her in his room, and preferably about something other than cancelled meetings and cretinous colleagues who could only benefit from having to take care of themselves and leaving him in peace.

'Have you heard anything more about Rosita?' Bäckström asked, as a suitable and introductory diversionary manoeuvre. 'Are there any grounds for serious concern?'

However, Annika was unable to provide an answer to this question. And she wasn't able to go into why. But it was her decided opinion that their colleague Rosita Andersson-Trygg was likely to be off sick for some time.

'She hasn't caught bird flu or some shit like that, has she?'

'No, why would she have?' Anchor Carlsson replied, unable to conceal her surprise.

'Oh, I was just thinking that she's so interested in animals, of course, and there are loads of weird things that animals like that can infect us with. Impetigo, rabies, foot and mouth, parrot fever, you know,' Bäckström said, shrugging his shoulders. Or rabbit fever, he thought. Why the hell would anyone want to stroke a rabbit?

'Take it up with Holt,' the Anchor said, shaking her head dismissively. 'If you ask me, it's got more to do with everything that's been in the papers. The fact that the photofit picture ended up in the media wasn't terribly smart, considering what happened to our witness, because we can't really assume that both Åkare and García Gomez were entirely illiterate.'

'No, those journalists are terrible, they're just vultures.' Bäckström sighed. 'I solve that problem by never reading the papers.'

'No, why would you need to?' Anchor Carlsson replied, for some reason. 'Well, you'll have to excuse me. I've got a lot to do.'

The Anchor was evidently having one of her special days, and it was time he himself got something done, Bäckström thought with a contented sigh as he contemplated the activities that lay ahead of him. Tapas for lunch, he thought. Followed by Little Miss Friday, an afternoon nap and a decent dinner with GeGurra as a suitable conclusion to a week that had been full of hard work.

Time for a taxi, he thought. He stood up with a jerk and pressed the quick-dial button for Taxi Stockholm.

While Superintendent Evert Bäckström was sitting in a taxi on his way to have lunch, his colleague Detective Inspector Annika Carlsson got in touch with Superintendent Jan Lewin at the National Murder Unit, the officer leading the preliminary investigation into the triple murder down in Södermanland. Lewin began by apologizing for the fact that he hadn't been in touch himself, but that he'd simply had too much to do, as was usually the case in the opening stages of a murder investigation. Not least when it was an investigation of this size.

Then he thanked her for the information that she and her colleagues in Solna had passed on to them. He shared her belief that there was a lot to suggest that their witness, the taxi-driver, was the link between the other two victims, Åkare and García Gomez, and the most likely perpetrators, Afsan Ibrahim and those in his circle. The motive would have been the several-years-long blood feud that had arisen between the Hells Angels and the Brotherhood of the Ibrahims. And the opening shot would have been the murder of Afsan Ibrahim's legal advisor, Thomas Eriksson.

'Most of the evidence would seem to suggest that Åkare was the one they really wanted to get,' Lewin said. 'According to our forensic medical officer, they hung him from a wire noose, then, while he was still alive, entertained themselves with taking pot-shots at him and stabbing and cutting him.'

'What about García Gomez and the taxi-driver? Have you found out any more about them?'

'They were lying in the hall on the ground floor of the house. Both shot in the head, from very close range, execution-style, as our American colleagues say. The evidence suggests that García Gomez was shot first. Our taxi-driver Ara is covered in his blood, so García Gomez was probably shot while he was attacking Ara. After which Ara was also shot.'

'Same weapon?'

'Looks like it,' Lewin said. 'Nine-millimetre, hollow-tipped bullets, pistol by the look of the cartridges, but we'll get a definite answer on that this afternoon. We'll email you as soon as we know.'

'Anything else?'

'Nothing, except that I think the same as you,' Lewin said. 'That your witness was used as bait to lure Åkare and García Gomez and, as soon as they'd been dealt with, he went the same way. There's no other explanation that makes sense, given everything that's happened.'

Omar ben Kader seems to be a charming sort, Annika Carlsson thought. A really good mate.

126

First the tapas bar on Fleminggatan. A concluding cognac out in the sun on the terrace.

Then Little Miss Friday, where Bäckström pulled out a little surprise and commenced by shaving her before embarking on the usual downstairs picnic and finishing with the traditional salami ride.

Finally, a gentle stroll home in the sunshine to his cosy abode, his nice wide Hästens bed, but as soon as he stepped in through the door his phone rang.

'Listening,' Bäckström grunted.

'Am I speaking to Superintendent Bäckström?' the voice at the other end asked.

'That depends,' Bäckström said. 'Who are you?'

'Ronny,' Film Ronny said, 'aka Ronny the Reel. You left a message for me. You said there was something you wanted help with?'

'Good,' Bäckström said. 'I'm assuming that this will stay between us.'

'Of course,' Ronny said. 'Discretion, a matter of honour,' he added.

'If I say the name Genco, what does that make you think?'

'The best movie in film history,' Ronny said. 'Swedish premiere 28 July 1975, simultaneously at Rigoletto,

Draken and Spegeln in Stockholm. The American premiere was 12 December the previous year. In New York.'

'Anything else?' Bäckström said. What the fuck's he going on about?

'Genco Olive Oil, import and export. That was Vito Corleone's first business after he emigrated to the USA. He was born Vito Andolini in the village of Corleone on Sicily, and the best film in the world is the story of his life.'

'*The Godfather*,' Bäckström said, practically able to hear the penny drop inside his head.

'*The Godfather: Part II*,' Ronny corrected.

'Thanks very much,' Bäckström said. Must have been a class monitor when he was at school, he thought.

'Can I ask why you wanted to know?'

'You can,' Bäckström said. 'But it's probably best not to expect an answer. Anything else I can help you with?'

'Maybe that Hawaiian shirt you were wearing when you were on the summer series of *Crimewatch*?' Ronny said.

'By all means,' Bäckström said. 'Where should I send it?'

'My name, to the newspaper's office,' Ronny said.

'It's in the post,' Bäckström lied, seeing as even someone like Film Ronny ought to know that postmen stole like magpies these days, and that something as valuable as that would be lost the moment you put it in the post box.

'Thanks, thanks very much,' Film Ronny said, sounding like he really meant it.

'Don't mention it,' Bäckström said. Evidently, he didn't know, he thought as he ended the call.

That evening's dinner at GeGurra's turned into a fine conclusion to the day. First, they imbibed some light refreshments, with a mixture of hot and cold canapés.

Then there was a traditional, bourgeois three-course dinner in GeGurra's dining room, before they concluded with coffee and cognac in the library as they discussed their mutual business project.

'How is it going with the search for Pinocchio and his nose?' GeGurra enquired with a look of curiosity.

'Things are happening,' Bäckström said with a heavy nod. 'Even if it's far too early to be talking of any kind of breakthrough.'

'But I understand from the newspapers that the trail is leading towards the court and His Majesty the King,' GeGurra persisted. 'Even though I have to steel myself at the very thought that His Majesty would have had any dealings with a character like Eriksson.'

'Absolutely, that's right,' Bäckström assured him. 'Sadly, it's all too often the case that people end up in the hands of men like Eriksson when it comes to business of a more sensitive nature. So you probably don't have to worry about the province. Unfortunately, the problem is that the trail goes cold in the home of the ghastly Eriksson.'

'Let us hope that that isn't the case,' GeGurra said, looking like he really meant it. 'That would be a catastrophe for the whole of Western art history.'

'Oh, it's probably not as bad as that,' Bäckström said, rubbing his round nose. 'But there is one thing that you could help me with.'

'I'm all ears.'

'The name of your acquaintance. The one who was interested in that painting of the fat monk.'

'Alexander Versjagin's painting of Saint Theodore?'

'That's the one,' Bäckström said.

'Under an oath of silence, strictly between us?'

'Of course,' Bäckström said, with a nod of encouragement.

'In that case,' GeGurra said with a light shrug. 'In that case, I shall have to deviate from my principles. But I have a feeling that you'll know who it is as soon as I say the name. He's supposed to be something of a legendary figure where you work, out in Solna.'

'So what's his name, then?'

'Mario Grimaldi. You know, the Godfather.'

127

Bäckström spent most of the weekend thinking about his case, and lawyer Thomas Eriksson's tragic demise, although he was happy to leave the finer judicial details of this to Lisa Lamm and her associates. There were other aspects that were more interesting. He also made sure to stick to his usual routines as far as food, drink and exercise were concerned. 'A healthy mind in a healthy body' had become something of a mantra for him, and the slightest deviation from that rule was unthinkable.

He spent the remainder of his time reducing the now endless queue of women longing for a go on the super-salami. Two fresh and hitherto untested talents. On Saturday afternoon a 25-year-old nail technician who, to judge by the pictures she had taken of herself with her webcam, seemed extremely promising, although unfortunately she turned out to be a definite disappointment when it came to the real practical test.

At best a four, a weak four, a very weak four, Bäckström thought when it was finally over and he could send her home to the run-down suburb where she probably lived. He was obliged to cancel the promised dinner because he received an urgent call from work requiring him to attend the scene of a new murder out in Rinkeby immediately.

'God, that's awful,' the nail technician said in the hall

when she was on her way out. 'We're so lucky to have people like you. Promise we'll meet up again soon.'

'Of course,' Bäckström lied. 'You must do this again.'

For the rest of the day he resumed his usual routines and rounded off the evening with a decent dinner at Operakällaren in his own company.

Sunday was an improvement. A considerable improvement. He ate lunch with a 35-year-old self-employed accountant, and when they finally got down to business she turned out to be a completely uninhibited sex maniac, the sort he would never dream of entrusting with his money or financial documents. Not that he could imagine why she would want those, given her other talents. A strong eight, possibly even a weak nine, which probably put her at the very top of all the number-crunchers in the world. In his mind's eye he saw her standing at the top of the podium at the end of the sex world cup for accountants. Perched up there on all fours sticking her arse in the air coquettishly, her pendulous breasts swinging freely and her steamed-up spectacles sitting askew on the end of her nose.

'Promise we'll meet up again soon,' she said in the hall when she was on her way out.

'You can be pretty confident of that,' he replied, having already added her number to the quick-dial list on his mobile.

He let himself have an early night and, as on so many previous occasions, the truth sought him out in his dreams without him having to make the slightest effort. That was just the way it was for the privileged few who, like him, had been given the gift of seeing what was actually going on instead of allowing it to be obscured or hidden by things that only appeared to be going on. And considering who his so-called murder victim was, he could hardly think of a better end to that part of the story.

On Monday morning, when he was sitting in the back of the taxi that was taking him to the police station in Solna, he was more or less sure of how the whole thing had happened. All that remained was to slot the final pieces in place before he could devote himself to what this was all really about. To finding a sufficiently secure and discreet way of making sure that little Pinocchio and his long nose remained in the possession of his new owner, Detective Superintendent Evert Bäckström.

VII

The prosecutor concludes the investigation into the murder of Thomas Eriksson the lawyer

128

The first thing Bäckström did to start the new working week was to talk to Nadja.

'What do we know about the company that owns the Merc we were tipped off about?' he asked.

According to Nadja, they now knew a fair bit. Genco Ltd had been founded in January 1976, almost exactly six months after the film *The Godfather: Part II* was released in Swedish cinemas. Since then it had been mainly engaged in importing and selling Italian food and delicacies: olive oil, pasta, wine, salami, ham, cheese. It appeared to be a well-run and profitable company.

A wholesaler in the grocery business, with its head office and warehouse outside Malmö, a dozen employees, and during its almost forty years of operation it had never made a loss or had any difficulties at all with the authorities. They paid their taxes and national insurance contributions on time, and all the permits they were required to have seemed to be in good order. For the past few years annual turnover had been in the region of twenty million kronor per year.

'There really isn't anything remarkable about that, and the company makes something like a million in profit each year,' Nadja concluded.

'So what are they doing leasing out cars?' Bäckström asked.

According to Nadja, that appeared to be a lingering remnant from the business's early days, when it was involved in more varied activities. It also used to be involved in financing restaurants and catering companies, and similar enterprises. At some point they acquired a smaller company that hired out limousines. Those parts of the business had all been wound down in an orderly fashion now, and all that remained of the leasing company was the Mercedes in question.

'Four years old, cost around a million when it was bought, excluding VAT. Its current value is somewhere close to half a million,' Nadja said.

'Sounds to me like a bit of basic money laundering,' Bäckström replied.

That thought had also occurred to Nadja, even if she was far from sure that was actually the case.

'The simplest explanation is probably still that they really are engaged in the activities that they claim to be involved in. After all, they've been doing it for a fair few years now, and neither the police nor the tax office seem to have raised any objections.'

'Who owns the business?' Bäckström asked.

'Seems to be owned by a tough old bird,' Nadja said with a slight smile. 'Andrea Andolini, ninety-two years old. She's lived in Malmö for the past fifty years and has been a Swedish citizen for the same length of time. She's spent her whole life in the restaurant business, and at a guess probably arrived as part of the first wave of workforce immigration in the sixties. Never married, no children, and she's still chair of the company's board.'

'Yes, they're supposed to be tough, those old pizza-bakers.' Bäckström sighed.

'And now of course you're wondering how she's related

to the Godfather,' Nadja said. 'Even I watch the occasional film, you know,' Nadja declared when she noted Bäckström's look of surprise.

'Yes, I'm listening,' Bäckström said. That Russian's as sharp as a scimitar, he thought.

'There was something about the name of the company that made me react. I got the rest from the internet. Andrea Andolini is the Godfather's aunt. Not Vito Corleone, born Andolini, but our very own local godfather here in Solna, Mario Grimaldi. Who actually comes from Naples rather than Sicily.'

'Who'd have thought it?' Bäckström said.

'Quite. Funny the way things turn out sometimes,' Nadja agreed.

'Get some good pictures of Grimaldi and we'll go round Eriksson's neighbours again. Wasn't there a witness who saw an old man with white hair sitting on the steps of Eriksson's house? Around the time Eriksson died?'

'Already underway,' Nadja said. 'Felicia was going to talk to our witness this morning.'

129

A seriously depleted investigative team that didn't seem especially energetic, even when you took into account the fact that it was Monday morning and that their two forensic medical officers had in all likelihood deprived them of a murderer and a probable lifetime sentence and had at best given them a standard-issue thug and a couple of years in prison instead.

'It's a genuine pleasure for an old policeman like me to be confronted with so much enthusiasm,' Bäckström declared, glaring bitterly at the meagre gathering.

'Well, considering what our medical officers told us and what happened down in Nyköping with Åkare, García Gomez and our witness, perhaps that isn't so surprising,' Annika Carlsson said.

'That may apply to you,' Bäckström interrupted. 'As for me, I don't leave anything half done. I want to get hold of the as yet unidentified perpetrator who beat Eriksson up so badly that his heart decided to give out. That's the first thing.'

'Noted,' Annika Carlsson said.

'Don't interrupt me. I also want to get hold of his similarly unidentified accomplice who shat himself on Eriksson's sofa, and even if he only did that to cause trouble, I want him charged with criminal damage. That's the second thing. Have I expressed myself clearly enough?'

'Abundantly clearly,' Annika Carlsson said. 'Is there anything else we can do for you, boss?'

'Find out what really happened that evening in Eriksson's house. How come a bit of squabbling about some paintings ended up leading to a full-blown gang war? That's the third thing.'

'Of course, boss,' Annika said. 'Anything else?'

'I'm more than happy to let you deal with the administrative details and paperwork,' he said. 'Make sure we hand everything we've got on Åkare, García Gomez and Afsan Ibrahim to our colleagues down in Södermanland. Don't forget to ask them if they can take over responsibility for those threats, the ones made against Danielsson and that girl who works at his office.'

'That's already being taken care of,' Annika Carlsson said.

'Good. The time of tomorrow morning's meeting will be announced later today. I'll expect to see everyone here so that we can finally bring this miserable business to an end. You just need to do as I tell you. That's really all there is to it. Is that really so hard to understand?'

130

Little Felicia seems happy, Bäckström thought as he walked out of the meeting and saw her smiling and waving to him.

'My room,' Bäckström said, gesturing with his hand.

Their witness had picked him out as soon as Felicia showed him the pictures. He hadn't shown any sign of hesitation and was quite prepared to testify under oath, even though the elderly man he had seen sitting on Eriksson's front steps with his white-haired head in his hands didn't look anything like an ordinary murderer.

'Mind you, I don't suppose he is, if I've understood correctly,' Felicia said.

'No, but there's one more thing,' Bäckström said. 'A favour I was wondering if I could ask from you. I want this to stay strictly between us for the time being. I want you to go and talk to this person.'

He jotted a name, address and mobile number on a blank page of his black notebook, tore it out and gave it to Felicia.

'Ask him if I can take him out for lunch. At that bar out in Filmstaden where he and his associates usually meet for a drink whenever AIK are playing.'

'Alphyddan?'

'That's the one. If you're wondering why I can't just call him and ask, it's because there's a certain risk that he'd just put the phone down on me. So go and see him, convince him of my friendly intentions, then make sure he gets a pilsner and a decent short on the side as soon as he's there. I want him in a good mood. Then you call me, and I'll be there in ten minutes.'

'You think this is the other man we're trying to get hold of, boss?' Felicia asked, holding up the note she'd been given.

'Do you usually watch the Disney cartoons on Christmas Eve?'

'Always,' Felicia said with a smile. 'Ever since I arrived in Sweden.'

'Then you'll be familiar with Chip 'n' Dale. You know, those two chipmunks. The ones who keep causing trouble for Mickey Mouse when he tries to decorate his tree.'

'Yes, and his dog too, Pluto,' Felicia said, unable to conceal her delight.

'Can you imagine Chip without Dale?'

'No,' Felicia said, shaking her head.

'Me neither.'

131

As soon as Felicia left him, Lisa Lamm called his mobile and asked if they could meet for a chat. She needed at least fifteen minutes of his valuable time.

'I thought you were still here,' Bäckström said. 'In the building, I mean.'

'I am,' Lisa Lamm said. 'I just wanted to check I wouldn't be disturbing you first.'

'I'm in my office. You're more than welcome, no problem,' Bäckström assured her.

Our meek little Prosecutor Lamm really isn't much like Officer Carlsson, he thought, shaking his head.

From the little that Bäckström had said during their meeting, Lisa Lamm had formed the definite impression that things were beginning to come together. That it would soon be time for her to clear her desk and get on with her life. Bearing in mind her own role in proceedings, she would obviously be very happy if Bäckström could satisfy her curiosity. That was the first reason why she wanted to see him.

She had a better understanding of the second reason why she wanted to see him. Bearing in mind Bäckström's own role, she wanted to bring him up to date with the latest legal developments in their case.

Bäckström replied by first apologizing. He certainly wasn't trying to withhold any information from the head of his preliminary investigation. On the contrary, he had been thinking of informing her once the morning meeting was out of the way. As soon as he had dealt with a few pressing matters, which he had now done.

'You only have to open any newspaper to see what I mean,' he said, looking at her seriously. 'This investigation's leaking like a sieve,' he added.

'I hope you're not worried about me?' Lisa Lamm said.

'Not in the slightest,' Bäckström said, shaking his head very firmly. 'I'm worried about the others. We've got thirty people in our investigative team, and probably another thirty in the building who have a reasonable idea of what we're doing. Sadly, there appear to be a few of them who don't seem to know how to keep their mouths shut. And what can we do about that? You and I, I mean. Nothing. Not a sausage,' he concluded, now red under the eyes and evidently having trouble concealing how upsetting he found this.

Lisa Lamm was in full agreement with Bäckström. It was a sorry state of affairs. Especially in a case that was as sensitive in terms of media coverage as this one was. But it was a situation that they would probably both just have to put up with.

'I hear what you're saying,' Bäckström said. 'My problem is that it only takes one blabbermouthed colleague to ruin what would otherwise be a perfect investigation.'

'A delicate situation,' Lisa Lamm said with a nod of agreement. 'Do you want to start, or shall I?'

'Why don't you start?' Bäckström said.

Lisa Lamm was thinking of releasing von Comer from

custody after lunch. They had enough evidence on the charge of aggravated fraud. All that remained were a few details. Such as finding out who Eriksson's employer was – the ultimate victim of the fraud.

Bäckström had no objections.

Both Afsan Ibrahim and Omar ben Kader had been in touch, via their legal representatives. It had come to their attention that they were being sought by the police on suspicion of making illegal threats. Something which they naturally both denied, and the simplest solution was surely that the police suggest a time for them to come to the police station in Solna to discuss the matter.

'I've already spoken to Lewin, who's promised to take over that part of the case as well. So as not to alert them unnecessarily, he wants his detectives to interview them out here in Solna.'

'Sounds sensible,' Bäckström said. 'You'd never be able to bring charges against them for that.'

Lisa Lamm agreed with him on this point as well. Danielsson had already been in touch to say that he didn't want to press charges about what had happened in his office. There was no question of them having made unlawful threats. Possibly an intermittently animated discussion, but as both he and the prosecutor were well aware, that wasn't currently an offence covered by the Swedish Penal Code.

'What about that girl who works there, then?' Bäckström asked. 'The one they paid a home visit to? If you ask me, I get the distinct impression that she was seeing Eriksson.'

'Worked there,' Lisa Lamm corrected. 'Apparently, she resigned the same day she was interviewed out here. She seems to have gone abroad for a long holiday. Not sure where. As far as her relationship with her former boss is concerned, I'm inclined to agree with you.'

Bäckström contented himself with a gentle sigh and a nod. Where have I heard that before? he thought.

'Did Danielsson have anything else he wanted to tell us?'

'Two things,' Lisa Lamm said. 'Firstly, that Eriksson and Partners will no longer be representing Afsan Ibrahim and his friends. Secondly, that he is relinquishing the post of executor of Eriksson's estate. If you ask me, I'd say those two facts are related, given Eriksson's business dealings with Afsan.'

'So what can I do for you, then?' Bäckström asked.

'You can't wriggle out of it any longer, Bäckström,' Lisa Lamm said, making herself comfortable on her chair.

'In that case, I've got two things to tell you as well. As far as the two men we're looking for are concerned, I'm fairly certain I've found them. Considering the amount of evidence they left behind them, it shouldn't be too difficult to find out if I'm right or wrong.'

'I interpret that to mean that you're absolutely certain.'

'You can never be absolutely certain,' Bäckström said with a carefully judged shrug of the shoulders. 'I've occasionally been wrong in the past.'

'How often does that happen, then?'

'To be honest, I can't remember. It's so long ago that I've forgotten. I'd like you to bear with me for just a few more hours. There are a couple of things I need to check first.'

'The tension is quite unbearable . . .' Lisa Lamm said.

'I'm afraid this so-called murder has simmered down to a rather dull business, and that's where I'm in serious need of your legal expertise. If you'll excuse me, I was thinking of approaching it as a hypothetical case.'

'Shoot,' Lisa Lamm said. God, this is exciting, she thought.

'Just before nine o'clock someone rings on the door of Eriksson's house,' Bäckström began, sinking deeper into his chair. 'The meeting's been arranged in advance, but his visitors are in the process of pulling a fast one on Eriksson . . . so when he opens the door and lets them in, he doesn't suspect that there's anything wrong . . .'

'What do you make of that?' Bäckström asked a quarter of an hour later as he concluded his outline of the hypothetical case. 'More particularly: what crime has been committed?'

'There isn't one,' Lisa Lamm said, shaking her head. 'Assuming everything happened the way you described, there's no punishable offence. It's a different matter with Eriksson, of course, but given that he's dead . . .'

'That's what I suspected,' Bäckström said, just as his mobile started to ring.

'Bäckström,' he said. He had already worked out who was calling.

'Felicia here,' Felicia said, sounding just as happy as she had done an hour earlier. 'We're in position.'

'See you in a quarter of an hour,' Bäckström said. 'You'll have to forgive me, Senior Prosecutor.' Bäckström got to his feet. 'I promise to call you in a couple of hours.'

'Time to take the bull by the horns,' Lisa Lamm said, more as a statement than a question.

'Yes.' You don't know how right you are, he thought.

* * *

An unusual man, a very unusual man, Lisa Lamm thought as she watched Bäckström go.

Not bad-looking, really, Bäckström thought as he stepped out on to the street and got into the waiting taxi.

132

Felicia met Bäckström at the door, and told him his guest was sitting in the back room, waiting with a large glass of beer and a whisky on the side.

'How is he?'

'He seems happy. When I told him what it was about, he seemed pretty surprised at first. But after that there were no problems. And he has to have lunch somewhere, after all.'

'Do you think he knows why I want to meet him?'

'Yes,' Felicia said with a nod. 'He even said he was looking forward to talking to you, boss, and explaining what really happened. He was surprised it had taken you so long to contact him.'

'Anything else?'

'He seems like a cool guy,' she said, looking up at the ceiling. 'That business about him being a legend isn't hard to understand. If he was fifty years younger I'd have clambered through his bedroom window myself. By the way, boss, do you want me to stick around?'

'Stay in the vicinity,' he said. Brazilian women, he thought. It's the only thing they've got on their tiny minds.

'Superintendent Bäckström,' Roly Stålhammar declared. 'Little Felicia told me you wanted to buy me lunch.

You haven't found the Lord, have you, or anything like that?'

'There's something we need to talk about, you and me,' Bäckström said. The rest of it is none of your business, he thought.

'Well, yes, I realize that, even if it took a hell of a time for you to get in touch.'

'What do you want to eat?' Bäckström asked by way of a diversion.

'Steak and onions,' Roly said. 'And when it comes to drinks, I was thinking of carrying on the way I've started.'

'Steak and onions sounds good,' Bäckström agreed, nodding to the waiter who had just appeared. 'And I'll have the usual to drink.'

'One more thing,' Roly Stålhammar said. 'Before we start eating, I mean. If you've got it into your head that I killed Eriksson, you can forget all about this little meal.'

'No,' Bäckström said. 'The reason we're sitting here is that I've got it into my head that the exact opposite is the case. I thought I'd give you a chance to tell me what happened so I can write it down.'

'That's good to hear,' Roly said, looking like he meant it. 'Mind you, if you ask me, it's a total fucking mystery,' he added, shaking his head.

'I'm listening,' Bäckström said, gesturing with the glass that had just arrived.

'When I said goodbye to Eriksson, there was nothing much wrong with him. Okay, so he was shouting and screaming and generally being uncouth, and he had a bit of a nosebleed, but that's not the sort of thing that kills you. Especially not if you're used to working for gangsters the way he was. Definitely not the sort of thing that kills you.'

But on this occasion it evidently did, Bäckström thought, and nodded.

'I'm listening,' he said.

133

A sad business, and a complete mystery, according to Roly Stålhammar. Considering what had happened, he regretted getting involved at all. Quite regardless of the fact that it concerned his best friend, and that that was what life was really all about when it came down to it.

'You can forget all that crap about right and wrong when it's your best mate,' Roly Stålhammar explained.

In this particular instance, a lawyer – 'nothing but a gangster, a massive arsehole' – had tried to con his best friend out of an art collection that was worth a fair bit, and once Mario Grimaldi had realized that he decided to get it back without delay. To help with the practical details he had contacted an old acquaintance who owned a security company which, among other things, dealt with this sort of thing. Fredrik Åkare and Åkerström Security, whom Mario had used on various previous occasions when he had had to sort out similar situations.

'When Mario told me he'd contacted Åkare and his friends I just shook my head. To start with, it would be lethal taking them to Eriksson's house, because there was no way Eriksson was going to let them in if Mario showed up there with blokes like Åkare and García Gomez. He'd have pulled up the drawbridge and called his mates in the

Taliban, and then you'd have had even more to deal with, Superintendent – I can assure you of that,' Roly said, fortifying himself with a couple of deep swigs.

'So you offered to go instead,' Bäckström said.

'Of course. What would you have done?'

'If it's a mate, then obviously you volunteer,' Bäckström lied. If you're really that stupid, he thought.

'Yes, well, this time it didn't turn out too well.' Roly sighed.

'One question, out of curiosity,' Bäckström said. 'How come Eriksson agreed to meet Mario?'

'That's not so strange,' Roly said, having trouble concealing his surprise. 'If Mario gets in touch and wants to meet you, that's what happens. That's all there is to it. Mario isn't the sort of man you say no to. All the same, I'm fairly sure he hadn't told Eriksson what it was really about. I reckon he spun him some yarn about a few bits of business. A bit of buying and selling – random stuff, you know,' Roly Stålhammar said, raising his huge right hand.

Roly Stålhammar had gone round to Mario Grimaldi's at eight thirty that evening. Because Mario didn't have a driving licence, Roly drove. Just before nine they rang on Eriksson's door, and Eriksson opened it and asked them inside. No problem at all. They sat down in Eriksson's office upstairs, and the pictures they had really come to collect were standing against one wall of the room they were sitting in.

'If you're wondering why he had them out, I think it was pure coincidence. He didn't seem to have a clue that Mario had come to pick them up.'

'So what happened after that?'

'Eriksson offered Mario a whisky. He took one himself, and if you ask me, I think he'd been on the bottle before we arrived. Not that he was hammered, exactly, but he'd certainly had a few. I declined the offer. I was driving, after all. Well,' Roly said, then sighed deeply and flexed his broad shoulders. 'There were no problems for the first five minutes. It was all nice and relaxed, if you ask me, a bit of chit-chat about this and that, then all hell broke loose. The minute Eriksson realized why we were there.'

'How did he realize?'

'Mario got out the power of attorney Eriksson had been given. He explained that it was no longer in force, with immediate effect, and that we'd come to take back the pictures.'

'How did Eriksson react to that?'

'He went crazy, started shouting and yelling. But Mario was perfectly calm, as usual. He just explained that that was the situation now. Nothing more to discuss.'

'What about you?'

'I started to put the pictures in a couple of boxes that were over in the corner. Ordinary white removal boxes. I wasn't going to get involved in all that talk. It was none of my business, after all. I was supposed to drive Mario there, then take him home. Carry the stuff out. That was all. Eriksson must have been mad. To contradict Mario? You might as well save yourself a whole load of suffering and cut your own throat.'

'Eriksson refused to listen?'

'Are you kidding? He went totally fucking batshit crazy. When Mario wanted him to sign the power of attorney to acknowledge that he'd just been relieved of it, he suddenly pulled a revolver out of his desk and started waving it about. Yelling at us to get out of the house.'

'So what did you do then?'

Roly Stålhammar's old reflexes had kicked in. The same reflexes that had made him a legend both in every police station in the country and among all their adversaries. As soon as Eriksson started waving his revolver about, Roly had put down the box he was about to carry downstairs, walked straight up to Eriksson, and loudly and clearly told him to put the gun down.

'And do you know what the bastard does then?' Roly asked. 'When I go up to him and tell him to put his piece down, nice and calmly?'

'No?'

'He points at me and raises his left hand, like some fucking traffic cop, while he raises the revolver above his head, then he yells at me: Stop! Stop, or I'll shoot.'

'Stop, or I'll shoot?'

'Stop, or I'll shoot,' Roly repeated, shaking his head. 'What the hell did he think he was playing at? That he was one of the guards at the Royal Palace, or what?'

'So what did you do next?'

Stolly the legend had let his reflexes take over. He threw himself at the lawyer. Grabbed his right arm and tried to twist the gun from his hand. Eriksson fires a shot straight up at the ceiling. Roly slaps him in the face. With his hand open, right across the nose. Eriksson refuses to give in. Another shot goes off.

'I started to get a bit annoyed then, so I gave him a few serious right hooks in the jaw, twisted his wrist again and got the gun off him. I put it in my jacket pocket. Then I sat him down on his chair behind the desk and explained the situation to him.'

'What was the situation, then?'

'That he needed to be nice and polite, unless he wanted me to start breaking bones,' Roly said.

'And he followed that advice?' Weird that Eriksson didn't shit himself as well, Bäckström thought.

'Yes, although I may have given him a little reminder while he was sitting there.'

'A little reminder?'

'I twisted the bastard's nose. Cheers, by the way,' Roly said, raising his glass of beer.

'So that was how it all happened?'

'Pretty much, as I remember it. Is there a problem?'

Quite a few, Bäckström thought. Among them the fact that you might just have talked your way into a prison cell, where I really don't want you. Not this time round, anyway.

'What do you say to a bit of food?' he asked.

'Definitely,' Roly said. 'And another beer each, and a couple of proper drinks to go with the food.'

134

Steak and onion and fried potatoes, another large beer and a small vodka, the worst of his hunger sated and high time he made some proper sense out of Roly Stålhammar's story, seeing as – unfortunately – it might well be completely true.

Bäckström dealt with it piece by piece, taking care to emphasize his pedagogical intent. As a general observation, he was prepared to buy Roly's version of events. That just left a few minor details that he feared Roly might have misinterpreted. With all due respect, of course, because, naturally, the situation was highly charged and chaotic, and all that.

'How do you mean?' Roly asked, looking the way honest people usually do when they don't understand what everyone else is talking about.

There were a number of things that didn't match what Niemi and his colleagues and their forensic medical officer had said. Nor with Bäckström's own thoughts about what had happened. Because there was actually a lot of evidence to suggest that Eriksson had suddenly pulled out a weapon, taken aim at Mario as he was sitting on the sofa and quite simply tried to blow his head off. That that was how things had really started. Like a bolt from the blue, so to speak.

And then Roly, at risk of his own life, tried to disarm Eriksson, and Eriksson, while they were struggling for his gun, managed to fire a shot straight up at the ceiling before Roly finally managed to disarm him. And Roly had tried to distract Eriksson by slapping him across the face with an open palm that struck Eriksson on the cheek and nose, before eventually twisting the gun from his hand. And Bäckström really didn't believe that business about Roly – after everything was over – twisting Eriksson's nose. According to their medical officer, there was no evidence to suggest that had happened.

'I understand what you're saying,' Roly said with a nod, looking as if he were thinking hard.

'Yes, it's very easy to get the details muddled up,' Bäckström said.

'On reflection, I think it happened exactly the way you said it did,' Stolly said, brightening up considerably and raising his glass. 'Now I come to think about it, I'm totally sure that's what happened. Cheers, Bäckström!'

'Cheers, Roly.' At last, Bäckström thought.

As they drank their coffee and cognac, Bäckström and Roly Stålhammar reached the end of the sad tale. And also cleared up a few practical details. What had happened after Roly disarmed Eriksson and they left the scene?

Not much, according to Roly. First, he helped Mario downstairs and out of the house. He left him sitting on the front steps. Mario hadn't been feeling very well. He kept going on about a bullet whistling through his hair. Unfortunately, he had managed to piss and shit himself when it happened. Roly had gone back upstairs to fetch the two boxes of paintings they had come to collect.

'There was nothing much wrong with Eriksson, if you're

wondering. His nose was still bleeding a bit, and I lent him my handkerchief so he could wipe it, then when I asked him if everything was okay he just yelled at me. Told me I could go to hell.'

'What did you do after that?'

'I left,' Roly said. 'What else was I going to do? Then, as I was about to step out of the house, I realized I still had the bastard's revolver in my pocket. So I went back into the hall and dumped it in some old vase of flowers in there. I wasn't about to give it back to Eriksson, as I'm sure you can appreciate.'

'Then what?'

First, he had helped Mario to the car. He laid him down in the back seat before putting the boxes of paintings in the boot. Then they left and went back to Mario's. He helped Mario up into his apartment, then carried up the boxes of paintings. He made sure Mario was feeling better, then left him and walked home.

'What time was it when you left Eriksson's house?'

'Half past nine, pretty much on the button,' Roly said. 'If you're wondering how I know that, it's because I wanted to watch a programme about old boxing champions, from the days when I was active myself, and that was on at eleven o'clock. Quite a bit had happened, of course, if I can put it like that, so I wanted to make sure I wasn't going to miss it. That's why I looked at the time when we left Eriksson's.'

'So what time did you get home, then?'

'Half past ten. So I set out some goodies in front of the sofa before it was time to switch on the idiot lantern.'

'Is there anything we've forgotten, do you think?' Bäckström asked.

'Possibly one last little cognac before we head up to the station and get all the forms filled in.'

'I'd suggest we do that bit tomorrow. I was thinking that the Anchor could take care of the practical stuff with the interview and so on. Then I dare say the prosecutor will want a few words with you. I want you to talk to Mario as well. Explain that we're going to have to interview him. Considering what good mates you are, that shouldn't be a problem.'

'No problem, not the slightest,' Roly said, unable to hide his surprise.

'There's one thing I'm still wondering about.'

'Go for it, Bäckström.'

'I had no idea Mario was interested in art.'

'Nor did I, really,' Roly agreed. 'I mean, Mario's an ordinary, decent person, completely normal. He likes food and drink and women and all the rest. Boxing, horses, football, hockey. But, like you say – art? Surely no normal person's interested in that crap? Only old women and poofs.'

'But he evidently had a whole collection of Russian art,' Bäckström persisted. 'Where did he get it from?'

'Probably something he bought,' Roly said, shrugging his shoulders. 'Mario would buy pretty much anything, if you ask me. Probably easiest for you to ask him straight out.'

'I've got the impression that talking to him isn't altogether straightforward. According to various medical certificates that I and my colleagues have seen, he's supposed to be suffering from Alzheimer's.'

'Who'd have thought it?' Roly Stålhammar said with a wry smile. 'If you ask me, it's much simpler than that. Mario only talks to people he wants to talk to, and when he talks to them he only talks about things he wants to talk about. The problem isn't that Mario is stupid. Mario's smarter than everyone else in this country put together. But of course that isn't his problem, but everyone else's. You get what I mean?'

'I certainly do,' Bäckström said. 'How is he otherwise? As a person, I mean?'

'Mario and I have known each other since we were this small,' Roly Stålhammar said, holding his right thumb and forefinger apart. 'Mario's a friend to his friends and an enemy to his enemies. Because he and I have been best mates since we were snotty little kids, I've never encountered any problems in that regard.'

'What about his enemies?'

'Let me put it like this,' Roly Stålhammar said. 'If there's one person on the planet that you should avoid falling out with, it's Mario Grimaldi. That business about him wetting himself when Eriksson tried to part his hair with the help of his revolver isn't something you should get hung up about. It could happen to anyone. Not least an old man like Mario. It even happened to me.'

'It happened to you?'

'Forty years ago. A colleague and I were about to pick up a mental patient who'd escaped from Långbro. A woman, she'd gone straight home to her mum, who called and asked us to collect her. A skinny little thing, twenty at most, looked younger, said nothing, just stood there looking at me with her big blue eyes. And it's in that sort of situation you sometimes drop your guard. So when I pulled out my ID and was about to explain who I was, she stuck a hunting knife straight into my stomach. If she'd aimed a couple of centimetres to the right she'd have hit my aorta.'

'So you shat yourself?'

'Yes,' Roly Stålhammar said. 'Mind you, I can't

remember if that happened when she stabbed me or when I was in the ambulance.'

'Cheers,' Bäckström said. What the fuck am I supposed to say to that?

After a couple more final cognacs, Bäckström ordered a taxi and made sure his companion got home in one piece. Roly Stålhammar even gave him a bear hug as they parted. And gave him a piece of advice with regard to his ongoing investigation.

'There's something I've been thinking,' Roly said.

'I'm listening.'

'Asking Mario about his interest in art may not be such a great idea. Answering questions isn't really Mario's thing, I mean.'

'What do you suggest, then?'

'My advice would be to talk to Pyttan.'

'Pyttan?'

'Yes, you know, Pyttan. The love of Mario's life. You've met her. When you gave that talk for that property developer. A few weeks back. Tall, good-looking woman. And she's really damn nice as well, even though she's posh. She's supposed to be some sort of countess.'

'Yes, I remember,' Bäckström said. The one with all those diamonds the size of hazelnuts, he thought.

'I'll give you her number. Talk to Pyttan. She knows everything Mario gets up to. She's got him eating out of her hand. He's like a love-struck puppy.'

A godfather who's like a love-struck puppy, a countess who hand feeds an old dago, this country's already shot to hell, Bäckström thought as he sat in the taxi on the way home.

135

Once he was home, Bäckström got to grips with the practical details. He called Anchor Carlsson and told her all she needed to know, and then gave her instructions for the following day. They were to hold thorough interviews with Roly Stålhammar and Mario Grimaldi. Make sure they gave DNA samples, check the GPS of the Mercedes in question, talk to the forensic medical officer and Niemi, to make sure their stories fitted. And make sure Lisa Lamm didn't start to make trouble and simply dropped the whole case as soon as possible.

'It's an extremely tragic business, considering what happened to our witness,' Annika Carlsson said.

'I hear what you're saying,' Bäckström said. 'But what can we do about that?'

'Nothing,' Annika Carlsson said. 'What are we going to do about tomorrow morning's meeting?'

'Cancel the bastard,' Bäckström said. 'And they won't get any cake until they've finished filling in all the paperwork. You can tell them that from me.'

'What were you thinking of doing?'

'Time owing,' Bäckström said. I've got considerably more important things to grapple with, he thought.

* * *

Bäckström spent the evening and half the night submerged in gloomy thoughts. Suppose things were so bad that Mario Grimaldi did really own all the art. Or worse, that he and his family had owned it the whole time, because one or more mafiosi of an older generation of the Grimaldi family had broken into Prince Wilhelm and Maria Pavlovna's palatial villa out on Djurgården and helped themselves to whatever they could carry. There are far too many dagos in this story, he thought, pouring himself another drink.

He himself had been hoping for His Majesty the King of Sweden, or at least one of all the other princes and princesses in his vicinity. Even that bodybuilder from Ockelbo would have been a blessing from above compared to Mario the Godfather Grimaldi, and he himself had entered the chain of ownership far too recently for that to have affected the price in a positive direction.

As an art connoisseur of long standing, since his time in the police's lost property store, he knew better than most people how much difference the province could make to the value. What would the heirs of that old fisherman have got for his sealskin slippers at the bog-standard estate sale they'd have ended up in if that film director hadn't stuffed his frozen blue feet in them? Five kronor at most, from the chairman of the foot fetishists' association, Bäckström thought. Then, full of these mournful thoughts, he finally fell asleep.

136

At eight o'clock on Tuesday morning Detective Inspectors Annika Carlsson and Johan Ek conducted an interview with former Detective Inspector Roland Stålhammar about his visit to the home of lawyer Thomas Eriksson on the evening of 2 June. The purpose of the interview was to gather information, and in the observation room next door sat Senior Prosecutor Lisa Lamm, Detective Superintendent Peter Niemi and their forensic medical officer, Dr Sven Olof Lidberg, watching the interview.

The interview took about an hour, and gave neither of the interviewers any reason to cast the slightest shadow of a doubt on anything Stålhammar told them. He even had a perfectly plausible explanation to the final question he was asked: how come he hadn't contacted the police at once when he heard about what had happened? Especially considering his background in the force?

'There was nothing wrong with him when Mario and I left,' Roly Stålhammar said. 'But, as you ask, I still don't understand what he died of.'

'I can't help thinking it seems a bit odd,' Annika Carlsson retorted. 'That you didn't come and tell us what had happened, I mean.'

'If you switch the tape recorder off, I'll tell you,' Roly

said. 'Otherwise, I won't bother. Because it's not about me, but Mario.'

'Okay,' Annika said, as the loudspeaker in the observation room was still working and both she and Ek had ears that were perfectly good enough to stand witness to anything he said.

'He tried to blow Mario's head off,' Roly Stålhammar said. 'Mario's an old man. He could have died. I asked him the next day if he wanted to report Eriksson, but he said we shouldn't, so that's what happened.'

'Why did he say that, then?'

'It's hardly that difficult to understand,' Roly Stålhammar said. 'He shat himself. He was bitterly ashamed. He could live with all the rest of it.'

'I see what you mean,' Annika Carlsson said.

'Good,' Roly Stålhammar said. 'If I ever hear a single word about what I've just told you, I swear I'll tear down Solna police station with my own hands.'

'I don't think that will be necessary,' Annika said with a smile. 'Well, I'd like to thank you for coming, and that last part will stay in this room.'

'What do we think about that, then?' Lisa Lamm asked a quarter of an hour later.

'I don't have any objections,' the medical officer said. 'Stålhammar's story fits the results of the forensic medical examination.'

'I agree with you,' Peter Niemi said. 'And for once we're in the fortunate position of being able to tick off his story against the results of the forensic search. I don't think there'll be any surprises on that score.'

'Fine with me,' Annika Carlsson agreed, while her colleague Johan Ek simply nodded his agreement.

'Well, in that case,' Lisa Lamm said, 'considering the circumstances, I judge that the force Stålhammar used against the lawyer is within the bounds of the paragraphs of the Penal Code governing self-defence. By quite some margin, I might add. I don't have any reservations about closing the case. All I need now are the results from the National Forensics Lab, the DNA samples from that handkerchief and the sofa cushion.'

'We should be getting those tomorrow, believe it or not,' Peter Niemi said. 'Bearing in mind the media pressure, we'll drive the new samples down as soon as we've interviewed Grimaldi and taken a swab.'

'In that case, I'll make sure Stålhammar gets his handkerchief back,' Lisa Lamm said. 'Nice to be able to surrender a piece of evidence for once.'

'What if Eriksson had survived?' Annika Carlsson asked. 'What would you have done then?'

'I'd probably have charged him with attempted murder, or attempted manslaughter,' Lisa Lamm said.

Three hours later Carlsson and Ek were finished with their next interview with an unusually garrulous Mario Grimaldi, who had also brought along a lawyer. It took thirty-five minutes, and everyone who heard him drew the same conclusions as after the interview with Roland Stålhammar, even though he refused to answer the question of who owned the paintings he had gone to collect.

According to Mario, he got involved on behalf of an old friend. Before he gave them his friend's name, he wanted to obtain their approval. Because he had taken with him the power of attorney that Eriksson had been given when he was commissioned to sell the items, Eriksson must have realized that Mario was authorized to be there in that capacity. His lawyer was able to confirm this, because he had signed the immediate withdrawal of Eriksson's power of attorney and made sure it was properly witnessed. The reason for the withdrawal was that Eriksson had tried to defraud his employer. They were planning to return to the matter of their financial claim against Eriksson's law firm and his estate.

Mario Grimaldi began by telling them that he was an old man. That what had happened that evening inside the lawyer's home was the worst thing he had experienced in his whole life. In spite of all the terrible things he had been through in his native Italy at the end of the Second World War, when he was just a little boy.

'He suddenly went mad,' Mario said. 'He pulled out a pistol and aimed it right at my face while I was sitting there. The bullet flew past my head, and if my old friend Roly hadn't thrown himself at him and disarmed him, I wouldn't be sitting here today.'

'Someone must have borrowed your car later that night,' Johan Ek said, as the last question of the interview. 'That much is apparent from the vehicle's GPS. Do you have any comment to make about that?'

No comment. He had given up driving twenty years ago, and handed his licence in more than ten years ago. Entirely voluntarily, and as soon as his doctor had advised him to do so. But it did happen that people he knew sometimes borrowed the car from him. Among others, a nice Chilean lad who worked as an odd-job man and had recently helped him hang some new curtains in his kitchen. That must have been when he borrowed the car keys from him. His spare keys, that is, because he was fairly sure that he still had a set of keys at home in his apartment.

'His name is Angel,' Mario said. 'Like the heavenly host,' he explained. He couldn't remember the lad's surname, but it was one of those common names that Spanish-speaking people often had. His mother had worked for him many years ago, when he owned a restaurant in Solna. She was a very pleasant woman, very reliable. Not long ago, Roly had told him that she had passed away.

'We shall all tread that path,' the Godfather declared with a sad sigh.

That afternoon, interviews were also conducted with Omar ben Kader and Afsan Ibrahim, who arrived in the company of their respective lawyers.

Omar ben Kader left the police station within half an hour, a free man. He had been unswervingly friendly the whole time, and had expressed his surprise that they wanted to see him. The fact that he had accompanied Afsan Ibrahim in his capacity as his financial advisor to a meeting with Peter Danielsson, a lawyer with the firm of Eriksson and Partners, was hardly a secret. That much ought to be clear from the law firm's visitors' book, but if they had been neglectful on that score, he was very happy to confirm that he had been there. Because the meeting with Danielsson had actually been booked by him. He wasn't prepared to go into the reasons why he had done so. Before he left, he gave them his business card and said that the police were welcome to call him if there was anything else they were wondering.

The spitting image of his father, Jan Lewin thought as he sat in the observation room watching him.

* * *

His employer, Afsan Ibrahim, remained in the interview room for approximately an hour. The reason he had gone to visit Isabella Norén was that Thomas Eriksson had told him to talk to her if anything happened to him. According to what Eriksson had told him, he and Norén had been in a relationship for the past couple of years, so she would be able to help him with a few things that his colleagues in the office knew nothing about.

In this instance, it was about whether she could possibly help him find the money that Eriksson had borrowed from a Cypriot bank, because Afsan had been charged by the bank to demand that the money be repaid. It had been a very short visit, ten minutes at most, and nothing remotely untoward had taken place. If Norén was claiming otherwise, he was more than happy to participate in an open interview with her.

As far as their questions about two of his employees, Ali Ibrahim and Ali Issa, went, unfortunately he wasn't in a position to say very much. Ibrahim had had to go back to Iran suddenly because his father had been taken ill. When he spoke to him on the phone the previous day, Ibrahim had told him that he expected to have to stay for at least a month in order to take care of his mother and the rest of the family.

Ali Issa and his girlfriend had been abroad on holiday for the past week or so. It was both much needed and well deserved, because Ali Issa had worked hard all winter and spring opening a restaurant on Södermalm that was owned by one of Afsan's businesses. If he got in touch, of course Afsan would tell him that the police wanted to talk to him.

'Well, Jan. What did you get out of your visit?' Lisa Lamm asked.

'Hopefully, my colleagues got some good moving footage of Afsan and Omar,' Jan Lewin said with an amiable smile. 'Otherwise, it was pretty much what I was expecting.'

'If you don't insist on taking over my complaint against them for making unlawful threats, I was thinking of dropping it.'

'Sounds sensible,' Jan Lewin said.

'How are you getting on down in Nyköping? Anything you can talk about?'

'It's going badly,' Jan Lewin said. 'Right now, we're pinning our hopes on the possibility that those most closely involved are going to use their freedom to do something else stupid. I don't find that very reassuring.'

'There's not much there to make the most of,' Lisa Lamm said.

'No, there isn't,' Jan Lewin said, and shrugged his shoulders.

137

While his colleagues were busy conducting interviews, Bäckström had considerably more important matters to deal with. In this instance, a crisis meeting with GeGurra at his office in Gamla stan, where they discussed the significance of provenance to the price of an item.

'How can I help you, my dear friend?' GeGurra asked, as amiable and obliging as always.

'There's something I've been wondering. How important is the province in this case? The musical box, I mean.'

'The importance of the provenance in this case . . .' GeGurra said, making a conscious effort to pronounce all three syllables in the word but without actually inscribing them on Bäckström's nose.

'Yes, the provenance,' Bäckström repeated. 'Isn't that what I said?' Why are faggots always so fucking stuck-up? he thought. Especially arty faggots.

'How do you mean?' GeGurra asked, arching his fingers and resting his elbows on his extremely valuable rococo desk.

Bäckström wanted to try out a hypothesis on GeGurra. It was, admittedly, entirely theoretical, but at the same time it was based in part on his hitherto unsuccessful search. Suppose the king or some closely related member of the Bernadotte family had never actually owned the musical box. And that someone like Grimaldi had owned the collection in question, and that he had acquired it in a way that wouldn't stand up to close scrutiny. If Bäckström had understood correctly, that would be nothing short of a catastrophe for the value of the musical box of Pinocchio and his nose.

'I've been thinking about what you said about that film director and his slippers,' he said. 'If I've got this right, it would mean that the price would collapse, wouldn't it?'

GeGurra had no problem understanding either his question or the general point he was making. Obviously, it would be extremely significant if three generations of a royal dynasty were to be replaced by Mario Grimaldi and his forebears. Especially if they had acquired the artefact by nefarious means.

'"Catastrophe" is perhaps a rather strong word,' GeGurra said with a precisely judged shrug. 'At worst, perhaps it would halve the price. And of course it might be more difficult to find a buyer. A lot of institutions and museums wouldn't be interested.'

'As bad as that?' Bäckström said, looking like someone who'd just had half his fortune stolen.

'Yes. Not a catastrophe, but of course it wouldn't be good.'

'On a completely different subject,' Bäckström said. 'That painting of the fat monk. You wouldn't let me borrow it, and take it home?' Got to make the most of a bad situation, he thought.

'By all means,' GeGurra said. 'You won't be upset if I ask why?'

'I'm actually thinking of buying it from you. Just want to see if it would work above my sofa first.'

'By all means,' GeGurra said, barely able to hide his surprise. 'I'll ask my secretary to fetch it. It's in the storage facility.'

Bäckström and Saint Theodore went straight back to Bäckström's home, where Bäckström ate lunch while he stared at the fat Greek priest who was perched on the kitchen worktop a few metres away. Brown beans and fried pork chops, and a couple of emergency vodkas that were urgently required as a result of his forced involvement with thieving priests and Italian pasta cooks who shat on people's sofas and didn't even have the decency not to steal from an honest, hard-working police officer like him.

He woke up from his much-needed afternoon nap to find someone ringing on his door, and, once he had pulled on his dressing-gown and gone to open it, he realized that he was being dealt a terrible blow, and that the domestic tranquillity that he treasured more than anything was lost.

138

The visitor was Edvin's mother, Dusanka. She had brought Isak with her and, judging by the size of the cage he was in, he had ended up in the parrot equivalent of an isolation cell. He also seemed 'subdued', as his little surrogate custodian had described Isak's emotional state to Bäckström during his earlier visit.

Dusanka said she would be brief. In spite of Edvin's protests, she had decided to return Isak to his rightful owner. They simply weren't suitable company for each other, and at the ceremony to mark the end of the school year the previous day, sadly they had embarrassed both themselves and Edvin's parents, Slobodan and Dusanka.

'Come in and sit down,' Bäckström suggested, gesturing invitingly with his arm towards the large leather sofa in his living room. 'Can I get you anything?' he went on with a generous nod towards the well-stocked antique dresser on which he currently stored the majority of his more expensive strong liquor.

Considering what she was about to tell him, Dusanka wouldn't say no to a rum and Coke, with plenty of ice and a slice of lemon. Bäckström hurried out to the kitchen, fulfilled her wishes and – just to be on the safe side – armed himself with both a large Czech pilsner and a vodka of truly Russian dimensions.

'I'm listening,' Bäckström said, contorting his moon-face into an amiable and understanding expression.

On the last day of the school year, Edvin and his class-mates had been given the chance to present a talk about their favourite hobbies, and because Edvin went to a 'non-profit-making free school for particularly gifted children', there were approximately three parents for every child, and at least one teacher for every half-dozen young pupils. The classroom was packed, and expectations were high when it was time for the climactic high point of the pro-gramme, when Edvin was going to show the audience how to teach a parrot to talk.

Edvin had started rather cautiously. He got Isak to say 'Hello' to the audience, and say that he was a 'clever boy', then claim that 'AIK are best'. In short, he garnered both laughter and applause until the highly anticipated finale, which Edvin introduced by saying that it was possible to teach a parrot to say sentences of up to nine syllables, and possibly more if you really tried.

He had asked for silence, snapped his little fingers, and looked encouragingly at his blue and yellow partner.

Isak reacted instantly with a loud, cackling utterance, and there was no doubt whatsoever about the meaning of his message.

'It was terrible.' Dusanka sighed, crossing herself and taking a couple of large, fortifying gulps of her rum and Coke.

'What did he say, then?' Bäckström asked. Nine sylla-bles? What did Edvin mean by that?

'Little Willy in the lady-cave,' Dusanka said in a muf-fled voice.

'Ah, perhaps that was a little unfortunate,' Bäckström

said, and downed half his vodka. That lad's going to go far, he thought. Nine syllables, he thought with reluctant admiration. Not the usual five he used to shout when he would sneak after his religious education teacher while she was walking home at night to the parish house from school.

'What happened after that?' he asked with a serious expression. He's definitely going to go far, he thought.

All the children had been delighted. They jumped about, howling with laughter, and their behaviour suggested that the whole thing might have been planned in advance. Their parents, teachers and school governors were less amused, and once Isak had been banished to a neighbouring classroom and order had been restored among the children, and they had sung the obligatory 'Ida's Summer Song' by the great Astrid Lindgren, and handed out certificates, the headmaster had concluded events by summoning all the parents to an extraordinary meeting with the teachers and governors later that week.

'At first we thought Edvin was going to be expelled.' Dusanka sighed. 'But now Slobodan has spoken to the headmaster, and he's promised that Edvin will be allowed to go back in the autumn. On probation. The headmaster was concerned about him knowing phrases like that.'

Expelled? Fucking upper classes, Bäckström thought. If that was how it was going to be, perhaps he could intervene with a bit of music-box money and send the lad to Lundsberg, so he got the chance to behave like every normal young man of his age.

'I see,' he said. 'So what do we do now?'

Dusanka was happy to leave Isak's owner to find a solution to that problem. But, for Edvin and his parents,

Isak was a closed chapter. Bäckström took the opportunity to suggest that the simplest solution would be to wring Isak's neck. Slobodan had evidently been thinking along the same lines, but because Edvin would never forgive his parents if they did anything like that, they had decided to hand responsibility back to Isak's rightful owner.

What the fuck am I going to do now? Bäckström thought when Dusanka left him, after downing another rum and Coke.

Bäckström spent a couple of hours in front of his computer in a vain search for a discreet and competent parrot exterminator. Isak clearly realized the seriousness of the occasion, and kept his beak shut the whole time.

Then Bäckström returned him to his usual cage. He put on a fresh set of clothes and strolled down to his local bar to get something to eat while he considered the dangerous position in which he had clearly ended up. When he got home shortly before midnight things were still calm, until he was woken at four in the morning, when Isak was evidently back to his old self again.

139

At nine o'clock on Wednesday morning, the last meeting on the subject of the Western District's investigation into the murder of lawyer Thomas Eriksson took place. The head of the preliminary investigation, Senior Prosecutor Lisa Lamm, had brought coffee and cake, and thanked her detectives for their hard work. What had at first looked like an unusually brutal murder had, on closer inspection, turned out to be a forgivable use of force that was more than covered by the Penal Code's definition of self-defence.

If there was anyone who could be criticized for what had happened, it was the dead man himself, Thomas Eriksson. If he had survived, Lisa Lamm would have had no hesitation in prosecuting him for attempted murder, or attempted manslaughter, but seeing as Eriksson was dead that was obviously no longer an option.

After consulting her own boss, the Chief Prosecutor for Stockholm, as well as the head of the Western District Police Force, Police Chief Anna Holt, Lisa Lamm had decided to close the case the following morning, on the grounds of 'no crime committed', which was the strongest of the options open to her. Considering the vast amount of media interest, she had also decided to hold a press conference in conjunction with the publication of her decision.

All that remained, from a legal perspective, were little more than minor details when seen in the wider context. She had also decided to drop Isabella Norén's complaint against Afsan Ibrahim, Ali Ibrahim and Ali Issa for threatening behaviour, or for perverting the course of justice, as 'crime not proven'.

The suspicions of financial irregularities that had arisen concerning Thomas Eriksson and Baron Hans Ulrik von Comer had been handed on to the Economic Crime Unit. Responsibility for the triple murder of Fredrik Åkerström, Angel García Gomez and Ara Dosti was in the hands of the police and prosecutor's office in Södermanland. That left the charge against Hans Ulrik von Comer for assaulting a public official, and that investigation was being dealt with by one of her younger colleagues.

She was happy to move on with her life, richer from this interesting experience, and was now planning to take some holiday. From the cheerful expressions around the table, she understood that she wasn't alone in planning to start the summer that way. Lastly – but by no means least – she wanted to express particular gratitude to her right-hand man for the exemplary way in which he had conducted their investigation.

'Detective Superintendent Evert Bäckström, the Man, the Myth, the Legend,' Lisa Lamm said, directing a broad smile at the man in question.

Bäckström, on the other hand, wasn't his usual self. He seemed almost distant, in an amiable but very peculiar way. He thanked the prosecutor, all of his dear colleagues, and said that this had been an arduous case, not least for him personally, although he didn't want to go into that in detail, but that there were far worse things that could happen to you. When he went on to excuse himself by saying that he had an important meeting to go to, there were a number of his colleagues who felt genuinely concerned on his behalf.

Isak, however, was most definitely his usual self, and when he was at his worst, Bäckström seriously considered abandoning his own home and moving into a comfortable local hotel, leaving the fucker to slowly starve to death. Once he got that far with his thoughts, Isak suddenly went quiet. He just sat there on his perch in total silence, glaring at Bäckström. In spite of everything he had done beforehand, this complete silence was almost unbearable.

In the midst of all this, his tame reporter had called to moan. He'd heard rumours that the investigation into the murder of Eriksson the lawyer was suddenly about to be dropped. The palace press officers were also behaving in a much more forthright manner, to the extent that you might almost imagine they were gearing up to win a rerun of the battle of Poltava. The editor-in-chief was getting cold feet. He had taken to padding round the corridors like an unquiet spirit, constantly asking what was really going on.

'So what do we do, Bäckström?' his tame reporter asked.

'That's hardly my fucking responsibility, is it?' Bäckström replied. 'I'm not the one who publishes your rag, am I?' It is to his credit that he didn't actually have any idea that this was precisely the situation at the largest paper in the country, and had been for the past week.

'You could at least give me a bit of good advice, though, couldn't you?' his tame reporter pleaded.

'Okay,' Bäckström said, having finally made up his

mind. 'See you in the bar of the Grand Hotel at six o'clock. Make sure you've got paper and a pen.'

Then he packed a bag with the bare necessities, left Isak to his fate and fled the field for a different, better life.

140

On Thursday morning there was a press conference in the police station in Solna. Senior Prosecutor Lisa Lamm opened proceedings by explaining that the preliminary investigation into the murder of Thomas Eriksson the lawyer had been closed. Then she gave a fairly exhaustive description of what had happened. That Thomas Eriksson had died as a result of a combination of his own violent conduct, it had been fully justified self-defence, and the poor state of his heart.

The whole event was actually entirely unnecessary, as everything that was said in the press conference was already available to read in the largest of the country's evening papers. Even before the press conference began, readers of that day's edition of the main evening paper could learn both what Lisa Lamm was going to say an hour later, as well as a considerably more dramatic and detailed story that bore a conspicuous resemblance to what Roly and Mario had said during their interviews with the police two days before.

The headline almost wrote itself: 'Desperate Gangster Lawyer Tried to Rob and Murder Pensioner'. Once again, the biggest paper in the country had wiped the floor with its competitors, and the fact that Bäckström the legend was absent from the press conference itself looked as if it was the result of conscious thought.

VIII

The true story of Pinocchio's nose. Part II

141

When Bäckström woke up in his large suite in the Grand Hotel, he was in a quite excellent mood. He had ordered breakfast in his room and, as he stuffed himself with scrambled eggs, sausages and bacon, he improved his already good appetite with the help of giddy fantasies about the starvation which ought by now to be afflicting Isak.

Then he called Mario's girlfriend, Pyttan, and asked if he could meet her. There were a few questions he wanted to ask, about a collection of Russian art that she might have read about in the papers.

Pyttan seemed to be in a good mood as well. Superintendent Beck was 'ever so welcome', and she could see him in an hour in her and Mario's new apartment by the Karlberg Canal, where she had been fully occupied recently with the final details of the furnishings.

Bäckström packed what he needed in Superintendent Pisshead's old briefcase and ordered a taxi to the palatial building overlooking the Karlberg Canal, where his old property-developer friend could offer the most secure housing in the land to the elite group of senior citizens who owned most of Sweden, and where the Godfather and Pyttan had evidently laid claim to the entire top floor of the building. 'Hamilton – Grimaldi', Bäckström read on the large gilded sign on the front door. Which ought surely to mean that Pyttan was related to that special agent, Carl Hamilton, in all those books by the only writer in the country worthy of the description, Bäckström thought. In spite of all the malicious rumours he had heard recently about him switching to writing faggot novels. How likely was that? About as likely as the pope handing out sacramental wafers wearing the esteemed author's hunting cap, he thought, shaking his head and ringing the doorbell.

Pyttan was just as charming as she had been on the previous occasion. Suntanned and bedecked with diamonds. After a mere fifty-metre walk she and Bäckström sat down on a large suite of sofas and chairs with a view of both Karlberg Palace and the canal below. He put his little tape recorder on the big glass coffee table where they were sitting, and asked if she had anything against him recording their conversation, because over the past few years he had started to have a bit of trouble with his memory.

Pyttan knew exactly what he meant. Some days it took her until lunchtime before she could remember what Mario's first name was. 'God, how exciting!' Pyttan said, flashing her eyes, teeth, rings and necklaces all at the same time. Finally, a proper police interview, and with one of her great idols as well.

'Shoot, Detective,' Pyttan said, then lit a cigarette, crossed her long legs and leaned back in the Gustavian armchair she was sitting on.

Bäckström started by showing her pictures of all the icons, the remnants of the hunting service, two canteens of cutlery and a gold cigar-lighter. The only thing missing was the picture of Pinocchio with the long nose, which he was planning to hold back as long as he could, and hopefully keep to himself for ever. The first question was obvious: did she happen to know who owned the paintings and other objects in the pictures?

'Yes, of course,' Pyttan said. 'They're all mine. I got them from my daddy, Archie, when he died. He got them from his mother, Ebba, my grandmother, who in turn got them from that Russian, Maria Pavlovna, when she got divorced from Prince Wilhelm.'

'Could you tell me a bit more about that?' Bäckström asked, giving her a friendly smile. This is more like it, he thought. Admittedly, not kings and queens, princes and princesses, but plain old counts and barons weren't to be sniffed at in a situation like this. They were at least several million kronor better than a load of pomaded brilliantinos of mixed Mediterranean extraction.

'Could you tell me more?' he repeated, as Pyttan suddenly looked as if she was in a better, long-lost world.

'Of course,' Pyttan said. There were no problems with her memory on that point. She could list the Swedish aristocracy even if you woke her up in the middle of the night, as she was related to pretty much all of them and had met most of the ones it was possible to talk to. Her grandmother had been born in 1880, her maiden name was Lewenhaupt, and she was born a countess. At the age of twenty she married Count Gustaf Gilbert Hamilton, who was twice her age. He was head of the Västergötland branch of the great Hamilton family, a big landowner, rider, hunter and courtier, and a personal friend of both Oscar II and Gustaf V.

'My grandfather was a very stylish man,' Pyttan declared. 'He had the typical Hamilton look, as we usually say in the family. Unfortunately, he also had the typical

Hamilton brain, so my dear Grandma Ebba perhaps didn't always have things terribly easy.'

'What did she do, then? Ebba, I mean?'

'I suppose she did what everyone else did,' Pyttan said, unable to hide her surprise at the question. 'She socialized with everyone one was supposed to socialize with at the time. She was at court when Gustaf V ascended the throne after Oscar. By some years, she was the youngest of the ladies-in-waiting to his wife, Queen Victoria. That was probably why she ended up with Prince Wilhelm and Maria. Of course, Maria Pavlovna was even younger than Grandma. And by then Ebba already had three children, so she was able to offer advice to Maria when the time came. My daddy, Archie, was the eldest, actually. He was born in 1901, I'm sure about that. After all, it's an easy year to remember.'

'Did anything special happen in 1901?' Bäckström asked. 'In the family, I mean.'

'No,' Pyttan said. 'Why should it have done?'

'You said it was an easy year to remember. That's what made me wonder.'

'I always find it easier to remember years at the start,' Pyttan explained. 'Like 1901, right at the start. But if you asked me when my daddy, Archie, died, I wouldn't have a clue. I know it must have been sometime during the seventies, but of course I can't remember exactly when. And that's not at the start, if you understand what I mean, Superintendent.'

'I understand,' Bäckström said, who by now was certain that Pyttan had been blessed with the typical Hamilton brain as well.

'I understand that your Grandma Ebba and Maria Pavlovna became good friends,' Bäckström went on, keen to avoid getting stuck in a Hamiltonian dead end.

'What makes you think that?' Pyttan asked.

'Considering all the gifts she got from Maria when Maria returned to Russia.' Bäckström pointed at the pictures on the table in front of them.

It wasn't that remarkable really, according to Pyttan. It was mostly rubbish, and the only reason Maria gave it away was probably that she couldn't be bothered to drag it all back to Russia again. There was never any question of there being a great friendship between Ebba and Maria Pavlovna.

Neither the Hamiltons nor the Lewenhaupts were terribly fond of Russians. For the perfectly understandable reason that they had pretty much only encountered them in connection with various battles over the course of three centuries, and that a thousand or so of her older relations had lost their lives during these very masculine encounters.

Nor did they ever seem to have got terribly close to each other. Admittedly, when Maria first arrived in Sweden they had competed in sliding down the grand staircase in the entrance hall out at Oakhill on silver trays, but after Grandma Ebba had beaten her three times in a row Maria got fed up and replaced her with one of her chambermaids, who was so terrified that she went down backwards with her eyes closed.

Pyttan's grandmother was an excellent rider, particularly at jumps and dressage, and was very careful with her health. Ebba didn't smoke or drink, whereas Maria smoked like a chimney and drank as much as all the male members of the Romanov dynasty.

'Take that cigar-lighter, for instance,' Pyttan said. 'I'm fairly sure she gave that to Grandma to tease her, because she knew she didn't smoke.'

'What about the dinner service?'

That was even easier to explain: her grandmother had been given it by Prince Wilhelm, not Maria. Among the family records was the letter confirming the gift. Prince Wilhelm was a fine, sensitive young man, several years younger than Grandma Ebba. The divorce from Maria had hurt him badly. Eating off the dinner service that his former wife had given him as a wedding present was quite out of the question.

'He couldn't get a thing down, poor man.' Pyttan sighed. 'So he gave it to Ebba, who he seems to have been rather more fond of than he dared admit. That's how it ended up in the porcelain cabinet at home in Västergötland. The Hamiltons have never had to worry about having enough plates.'

Time to change tack, Bäckström thought, and went on to talk about Eriksson the lawyer. How come she had commissioned him to sell her art collection? Not least considering the regrettable consequences that ensued.

If Pyttan were to blame anyone apart from herself, it might perhaps be her father and grandfather. The Hamiltons had always been warriors, and they fought with cannons, rifles, pistols, swords, sabres and rapiers. But it was a different matter when it came to fighting with legal documents and money. That was a battle that demanded a different sort of soldier.

'Grandpa Gustaf was very clear about that. You should always have judicial advisors as soon as legal documents and money were involved, and in the family we've always used Goldman's law firm. First, old man Albert, then his son Joakim. Splendid people. As long as you've got a Jew by your side, your opponent doesn't stand a chance. That was why I turned to Thomas Eriksson and asked him to sell those things for me. I'd moved house, after all. From a big house to a small apartment, only five rooms and a kitchen. There wasn't even room for them in the attic. So I asked Thomas to sell them for me.'

'So Thomas Eriksson was Jewish?' Typical, Bäckström thought.

'No, he wasn't,' Pyttan said. 'If only he had been.'

According to a Hamilton family rumour, Thomas Eriksson was supposed to be the illegitimate son of the lawyer Joakim Goldman. Which explained why Eriksson started out at the Goldman law firm when he was a newly graduated lawyer, and the fact that he changed the name of the business after old man Goldman's death had been explained away as another little act of rebellion against his father.

'Sadly, it was rather worse than that,' Pyttan declared. 'Young Eriksson wasn't remotely Jewish, because then I would never have ended up in this sorry mess. Eriksson was a common Swedish crook and a thief, and it was actually Mario who found him out. That rumour that Goldman was his father was probably something Eriksson made up himself.

'But of course I don't have to tell you that, Superintendent,' Pyttan said. 'That you need to be careful with people like Eriksson. All these Anderssons and Erikssons and Svenssons and Perssons and all the rest of them. We Hamiltons always fight without visors.'

Mario the Godfather Grimaldi seems to have ended up in the right place, Bäckström thought, but simply nodded in agreement.

'By the way, I just thought of something,' Pyttan said, holding a long, neatly manicured forefinger up in the air. 'That picture of the fat Greek priest, the one that led to

Mario working out what that fraudster Eriksson was up to, I was given that by Archie, my daddy. He bought it at auction at Christie's, in London. He lived there for a couple of years towards the end of the war. He was the naval attaché at the Swedish Embassy.'

'Tell me,' Bäckström said, leaning back and clasping his hands over his round stomach. Another piece of the puzzle falls into place, he thought.

142

Pyttan's father, Count Archibald 'Archie' Hamilton, was born in 1901, which was of course practical because it made it easy to remember. Like all those who had gone before him, he grew up on the family estate in Västergötland. He graduated from Lundsberg private boarding school in 1920 and went on to study at the Royal Naval Academy, like so many Hamiltons before him. Not all of them, but enough.

At the outbreak of the Second World War he was appointed commander of a flotilla of torpedo boats stationed in Gothenburg, and was soon deeply involved in the clandestine smuggling of ball bearings from the Swedish Ball Bearing Factory in Gothenburg to Britain. Given the circumstances, it would have been hard to find anyone better suited to the job than Pyttan's father.

The Hamiltons were on the side of the British. This was a consequence of their background, and they had had their roots, relations and close friends in England for the past thousand years. Grandpa Gustaf was on the board of the Swedish Ball Bearing Factory, and considering the cargoes his son would be transporting, the typical Hamilton brain was hardly a disadvantage but more a prerequisite for success. Nocturnal sorties at high speed across the icy, storm-swept waters of the North Sea, lights switched off to evade all the German cruisers, destroyers and U-boats that were trying to sink them along the way and stop the British from getting the Swedish ball bearings that kept their military functioning.

'People can say what they like about Daddy, but he wasn't a coward. Archie was a daredevil, and if my mummy, Anna, hadn't protested, he'd have stayed on that bridge for the rest of the war,' Pyttan said, with evident pride in her voice.

'But your mum disagreed,' Bäckström said.

'They had three children. I was the youngest when it all started. Before the war was over there were six of us, so Daddy was home a bit more regularly, if I can put it like that.'

'You said your dad worked at the embassy in London,' Bäckström said. 'How did he end up there?'

It had been arranged by Pyttan's maternal grandfather. He was not only a count, but also a general in Defence Command in Stockholm. First, he saw to it that his son-in-law was promoted to the rank of commander, meaning that he had to be dragged off the torpedo boat he was clinging on to so tenaciously. To make sure Archie remained in a remotely tolerable mood, he then arranged for him to be given a secret posting as naval attaché at the embassy in London, with special responsibility for the transportation of Swedish ball bearings. Close enough to the war that lent meaning to his son-in-law's life. Far enough away to keep him alive and not make the count's own daughter the widowed mother of half a dozen fatherless children. That was all there was to it, according to Pyttan. But the purchase of that painting of the fat priest, and all the rest of it, for that matter, had nothing to do with any of that.

The reason why Archie Hamilton, commander and count, had bought Versjagin's painting of Saint Theodore was that Theodore bore a striking resemblance to the vicar in the village back home in Västergötland where the family estate lay. The commander and count didn't get on with the parish priest, who was both hypocritical and sanctimonious, in Archie's opinion. And he was no good at hunting either, which was pretty much a prerequisite if you were going to be in charge of a church and graveyard in the middle of the Hamilton estate, and one hundred pounds was a perfectly defensible price for one of the Hamilton counts who wanted to have a bit of fun with a servant of the Lord on the occasion of his fiftieth birthday.

The priest hadn't found the joke amusing. He returned the gift at once, with an indignant letter in which he encouraged Pyttan's father to call in the Church authorities immediately to inspect his activities if he really did suspect him of stealing from the collection box.

'Was he, then? Stealing from the collection box?' Bäckström asked.

'I'm quite certain he was,' Pyttan snorted. 'They all do, don't they? And a hundred pounds wasn't the end of the world. Because he got the painting back, of course, and he used to read the vicar's letter out loud to us when he was in the mood. It was one of Daddy's favourite stories.'

'I was just thinking about something else,' said Bäckström, who had suddenly been struck by a thought. 'Your dad wasn't bombed when he lived in London?'

'Bound to have been,' Pyttan said. 'Wasn't everyone who lived there? But that's probably not the sort of thing you tell your children.'

'I was wondering if that might have been why the

hunting service got wrecked,' Bäckström said, as another piece of the puzzle slipped into place.

The tragic remnants of what had once been a hunting service for maritime use, 148 pieces from the imperial porcelain factory in St Petersburg, which – in its original condition – would have been worth over ten million kronor.

'You can blame Hitler for a lot of things,' Pyttan said, shaking her head, 'but he's entirely innocent when it comes to that dinner service. I'm afraid the truth is much worse than that. If you want to track down the culprit, Superintendent, I think you should start with my brother, Ian.'

The hunting service was kept in four large wooden trays that were marked with the Romanov coat of arms. When it left Prince Wilhelm and Oakhill, it ended up being stored in a cellar at the family estate in Västergötland, and there it remained untouched until the fire.

Pyttan's brother was home from Lundsberg for the Easter holidays. He had borrowed an illicit still from one of the farmhands, and began distilling alcohol in the cellar of the main house. While he was producing the alcohol that he intended to take with him when he returned to school, unfortunately a minor fire broke out, in which most of the 148 pieces were lost.

Archie, their father, had taken the matter calmly. The house and his wine cellar had survived, after all, and he preferred to eat off the family's own porcelain anyway. The remnants of the service ended up in the children's playhouse, where it was used for a number of children's parties. Pyttan herself used to wash her dolls in one of the soup tureens, and on one occasion her brothers held a porcelain-smashing contest.

When Archie's estate was being sorted out after his death, the remnants had been collected and packed in one of the original four trays. Pyttan had been given it by her brother. He didn't want it. He thought it brought bad luck, he was missing his dad – it basically just nagged at his conscience.

143

'Sad story,' Pyttan said, with a shrug of her shoulders. 'I heard from Mario that one of those nouveau-riche Russians bought it. He's welcome to it. If you ask me, it never had any business being in Sweden. But would you like something to drink, Superintendent? I see we've already missed lunch, but I could imagine having a little glass of champagne.'

'Well, I wouldn't say no,' Bäckström said, as he was keen to stay on the right side of Pyttan, even if it had to be at the cost of a glass of fizzy wine at ten o'clock in the morning.

She must have put her watch on upside down, he thought.

In the absence of domestic staff – Mario had promised to take care of that particular detail as soon as they were properly installed – her guest would have to make do with Pyttan herself serving him. A quarter of an hour later she returned with a tray bearing a large ice bucket and an assortment of bottles and glasses.

Bäckström leapt up to help her, but Pyttan just shook her head. In her home, that wasn't the guest's job.

'I brought whisky and vodka for you, Superintendent,' Pyttan said. 'I'm thinking of having a glass of bubbly, but I don't imagine that's the sort of thing you drink?'

'It has been known,' Bäckström lied. 'But, given the choice, I'd love a small vodka.'

'Wise decision,' Pyttan said. 'Daddy used to drink whisky, but that was probably only because he was so fond of boats. I mean, it tastes like freshly tarred oak, doesn't it? But he did use to drink vodka with meals.'

Pyttan poured drinks for them both, and didn't hold back when she filled Bäckström's glass. Her daddy used to say that a proper man deserved a proper drink, and she could see no good reason to deviate from that.

'Well, then,' Pyttan said. 'Is there anything else I can help you with, Superintendent?'

'Well, there was one thing I've been wondering about,' Bäckström said. 'On that list I saw, there was mention of some sort of musical box. Do you remember anything about that?'

'Money,' Pyttan said, evidently thinking about something else entirely. 'Apart from the money that little bastard Eriksson, the bloke who tried to shoot Mario, tricked me out of. Mario's promised to take care of that. Whenever there's a practical problem like that, I always ask Mario to sort it out.'

I can imagine, Bäckström thought.

'As far as the money is concerned, I don't think you have any cause for concern,' he said. 'According to my colleagues who are working on the matter, Eriksson seems to have tricked you out of around a million kronor.'

'Really?' Pyttan said, pouring more champagne. 'A million. Who'd have thought it?'

'But you don't have to worry about the money. You'll get it back as soon as we've worked out how much you should get.'

'I suppose I've got enough to get by on. But of course I could always give it away to someone who needs it more than I do.'

Like little Mario, Bäckström thought.

'Anything else?' Pyttan asked, still sounding like she was somewhere else.

'Yes, that musical box,' Bäckström prompted. 'You don't remember anything about it? According to the notes I saw, it doesn't seem to have been of any great value but, as I'm sure you can understand, we need to have our papers in order.'

'Musical box, musical box, musical box,' Pyttan said. She had evidently switched to thinking out loud now that she was well into her second glass of champagne.

She honestly couldn't remember a musical box. But she did have a vague memory of a little enamel elf with a red hat on his head. It was far too heavy to hang on the Christmas tree, so perhaps it was one of those ornaments you got out for Christmas?

'But no musical box?'

'Daddy used to tell a story about a musical box,' Pyttan said. 'He was given it by his mother when he was a little boy. I think he had several musical boxes, now I come to think of it. I think he gave one of them away as a present when he was in London during the war.'

'You don't remember the name? Of the person he gave it to?'

'Name, name, name,' Pyttan said, shaking herself irritably. 'Just think how practical it would be if everyone had the same name. I have a feeling it was that politician. The one who was in charge of everything. That fat bloke who was always smoking a cigar. The one who's like a toilet.'

'A toilet?'

'Yes, WC, I mean.'

'Winston Churchill?'

'That's it. That was his name. We're related, by the way. My grandmother's sister was married to one of his cousins. People like us are always related to each other.'

'Your father gave Winston Churchill a musical box?' Must have been another one, Bäckström thought.

'Yes, unless Churchill gave it back to Daddy? Like that miserable old vicar. You'll have to forgive me, Superintendent, but I don't remember. I know Daddy met Churchill several times when he lived in England. Mostly at private functions, of course. I know he wrote about it in his diaries. And there was some English historian who wrote a book about Churchill, and he mentioned Daddy as well. Remind me before you go and I'll dig it out for you. I saw it in one of the boxes in the library. Must have been fairly recently, I suppose.'

'That's very kind of you.'

Half an hour later, after Pyttan had drunk a third glass of champagne and refilled Bäckström's glass, Bäckström left her. He was carrying a total of four diaries written by her father. Ordinary, fat notebooks with black wax-cloth covers. And a book about Winston Churchill written by an English historian. It had been a lovely meeting, Pyttan declared. As soon as she and Mario had sorted things out a bit, Superintendent Beck was welcome to come again. But at the moment she was run off her feet, there was so much to do. But soon things would be better. When all the furniture was in place and Mario had employed someone to take care of the practical details.

She was thinking of getting a pet to keep her company

when Mario was away. A dog, perhaps. Pyttan had always been fond of animals. She'd had loads of animals, ever since she was a little girl. Back home on the estate in Västergötland where she grew up there had been considerably more animals than people. Horses and cows, pigs and hens, cats and dogs . . . All sorts of other things too. Lots of those little animals.

Bäckström understood exactly what she meant. He too was hugely fond of animals. For many years he had been particularly fond of parrots. He actually had several at the moment, and he couldn't wish for better company. 'The sort you can talk to,' Bäckström specified. Who cares, as long as it works, he thought.

Pyttan had never had a parrot. She had owned both canaries and budgerigars, but never a parrot that could talk. The closest she had come to that was a tame raven that she was given by her brothers, but he could only caw, and then he croaked shortly after that.

'A parrot that can talk, that must be absolutely wonderful,' Pyttan said, looking as if she really meant it.

This is going to work out nicely, Bäckström thought as he sat in a taxi on the way to the police station in Solna.

144

As soon as Bäckström arrived at work he went and spoke to Nadja, who had some news for him. Interesting news about Mario Grimaldi and his new woman, Countess Astrid Elisabeth Hamilton, born 1940, who preferred to be called Elisabeth but was known to her friends and family by the nickname Pyttan. And born a countess, which was not entirely irrelevant under the current circumstances, but presumably Bäckström knew all this.

'So what don't I know, then?'

What he didn't know was that she already existed in the files of the Solna Police under the name Astrid Elisabeth Linderoth. Linderoth from her late husband, who had died five years ago. A highly respectable man who appeared to have spent his career as a doctor and professor of internal medicine at the Karolinska Institute.

'Hang on a minute,' Bäckström said, raising his hand to stop her. 'Astrid Linderoth? Wasn't that the name of that crazy old bag who was reported for animal cruelty?'

The very same, Nadja confirmed. A month ago Astrid Elisabeth Linderoth had changed her name back to her old maiden name, Hamilton, at the same time that she and Mario Grimaldi had the banns read in advance of their marriage, and so far there hadn't been any problem, not regarding the change of name, her title, or their impending marriage.

'Apparently, they're getting married tomorrow, on Midsummer's Eve. At the Swedish Embassy in Rome.'

'I see,' Bäckström said. How the hell were we supposed to know about that? he thought.

'That explains quite a lot. Not least that home visit García Gomez paid to Fridensdal, her neighbour, after she'd reported her for animal cruelty.'

'What do we do about that, then?' Bäckström asked. That nice young man who helped Mario put up his kitchen curtains, even though Mario was such a practical man, according to Pyttan, he thought.

Nothing, according to Nadja. All the charges had been dropped. García Gomez was dead. Grimaldi was impossible to talk to. His wife-to-be was probably unaware of the help he had given her. But it was still interesting. Being able to answer the questions in one's own mind.

Nadja doesn't give up, Bäckström thought. Someone really ought to talk to her about those gold teeth. Get them replaced with ordinary porcelain crowns. If nothing else, she should consider the risk of being mugged. It was like going around with a wad of notes in your mouth. But as he had just had a brilliant idea, it was high time for him to get down to work. Best to strike while the iron's hot. Anyway, Pyttan's probably already forgotten she's going to Rome tomorrow to get married, he thought. He put what he needed in his old briefcase, called for a taxi and left the police station in Solna in something of a hurry.

First, he stopped off at GeGurra's office and left the books Pyttan had given him with GeGurra's secretary. He also asked her to say that his investigations were proceeding, and that the provenance had been clarified. Albeit at the cost of replacing three generations of Bernadottes with two countesses and one count in the Hamilton family.

Then he went home, calling Pyttan en route, and asking if he could stop by and drop off a present for her. Pyttan thought that sounded quite marvellous. She looked forward to seeing the superintendent again.

Isak didn't seem quite so perky. He just sat in his cage glaring at Bäckström as he put him in the back seat of the taxi for onward transportation to his new custodian.

'Goodness, how cute!' Pyttan said, clapping her hands in delight. 'And such lovely colours! Are you quite sure you want to give him away, Superintendent?'

Because Bäckström had several parrots, that wasn't a problem at all. Even if this particular one was one of the most talented when it came to the gift of speech.

'What's his name?' Pyttan asked.

'Isak,' Bäckström said. 'But I'm sure he wouldn't mind if you wanted to call him something else.'

But Pyttan said there was no question of changing his name. On the contrary, she thought the name very fitting. You could see straight away why Isak was called Isak. And he looked exactly like old Goldman, the lawyer.

It should be noted that Isak, to his credit, gave no grounds for complaint. At the critical moment when she stuck her hand in and tickled him under his chin, he merely laid his head to one side and chuckled happily. When he was given a peanut, he opened his beak and behaved precisely as one had a right to expect of a parrot like him. 'Many thanks,' Isak said, tilting his head and clucking at his new owner.

'He's quite wonderful!' Pyttan said, her eyes sparkling

to match her diamonds. 'Are you sure there's nothing I can do for you in return, Superintendent?'

'Please, don't mention it,' Bäckström said. That would have been the musical box, he thought, but you've already forgotten all about that.

Then Bäckström left the pair of them before Isak got back to normal again. He had a long lunch, followed by an afternoon nap, and didn't wake up until GeGurra called. He began by thanking Bäckström for enabling him to hear the wings of art history fluttering. He also wanted to meet him as soon as possible. Dinner, eight o'clock, Operakällaren. The private dining room, as it was high time to discuss matters of decisive importance for the history of the Western world.

145

That evening Bäckström and GeGurra had dinner in the private dining room in the Opera House. A simple meal, seeing as it was the middle of the week. Bäckström made do with assorted fried titbits for a starter and swapped the veal steak for plum-glazed pork collar, but GeGurra went even further, assuming an almost ascetic attitude and ordering salad and fried sole.

An evening devoted to work, which was underlined by the fact that they had both brought their briefcases with them. Bäckström's was considerably fatter than GeGurra's, which was eminently practical, because it was more than big enough to contain what this whole business was about.

After the introductory toast, GeGurra began by praising Bäckström for his efforts. As soon as his secretary had rung to tell him of Bäckström's visit, he had dropped everything else he was doing. He raced to the office, then spent the rest of the day studying Archie Hamilton's diaries of his time as a clandestine attaché at the Swedish Embassy in London.

'It's a quite remarkable story,' GeGurra sighed. 'I doubt whether even you have heard anything to match it, Bäckström.'

Do I have a choice? Bäckström wondered, but contented himself with a nod.

* * *

Count Hamilton had spent just over a year in London, from the spring of 1944 to the summer of 1945, and during that time he met Winston Churchill on half a dozen occasions. The meetings always took place in private, and they appeared to have spent most of the time talking about the war and, in particular, deliveries of ball bearings from Sweden. During each of their meetings Churchill had taken care to ask how things were going with the clandestine operations for which Hamilton was responsible.

Hamilton and Churchill shared the same aristocratic background. There were family ties between them stretching back three centuries. On a personal level, they shared a deep and mutual admiration. Values, family ties, personal respect. All the things that mattered to people like them.

Hamilton admired Churchill for who he was and what he was doing. A younger man's respect for someone twenty years older than him. Somewhere between an older brother and a young father. For Churchill, it was simpler. He liked Archie Hamilton because he was a daredevil, the perfect choice to command a ship if you needed to order an attack. It was highly likely that he reminded him of his own younger self when, thirty years before, he had been appointed First Lord of the Admiralty, the first major political challenge of his life and the one he always remembered most fondly.

At the end of December 1944, a few days before Christmas, they met at a dinner at Blenheim Palace outside Oxford. Towards the end of the evening, Churchill, Hamilton and a select few other guests had withdrawn from the rest of the gathering to round off the evening by discussing things that were for their ears only, smoke one last cigar and have a final nightcap.

Churchill was in a bad mood, on the verge of grouchy. The offensive in the Ardennes that the Allies had launched a few days before had ground to a halt. The Germans were gathering for a counter attack, and it wasn't looking remotely like the victory procession his generals had promised him. Not that he feared for the final outcome but, with each passing day, he found himself with less room for manoeuvre at the forthcoming Yalta Conference in a couple of months' time, where he was due to meet his two allies, the US President Franklin D. Roosevelt and the Russian leader Josef Stalin, and where the first point on the agenda was to redraw the map of Europe and decide its political future.

It wasn't the American president who was Churchill's problem. It was his Russian ally, Josef Stalin, and on that point everyone in the present company was touchingly unanimous. Dealing with Russians was very straightforward. You couldn't trust them. It was highly likely that this was when Count Archie Hamilton got the idea of cheering up Winston and preparing him for future meetings with Stalin, a man who came from an entirely different world to them. A man who couldn't be trusted.

At least, that was how Hamilton described the background to the story in his own diary when he wrote of how he sent his adjutant to Churchill's headquarters immediately after New Year to give him a musical box as a present, with an accompanying message to the eminent recipient of the gift. A reminder of the conditions that applied whenever they met someone who wasn't like them. And a hope that Stalin had the same sort of nose as Pinocchio.

One week later Hamilton's gift was returned to him, with a friendly, personal letter in which Churchill thanked him for the present and his words of warning but explained that he couldn't accept it. Fabergé's musical box had a history which sadly rendered that impossible.

Hamilton's diaries, his own handwritten copy of the letter he had sent to Winston Churchill, Churchill's letter to Hamilton. In the original, typewritten on the prime minister's own notepaper, signed by Churchill and tucked inside the envelope from the Cabinet Office in which Hamilton received it. All of this was now in one larger envelope bearing the Hamilton coat of arms. Tucked inside the book that Pyttan Hamilton had given Evert Bäckström in the hope that he might find something inside it that he could be bothered to read. They must have been put there by her father, the count. A man who was more concerned with firing guns than filing cabinets.

'It's quite wonderful,' GeGurra said, holding up the book that Pyttan had given Bäckström. 'Funny how easy it is to find what you're looking for when you know where you should be looking.'

'I know,' Bäckström said. He had been a police officer his whole life.

'I presume you haven't had time to read the book yet, my dear friend?'

'No,' Bäckström said. 'I've had other things to deal with.'

'Then I shall tell you,' GeGurra said. 'It really is quite wonderful.'

What choice have I got? Bäckström thought again, and gestured to the maître d' that his glass needed refilling.

The author of the book was a very well-known English historian, Robert Amos, later Lord Amos, who ended his days as professor of history at Balliol College, Oxford. During the Second World War Amos had been a member of Churchill's staff and, on a number of occasions towards the end of the war, also acted as his personal secretary. Twenty years after the war ended he published a book about his former boss, entitled *Winston Churchill: Political Thinker, Rhetorician and Strategist* (Oxford University Press, 1964), in which he focused on Churchill's often overlooked talent for strategic thinking in political situations. Churchill may have been regarded – with good reason – as one of the finest rhetoricians in global history, but he was also a careful and precise politician, even when it came to the question of what gifts one could accept from those around one.

The example he gives in the book is a musical box the prime minister was given by a Swedish count and naval officer. A man who, at risk to his own life, had done great service to England and Englishmen during what might well have been the most difficult time in the long history of the Empire. He was also a distant relative, and a personal friend, and so was beyond any suspicion of harbouring a hidden agenda. Yet it was still a gift that it was impossible to accept. Because of its origins and history, because of the message it conveyed between giver and recipient the moment it was accepted. Because of the political situation that pertained at the time between Churchill and Stalin. In short, it was a good example of Churchill's skill at political and strategic thinking.

'Straight from the horse's mouth,' GeGurra declared. 'Lord Amos was present at that dinner at Blenheim. He also wrote the draft of Churchill's letter in which he declined the gift, and he and Churchill spent a whole hour discussing the matter, even though they were fully occupied almost round the clock with preparations for the Yalta Conference.'

'So he sent the musical box back?' How stupid can you get? Bäckström thought.

'Yes, that's exactly what he did,' GeGurra said. 'To the great benefit of posterity, and not least you, my dear friend, whose finely honed mind has at last managed to deduce the remainder of our story. All that remains now is to find the musical box itself.' And, for some reason, GeGurra glanced at the large briefcase that was sitting next to Bäckström on the sofa where he was seated.

'Well, you can relax now,' Bäckström said. He opened the briefcase, took out the dark wooden box and put it on the table between them.

146

The remainder of the evening was spent discussing financial terms, which fairly soon reached a point where they took their toll on both food and drink, and the harmonious relationship between the two parties.

GeGurra began by putting on a pair of white cotton gloves, before carefully starting to examine Pinocchio with the help of a magnifying glass and an extra reading lamp provided by their maître d'.

'Not a single scratch.' GeGurra sighed.

'There's nothing for you to worry about,' Bäckström said. 'It works, too.'

'How do you know that?' GeGurra said, looking at him with wide eyes.

'I tried it out,' Bäckström said. 'It sounded fucking awful, but the nose came out and went back in, whistling the whole time.'

GeGurra put Pinocchio back in his box. He asked for a large linen cloth, and gently wrapped it round the box. He left the package on the table.

'Make me an offer,' Bäckström said.

Considering the circumstances, and not least the fact that his dear friend had just made a crucial contribution to the history of art, for the first time in his long life as an art dealer he was prepared to abandon a principle that he could never have imagined giving up, even in his wildest dreams.

'I'm willing to split my fee with you. Fifty–fifty.'

'What sort of money are we talking about?' Forget it, Bäckström thought.

Considering the documentation they had at their disposal, and bearing Winston Churchill in mind, they were now dealing with a market value in the region of a quarter of a billion kronor – so the commission would be around fifty million kronor. Twenty-five million each.

'In that case, I have a better suggestion,' Bäckström said.

'I'm listening.'

Pyttan Hamilton didn't have a clue about either the musical box or the amount of money she was sitting on. Her short-term memory was like a very small child's and, as far as the rest of her mental faculties were concerned, it was doubtful that she could even tell the time.

The simplest solution would be for GeGurra to dig out one of the many collectors who might conceivably be prepared to buy Pinocchio straight off, then take him off to their private bank vault and sit there looking at him in splendid isolation for the rest of their lives. They could even let him have a discount if necessary. And content themselves with sharing the two hundred million, where GeGurra could keep all of twenty per cent while Bäckström made do with the remaining eighty. Considering the division of labour between them, that seemed an entirely reasonable share of the spoils.

Not entirely unexpectedly, GeGurra had a rather

different view on the matter. The problem with a deal of this nature was comparable to trying to sell the ceiling of the Sistine Chapel by putting an advert on eBay. Which was just as irrelevant to the current situation as Pyttan Hamilton's mental state.

'Why?'

'Because tomorrow she's getting married to my old acquaintance Mario Grimaldi. He called me himself yesterday to tell me about their impending nuptials. From what he told me, she's the love of his life and, because Mario never lies, we can only assume that this is indeed the case.'

'I know they're getting married,' Bäckström said with a shrug. With a bit of luck, little Isak will have them both packed off to the madhouse within a couple of weeks, he thought.

'But what you don't know is that he was the person who commissioned me to ask you to find the musical box for him. He did that as early as Monday, 3 June, the day you opened your murder investigation. He and Stålhammar evidently missed it when they were there to pick everything up. All being well, the forensics team would find it. But if they didn't, I was to talk to you and make sure that you found it for us. The main concern was to make sure it didn't go astray during the disposal of Eriksson's estate.'

'I hear what you're saying,' Bäckström said. 'In that case, I suppose I could always find someone else to help me.'

If Bäckström were to decide to do that, naturally, it would be a decision that GeGurra would find deeply regrettable. The reason wasn't just that he had promised to call Mario after his meeting with Bäckström and tell him how it had gone. Quite regardless of whether or not he chose to keep the truth from him, it would only be a matter of time before Mario worked out what was really going on. GeGurra might as well sign his own death sentence, quite literally. And as he was extremely happy with his life the way it was, he wouldn't have any trouble sticking to the truth.

'I don't think there's any danger of him filing charges against you with the police,' GeGurra said.

'No,' Bäckström said. 'If I understand you correctly, you're telling me that he'd kill me.'

'Of course. But I'm not sure that's what you should be worried about.'

'So what should I be worried about, then?'

'The manner in which he would do it. But I'll spare you the details. Mario isn't the figure of fun that you and all your colleagues have decided to regard him as. He and his brothers are members of the Neapolitan mafia and, if anyone can keep their Sicilian colleagues awake at night, it's men like Mario.'

'What do you think I should do?'

'Before we part, I will give you a receipt stating that I have taken delivery of a musical box made by Carl Fabergé, in the shape of Pinocchio, so that I can – on the instructions of the police – ascertain whether it is the musical box identified on the list of artistic artefacts that former lawyer Thomas Eriksson was commissioned to sell on behalf of Countess Elisabeth Hamilton. I'm quite convinced that you'll manage to sort out your paperwork in good time. Before we part and I take the musical box with me, I thought we might shake hands on the deal. Hopefully, you will soon be in possession of twenty-five million kronor for your efforts. And I promise to help you with the practical details so that we don't have to trouble either the tax office or your employers on that score.'

IX

Have you heard the true story of Pinocchio's nose?

147

Bäckström began his Midsummer celebrations at work. He made sure he filled in all the records of property seized and other documentation in such a way that he, if it proved necessary, could cover his back by blaming his inhuman burden of work if anyone were to comment on the delay in recording what he had done. As he did so, he swore without interruption about the crooks in whose company he had ended up. He concluded by calling Nadja, the only one he could trust, to ask her to check there wasn't anything he had missed. Then he went home and made a concerted effort to get back into his usual routines. To get back to a decent life.

Lunch functioned the way it always did. After that, he suffered one blow after another, found himself stabbed in the back and, towards the end of the night, was the victim of an occurrence that shook his entire worldview.

When, after a sufficiently long walk at a comfortable pace, he was standing outside the door of Little Miss Friday's physiotherapy establishment, he was confronted with a note saying that the business had stopped trading for the foreseeable future. Who the note had been written by and why was not clear but, because Bäckström could think of more than one possible candidate whom he had no desire to encounter, he walked away without any fuss.

In the absence of any better options, he went home. He sought consolation in perhaps rather too many emergency drinks, before finally falling asleep on his sofa. When he woke up it was already eight o'clock in the evening, the situation was desperate, good advice was expensive, and – as on so many previous occasions – he had a brilliant idea and called the female accountant he had met the previous weekend.

He didn't even get through to her voicemail. The number was no longer in operation, and the only remaining option was to seek solace among his online fan club.

If it comes down to it, I could always have a randomly selected member brought over by taxi, he thought as he read through the latest contributions to the forum.

There was one that stood out. It had been posted by someone using the name 'number-cruncher' who now had personal experience of the Bäckström super-salami, which – in the interests of consumer information and sisterly solidarity – she wanted to share with a wider audience. In terms of volume, she had no conclusive opinion to offer. Notwithstanding customary male exaggeration, the bearer of the super-salami was much like any other Tom, Dick or Harry. Well, perhaps a smaller than average Tom, Dick or Harry, as far as his nether regions were concerned.

The problem was that there were other similarities. The choice between the Man with the Super-Salami and the equivalent product from a delicatessen wasn't difficult. From experience, if she had to choose again, she would prefer the latter, because then she wouldn't have to deal with the bearer of the item in question. She had no intention of going into his view of women. Considering his views on humanity in general, this was sadly only a tiny detail in a far larger context.

One hour later Bäckström was sitting at the bar of one of the floating hostelries down at Norr Mälarstrand. He ordered several cold beers, large vodkas and toasted sandwiches so that he would not, at least, fall down dead from hunger and thirst. For safety's sake, he was also wearing his surveillance sunglasses, to avoid attracting too much attention.

When he left the bar a couple of hours later he came close to missing the gangplank and, when he was finally back on solid ground again, it was swaying alarmingly. He didn't manage to get hold of a taxi, and was slowly making his way unsteadily up the road when things took a serious turn for the worse. Further down the street a huge black man appeared, shouting and gesturing at him. He was black as soot, big as a house, quick as a gazelle, and obviously out to mug him. When Bäckström bent over to get a bit of assistance from little Siggy, he ended up falling flat on his backside.

There he remained for several seconds until the black mugger came over and helped him up, brushed him down, handed him the note-clip that he had managed to leave behind him in the bar, and asked if he should call for an ambulance, or would an ordinary taxi be okay?

Bäckström ended up spending most of the weekend in bed, trying to make some sense of the thoughts that kept flashing like summer lightning through his aching head, but without really succeeding. He even conducted an empirical experiment and carried the portrait of Saint Theodore into the bathroom, put on his surveillance sunglasses and turned out the light in order to find out if the fat, pasty-skinned Theodore would change his skin colour as a result of the fact that they were surrounded by pitch-blackness. All to check if the man who had come to his aid that night was a perfectly ordinary Swede, and he had fallen victim to an optical illusion.

Theodore shone like a candle in the darkness.

It's quite unbelievable, Bäckström thought, shaking his head and returning to bed.

On Sunday his tame reporter called to ask for his help. The palace press office was on a war footing. They were denying all involvement with organized crime, assorted Russian artworks and an art expert who had previously been employed on a freelance basis. They also had the support of the newspaper's hitherto becalmed competitors, who had suddenly changed tack, had the wind in their sails and had filled the whole paper with the usual royal stories.

'So what do we do?' the reporter asked.

'Don't ask me,' Bäckström said. 'I'm not a journalist. I'm a police officer.'

148

On Monday he arrived at work to find that a report had been filed against him. The report was in his pigeonhole. It was from the Animal Protection Unit of the City Police, and informed him that he was under suspicion of aggravated animal cruelty. According to an anonymous complainant, Bäckström had been 'neglecting and tormenting' a parrot that had been in his care for the past two months. As a result, they wanted him to contact the investigating officer as soon as possible, acting Detective Superintendent Rosita Andersson-Trygg, to arrange a time for the inspection of the crime scene – his flat on Inedalsgatan in Stockholm – as well as an interview with him.

Must be little Edvin, Bäckström thought. After the weekend that had just passed, he was fully aware of the extent of the evil surrounding him. Forget it, he thought, and pressed the quick-dial number for Anchor Carlsson and asked her to come to his office.

'What do you want me to do?' the Anchor asked.

'Give them a call, say hello from me, and explain to them that I don't own a parrot, then tell them to shove the complaint where the sun doesn't shine.'

'Of course,' the Anchor said. 'Is that all? You don't want me to break any bones?'

'Feel free,' Bäckström said.

* * *

The Anchor barely had time to close the door behind her before the next visitor knocked on it. It was Jenny Rogersson, looking the same as ever, keen to discuss their latest case. What case? Bäckström thought, gesturing to his visitor's chair. It was time to find something for little Jenny to do before she disappeared on holiday, with all the risks that involved for a young woman, he thought.

'Was I right or was I right?' Jenny said.

'How do you mean?'

'About our case, I mean. If I'm allowed to say what I think, I was on the right lines right from the start. The connections between that old lady, Linderoth-Hamilton, and von Comer and Eriksson. The Godfather was behind it all. I had a word with Dad. He congratulated me, and said to say hello, of course. How about going out to celebrate? Discreetly, of course.'

'Let me think,' Bäckström said. Is it possible to have more than ten points on a ten-point scale, and how do I avoid attracting more misery by ending up in bed with old Rogersson's daughter? he thought.

'Say hello back,' Bäckström said. 'On an entirely different subject, and please don't take offence, but are you absolutely sure that he's your father? I mean, there's not much resemblance between you, if I can put it like that.'

It wasn't the first time Jenny had heard that suspicion. She was only ten years old the first time it happened. Her dad was refusing to pay child maintenance and was using the same argument. So her mum, Gun, had taken him to court and forced him to provide a blood sample and have his paternity verified with a DNA test.

'How did that go?' Bäckström asked, refusing to give up

hope of a better world, even though he already knew the answer.

No doubt at all. The possibility that it could have been anyone but him was pretty much zero.

'But I do see what you mean,' Jenny said. 'So, what about grabbing a bite to eat? Before I go off on holiday at the weekend.'

'That would have been nice,' Bäckström said, 'but I'm afraid I'm going to have to pass. Bit too much going on at the moment.' I suppose we could always do another DNA test. Technology is improving all the time, he thought.

That afternoon he had a call from the second largest evening paper, asking if they could interview him. From what they had heard, Bäckström had got to the bottom of the false accusations that had been levelled at the king.

'In that case, you've come to the right man,' Bäckström said. Time to change sides, he thought.

That evening GeGurra called Bäckström at home, sounding almost high, and hissed something incomprehensible about 'the circle being closed'. He happened to be in St Petersburg, where he had just concluded the quickest deal in art history. He would rather save the details until they were alone.

'What do you mean by that?' Bäckström asked. The circle is closed, he thought. What circle?

'From the last tsar, Nicholas II, to the latest little daddy of all Russians,' GeGurra said. 'If you understand what I mean?'

'Obviously,' said Bäckström, who had no idea.

'What do you say to lunch tomorrow? Have a bite to eat, celebrate our victory, sort out the details.'

'Sounds good,' Bäckström said. As long as he didn't get mugged before then, he thought as he hung up.

149

On Tuesday Bäckström was the lead story in Sweden's second biggest evening paper. In an exclusive four-page interview, 'the country's most famous homicide detective' gave a detailed account of the circumstances surrounding the art fraud perpetrated by a 'now deceased celebrity lawyer'. There was no indication of any connection to the king or any of his relatives. The artworks in question had been inherited by an elderly female Swedish pensioner and, because she wanted to remain anonymous, obviously Bäckström was prohibited from revealing her identity.

Towards the end of the interview, Bäckström addressed the fundamental principles by which the free press acted and survived in a democratic country like Sweden.

For him, the freedom of the press was sacred, and the anonymity of sources its most important foundation. But, naturally, he lamented the fact that poorly supported articles could harm individuals, and, as a long-time supporter of the Swedish monarchy, it had saddened his heart when he saw that this had now afflicted even the King of Sweden, Carl XVI Gustaf.

While the country's newspaper readers were enjoying the fruits of Bäckström's wisdom, he himself was having lunch with GeGurra as the latter told him about the deal he had concluded in St Petersburg the previous day with the representative of a very prominent Russian buyer who wished to remain anonymous.

To start with the financial side of things, after tough negotiations they had agreed a price of two hundred and fifty million Swedish kronor. As soon as GeGurra had completed the formalities, he would of course ensure that Bäckström received the twenty-five million that he and GeGurra had shaken hands on. So that he didn't have to suffer any hardship in the meantime, he had arranged a small cash advance of one million, in case Bäckström was wondering why the brown envelope on the table in front of him looked so much fatter than usual.

'The circle is closed,' GeGurra declared, winking and raising his glass.

The new buyer, the latest daddy of all Russians, wasn't actually intending to hide little Pinocchio away in his private bank vault. In the autumn, he and Pinocchio would be appearing in front of all the art-lovers of the world at a special exhibition at the Hermitage in St Petersburg. Bäckström could count on being invited as one of the guests of honour.

'Is there anything you're wondering about?' GeGurra asked, as Bäckström had sat in silence more or less throughout.

'No,' Bäckström said, shaking his round head. 'Should there be?'

150

While Bäckström was having lunch with his old acquaintance GeGurra, Lisa Mattei was reading that day's edition of the country's second largest newspaper, and became aware that she was suddenly losing control of herself. That man defies all description, she thought, standing up with a jolt, grabbing the paper and marching straight into her boss's office.

'Please, sit down, Lisa,' the general director said with a friendly smile. 'If you're wondering if I've read today's paper, the answer is yes.'

'What do we do?'

'Nothing,' the general director said, shaking his head. 'Don't let's underestimate Superintendent Bäckström. If you were to ask me for my personal opinion, I might even concede that the man has a certain entertainment value. Such as that photograph in today's paper, where he's standing on the bridge leading to Lovön, with Drottningholm in the background, holding up his hand in a stop sign towards the camera. Like an old-fashioned traffic cop determined not to let anyone cross the bridge.'

'Yes, I've seen it,' Lisa Mattei said. 'It's hard to avoid, to put it mildly.'

'Or perhaps like a latter-day Sven Dufva, coming to the rescue of the Crown,' the general director declared, chuckling happily at his literary reference. 'But there's one thing you ought to know about. For the time being, for your knowledge alone.'

'I'm listening,' Lisa Mattei said.

A few hours ago their contact in Moscow had got in touch to inform him of rumours that the Russian president, Vladimir Putin, was planning to award the Pushkin Medal to Superintendent Bäckström.

'The Pushkin Medal?'

'The Pushkin Medal is the highest honour that Russia can give to a foreigner.'

'To Bäckström? What for?'

'The Pushkin Medal is awarded to people who have made a unique contribution in the field of art, culture and the humanities. Only contributions that are of definitive significance to Russia and its people are considered. To date it has only ever been awarded on a very few occasions, and this will be the first time it has been given to a foreign citizen. And the first time that the president himself has awarded it. From Vladimir Putin to Evert Bäckström. We ought, perhaps, to ponder the reason why.'

'From Vladimir Putin to Evert Bäckström?'

'Yes.'

Or vice versa, Lisa Mattei thought, but just nodded.

151

When Bäckström opened the door of his flat on Wednesday morning to go to work, he discovered that someone had hung a plastic bag on his door-handle. A white plastic bag, no writing, and inside it was a white shoebox, also without any writing. If it had contained a bomb detonated by the usual motion detector, Bäckström would have been dead by now.

Instead, he let his curiosity get the better of him, and weighed the bag carefully in his hand before carrying it into the flat, putting it down on the hall table and lifting the lid. Inside the box lay little Isak. Lying peacefully on his back, his tongue sticking out of the side of his hooked beak, a wire noose pulled tight around his throat and a neatly handwritten note on his chest.

'*Parlava troppo*,' Bäckström read.

Bäckström put the bag, box and Isak in the briefcase in which he had secreted various sensitive items over the years. He asked Nadja to come to his room, showed her the contents of the box and asked if she could help him interpret the message on the note.

Of course she could. *Parlava troppo* was a common expression within the Neapolitan mafia.

'Italian,' Nadja said. Translated, it basically meant that he talked too much.

Bäckström had received a message from someone who, in all likelihood, knew what he was up to. If he wanted to put a positive spin on it, at least it wasn't Bäckström himself lying there, so it was more a friendly exhortation to keep his mouth shut from now on.

'Do you want to file a complaint?' Nadja asked.

'No.' Bäckström shook his head. 'I want you to get rid of the body.'

'You've come to the right person.'

'How do you mean?'

'I'm Russian,' Nadja said with a smile. 'I thought I might do it the Russian way. In five minutes there won't be any parrot, nor any box or plastic bag, and this conversation between you and me never happened.

'Thanks,' Bäckström said.

'On one condition,' Nadja said.

'I'm listening.'

'Non parlerai troppo.'

'I promise.'

152

Bäckström spent the rest of the day behind his carefully barricaded door.

He ate both lunch and dinner in the company of little Siggy, as he tried to sort out the new financial situation in which circumstances had left him. To be on the safe side, he used paper and pen to list all the practical problems that occupied the everyday life of a multimillionaire. The new company that GeGurra had promised to help him with, Slobodan's suggestion of discreet partner ownership of a highly profitable betting shop, perhaps even some new teeth for Nadja.

Bäckström was sitting there with a list that just kept getting longer and longer, and he only interrupted his work when Anchor Carlsson phoned him.

'Are you at home?' the Anchor asked. 'There's something we need to talk about.'

'No, I'm on my way to my local to have dinner,' Bäckström lied. He was still waking up in a cold sweat in the middle of the night from having nightmares about the Anchor's last visit to his home.

'See you there, then,' the Anchor said, and because she ended the call immediately it was too late for further excuses.

* * *

Bäckström more or less had to shovel his food down and, when the Anchor showed up an hour later, he got away with only having to offer her a beer.

'How did you get on with the complaint from the Rabbit Unit?' he asked.

'Sorted,' the Anchor said. 'The charge has been dismissed.'

'How did you sort that out, then?'

'I explained to them that you'd got rid of the bastard. And I gave them a few choice words of advice, so I don't think it will be happening again.'

'Thanks very much. Let me know if there's anything I can do for you.'

'Okay,' the Anchor said with a nod. 'That's actually why I'm here.'

'Go on,' Bäckström said, leaning back and sipping the modest glass of cognac that had just appeared in front of him.

Anchor Carlsson was going to move house. She wasn't happy in her cramped two-room flat out in Bergshamra, and a few days ago a friend whose family had just grown got in touch, wondering if she would like to buy their flat in Filmstaden, in Solna. It was twice the size of hers, good location, its own balcony, as good as new, walking distance from work, and all she needed was three million.

'I don't understand,' Bäckström said. 'What does this have to do with me?' Three million, he thought.

'I was thinking you might like to lend me the money,' the Anchor said.

'You were, were you?' Bäckström said. 'Just one question. What rate of interest were you thinking of?'

'Zero per cent,' Anchor Carlsson said, giving him a friendly smile.

'Zero per cent,' Bäckström repeated. 'Why would I do that?'

'Have you heard the true story of Pinocchio's nose?' Anchor Carlsson said.

The Dying Detective

Leif G.W. Persson

Lars Martin Johansson has just suffered a stroke. The retired Chief of the National Crime Police and Swedish Security Service is paying the price for a life of excess – stress, good food and fine wine. With his dangerously high blood pressure, his heart could fail at the slightest excitement.

In the hospital, a chance encounter with a neurologist provides an important piece of information about a twenty-five-year-old murder investigation and alerts Lars Martin Johansson's irrepressible police instincts. The window for prosecution expired just weeks ago and that isn't the only limitation. Lars Martin Johansson is determined to solve the atrocious crime – even from his deathbed.

The inimitable style, distinct voice and dark humour of Leif G.W. Persson, along with the fascinating exploration of a long-cold murder case, serves to make *The Dying Detective* a true masterpiece of the genre.

Linda, as in the Linda Murder

An Evert Bäckström Novel

Leif G.W. Persson

In the middle of an unusually hot Swedish summer, a young woman studying at the Vaxjo Police Academy is brutally murdered. Police Inspector Evert Bäckström is unwillingly drafted in from Stockholm to head up the investigation.

Egotistical, vain and utterly prejudiced against everyone and everything, Bäckström is a man who has no sense of duty or responsibility, thinks everyone with the exception of himself is an imbecile, and is only really capable of warm feelings towards his pet goldfish and the nearest bottle of alcohol. If they are to solve the case, his long-suffering team must work around him, following the scant leads which remain after Bäckström's intransigence has let the trail go cold.

Blackly comic, thrillingly compelling and utterly real, *Linda, as in the Linda Murder* is the novel which introduces the reader to the modern masterpiece that is Evert Bäckström, a man described by his creator as 'short, fat and primitive'. He is, without doubt, the real deal when it comes to modern policing.

> 'Leif G.W. Persson is unique in this genre; as an author he is exceptional. This is grand reading.'
>
> Borås Tidning

He Who Kills the Dragon

An Evert Bäckström Novel

Leif G.W. Persson

It should have been an open and shut case: Two drunks meet for a bite to eat and considerably more to drink, fall into an argument. And then one of them brings their evening together to a close by beating the other to death.

A strangely routine and yet puzzling scenario to Detective Superintendent Evert Bäckström, whose legendary poor temper has not been improved by strict orders from his doctor to lead a healthier life. His gut feeling proves him right: within days, his team has another murder linked to the first on their hands.

Suddenly the nation needs a hero. Who better to save the day than Evert Bäckström, misanthropic, ostentatious, devoid of morals, Hawaii shirt-clad, and, latterly, armed? Once again an unholy combination of laziness, luck and an unbelievable sense of timing may yet rescue him from the perils of his fifteen minutes of fame . . .

'Persson outperforms most of his competitors in the Swedish crime genre by miles . . . Hardboiled, clever, suspenseful'
SVENSKA DAGBLADET

'Just what fans of Jo Nesbo and Stieg Larsson are looking for'
BOOKLIST